Praise for Catriona McPherson's Dandy Gilver series:

'Guaranteed to
appeal to those who have never
got over the death of Dorothy L Sayers . . .
That McPherson has an ear for mellifluous language is obvious . . .
The story bristles with clues, and the resolution – arrived at by agonised
brain-racking on the part of our tenacious heroine rather than any
brilliant leap – is unguessable.' – *Financial Times*

'For all their cheerfulness, her books – unlike the works of the
Christies and Allinghams – are infused with the lingering
sadness of the inter-war period … It is this underlying sadness
that lifts McPherson's books out of the "cosy crime"
sub-genre where they sit alongside Agatha Christie and
Alexander McCall Smith.' – *Scotsman*

'McPherson's books are always strong on period detail, with
nifty sleight-of-hand plotting and plenty of interesting
secondary characters, but it's Dandy herself who makes them
shine: witty, briskly humane and quietly subversive,
she is a continuing delight.' – *Guardian*

'McPherson is an exemplary crime writer, effortlessly balancing the
driest wit with melodramatic suspense. Her range of reference is
seriously literary, her research impeccable, and her exuberance with
period detail utterly beguiling. And Dandy herself is wonderful: blundering
bravely through this mad and murky tale with perfect aplomb and a
drop-dead vocabulary, she is a lesson to us all.' - *Scotsman*

'Mrs Dandelion Gilver is a charming creation… dry wit… sparkling
dialogue and meticulous description' – *Herald*

'McPherson is on to a winner... The period detail is accomplished and
convincing, the crime is neatly convoluted and McP clever asides under a lucid surface... I can't wait
– *Scotland on Sunday* on AFTER THE AR

'Dandy Gilver is an enthralling heroine; part
Miss Marple, utterly engaging. Absolut
– *Kirsty Scott*, author of MOTHE

The Dandy Gilver Series

After the Armistice Ball
The Burry Man's Day
Bury Her Deep
The Winter Ground
Dandy Gilver and the Proper Treatment of Bloodstains

About the Author

Catriona McPherson was born in the village of
Queensferry in south-east Scotland in 1965 and educated
at Edinburgh University. She left with a PhD in
Linguistics and spent a few years as a university
lecturer before beginning to write fiction. The first novel
in her acclaimed Dandy Gilver series was shortlisted
for the CWA Ellis Dagger for historical crime fiction.

CATRIONA McPHERSON

Dandy Gilver and the Proper Treatment of Bloodstains

HODDER

First published in Great Britain in 2009 by Hodder & Stoughton
An Hachette UK company

First published in paperback in 2010

1

A CIP catalogue record for this title is available from the British Library

ISBN 978 0 340 99296 8

Typeset in Plantin Light by Palimpsest Book Production Limited,
Grangemouth, Stirlingshire

Printed and bound by Clays Ltd, St Ives plc

Hodder & Stoughton policy is to use papers that are natural, renewable and
recyclable products and made from wood grown in sustainable forests.
The logging and manufacturing processes are expected to conform to the
environmental regulations of the country of origin.

Hodder & Stoughton Ltd
338 Euston Road
London NW1 3BH

www.hodder.co.uk

For Catherine and Olivier, with love.

Thanks to:

Lisa Moylett and Juliet Van Oss.

Suzie Dooré, Imogen Olsen, Katie Davison, Jessica Hische,
Alice Laurent and Francine Toon.

Caroline Lyon, David Hicks and Kerrie Smith at the
Edinburgh World Heritage Trust.

Hil Williamson and Ruby Woods in the
Fine Art Dept of Edinburgh City Libraries.

Nancy Balfour, Jim Hogg and Ann Morrison in
the Edinburgh Room (again).

Bronwen Salter-Murison for the website.

All the staff of the Scottish Mining Museum at
Lady Victoria Colliery, especially Tam and John for their
memories of mining life and their wit – drier than coal dust.

Nancy and Jeff Balfour for allowing me
the use of their name.

Catherine Lepreux, for the sickroom recipes.
Fish custard, anyone?

And Neil McRoberts, of course, for everything.

I

I had been standing under this tree, against these railings, looking at that house from the corner of my eye for almost ten minutes now while I waited for my heart to stop dancing. It was beginning to dawn upon me that I waited in vain. I scanned the windows once more – all seventeen of them; I had counted – but saw no movement anywhere. I glanced along the street both ways, hoping for an excuse to abandon the enterprise, and found none. I looked down at myself, wondering whether my disguise would pass muster, and concluded that it would. So, ignoring the watery feeling in my legs, at last I marched across the road, mounted the steps and pulled hard on the bell.

Stupidly, I had imagined having to conjure up a performance of nerves for the looming interview. I had even doubted whether I could pull it off, for I have no dramatic experience beyond Christmas charades at home each year and one pageant at my finishing school in which I started as Clytemnestra but was so unconvincing that I ended up as a broken column, wrapped in a bed sheet and clutching a fern.

Today, I need not have worried: when the door swung open and my name was demanded of me there was nothing theatrical at all in my answering squeak.

'Miss Rossiter,' I said. 'To see the mistress.'

The butler did not answer – did not so much as blink as far as I could tell – but merely turned his back and sped away, leaving me to close the door and scurry after him.

Miss Rossiter, squeaking like that, was evidently a bit of a ninny for I had given her an impressive professional history and she might have been expected to take this new chapter more easily in her stride. I on the other hand, Dandy Gilver, could be forgiven. I had a handful of *cases* under my belt but this was, without a doubt, my first *job*.

The letter had come on an ordinary Tuesday morning at the end of April, in amongst a typical batch of thank-you notes, invitations and demands for subscriptions and looking so much like another of them that, as I slit it open and scanned it through, I was already moving it towards the 'bore' pile at my left elbow, always so much taller than the 'fun' pile at my right.

Dear Mrs Gilver, it began in a clear but feminine hand, the ink bleeding a little into the good, thick paper. *My husband is going to kill me, and I would rather he didn't.*

I had jerked up in my seat, sending the bore pile cascading and making Bunty – asleep on the blue chair – twitch her ears, although her eyes remained shut. I took a closer look at the address: *Mrs Philip Balfour, 31 Heriot Row, Edinburgh.* One of the most respectable streets in that most respectable of cities and a name to match it.

I cannot arrange to meet you, the letter went on, *because he would have me followed if I tried. I am followed whenever I leave the house now. Naturally, I cannot telephone either and I must implore you not to telephone to me. However, I have thought of a way to manage it. I have recently lost my maid and am seeing girls next Friday, hoping to find a new one. If you could come along, suitably attired, at 3 o'clock in the afternoon, we could be sure of some time in private when I might explain. Please do not send a reply to this – he would steam it open as he does everything.*

Until Friday then. Yours faithfully, Walburga Balfour.

The butler passed through the outer hall with its hat glass and umbrella stands and into the chilly grandeur of the stairwell, where a row of wooden chairs was set against the banister wall. He nodded me towards one of them and I sank down onto its edge, tucking my feet in and holding my bag handles in both fists. I had learned the pose from a girl on the train. (This was in the third-class carriage; I had decided to get into character good and early.) The butler was clearly beguiled by it, and he proceeded to set me at my ease by slipping his hands into his trouser pockets and putting one foot up on the spar of the chair beside mine.

'Come far?' he asked.

'Perthshire,' I said, in all honesty. 'And it was ever such a slow train.'

The butler gave me a long, enquiring look before he spoke again and I prayed that my face would not colour, for this of course was the greatest hurdle: my triumph or my undoing lay in the voice, in the quashing down of my own perfectly accentless, perfectly neutral way of talking and the cloaking of it in Miss Rossiter's words and Miss Rossiter's sounds – particularly in the strange notes of Miss Rossiter's vowels.

I had unearthed from a trunk the standard-issue grey wool coat and skirt from my days as a nurse-volunteer – they were still in excellent condition, since I had not worn the vile things above twice, and they smelled most appropriately of camphor and attic – and had daubed my oldest brown brogues with black polish to make maid's shoes of them (this was successful enough, but I did fear the polish coming off onto my stockings). No amount of scraping and pinning could produce a bun out of my short hair, but I had washed it straight, parted it in the middle and fixed it behind my ears with three grips each side until there was nothing of the shingled bob left about it anywhere. (And it felt delicious, I must say, to be free of setting lotions again after fifteen years of their fumes and itching.)

But all of this should be as nothing and as a thing of naught without the voice and I peeped up at the butler, once again free of the need for any acting. He was rather older than me, perhaps fifty, with a pleasant, open countenance – red cheeks, red lips, not quite the long nose which can be such a help to a butler when it comes to looking down it, and black hair in crisp curls across his head like a bad drawing of a choppy sea, but very short and twinkling at the back against his neck.

At length, he smiled.

'I'd have said you come up from the south, not down-a-ways,' he said and picking up the silver card salver from the hall table he breathed on it and then polished it by rubbing it hard on the seat of his striped trousers.

'Northamptonshire, prop'ly,' I said, trying not to boggle at the antics with the salver. My reply had the virtues of being true and of ending all enquiry, since the county of my birth and child-hood is as obscure as it is dear to me.

'Cornishman myself,' said the butler and I could tell that he revelled in his association with such an effortlessly more thrilling corner of England. 'Come up to London and kept on going, I did.'

Before we could continue the discussion, before I had the chance to regain some stock with news of my mother's Cornish relations, there came from one of the back rooms of the house, the unmistakable sound of a conversation ending: a voice lifted to deliver the closing courtesies and the movement of chair legs against a hard floor. I glanced at my wrist, but Miss Rossiter wore no watch.

'Don't you worry,' said the butler, seeing my sudden movement, 'you'll be all right.'

'What's she like?' I asked, hoping that this was not too familiar. Evidently not.

'No trouble,' he said. 'Just a kid, really. She married well – it's him that's got the money and the family, you know.'

A door opened and a stout girl in grey serge, holding her bag up under her chin, emerged. A voice drifted out from behind her.

'If you would see Miss Allan out, Faulds. Is the next . . . Oh, splendid.'

The butler, hands out of pockets, both feet flat on the floor, and nose as long as he could make it, swept away towards the hall doors. I shared a look with Miss Allan as she passed me and then turned to the voice.

4

'Miss Rossiter, mem,' I said.

'Indeed,' said the young woman in the doorway. 'Please come on through.'

She ushered me into a morning room, where another of the plain wooden chairs was set at an intimidating distance in front of a small papier mâché writing desk. It was a typical Edinburgh room, so recently decorated that the fussy Adam plasterwork which picked out the cornice and the chimneypiece in green and white had not yet had time to grow sooty. There was a very fine carpet – the thin kind which is treacherous if wrinkled, but which here was as smooth as a pond – and some good but dull pictures, badly hung. An exquisite long-case clock, gleaming with polish, ticked away a kind of endless bass lullaby.

Mrs Balfour herself, when I took a good look at her, struck me – thankfully – as a sensible sort of girl. (The letter had been so extraordinary that I had half suspected an hysteric, but there was no hectic flush nor twitch of unease about her.) She was in her mid-twenties, with a healthy figure just too full to be coltish, although there was something equine about it somewhere, and had that light Scotch hair which is not quite red and that thin Scotch skin which is not quite freckled. These are looks which go over very quickly, but for now she was pretty enough in an unremarkable way. As she folded herself into the seat at the desk she smiled at me.

'Mrs Gilver,' she said. 'Thank you so much for coming.'

I sat back in my seat, put Miss Rossiter's bag down on the floor and crossed my ankles.

'I could hardly do otherwise,' I said. 'Your letter was . . . rather compelling.'

'I didn't know where to turn,' said Mrs Balfour. 'But I remembered reading about that terrible business last winter.'

I could feel my face twist at the memory; it would be a long time before I stopped going over the Castle Benachally affair every night in bed and it was a source of pain that the first of my cases to be trumpeted in the newspapers should also have been the one where I stood by and watched murder be done.

Alec Osborne, my friend and Watson, always squashes me flat when I describe it that way (and I cannot help thinking that being firmly shut up, whenever one tries to talk about what is troubling one, is pretty cold comfort and not likely to bring a speedy end to the fretting).

'Sorry,' said Mrs Balfour, seeing the look. 'I've put my foot in it, but what I meant was that it would have been so much more terrible *but* for you that I was sure you'd be able to help me now.'

'Tell me about it,' I said, mentally shaking myself. I might have my regrets but this poor girl had a husband plotting her grisly end and deserved all of my attention.

'Yes, of course. Well, I've been married for five years and my husband is . . .' She stopped and looked around herself at the apartment. I waited. 'My husband is . . .' she said, and looked around again. I sat forward a little and looked around too. Of good fortune, I thought, judging by the clock and the pictures. Yet I had never heard of him, so he probably was not a gentleman as such, but then Edinburgh has lots of not gentlemen as such who have been beyond question for generations. A banker, perhaps.

Mrs Balfour sat up a little straighter in her seat.

'My husband is . . . a devil.' She gave a sound somewhere between a laugh and a sigh. 'There. I've said it. And finding out was so unexpected that it still seems not quite real. I didn't know him for long before we got engaged but I could see straight away – or thought I could – that he was a poppet. I mean to say, his name's Pip.'

'And when you say he's . . . unsatisfactory,' I prompted, but Mrs Balfour laughed and shook her head.

'He's a monster, Mrs Gilver. A nasty, brutish, bullying, philandering, dishonest, beastly . . . pig.'

'And you think he's going to kill you?'

'Oh, I'm sure of it,' she replied. 'He told me so.'

'I see. And can I ask why?' She stared dumbly back at me. 'Does he want to marry someone else?'

'That's an idea,' she said. 'I haven't seen any signs of it, mind you.'

'You said – just now – that he was a philanderer,' I reminded her.

'Yes,' she said, frowning. 'Yes, I did, didn't I? He is. Faithless, adulterous, underhand . . . it must be that. Why else, if not?'

'Well,' I said, 'to quote a police acquaintance of mine on the subject of murder: it's either love or money.'

'I haven't a bean.'

'Are you insured?' Mrs Balfour looked rather startled. It is difficult always to remember how far I have travelled along the road from where I used to be, where she still was, in that warm glade of gentle womanhood where such things would never occur to one. I felt as though I should have narrowed eyes and a cigarette in one corner of my red lips as I grilled her.

'I've no idea,' she said, blinking, 'but Pip has heaps of his own anyway.'

This was interesting; it is always interesting to hear how anyone manages still to have 'heaps of his own' in these dark days, but it was probably not to the point and so I passed on.

'And when you say he told you, do you mean he threatened you? Might he merely have been blustering? Was he very angry about something at the time? Or – forgive me – had he been drinking?'

Mrs Balfour laughed again.

'Pip? Drunk? No, that's not the kind of man he is at all. I shall try to explain.' She picked up a pen from her desk and fiddled with it as she spoke, gouging the nib into her blotter.

'It was at Christmas-time when it started – really started, I mean. It was Boxing Day, the servants' party, and if anyone had had too much "good cheer" I think it was me, because my memory of it is very peculiar, somehow. Mrs Hepburn had made her hot punch and I wonder if perhaps one of the other servants might have embellished it. Our chauffeur is a bit of a scamp. Anyway, the party was in its last stages, everyone rather hot and getting too tired for more dancing, and all of a sudden there was some kind of trouble with one of the maids – lots of shrieking – and Faulds, the butler . . . Oh, but of course you met him, didn't you? . . . had to haul her off and give her a talking-to. He was most displeased. And we all went to bed a bit flattened. But I couldn't get to sleep and I certainly couldn't face ringing down for someone to bring tea – it had all been so unseemly and embarrassing – so I went to fetch some for myself, or milk anyway which is easier, and when I got back up to my room, Pip was there, and he was . . . Well, he was . . . He was like a man possessed. He was in a complete rage and that's when he told me for the first time that he was going to kill me.'

I considered the story in silence. If I had heard it the morning after the events took place, I should have brushed it off without a murmur: servants' parties are notoriously ticklish affairs even without the adulterated punch, and what with maids and masters dancing together – mistresses and scamps of chauffeurs too, if I were reading correctly between the lines – then the lady of the house creeping back down in her nightgown, a husband breathing fire was hardly astonishing. However . . .

'For the *first* time?' I repeated.

'Yes, and since then it's been drip, drip, drip,' she said. 'He's perfectly ordinary during the day, when someone might see him, but sometimes at night he comes to my room and simply revels in it. Telling me that he loathes me, that he curses the day he met me, that he'll get rid of me if it's the last thing he ever does – you get the general idea.' Her smile was still brave but her voice had got a wobble in it and her eyes were shining. 'And the worst thing of all is that since that first time I've come to realise that there were hints of it all along rumbling away underneath that I was too naive or too trusting to see.'

'But he hasn't actually done anything,' I said.

'No,' said Mrs Balfour.

'Which is odd, if he really means it,' I said. 'I mean, he's had months. What do you suppose he's waiting for?'

I wondered if this was a little too callous, but Mrs Balfour merely shrugged.

8

'I have no idea,' she answered, 'but he's not going to wait much longer.'

'Oh?'

'He's going away to our place in the Highlands for the first of August,' she said. 'And, as I wrote to you, I can't leave the house any more unwatched and I can't telephone without being listened in to, but I taunted him – one beastly night when he was at it as usual – I said what made him think that I wouldn't pack my things and run off when he went shooting, and he said I'd be long gone by then. He said – I shall never forget it – he said, "Naturally, this will have to be tidied up by the end of July. I'm not going to miss the stags over it."' She gave a little sob as she spoke and then caught her bottom lip in her teeth.

'Mrs Balfour,' I began, after another long moment's consideration.

'Oh, Lollie, please,' she said. 'Not Mrs Balfour when I've just told you all that – too ridiculous for words. And certainly not Walburga.' There was a ghost of a smile.

'Well, Lollie,' I resumed, 'it's a most fantastical tale. He sounds not only insupportable – that almost goes without saying – but actually mad. He sounds as though he needs some kind of rest cure or some clever doctor. However, *he* is not my concern.' I gave her a stern look. 'You are. And your instincts are sound. You should do just what you threatened to. Pack your bags and go, my dear girl. Or leave your bags behind and go. Just go.'

'But go where?' said Lollie. 'My parents are dead, I have no friends that aren't his friends too, I have no means of getting any money without his approval. And besides . . .' Her voice trailed off.

'Are there children?' I asked, guessing that they would be a heavy anchor.

'Not yet,' said Lollie. 'I mean, no. See?' she went on wildly. '"Not yet"! I still can't convince myself that this is actually happening to me.'

'Is he in the house at this minute?' I asked. She shook her head. 'Well then, you can walk out of the front door along with me. Come home with me. And then telephone to a doctor, or to the police. To both.'

'You do believe me then?' said Lollie. 'He always reminds me that I have no proof or witnesses and tells me that anyone I speak to will think I'm mad. And that he'll give them lots of help to think it when they come to ask him about me.'

'Hm,' I said. She was right about the evidence and witnesses, of course, when I looked at the matter coolly. On the other hand, waiting until what they witnessed was her murder could not be recommended.

'Is there any way you can try to be even more careful?' I asked. 'Has he ever given any hints of his proposed method?'

'Oh yes,' said Lollie. 'I should have told you. It would be impossible to go on if I thought every dish might be poisoned or I might be shot in the back at any moment. No, I think he's going to strangle me at night in my bed.'

'He told you that?'

'Not in so many words,' she said. 'He whispers as he comes and goes, you see.' She leaned forward and spoke very softly. '*The rain set early in tonight, the sullen wind was soon awake, it tore the elm-tops down for spite, and did its worst to vex the lake.*'

I could feel a nasty prickling feeling creeping up my back towards my neck, where a nasty shrinking feeling in my scalp waited to meet it.

'What on earth?' I said, thoroughly rattled.

'I wondered for the longest time,' said Lollie, 'and then I found it. Well, a line of it – in a volume on the Carlyles.' I must have looked impressed at this example of her reading habits, because she went on: 'A volume that Pip left on my desk for me to find, open at the right page. It's Robert Browning: a horrid, horrid poem all about strangling his mistress.'

'I don't know it, I'm glad to say.' I shook my shoulders to drive off the last of the shivering. 'So. You need a reliable witness and you need protection in the night-time. You need, in fact, someone to sleep in your room with you. Do you have a sister?' She shook her head. 'An old nanny?' Another shake. 'A trusted maid of stout heart? Well, stout everything would be best, really.' Lollie opened her hands in a gesture of despair. 'Oh! Yes, of course,' I said. 'Your maid left, didn't she, hence today's interviews. Well, what about the girl before me then? She looked pretty sturdy.'

'The girl *before* you,' repeated Lollie, a beseeching look in her eyes. It took me a moment to see what was being besought.

'Ah, now,' I said. 'Well, as to that. I mean, I don't think that would be possible, I'm afraid.'

'Why not?' she asked me.

'One would have to . . . Well, one would have to know what one were doing,' I said, 'which I don't. At all.'

'But in the newspapers . . .' said Lollie.

'Oh no, I don't mean the detecting. I certainly know what I'm doing as far as that goes. And I can see that it would be wonderful to be stowed away in the heart of the household getting to the bottom of it – very practical – but as to the actual . . . I'd be seen through in a minute. I thought Faulds out there had uncovered me as soon as I opened my mouth. Gosh, if I tried to mix up freckle cream or launder lace . . .'

'But I'd help,' said Lollie. 'I wasn't brought up with my own maid and I know most of it. We could muddle along together. And if it's your fee that's worrying you—'

'I assure you it's not. No, my worry is Mr Faulds. And Mrs . . . Hepburn, was it? And the chauffeur? And you mentioned a maid or two at the Christmas party? That's too many to take into your confidence and I couldn't begin to fool them – not over days and weeks.'

'Twelve,' said Lollie.

'Twelve what?' I asked her.

'Servants,' she replied. 'Butler, cook, kitchenmaid, scullerymaid, tweenie, parlourmaid, housemaid, a valet, a footman, a hall and boot boy, and the chauffeur.'

'Twelve servants?' I echoed.

'Including you,' she said, smiling.

And a small part of me wonders even now how much of my agreeing sprang from a desire to find out how, in the name of heaven, in these days of desperate and universal retrenchment, they were managing it.

2

'*And all her hair, in one long yellow string I wound, three times her little throat around, and strangled her,*' said Alec, peering at the volume in the lamplight, and tracing the tiny print with the stem of his pipe.

'That's the one,' I said. 'Only it's red.'

'Not words you'd want your love to come cooing at you in your bedchamber,' Alec said. He turned the page. 'Good God, listen to this bit.'

'Oh, please, no more!' I said. 'What a man he must have been – and after his poor wife wrote all those *lovely* sonnets for him.'

Alec snorted and put his pipe back in his mouth. We were in his library, on the evening of the successful interview. (I had braved the hoots of derision over Miss Rossiter's adornments to commune with him, as I always did when a new case was stirring and at intervals while it wore on too.) At least, I thought to myself, the hoots of derision were all I should have to brave; there would be no frosty silence nor cutting remarks from Hugh when I got home since, after a great deal of glowering and muttering over the last four years, he had finally managed to find space inside his skull for the idea that Alec and I were friends, colleagues and nothing more, an idea I took great pains not to dislodge again.

'I have to agree with young Mrs Balfour,' Alec was saying now. 'Walburga, was it? – poor girl! It sounds so torrid and mad, she'd have a hard time convincing either the bobbies or docs until he actually strikes. I suppose you're convinced, are you?'

'I am but, as to the bobbies, it's even worse than having to convince them. I'm pretty sure that as long as he keeps to whispered threats she doesn't have a case. She doesn't even have a case for divorcing him unless she can unearth one of the philanderees and get him that way.'

'She can't divorce him for cruelty when he murmurs about winding her tresses round her little throat? That's a bit thick.'

'Apparently not,' I said, trying to hide my smile. Alec is younger than me and sometimes seems *much* younger, as when he is troubled and wounded by life's unfairness, by life's showing itself so regularly to be 'a bit thick'. 'I went to the National Library and looked it up before I caught the train home,' I told him. 'Apparently, he can be as cruel as he likes as long as it's only to Lollie – she doesn't encourage "Walburga", for obvious reasons.'

'Law books in the National Library *and* grey serge, Dan,' said Alec. 'You're flying all flags on this one, surely?'

'You haven't heard the half,' I said. 'Here's what I propose to do next, darling.' And I told him, to his evident and gratifying stupefaction; when I finished his mouth hung open, his pipe cooling, forgotten, in the ashtray.

'You don't stand a cat's chance,' he said at last.

'Well, thanks a lot,' I said, laughing.

'But seriously, Dan, how do you hope to pull it off? How can you propose to go in and do what amounts to making a fool of a man who is certainly violent and probably raving mad? And why? Why not say you're a girlhood friend or something?'

All of these were objections I had put to Lollie hours before, but she had answered them and, besides, I had come around to the notions for reasons of my own.

'He wouldn't let her have a friend to stay,' I said. 'And he won't take any notice of me. As long as I dress soberly and keep my head down I'll be fine. And I've decided not to attempt too much authenticity. I shall say I'm gently born and recently come down in the world. That should cover any amount of ignorance and unintended slips, don't you think?'

Alec nodded rather reluctantly.

'And most important of all,' I went on, 'there's this question of Lollie being followed whenever she goes out and eavesdropped upon whenever she's in the house. Do you see?'

'Ah, of course,' said Alec, who usually does see; it is one of the most comfortable aspects of our collaborations. 'It must be one of the servants, doing his master's bidding. Well, all right, you've convinced me.' He gave a short laugh. 'Oh, to be a fly on the wall though, Dandy, when you're . . . when you're busy . . . What exactly does a lady's maid do all day?'

'Don't ask me!' I said, rolling my eyes in not-completely-mock horror. 'I have tomorrow and Sunday cramming with Grant – and won't she adore it! – but for now I can't imagine.'

'I'm almost tempted to join you just to watch the fun. Would I make a footman?' Alec stood up and came to offer me the cigarette box, bending over from the waist like a jointed wooden soldier and clicking his heels together with a beaming smile.

'You look like a *Punch* cartoon of a bad waiter,' I told him. 'And anyway, there isn't another opening. The Balfours, if you please, have twelve servants in their Edinburgh house, and goodness knows how many more in the Highlands.'

'Twelve?' said Alec, standing up straight again and frowning. He ran Dunelgar on seven and a few locals for the rough work. 'What does he do, this Pip? Some kind of merchant or something, is he?' He sat back down again and knocked out his pipe.

'Well now,' I said. '*He* doesn't do anything, but listen to this and tell me if you don't agree that some earlier Balfour must have sold his soul to the devil.' I lit my cigarette and sat back to regale him with the history of the Balfours as it had been told to me. (The last thirty minutes of Miss Rossiter's interview had been taken up with it, almost as though Lollie could diminish the shortcomings of Pip himself by setting them against the triumphs of the Balfours in general.) It was quite a tale.

The first Balfour of any note came to prominence in the early days of the Georgian era, by setting up a bank in his native Edinburgh in 1717: the Edinburgh and Scottish Eastern Merchants' and Private Clearing Bank, whose name no one – from the founder, James Balfour himself, to the lowliest copying clerk – could be relied upon to reproduce with any accuracy (the pull of 'Eastern Scottish' in place of 'Scottish Eastern' being a particularly common pitfall) so that it is chiefly remembered among banking historians for the number of notes and drafts it issued with errors upon them. There is many a curio-cabinet which has, in one of its drawers, a family's famous 'bad banknote' folded up and yellowing but still taken out and shown to visitors.

Inevitably, the merchants of the day made life easier for themselves by dubbing Balfour's pet enterprise with a more descriptive title, and 'the Silk and Tobacco' flourished along with the trades which gave it its name. (There is still a public house in a back street of Edinburgh called the Silken Tab, whose hanging sign depicts a wigged and powdered old gentleman with a long pipe in his mouth, but since the associations have become blurred and the etymologies muddled, the current Balfours do not concern themselves about it.)

James Balfour Jr was a less cautious man than his father had been, a man who liked to be in at the start of things, and so it is unsurprising that in 1769 he was among the first to move down the hill, away from the smells and noise of the medieval Old Town, and into the stark majesty of a town house on Princes Street, with a view of the Castle and – once the draining of the old North Loch had finally been resolved, after many attempts and disappointments – as much fresh air as he, his wife and their seven children could hope for.

There was, however, to be little repose for Mr Balfour in his commodious new rooms, for he could not contain his eagerness to be part of the great expansion; new houses outside one's own window were simply that much more fun than holds of silk and bales of tobacco leaves half a world away and in 1770, when every other financier in the capital was feeling well cushioned and replete with success, Balfour found himself in company not with them but with the rather more hard-bitten speculative builders, who were poised to see if their fortunes would swell with the city or go like tapers up a newly swept flue. Balfour would never have sailed as close to the wind as to endanger his fortune, but he did what was to his peers even more amazing. He sold up his father's business: the Bank of Scotland opened its door with cold charity as to a waif on its step and the Edinburgh and Scottish Eastern Merchants' and Private Clearing Bank was no more.

So it was that the Balfour family got out of banking on the high tide just before the beginnings of the great long endless collapse and never had to underwrite a penny of it. And of course the New Town was the success story of the age and grew and grew until there was nowhere in his native city for the old man to put any more of his considerable fortune and his son – Robert Balfour – began to spread it around the land, and most notably to send it underground. From the lead mines of the Scottish uplands to the coal mines of the north of England, the Welsh silver mines and all the way to the tin mines of the West Country, Robert Balfour was chipping out of the earth more and more riches for himself and his own, sending the sons of lesser branches of the Balfour family to manage for him so that the name spread all over Britain and grew synonymous with a kind of far-seeing but hard-working massing of solid wealth.

In time, egged on by a son of his own with a taste for travel and adventure, Robert Balfour finally raised his gaze from the mine heads of Britain and looked to the East again, to India and to cotton, and grew richer still.

Now Robert's grandson, the first Philip Balfour, was as happy sailing back and forth between Bengal and Scotland as his wife was unhappy, whether accompanying him on the voyages or staying put at either end, for she suffered equally badly from the heat, the cold and the most excruciating, mortifying seasickness. Indeed, there was only one place on earth where she could imagine settling and turning her back on gangplanks and portholes for ever and that was the magical, almost mythical, island whither her more glamorous friends regularly sailed in search of fun and fashions and whence they returned with tales of both which made young Mrs Balfour's eyes and mouth water. Alexandra Balfour did not wish for the impossible: she could live without gold but every time she was forced onto the dusty streets of Calcutta or was carried through the mud of a mountain road in Kashmir on the neck of an elephant she pined anew for Manhattan, where the streets were paved.

In 1857, after a winter crossing which her husband called bracing but which reduced her to a state of such piteous and unrelieved sickness that their expected fourth child – whose arrival was the sole reason for the journey – came early and promptly left again, Alexandra prevailed. Philip was washed in guilt and grief but the spirit of his grandfather was lit in him as he began to ask around about the wonderful new city and the impossible new buildings rising up and up and up there and to write feverish letters to agents to secure for himself a patch of paradise while it was going.

And so it was that the Balfours made their second timely escape, from India this time, just before the Great Uprising which left every Company man with burned fingers and placed a mute in the neck of the jamboree for ever after.

Silk House – for Philip Balfour had a mind to family history – was to be the finest mansion in New York; he employed the newest and most daring of architects to plan its halls and cloisters and fountained courtyards, and the watercolour sketches of it, nestling in a green dip amongst hills with a cornflower-blue sky above and lush trees in the distance, had grown soft and faded from repeated rolling and unrolling, and rather grubby from the fingers of the three little Balfours choosing their bedrooms. Philip suffered one moment of disquiet in every ten of joy when he looked at the green dip and distant trees, for he could not quite make them fit into the other picture in his mind of lit streets and theatres and the vast emporia known as department stores. Once or twice, when he was regaling a chum at the club, he found himself not quite admitting of his half-built mansion that he had never set eyes on the place, and it did not bring him much comfort that – presumably because such a thing would never occur to them – none of the chums ever actually asked him.

They landed in November in 1858, in a gale which fired hail-stones up the wide avenues like peas from a shooter and turned every cross-street corner into a maelstrom, and it was clear right away even to the smallest Balfour child that the green dip had been fancy. Alexandra prepared to put a brave face on her dismay: there was certainly paving – there was little else. She paled and felt her eyes fill with tears, however, when she saw their mansion. It was the same familiar block of marble and porticoes from the watercolour drawings, but where the gardens should have been there were not only streets instead of glades but, on all four sides, railways. Their dreamed-of home was set about by railway lines like a pig penned in with hurdles and Alexandra began a bout of weeping which lasted on and off until the spring.

From their quarters in one of the Fifth Avenue apartment hotels, Philip wrote letter after furious letter and stormed the agents' offices, pored over street plans and maps, and even did his best with what scant volumes of American law he could lay his hands on, trying to find a hole through which he could wriggle. The names of the four railroad companies who owned one each of the hated tracks grew into a kind of bitter chant for him: Hudson, Central, Newhaven, Harlem, he muttered to himself as he scratched out another rage-filled letter. Hudson, Central, Newhaven, Harlem – that was the worst of the difficulty. There were four of the damned things and he was shoved around among them like the hot potato in the party game and could never pin down any one of the four owners or any one of their many managers and state his case fairly.

Actually though, Philip Balfour was not the only one incon-venienced by the four separate railroads passing one another in mid-town; it was becoming intolerable to everyone (except the hansom-men who shuttled passengers back and forth between the lines), but it took a man of immense riches, with an entre-preneurial vision greater even than that of the first James Balfour himself, to set matters straight. Mr Vanderbilt saw what was needed and Silk House, Philip Balfour's Valhalla, into which so much of the Balfour fortune had been poured, was a mere gnat to be swept away before the building of the Grand Central Terminus could begin.

'Blimey,' said Alec. 'So it's Vanderbilt money that's furnished the twelve servants?'

'Not quite,' I said. 'There's one more chapter to go. Balfour was still angry enough to drive a flinty bargain with the great man and he did recoup more of his outlay than he could possibly have dreamed of, then – so Lollie told me – they left New York with the laughter of all the Manhattan sophisticates still ringing in their ears and took themselves southwards to what – in April – must have seemed like a soft and balmy land where they could finally start up their life of lotus-eating as planned.'

'Where was this?'

'Somewhere in the vast southern territory,' I replied. 'Not a state as such.'

'Chumps,' said Alec.

'Indeed. They bought a huge spread with a white Palladian mansion on it, returned to New York to buy everything they needed to make life perfect there and arrived back neck and neck with the first heralds of summer – to wit, a swarm of biting insects of a size and ferocity never known in Calcutta. These were soon joined by things Lollie didn't know the name of but which sound like flying leeches if you can imagine anything so horrid, and black flies that followed them around in a column above their heads in the open air, and little fat things that flew in battalions all around their heads in the shade. Makes one almost glad of midges.'

'Speak for yourself,' said Alec. 'What happened next?'

'Alexandra, exhausted and dejected, refused to leave. She shut the doors on the wildlife and stayed there until she died. Philip travelled around a good bit, doing nothing very useful, and his son – our Philip's father – stuck it out until both parents were gone, planning to get shot of the place and come home to Scotland, which his mother had always made sound like absolute heaven to him.'

'So when did they leave?' Alec asked.

'1871,' I said, wondering if he would catch the significance of the date. He did not. 'Philip and Alexandra died and Alexander, their son, was just getting around to offloading the place when matters became rather more interesting.' Still Alec said nothing. 'Can't you guess? It's poetic really – an echo of Robert Balfour with all his subterranean adventures.'

'You're kidding!' said Alec. 'Oil?' I laughed along with him.

'The hundreds of thousands of sun-baked, yellow-grassed, insectiferous acres which were no good for anything except getting lost in happened to be smack on top of a perfect magic treacle pot of oil, that's still gushing out plumes of the stuff every day. So you see, twelve servants in an Edinburgh town house are really nothing.'

'And what does the current Pip Balfour do with the rest of it?'

'Counts it from time to time, I think. Too terrified by all the near misses to try anything more risky. Lollie says he felt the run of Balfour luck had to give out sometime and he doesn't want to be the one who finally lets it slip through his fingers on some wild scheme.'

'Well, that's a pretty poor show,' said Alec. 'He's hardly carrying the torch aflame, is he? Sounds like a bit of a ninny.' He paused. 'If ninnies went in for strangling their wives, that is.'

'Yes,' I said, agreeing with what he had not quite said. 'It's hard to come to a firm view from what we've been told, isn't it? I can't quite put him together somehow. I'm very much looking forward to meeting him for myself.'

'*I'm* not looking forward to you meeting him,' Alec said. 'Promise me you'll be careful, Dan.'

Tender concern for one's safety is always gratifying to behold. Hugh, in marked contrast, barely raised his head when he heard I was going.

'On Monday,' I added. 'To Edinburgh. I can't say for how long.'

'Good, good,' he said and turned the page of his newspaper.

I poked a hole in the top of one of my poached eggs and dabbed a piece of toast into it. I had only had one letter in the morning's post and was shamelessly lingering, putting off the evils of the coming day.

'You might know them,' I said. 'The people I'm . . . going to stay with.'

'Mm,' said Hugh. Then he added: 'Hah!' I waited. 'They've locked them out. Should have done it nine months ago. This'll bring them to their senses.'

'The miners?' I hazarded.

'I knew this would happen,' said Hugh, looking up at me at last. 'I predicted it from the start if you remember, Dandy.' I did not remember, but nodded anyway. 'There's no talking to these people and goodness knows how much money has been poured down the drain while everyone bent over backwards trying.'

It was my understanding – not firm but far from hazy – that both sides had their arms folded and their chins stuck out refusing to listen, but it was not worth starting an argument over it.

'Will the coal run out?' I asked.

'No, they'll be back at work before there's any chance of that,' Hugh assured me. 'And should think themselves lucky to have work to go back to. If I were a mine-owner, I should sack the lot and give their jobs to someone a bit more grateful.'

I judged another silent nod to be the best response to this. Hugh had never sacked anyone in his life, not even the mole-catcher who had once ruined Gilverton's lawns when, pushed beyond his limits by the little devils, he threw down his patented fumigation pump and testing rods and started digging wildly, swearing at the top of his voice and scattering divots of turf and sprays of soil for yards around him. Besides, the coal crisis was one of the few affairs of the day upon which Hugh and I saw eye-to-eye, or rather where our views happened to coincide: Hugh's view that the mine-owners could do what they jolly well pleased with what was theirs and my view that the wages one read about in *The Times* always seemed generous enough, pounds and pounds a week, and many of the families had half a dozen wage packets all told, between father and sons, and then they always lived in those dear little rows of cottages built for the purpose and enjoyed, one assumed, free coal.

Hugh turned another page and breathed in sharply, then started coughing to expel the inhaled toast crumbs. After a minute, I half stood to go round and bang him on the back, but he waved me into my seat again.

'Listen to this,' he croaked, eyes still streaming. '*The extraordinary conference of trade unionists currently convened in London will vote this afternoon upon whether to take sympathetic action in support of the miners.*' He took a gulp of tea and cleared his throat in a final-sounding way. 'The day is upon us. I always said it would come.'

'I'm not sure I understand.'

'A shutdown,' he said. All news was bad news with Hugh and his fears of an uprising were so oft expressed that I had ceased taking any notice of them. He had, for instance, continued to mutter darkly about Lenin even after he was dead and gone. This, however, sounded more definite than usual.

'Shutdown of what?' I asked.

'Everything,' Hugh told me with a thrill of angry pleasure. 'The whole country held to ransom, Dandy. No food in the shops, gasworks stopped, electricity dried up, hospitals in darkness, fires raging with no firemen to put them out, no teachers in the schools, factories silent . . .'

'But they can't do that,' I said. 'There must be laws.'

'Laws!' said Hugh, with a very dry laugh. 'The overthrow of the rule of law is the whole point, my dear. That's what they want and they've been champing for a chance to get started on it. The miners are just the excuse they've been waiting for.'

'But that sounds like . . .'

'A revolution,' he thundered. 'Which is exactly what it is. A workers' revolt.'

'Stop it,' I said, feeling genuinely scared now. 'That could never happen. Not here.'

'They're voting this afternoon,' said Hugh, tapping a finger on the newspaper where he had read it. I let my breath go in a great rush and shook my head at him.

'Well, exactly!' I said. 'They're voting on it. They'll never *do* it, Hugh; you're a fearful dramatist sometimes.'

'I shall remind you that you said so,' he said, much on his dignity, and with that the conversation was at its close.

'Grant,' I said, sidling into my bedroom again after breakfast. Grant started violently, and she and I both winced as her knuckles rapped against the inside of the drawer where she was carefully laying out newly ironed underclothes.

'Nothing wrong is there?' she said. 'Madam. Why aren't you out on your walk?' She glanced out of the window where the weather was as fine as could be hoped for, for May in Perthshire, that is, chilly and gusty but, for the moment, almost dry. I felt a small slump at the thought of my predictability, but I rallied myself before she could see it and set a bright smile on my face.

'I'm fine,' I said. 'What are your plans for the day?' Grant frowned at me, more perplexed than ever.

'My plans?' she said. 'I was going to start on changing over your wardrobe, laying away your winter things and seeing if any of your summer frocks from last year are worth airing out again.'

'I see. Well, I'm going to have to ask you to leave all that, I'm afraid, while I bend you to my will.' I smiled even wider; Grant frowned even deeper. 'I – I – I don't quite know, Grant, how much of what I do,' – I took a deep breath – 'professionally, I mean, has come to your attention in the last while.'

'You mean Gilver and Osborne Investigations?' My mouth dropped open. 'I thought you must be starting on a new case when I saw those shoes you dyed. How can I help you?'

'I see. Yes. So you *do* know about it then?' The name of Gilver and Osborne was pure servants' hall fantasy of course (although it had a ring to it) and I could not imagine how the newly black shoes, hidden in my sitting room while they dried and smuggled up to an attic the previous evening upon Miss Rossiter's return, .

had been rumbled but there was no question that Grant was fully informed.

'Oh yes, madam,' she said. 'We were all very proud of you downstairs over that last business. Even Mr Pallister, now that the master knows all about it and has given it his blessing.' Grant delivered all of this in her usual blithe tone, then finished it off with a belated and unconvincing: 'If you'll excuse the liberty.'

'Right, well, good,' I said. 'In that case, what I'm about to ask you will come as less of a surprise. I'm going undercover, Grant. Do you know what that means?' She nodded, looking thrilled.

'What as?' she breathed. 'I can drop everything this minute and get a costume run up for you, madam. When do you need it?'

'I'm starting on Monday. I'm going downstairs. I'm going to be a lady's maid.'

Grant's lips twitched once, twice, then she bit her cheeks and pulled her eyebrows very firmly downwards.

'And your "mistress", madam?' she said, with her voice under commendable control. 'Is it her you're investigating?'

'No,' I said, 'it's she who has employed me.'

'Oh, well then,' said Grant, lifting her hands high and then letting them clap down softly against her skirt again, 'in that case you'll be fine.' As votes of confidence go it was a stinker but, like most other people, I always claim to value honesty and so I could not refuse such a good dollop of it when it was served up to me.

By the time I fell into bed on Sunday evening, my head was heavy with great spilling heaps of new facts and long lists of outlandish preparations and I had a thick notebook full of daily, weekly and monthly chores.

'Crêpe de chine, satin, tussore – cold. Cashmere, chiffon, mohair – cool. Silk, faille, wool – warm. Lawn, cotton, linen – hot,' I repeated to myself. 'I've got it. And down again – wring, squeeze, press, drip. And up: sprinkle iron cool, sprinkle press cool, damp iron warm, wet press hot. It's easy!' I turned over, ignoring the crackling sound of the cold sugar-water waves in my hair; Grant had spent much of Sunday afternoon teaching me how to make them after a brief and alarming episode with the hot irons in the morning. I punched my pillow and clicked my tongue to make Bunty come up the bed a bit and let me put my arms around her. I had never been separated from her for more than a night or two since she had arrived – tiny, fat and wriggling – all those years before and I did not look forward to driving away and leaving her behind me. She would be quite happy with Alec and Millie, his spaniel, but I had slipped a photograph of her into my bag as a comfort to me. The bag was sitting in the middle of my bedroom floor with a plump black umbrella leaning against it and an extravagantly hideous hat balanced on top. The shoes, cleaned and re-dyed by Grant with much tutting, were lined up neatly under my chair, the grey serge suit laid out over its back. My tin trunk was already downstairs by the stable-yard door ready to be lifted onto the dogcart and taken to the station in the morning. I gave Bunty a squeeze, kissed her head and closed my eyes on it all, hoping that sleep would come swift and dreamless.

3

The train, at least the third-class part of it, was packed to the walls, every seat in every compartment taken, luggage racks bulging, corridors jammed tight and thick with pipe smoke. I had been banged on the elbow twice already by a sample case – I could not guess what its owner was selling but the case itself was painfully sturdy – and on shifting away from him had been dripped on by the melting iced lollipop of a child drowsing on its mother's lap to my right. I tucked both elbows in tighter, hugged the plump umbrella and peered out to see where we had got to.

'Today doesn't suit me at all as it happens,' said a woman opposite. She had been carrying on a conversation of loud complaint with her travelling companion since joining the train at Dunblane, or actually since joining the compartment at Bridge of Allan, after spending the first part of her journey standing in the passageway glaring in at two young men, silently demanding their seats. 'Half-day closing Wednesday is my usual day for Edinburgh and this has thrown me right out for the whole week. I'd not be surprised if I got one of my sick headaches tonight.'

'I did say that, Minnie,' her friend put in mildly. 'I was happy to wait and see what happened. I don't think they'll really stop the trains.'

'Transport, building, printing and heavy works,' said the salesman, in a thick Glasgow accent. 'Of course, there winnae be trains.'

'Och, they'll sort it all before midnight,' said an elderly man in the corner, speaking around his pipe. 'Mr Baldwin and Mr Pugh'll get it seen to between their two selves.'

'They might try right enough,' said the stout salesman, 'but what about Red Bevin and that wee Churchill toerag – they're just itchin' for a dust-up.'

With some relief I saw the large white lettering on the Jenner's depository building go by outside the window and felt a jolt as the brakes gripped and the train began the long slow pull in towards Haymarket station. The young salesman stood up, giving me a farewell bang on the knees with his case, and talk of the strike sank under the shifting of bodies and parcels and the general struggle of departure.

I was very glad to be leaving the train at its final destination, for I should have been at a loss on the question of how to extricate myself and my bag from a compartment and get my trunk out of the guard's van during a short station stop. Did servants summon porters? Grant's instructions had not covered this point but I hardly thought so, and even if a porter volunteered to help how was one to manage the tipping? As it was, I stood helplessly on the plat-form looking in at my trunk through the opened doors and wondering if I should try to shift it.

'Needin' a wee hand, hen?' said a voice beside me and the two young men – apprentice boys, perhaps – who had been ousted by Minnie hopped up into the guard's van and turned their caps backwards.

'Which one's yours?' asked one of them and, when I pointed, they hefted the small trunk between them and leapt back out onto the platform again.

'Where do you want it?' asked the other.

'I don't know,' I said. I gazed about myself. Lollie had not gone into any details about my arrival and I had no idea if I was to be met. I could not, obviously, hail a cab but nor could I manhandle this trunk onto a bus and off again.

'Startin' in a new place, eh?' said one of the lads, squinting at me past the smoke of his cigarette. I nodded. 'Maids' store, Sandy,' he said, and they set off towards the station building with me trotting after.

The maids' store was in a part of the station I had never seen before, under some brick arches with metalled walkways crossing overhead. A queue of girls in serge and bad hats shuffled forwards, kicking their trunks or rolling them on barrows, towards an opening with a counter where a middle-aged man in uniform was writing down details in a ledger and tearing off pink tickets from a roll.

'Name?' he said when I got to the head of the queue.

'Miss Rossiter,' I said. He looked up and frowned at me.

'Address?'

'31 Heriot Row,' I said. He put his pencil down, folded his arms and stared at me.

'There's no Rossiter in Heriot Row,' he said. 'Are you taking a lend o' me, lassie?'

'I'm sorry, I don't quite understand,' I began, feeling my face start to change colour. There was some tittering from behind me.

'Get yourself round to the left luggage and pay your tuppence,' said the man with the pencil. 'This is the maids' store.'

'I *am* a maid,' I told him. 'I'm starting today as a lady's maid for Mrs Balfour of Heriot Row and my name is Rossiter.' The struggle between wounded dignity and maid-like meekness was making my voice tremble.

The man explored the inside of his cheek with his tongue and regarded me.

'Aye, Balfour, that's right,' he said at last.

'I'm sorry,' I said. 'It's my first position, you see.'

His face softened with understanding and, I think, pity. He ripped off a pink ticket and closed my hand around it with a fatherly pat.

'I do see,' he said. 'Well, you take that there wee chitty and give it to the housekeeper. She'll get a pair of lads to lift your trunk round for you. And sorry I was that wee bit short, there. It's been going like a fair all day and I'm run off my feet with it.'

'It'll be a quieter day tomorrow for you,' I said. 'If this strike goes ahead anyway.'

'I'll be on the pickets, hen,' he said. 'On my feet all day and no' getting paid for it.'

I stared at him. A striker! I was face to face with one of them.

He did not look much like a revolutionary, with his uniform jacket open over a Fair Isle jumper in bright colours and with a stub of pencil behind each ear as well as the one in his hand.

'See if you can get the lads down for your case nice and sharp, eh?' he said. 'The store's fillin' up fast already and we've still the late rush to come.'

There was no front door and butler for me today, of course. The maids' store might have thrown me for a moment but I knew *that* much, and I passed through the iron gate and descended the area steps to the door below. It opened before I had reached the flagstones and a smiling face appeared round it.

'Miss Rossiter? I'm Clara, the parlourmaid.' She opened the door completely, came out into the area and took my bag from me. 'Mind they steps,' she said. 'They get right mossy when it rains.' She was a tall, vigorous girl in her twenties, with a long oval face and small dancing eyes, and her smile – perhaps to hide imperfect teeth – was more a bunching up of her lips into a bud than a stretching of them, which was most appealing.

'Mrs Hepburn's making toffee nests for tonight's sweet,' she said, 'and she cannae leave them, but come away back and say hello a minute, before you go to your room, and you can pick up a wee cup of tea and take it with you, eh?'

'That would be lovely, Clara,' I said, envisioning kicking off Miss Rossiter's shoes and lying back against pillows, sipping and dozing.

'So what's your Christian name?' asked Clara over her shoulder as she closed the area door behind us and started along a stone passageway towards the back of the house, squeezing past the filled scuttles and zinc liners which waited in a row there.

I stopped walking. What *was* Miss Rossiter's Christian name? I had not imagined that she would need one. Grant was Grant to me and Miss Grant to the others as far as I knew. Before I could speak, Clara turned around and gave me a cold look out of her little eyes, not dancing at all now.

'Oh,' she said. 'It's like that, is it?' and she flounced into the kitchen with her head held very high.

'It was Miss Rossiter you heard right enough, Mrs Hepburn,' she said. 'Here she is. *Miss* Rossiter.'

I stepped inside behind her. It was a cavernous room dominated by the black Eagle range which took up most of one wall and sent shimmering waves of heat to stir festoons of flypapers all around the ceiling. At the table, directly under the electric light, a formidable-looking cook in a rose-pink dress and enormous apron, with a bunch of keys twinkling at her waist, was letting ropes of syrup drop from a small ladle onto a wooden contraption like a large darning ball on a stick, held up by a kitchenmaid who was quivering with the effort of holding it steady and was cross-eyed from staring just in front of her face. By the range, a very young boy was sitting with his stockinged feet on the fender, plucking a chicken and throwing the feathers onto the flames.

'Fanny,' I said, rather louder than I had intended.

The young boy looked up, Clara bit her lip and the cross-eyed maid jumped.

'Millie-molly-moo,' said the cook, 'how many times have I told you?' She wiped up a blob of syrup from the table-top with her finger and stuck it out for the girl to lick. 'You have to hold the paddle steady.'

'Sorry,' I said, meaning it to take in all of them. 'I always tell myself that next time I meet someone I shall say Frances and I never do. I got close this time, though – said nothing at all!'

Clara was smiling at me again; she had swallowed it.

'Nothing wrong with Fanny,' she said. 'Better than Millie-molly-moo, anyway.'

Mrs Hepburn took the paddle and stuck it into a kind of pipe-rack affair where a few others were cooling, then she put the sugar pot on the back of the range to keep warm, wiped her hands on her apron and turned to greet me.

'Kitty Hepburn,' she said. 'And this wee chookie is my niece,

Amelia, the scullerymaid. She gets Millie, though. And Mattie, the hall and boot boy.'

'Miss,' said Mattie, dipping his head.

'Kitchenmaid now, Auntie Kitty,' said Millie. 'I mean, Mrs Hepburn.'

The cook's face clouded very briefly.

'Well, let's just see, will we?' she said. 'Make a cup of tea for Miss Rossiter to be going on with anyway.'

Millie trotted towards the scullery door then turned and took a few paces back in the direction of the large dresser which filled the wall opposite the range.

'What cup does a lady's maid get, Auntie Kit— Hepburn?' she said.

'I'll get it, Molly-moo,' said Clara, rolling her eyes at me. The scullerymaid, unperturbed by the teasing, sat down opposite Mattie by the fireside and put her hands between her knees, like a toddler who is trying ostentatiously to stay out of mischief. She was fifteen perhaps, with the face of a pink-and-white china baby doll and a round, dumpy figure that one could easily believe was made of stockinet stuffed with sand. Her brown hair was plaited and pinned over her head and her innocent eyes blinked from behind round spectacles. She caught me studying her and beamed at me with the guilelessness of a child.

'I've put two lumps in,' said Clara, holding out a teacup with the saucer balanced on top to keep it hot, 'seeing you've been on the train getting all trauchled.'

'There's a good girl,' said Mrs Hepburn. 'I'll take you down to your room now, Miss Rossiter. Clara, you better get into your blacks before Mr Faulds comes in. Coal scuttles, Mattie-boy. And potatoes, Millie – ten big ones and mind you set them in the salt water straight away and not leave them out on the bunker to brown.' Mrs Hepburn gathered up my bag and umbrella in one hand and taking my teacup in the other she swept out of the kitchen.

'Isn't she lovely spoken?' said Millie as I was closing the kitchen door behind me. The others shushed her furiously but I caught her eye and smiled.

'*Down* to my room?' I said, following the cook, and right enough she had crossed the passageway and was descending a set of worn steps, her wooden heels knocking on the stone with a rather mournful sound. 'I was expecting an attic.'

We arrived in the sub-basement, and I peered around waiting for my eyes to adjust to the gloom. When they did I saw dark green walls, dark brown doors and a dark red painted stone floor, covered with a narrow strip of grey hair carpet. There was no furniture, only two deep laundry hampers set against the wall, one open and half-filled with white bundles and one buckled shut, an address label tied to its handle, awaiting collection or just returned.

'You've never been in an Edinburgh house then?' said Mrs Hepburn. 'The nurseries are in the attics and our rooms are all down here.'

I had indeed noticed the almost subterranean windows below basement level in some of Edinburgh's houses but had never stopped to wonder what was behind them. Mrs Hepburn turned right and opened one of the brown doors.

To my surprise, light flooded out into the passageway.

'Here you are then,' she said, bustling in and putting my teacup down on a shelf to the side of the fire, which was burning cheerfully. 'You're at the back but there's no slight meant to it because the front rooms are black as caves and here you've a good view down the garden. Clara and Phyllis – she's the housemaid – are across the way and the rest of them – well, it's just the two of them now – have the front room.' She stopped and smiled at me. 'I'll let you get settled then,' she said. 'Servants' hall is in front of the kitchen and dinner's at six. Mrs Balfour said she'd not need to see you until seven, so there's a nice easy start for you. The – ahem – is just out the back there, up the steps to the walkway and on the left beyond the scullery and it's ladies only, so there's no need to worry about that. The menservants have their arrangements down at the mews.'

'Thank you, Mrs Hepburn,' I said. 'You've been very kind. And regarding the ladies' . . . arrangements, is the back door open?'

'Until Mr Faulds locks up at night it is. Now do you have your chit for your trunk? I'll get Mattie and John to slip down for it before tea.' I fished out the pink ticket and gave it to her. 'We're a happy house, Fanny,' she said, then hesitated as though wondering whether to say more. 'Young Mrs Balfour is a dear girl and you'll not have much to do with the master, I don't suppose.'

Which, I thought to myself once she had left, was commendably discreet but still spoke volumes. It need have no connection to Lollie's troubles, of course, but still I should have liked to know why my predecessor had left before a replacement could be found for her. The loss of a servant from a household of such friendliness, in which fires burned in bedroom grates on afternoons in May, needed at least some explaining.

My new home, now that I had a chance to look around it, was a great deal better than I had been expecting; a very great deal better than the attic rooms at Gilverton anyway. It was perhaps ten feet square, with a tall window, modestly clothed in muslin halfway up, which looked out over a patch of grass and a cherry tree. There was a black iron bedstead – exactly the same as those at Gilverton – with fat pillows and a fat quilt, an armchair near the fire, a chest of drawers with jug and basin on top, a bookcase and a hanging cupboard. A door beside the window revealed a tiny room housing a small china sink with hot and cold taps, a very small mangle fitted to it at one end and a clothes airer on a pulley above it. Boxes of Sunlight soap and packets of Robin starch lined up along the windowsill told me that this was where Miss Rossiter would lovingly launder Mrs Balfour's most delicate garments. I sniffed at the packets, of course. Armed with Grant's notes I would raid the kitchen for lemon and lavender; I knew the right way of things. I leaned over the taps and peered out of the window wondering if there might be a butt of rainwater I could lay claim to, but the fire, armchair and sweet tea were calling to me.

When I left my room at five minutes to six for dinner in the servants' hall, I had already made it wonderfully cosy. Photographs of Bunty – and one of Nanny Palmer whom I was proposing to pass off as my mother – were ranged on the chimneypiece; my clothes were folded away or hanging over the airer to uncrease themselves, and I had upended my trunk and covered it with a gay shawl as a nightstand, a trick learned at finishing school where the furnishers of our dormitory bedrooms had taken great care to discourage reading in bed by failing to provide anywhere to put a candle or cup of cocoa.

Before I was halfway up the stairs to the basement again I could hear talking – men's talking – and I hesitated, smoothing my hair under the restraining pins and patting flat the starched collar of my frock. When I pushed open the door a sea of faces turned towards me.

'Here she is,' said a jovial voice, and the butler I had met on the day of my interview stood up from a fireside armchair and opened his arms in welcome to me. Mrs Hepburn was sitting in a matching armchair on the other side of the fire with a small glass of some brown liquid in her hand. There was a third chair in a less exalted position just off to one side and a plump young man sprang out of it and began shaking up its cushions before turning towards me.

'Miss Rossiter,' he said, with a slight bow.

'Sherry, Miss Rossiter?' said Mr Faulds, taking out a fat watch and peering at it. 'There's just time before dinner, I see.'

Slightly bewildered, I sat down and accepted a glass with a thimbleful of thick, dark sherry in it.

'Now,' said Mr Faulds. 'Here's where we test your memory for you!' As he sat back down again he waved around the long table, covered in oilcloth but laid for a meal, where the rest of the staff were sitting.

'Clara, Millie and Mattie I know already,' I said, nodding at the three of them, the known faces in the crowd. As I spoke a young man in grey britches and braces, with his collar open and sleeves rolled, sat up very straight and whistled.

'Mind out for your glass with they vowels flyin' about, Mrs Hepburn,' he said.

One of the maids tittered and I smiled too, to show willing.

'That's John,' said Mrs Hepburn. 'He's the chauffeur. Cheek of a monkey but no harm in him.' John grinned at me and stretched out in his chair, crossing his legs at the ankle and lacing his hands together behind his head. Chauffeurs are most often chosen to complement an elegant motorcar and this one was no exception: tall and broad-shouldered with a square jaw and straight brows, as though the word 'strapping' had been invented to describe him.

'Next to him,' said Mrs Hepburn, 'is Harry, master's valet.' Harry took his nearly finished cigarette out of his mouth and saluted me with it, touching his fingertips to his temple in such a way that the insolence was as hard to define as it was to ignore. I smiled at him regardless and he looked away. He was as young as John and as tall, but nature had been less kind, giving him a weaker chin, a larger nose, a rather red and angry-looking complexion.

Beside Harry was the man who had vacated my armchair. He was clearly a butler-in-waiting, natty in dress, stout in outline, dressed in the same striped trousers, yellow-edged waistcoat and butterfly collar as Mr Faulds.

'Stanley,' he said to me, half rising to bow. 'I'm the footman.' He tweaked at his trousers as he sat back down and I noticed that Millie's eyes, soft behind her spectacles, were fastened upon him with something approaching rapture. I had to purse my lips not to smile. For if the scullerymaid was a china doll fashioned by Mabel Lucie Attwell, then Stanley the footman was made to match her with his large blue slightly pop eyes, his pink cheeks and his egg-like figure. They put one in mind of the carved couples who trundle out one on each side of a cuckoo clock to mark the halves and quarters with a bang of a mallet.

'And then there's Phyllis, the housemaid,' said Mr Faulds, gesturing with a broad smile.

'Nice to meet you, Miss Rossiter,' said Phyllis. She was a taking little thing, perched at the end of the table with her feet up on the spar of her chair and a small embroidery frame held up close in the dimness as she sewed. She had that very pretty Celtic colouring of dark hair, pale skin, light eyes and sparse pale brows, with curling lips which looked as though they had been rouged but were really just naturally pink, and a shiny little spade of a chin. I could not help glancing at John and Harry to see if there were any more rapturous glances to be intercepted, but I found none.

'And finally,' said Mrs Hepburn, 'Eldry, the tweenie.' Eldry, the tweenie, when she looked up and nodded a greeting – for she was sewing too – was revealed to be a plain girl with a bony nose and teeth which, at rest, were always visible against her bottom lip. She should have scraped her hair back, painted her lips red and pointed that sharp nose to the sky, I thought – I had seen girls who had managed to make themselves striking that way if they had enough confidence to pull it off – but Eldry had taken the much more common route of pressing her hair into little curls around her face, lowering her head to hide the nose and pursing her mouth to hide the teeth, after which of course there is no helping it.

'That's a very unusual name you have,' I said to her. Phyllis – I guessed that she was the giggler amongst the girls; there always is one – tittered again.

'Etheldreda,' said Eldry. 'Only my ma's Ethel and my grandma's Dreda so there was only the middle bit left for me.' She sounded so plaintive as she said it that the laughter spread around the room, even as Eldry blinked at us all wondering what the joke was.

'Eh, dear,' said Mrs Hepburn. 'Ah well, if you can't laugh, eh? Right then, girlies! It's sausage and onion pie and treacle pud, Fanny. Drop of pea and ham soup to start with. I knew you'd be wanting a good dinner after your long day.'

Eldry and Millie jumped up and Mrs Hepburn, one hand on each knee, hauled herself to her feet too. Clara, who had come to drape her long frame on the arm of the chair during the introductions, now slid into its seat and stretched her feet out towards the blaze.

'Is there someone missing?' I said, looking around and counting them off surreptitiously on my fingers. The butler, the cook and me made three, the four menservants – handsome John, plain Harry, round little Stanley and sweet Mattie – made seven and Clara, Phyllis, Millie and Eldry, the four maids, made eleven in all. Lollie had definitely told me there were twelve. Stanley and Mr Faulds glanced at one another, but it was Harry who spoke up, his voice as rough and awkward as his complexion.

'Maggie,' he said. 'Kitchenmaid. Done a flit on Saturday night.'

'Really?' I said.

'Silly wench,' said Mr Faulds. 'Didn't know when she was well off.' I saw Clara shift in her seat, her long face solemn and her small eyes beady, and Phyllis put her embroidery down and leaned over to squeeze the other girl's arm. 'Took off after a promotion, Miss Rossiter, down by Berwick in a big house with a chef and a lot of girls to boss about. Kept it to herself and didn't work a day of her notice. Mistress would have let her off with a week and given her a reference, but there's no talking to these young-sters.'

Privately, I agreed. To have left a post with no reference was a reckless move for any servant and if the Berwick job fell through, good luck to Maggie finding another.

'Mind you, Mr Faulds,' said Stanley, looking up from the news-paper spread over his place setting, 'if she'd stayed her week she'd never have got there. It says here there's no trains on tomorrow with this general strike.'

'It's not a general strike,' said Harry, sitting forward suddenly so that his chair legs banged against the floor. 'It's a selective co-ordinated industrial action.'

'Harry is our resident Red, Miss Rossiter,' said Mr Faulds.

'It's a menace is what it is,' said Stanley, folding up his news-paper in brusque angry movements. It is always pointless – either annoying or amusing – for the under-thirties to attempt pomposity and Stanley failed to do anything but make Phyllis giggle again.

'And you're the . . . valet?' I said to Harry. I was still trying to get them straight in my head after the whirlwind of introductions.

'He is indeed,' said John, grinning. 'It's all part of the plan.' Then he ducked as Harry aimed a punch at the side of his head.

'Now, now, lads,' said Mr Faulds, as Stanley looked on with his mouth pulled down in a cod-like pout of disapproval. The butler heaved himself up to his feet. 'There's a bottle of burgundy needs using up,' he said to himself, 'but sausage and onion pie wants beer, really.' Picking over a large bunch of keys, he left the kitchen and I heard the hobnails on his heels ring out against the stone steps as he descended to the sub-basement where, I guessed, the beer cellar must be.

'All part of what plan?' I asked the lads once he was gone. John grinned again and Harry gave me a long appraising look.

'Don't encourage them,' said Phyllis, who had taken up her sewing again.

'All the valets are Trots,' said John. 'Just waiting for the word and then ccrrrkkk!' He drew a finger across his throat. 'The lords and masters struck down while they get their morning shave and the revolution begins. Easiest way, really.'

'Disgraceful!' said Stanley.

'You should recruit Miss Rossiter, Harry,' said John. 'Get the lady's maids as well as the valets and you're laughing.'

'Eldry would have plenty to say if she caught you sweet-talking Miss Rossiter,' said Phyllis to John. I looked at her, startled. Poor plain Eldry and this rather arrogant young man? Surely not. But I thought, from John's shout of laughter and Phyllis's look of mischief, that this was a tease more than an indiscretion.

'You wouldn't dare go on like this if Mr Faulds could hear you,' said Stanley.

'Aye, we would,' said John. Stanley flushed.

'Well, you wouldn't dare if we had a butler like the butlers that trained me,' he said. 'Like the butler I'll *be* one day.'

'Oh Stan,' said Clara, stretching out a long leg and poking the footman with her toe. 'Don't let him rile you, he disnae mean anything by it.' But Stanley was not to be soothed.

'I'll go and help Mr Faulds,' he said, rising and patting at imaginary specks on his waistcoat. 'Heaven knows, he needs it.'

'That's my boy,' said Harry. 'We're all workers together. We shall surely overcome, united in toil.'

So Stanley's exit was marred by yet more giggling and his slightly pendulous cheeks were aflame as he passed me, his pop eyes shining.

'They were saying on the train that Baldwin and Pugh are meeting tonight,' I said, hoping to sound knowledgeable, wondering what Miss Rossiter would, and therefore what I should, make of the affair.

'Uncle Arthur'll never give in,' said Harry.

'Fingers crossed,' said a small voice. I started. It was the first time since I had come into the room that Mattie the hall boy had spoken. With his white-blond hair and his pale skin, he appeared not only childlike but positively elfin and anything less like a troublemaker could scarcely be imagined.

'They'll be awright, Matt,' said Phyllis, and she and Clara swooped down on him from each side and kissed a cheek each. 'Mattie's worried about his family, Miss Rossiter. With the lock-out, you know.'

'Mrs Hepburn'll give you such a basket to take to them on your day off, you'll not be able to carry it,' said Clara, trying to make him smile. 'You'll have to eat the lot to keep your strength up and then you'll have an empty basket and your ma'll leather you and call Mrs H. all sorts and you'll wish the strike was all you had to trouble you.' Mattie did, indeed, give a small chuckle at that.

'Who's this and what are they calling me?' said Mrs Hepburn, coming back in with an enormous tray, steam rising from six deep plates of soup. Eldry followed with another tray and Millie brought up the rear with a breadboard and butter dish. 'Where's Mr Faulds and his shadow got to now, then? This soup needs supped before the pies get over-browned. Come on, come on – get your legs under. You too, Fanny. Grub's up.'

★   ★   ★

The journey from the servants' hall after dinner was a long one. Of course, any upward journey is hindered by the recent ingestion of pea soup, sausage pie and treacle pudding – I was blowing like a whale by the second landing – but it was more than that. Across the linoleum, past the scuttles, up the worn stone steps, across the glittering tiles on the ground floor, past the hall table with its salvers, up the marble stairs with the gilded banisters, across the gleaming parquet of the drawing-room floor, up the carpeted stairs with the ebony banisters, all the way to where Lollie waited, peeping around her door, looking out for me, and when I arrived it took a moment for the idea to fall away that I was simply going to help her into an evening frock, stud her hair with a few ornaments and take her stockings away to rinse out for the morning. Miss Rossiter had possessed me body and soul.

'In here, Dandy,' she hissed. She drew me into the room beside her and closed and locked the door. 'How was it?' she said, looking searchingly at me, 'I haven't been able to stop thinking about you down there. Are you all right?'

'I'm fine,' I said. 'I like your Mrs Hepburn, Lollie dear. She calls me Fanny and plies me with drink. And the girls and boys are all very lively. I slightly let Miss Rossiter's accent fall by the wayside, but they've decided en masse to treat it as a sort of joke, so there's nothing to worry about on that score.'

'Splendid,' said Lollie. She crossed the room and sat at her dressing table where an overflowing ashtray spoke of her nervous afternoon. 'It's just a couple of Pip's friends for dinner tonight – nothing too fancy. But let's talk while I change.' I thought of Mrs Hepburn's spun toffee nests and the coconut ice she had been finishing off to fill them with when I had left her, and I wondered what 'fancy' would have looked like.

'Very well, then,' I said, taking out my little notebook and sitting down on the end of her bed. 'First of all: do you have any suspicions about who it is that's following you when you go out?'

'None,' said Lollie, stopping with her shirt halfway off over her head and staring at me.

'Male or female, even?'

'Why?'

'I was trying to think who it might be myself,' I told her. 'Some of them are absolutely impossible: Millie and Mattie, for instance. Their innocence shines out of them.' I nodded to myself. Of course, it was terrible detective work to discount a person on that score but, more pertinently, a scullerymaid is always under the eye of the cook and a hall and boot boy hardly less so; harried and chivvied and nagged and kept up to the mark with endless little jobs all day. I could not imagine that young Mattie could easily slip away.

So perhaps the only candidates were Mrs Hepburn or Mr Faulds, with no one above them to check their movements and demand accounts of missing time? But as soon as I had thought it I could see how hopeless it was, for a butler is always there, upstairs and down, drawing room and servants' hall, always at the other end of a rung bell, opening doors, bearing trays, bowing over salvers. If Pallister, at home at Gilverton, were to take up secret missions the very walls would crumble by teatime. And if a butler is the walls and floors and door bells of a house then a cook is the foundation stone, square and solid and always down there, in the kitchens, toiling away. I am not often in the kitchens at Gilverton, it is true, but I had certainly never been there when Mrs Tilling was not, could scarcely imagine such a thing.

No, if anyone were slipping out and following Lollie it was to the middle ranks I should be looking. Not perhaps the footman, for footmen are as visible as butlers all day long, and not the tweenie who, even though she spent half her time above stairs and half below, had a daily round not of her own devising. Besides, poor shy Eldry, biting her lip and blushing, did not seem the girl to dash out and then cover her tracks upon her return. The two upper maids, languorous Clara and pert little Phyllis, were a livelier pair of prospects; I should have thought either of them quite equal to a bit of spying. But then I thought again of Clara's flouncing huff over Miss Rossiter's Christian name. Surely that sprang from some quite solid sense of fair play? And then think of Phyllis giggling and stitching her embroidery and comforting poor Mattie with cuddles. A snooper? It did not seem likely.

Which left those two boys: John and Harry. John, being the chauffeur, could certainly – easily – be sent off on errands by his master without the other servants missing him. And I knew from my own experience how much time Grant spends mysteriously employed away from the house, even with only a dressmaker in the village to absorb her attentions. If we lived in a town she would never be out of the shops, buying up yards of ribbon and stockings by the score, and I imagined the same was true of a valet, if not even more so, what with shaving soap and tobacco and hair brilliantine. Again though, apart from the free time at their disposal, neither of them seemed all that likely: John had the easy, open manners which come from good looks and early advancement and Harry the brusque insolence of plain features and too much politics, but of watchful cunning and furtiveness I had seen not a whisker.

Lollie's thoughts must have been running along the same lines as my own.

'It never occurred to me it was one of the servants,' she said, rousing me from them. She had got herself out of her shirt and skirt and had wrapped herself up in a dressing gown to sit at her table.

'Who else?' I asked her. 'It was the first thing that occurred to me.'

'I suppose a private detective?' said Lollie. 'Someone could easily wait across the road for me to come out.'

I stepped over to the windows and looked out. Her bedroom was at the front, on the sunny side, and had an excellent view over Queen Street Gardens where a private detective might indeed pass endless unseen hours behind a tree watching her, so long as he had a key. These gardens were not open to the hoi polloi, naturally, but kept scrupulously for the use of the residents, even nannies with perambulators being frowned on in some of the grander squares and crescents in the town. I turned back to the room.

'I'm not even sure it's the same person every time,' said Lollie, who had started brushing her hair.

'Here, let me do that.' I came back from the window, took her hairbrush out of her hands and set to work with it.

'And doesn't that suggest a firm of detectives, rather than a servant?' she asked.

I did not answer; her fine, silky hair had responded to my brushing by flying up in a cloud like a dandelion head all around her parting. I dabbed the brush at it trying to make it flatten down again and caught her eye in the mirror.

'Sorry,' I said. 'Do you have a rose-water spray? I'm almost sure I could make some little waves if we dampen it.'

We went together to look and see what there might be in her bathroom, Lollie saying it was a good idea for me to get the lie of the land.

'And don't worry,' she said. 'Pip won't be up for half an hour.'

It had once been the dressing room and – although window-less in the middle of the building and surely rather stuffy as a result – made a very comfortable bathroom now. I looked with interest at the little hooded alcove on one end of the bath, something between a sedan chair cover and a grotto.

'Gosh,' I said. 'A stand-up shower-bath! How lovely.'

'Yes, we had them in our suite in Turkey on our honeymoon,' said Lollie, 'and Pip put one in for me. It's rather delicious, except when the hot water suddenly runs out. I don't think I'll chance it while our coal's being rationed. Now come and see my boudoir.'

She cannot have needed it, what with four rooms downstairs and the ground-floor parlour too, but there it was: a little oasis of satin- and tulip-wood, with Louis XIV salon chairs and floral plaques stuck on to any cabinet, cupboard front or sewing table which presented a flat space for the sticking.

Across the landing to the back, Pip had the larger of the two bedrooms, north-facing like Miss Rossiter's room four floors beneath it, but with a view down over the Forth to the hills of Fife. I stepped close to the glass and peered downwards, seeing my little cherry tree and patch of grass far below. Then I turned

44

around and studied the room closely. One could surely learn a great deal about a person from his bedroom.

What I learned of Pip Balfour was that he took rather less interest in his own surroundings than in those of his wife. Lollie's bedroom, no less carefully fitted up than her boudoir, had walls freshly covered in pale lavender silk, with white and lavender chintz at the windows and bed and sumptuous Aubusson carpets scattered about wherever her feet might be imagined to rest for more than a moment, but in here the walls were papered in stripes, the curtains were lined velvet and the floor was covered in a warm but far from beautiful Turkey rug. The furniture was mahogany in both rooms, it was true, but Lollie's was Georgian mahogany with legs like toothpicks while Pip's bedroom contained great hulking boulders of the blackest, most bulbous excesses the Victorian age can ever have mustered, from a very strong field.

'It's fearsome, isn't it?' Lollie said. 'He's had it since he was a boy. He told me he once managed to shut himself in the bottom drawer of the chest and slept the night there.'

I nodded but said nothing, still busy studying the room. There were books on the bedside table – Walter Scott, which suggested that Pip read to help with bouts of sleeplessness – and photographs on the chimneypiece – Lollie in various forms and a few of the right vintage and composition to be parents and siblings – but there were no toilet articles anywhere, I was disappointed to note. (Nanny Palmer had dinned it into me that the state of one's hairbrush and toothbrush was a window on one's soul – or moral character anyway – and I suppose I thought I might find evidence of Pip Balfour's villainy near his washstand.)

One thing I did notice was the great number of keys on view. There was one in each of the two doors in the room and one in every drawer and cupboard too, and they had given me an idea.

'Why don't you simply lock your door at night?' I said, thinking that if this were a house in which keys stayed where they were put, there was sure to be a key for Lollie's room as well as this one. I have always admired such houses; Gilverton is of the other sort, where every lock is empty and there are jars and drawers and boxes full of miscellaneous keys all over the place and no one ever has the time or the patience to put the sundered pairs back together again. Hugh once got a locksmith in to redo the locks on the gun room, wine cellar and silver cupboard, but within weeks the keys had wandered off again and gone to join their chums in odd vases on distant windowsills.

Lollie was shaking her head at me; not just her head either – she was trembling.

'I couldn't bear it,' she said. 'I've never been able to sleep in a locked room – not even in hotels – not since I was a child and my nursemaid slipped out one night to meet her young man and left me locked in my nursery. There was a thunderstorm and I couldn't get out of my room to find my mother.' She grinned at me. 'Pip always says we are Jack Spratt and his wife. I used to hate knowing that Pip locked his door at night, until we came to a compromise.' She led me back out onto the landing.

Nothing, she told me, could persuade her husband not to turn the key in his bedroom door at night, following a lifelong habit, but there was another door just outside at the top of the stairs which led into a small back hall, thence into Pip's bathroom – another former dressing room – and from there back into his bedroom again, and Lollie explained that he had consented to a night latch on the outer door, rather than a lock proper, with the little key kept on top of the lintel in case of emergencies.

'I should be far more wary of that arrangement,' I said. I did not trust these new-fangled cylinder latches with their flat little keys all looking exactly the same and always thought one could get into much more of a pickle from doors slamming shut with the key on the wrong side or from leaving the little knob up when it should be down or putting it down when it should be up.

'*I* wouldn't have one for a king's ransom,' Lollie agreed.

'Did he have an ayah?' I asked. 'Perhaps he got a complex from tight swaddling?' Lollie laughed.

'No, an ordinary nanny,' she said, 'but she told terrifying tales of monsters and burglars, while my nurse stuck to lullabies, so perhaps there's something in it.' With that, we returned to her room to choose a dress and some jewels and I noticed that her hair, without any rose-water or fussing, had lain down upon her head again. I left it well alone.

I had just fastened her shoes and was still kneeling on the floor, admiring her, dressed and decorated although with rather more rouge on than usual she told me, when there was a light tap on the door.

'Pip,' she mouthed to me, then she turned her head and raised her chin as the door opened.

I sat back on my heels, feeling my mouth suddenly dry and my palms damp. Here was the moment I had been dreading! Thankfully, I told myself, he would not take any notice of me and I should be spared having to converse with him. The bedroom door opened, scraping a little over the luxurious carpet, and Pip Balfour entered the room.

47

4

There was my villain. He looked even younger than his wife, with a long, lozenge-shaped face and three black dashes – two eyebrows and a moustache – very stark against his skin, which was smooth and pale down to his cheeks and then rather blue, needing its evening shave. His black hair was extremely smooth too and his eyes as he came closer I saw to be brown, like a spaniel's. It suddenly seemed very unlikely that a devil could have such brown spaniel eyes.

'Well,' he said to Lollie, 'don't you look lovely!' Lollie said nothing. As he had approached, her defiance had retreated until her chin was tucked down and she was looking up at him from under her lashes, breathing quickly. He gave a quick frown – of puzzlement or irritation, it was impossible to say – but then with visible effort managed another smile and even rubbed his hands together as he continued. 'Yes, lovely,' he said. 'Thank you for putting on such a good show for me. It's bound to be dull.' Then he turned towards me, still at Lollie's feet, and put his hand out, bowing slightly.

'Miss Rossiter,' he said. 'Welcome.' I shook his hand before I could help myself and he turned the handshake into a gallant gesture of helping me up. He had remarkably rough hands for a gentleman and his shirtsleeves – he was coatless for some reason – were rolled up just a little too far, well beyond the elbow, which is a very endearing trait in a grown man. 'You must excuse me,' he said. 'I've been sanding my model sailing ship. Lollie always tells me I look like a docker, don't you, darling?'

Lollie gave him an uncertain smile and spoke up at last.

'Harry will straighten you out in no time.'

Pip laughed.

'Gosh, yes indeed,' he said. 'Harry will certainly put me to rights. Wash and brush up and the rudiments of the Labour movement.' My smile, which I could not help, appeared to please him enormously and he beamed back at me. 'But peculiar valets notwithstanding, Rossiter, I hope you'll be very happy with us. And take good care of my beloved girl for me.' Then he glanced at his watch, blew a kiss towards his wife and withdrew.

That, I thought to myself, was more conversation than Hugh had had with Grant in the last twenty years. I looked wonderingly at Lollie and she caught the look and threw it back to me.

'I know,' she said. 'He's very convincing. Now do you see why I could never get anyone to believe me?'

I descended the stairs slowly and spent a good ten minutes staring out at my cherry tree before I wrote another word in my notebook. When Phyllis knocked on my door to tell me it was supper-time I was still puzzling.

'Mistress looked lovely,' she said to me as we climbed the stairs. 'I saw her come down. The last one – Miss Abbott – didnae hold with rouge and lipstick and mistress never could put her foot down, but she looked a picture tonight.'

'Thank you,' I said. 'I'll show you sometime if you like.' I had correctly interpreted Phyllis's wistful tone.

'Oh, Miss Rossiter, would you really? Would you do me for my day out? Not to go and see my ma and fa because my fa would kill us both but every other week I go to the dancing with my pal and she aye tells me I look like a milkmaid.'

I scrutinised her face as we passed under a lamp in the kitchen passageway, and wished I had made Grant instruct me in the mysteries of the kohl pencil and lash black, but I had hardly foreseen the respectable Mrs Balfour needing such attentions. Could I remember it from the times Grant had insisted on painting it onto me? (For the disposition of power between 'mistress' and Miss Abbott had its reflection in my bedroom at home.)

That first evening in the servants' hall was a perfect admixture of comfort, tiredness and boredom, and if one can get these three ingredients in proper proportion nothing is nicer; to be too tired to mind that one is bored and too comfortable to mind that one is tired makes for an evening of guilty pleasure that comes my way rather seldom. Mrs Hepburn and I occupied the armchairs once more, with Mr Faulds joining us between bursts of duty in the dining room; Mattie, Harry and John played gin rummy; Clara was nowhere to be seen – busy upstairs with the dinner guests, I supposed, as was Stanley – but the other girls sat sewing and chatting until the dirty plates began to come down again, then Millie and Eldry returned to the scullery with groans and yawns and Mrs Hepburn sauntered after them to supervise and plan for the following day.

Phyllis immediately took up Mrs Hepburn's place in the armchair; I was fast beginning to see that these soft chairs were the prize of the servants' hall and that no amount of time was too short to make it worth claiming one whenever all of one's seniors had left the room.

'So have you met master then?' she said softly to me. The lads at their card-game were not listening. I nodded, trying not to perk up too visibly. 'And what did you think of him?' I took a while before I answered.

'He seemed very nice,' I said. 'Very friendly. But I did wonder . . .'

'Oh, he's friendly all right,' said Phyllis. 'Just make sure you lock your door tonight, that's all.'

'Really?' I said. 'One of those, is he?' I felt a thrill of sophistication as I said this and Phyllis nodded, her eyelids half-closed and her tongue exploring her cheek in a triumphal show of ennui.

'And who goes in to light his fire of a morning?' I said. 'Not you, dear, is it? I hope not.'

'He's never bothered me – thank goodness,' Phyllis said. 'Not in that way.'

'But Miss Abbott?' I said. She nodded.

'And Mr Faulds can say what he likes about that baronet in North Berwick being a step up,' she said, 'but we all know why Maggie didn't work her notice.'

'Forgive me prying, dear,' I wriggled forward in my chair and spoke even more softly to her, 'but when you said he didn't bother you *in that way*, what did you . . .'

'I'm on notice,' said Phyllis, 'for giving him cheek. I'm on my last warning and if I don't behave I'll be out on my ear with no character.'

'Well, I like that!' I said. 'For sticking up for your chums? For telling him to leave the others alone?'

'No . . .' said Phyllis, slowly. 'It's a funny thing, Miss Rossiter, but I can't even remember what it was that riled him up so, what it was I'm supposed to have said or done.' She shook her head. 'He must have made me so angry I had some kind of a brainstorm. Well, it would be like him.'

'Right then,' said Mr Faulds's voice, making us both jump. He was standing in the doorway, cradling a Schweppes bottle in his arms like a sleeping baby. 'This is nearly empty,' he said. 'We'll finish it off down here to let me send it back for filling. But not tonight.' He flicked the central light off from the switch plate by the door, setting off a chorus of tutting and injured sighs.

'You might have let us finish the hand, Mr Faulds,' said John.

'You can get up early and finish it in the morning if you've a mind,' replied the butler.

'Oh, Mr Faulds,' said Phyllis, 'what about our sing-song?' She nodded towards the far end of the room where, in the corner by the window, there was a small and rather battered piano.

'That's right,' said Mattie, jumping up and trotting towards it. 'You promised, Mr Faulds. And it's my turn to play. I've been practising two hours a day, every day.'

'Mattie MacGibney!' said Phyllis, staring at him with her eyes crossed in a comical way. 'When do you ever get two spare hours a day to practise without bothering anyone? Don't tell such fibs.' Mattie blushed and mumbled an apology. 'We usually have songs at the piano on a Sunday, Miss Rossiter,' said Phyllis, turning to me, 'but we were all upside down yesterday with Maggie and everything and we missed it. We go to pieces when it's Mr Faulds's Sunday off sometimes.'

The butler gave her a fond smile but said nothing. Mattie was on the piano stool now, twirling himself around on his tiptoes to get the thing to the correct height for his slight frame. Mr Faulds stood with his hand still up at the switch, half frowning and half smiling at Phyllis.

'Not tonight, Phyllis,' he said, jerking his thumb upwards. 'Master's sitting on in the dining room with the port and you know how the sound carries.'

'Any road,' I said, 'who wants hymns of a Monday night, really?'

'Oh, it's not hymns,' said Phyllis.

'Anything but!' John put in.

'Now, now,' said Mr Faulds, 'you'll be giving Miss Rossiter the wrong idea of us all.'

'Mr Faulds was on the music halls,' said Mattie. He had stopped twirling round and was hanging on to the edges of the stool waiting for his head to stop spinning.

'For a while, Fanny,' said the butler, 'in my distant youth, and I know a good lot of songs, but I'm careful what ones I pass on to the youngsters. "Boiled Beef and Carrots" kind of thing. And "All the Nice Girls Love a Sailor". None of the ripe stuff.' He winked at me and I tried a wordly smirk back at him even though I had never been in a music hall to hear any of the other songs that he might be suppressing.

'Aye, there's an iron fist of censorship, right enough,' said Harry, to a chorus of groans and a raspberry from John. 'Mattie and me know a wheen of good songs too.' He lay back in his chair and broke out in a confident baritone, sending the words straight up in the air towards the ceiling and the dining room above. '*The people's flag is deepest red, it shrouded oft our martyred*—'

'Quiet!' As lusty as Harry's voice was, Mr Faulds drowned him out, all that projecting from his diaphragm to the back row of the upper circle, I supposed. 'Now, come on, lads, and don't keep me waiting, Stanley's off down the garden already.'

Harry stood up grinning and he and the other two filed out, looking sleepy enough to convince one that they welcomed bedtime really. Mr Faulds gathered up the pack of cards once they had gone, shuffled them efficiently and slapped them down onto the chimneypiece with a wink for Phyllis and me, then he followed the lads out of the room.

'They sleep upstairs in the carriage house,' Phyllis told me. 'So Mr Faulds has to lock the back door behind them at night. He's always chivvying them away to their beds so he can get to his. Mind you, he's not usually as sharp as all this – it's not ten yet.' She shrugged. 'But if he's at them he'll come back and start on at me, so I'd better shift myself.' She yawned extravagantly and stretched her arms above her head. 'You can suit yourself,' she said, 'but Mr Faulds puts the lamps off when he turns in, so . . .'

I was well used to creeping around with a candle but my night's work was far from over and I could not afford to linger. I shared a few words with Mrs Hepburn who was standing in the doorway of the larder just outside her kitchen, marking off orders for the morning on a slate, and popped my head into the scullery to say goodnight to Eldry and Millie, who had got as far as scrubbing out the sinks with sand and sluicing the floor and who looked pleased to be paid the attention. I called up a soft greeting to Clara who was coming down from the dining room at last, white in face and slow of step with tiredness, then I retired. As I stood splashing my face in my little washroom – with a candle, in fact, since it turned out that the electricity which surged so luxuriously around the rest of the house had not yet reached that corner – I could see Mattie's pale hair gleaming in the moonlight as the three boys made their way down the garden and could hear Mr Faulds locking up the back kitchen door above my head and trying the handles. A few minutes later, as I sidled out into the passageway with my nightdress over my shoulder, he was coming along the corridor towards the sub-basement door.

'Goodnight then, Miss Rossiter,' he said. 'I hope you've had a pleasant first day.'

'Indeed I have, Mr Faulds,' I said. 'It seems a very happy household. I'm glad to have joined it.' He locked the door, making an echoing clunk all around us, then removed the key, hung it on a hook and shot the bolts, top and bottom, with the kind of resounding clang one can feel in one's teeth.

'Your windows closed, Miss Rossiter?' he said. I nodded. 'Lovely job. I'll bid you goodnight, then. And I hope you sleep soundly. Oh but, Miss Rossiter?' I waited. 'It's not my place but we've no housekeeper to say it so I hope you'll forgive me.' He gestured towards my nightdress. 'You should really have mistress's things folded and in a muslin bag for carrying through the house. That there doesn't look good, if you ask me.'

The stairs from the kitchen floor emerged opposite the dining-room doorway, as one would expect, and coming up them I saw that the door was open. I lowered my eyes in proper maidly fashion and prepared to scuttle past, but was arrested by Pip Balfour calling my name. He had evidently been lying in wait for me; had, in fact, drawn his chair far back from the table to be sure of spotting me.

'A moment, Rossiter,' he said, rising and beckoning me into the room. With my nightie behind my back, I stepped forward and bobbed a faint curtsey. 'I just wanted to say,' he continued, 'that is, I mean, to say again, how very welcome you are. My wife . . .' He paused and fiddled with the stem of his brandy glass. '. . . my wife is in great need of you.'

'I'm sure,' I said, giving Miss Rossiter's vowels my all, for here was a test of them. 'Most discommoding to have been left without her maid, sir.'

'It's not that, Miss Rossiter,' he said. 'It's more than that. She hasn't been herself lately. Not at all.'

'I wouldn't know, sir,' I said, and from the way he let his breath go in a short sigh I saw that this conventional answer had disappointed him, which was, of course, a triumph to me.

'Well, anyway,' he said. 'I'm very glad you're here. She needs companionship, you know. It's not good for her to be so much on her own.' He was a master of his art, if art it were, because even knowing what I knew I could not fault the words, the voice,

54

the look, the slight suggestion of fidgeting (far short of any histrionic hand-wringing but a nod in its direction). Thankfully, I knew exactly what to say; one never forgets the sting of being snubbed by a servant with whom one has been too chummy. I even rather relished the chance to give it a go.

'Very good, sir,' I said, eyes flat, voice wooden. Flushing a little, he dismissed me.

Lollie was already undressed when I let myself into her room, and was sitting on her bed in a pair of yellow flannel pyjamas, hugging her knees to her chin. The blinds were down – the lavender and white chintz was clearly just for show – and they shifted a little as the breeze blew through the open window.

'Is there anything for me to do?' I said. 'Hanging things up or brushing or anything?' Lollie shook her head.

'I told you I hadn't always had a maid,' she said. 'I've shaken out my evening clothes and put them away and I've washed some small things and hung them up in the bathroom but you might take them downstairs in the morning and let them finish off drying there in case anyone should wonder.'

'I'll just change then,' I said, heading for the bathroom.

'And I'll make up your bed,' said Lollie. 'I've pilfered some pillows and blankets. Will you be all right on the chaise or would you rather have this? I don't mind which for me.' I hesitated. The chaise was wide and long and I was used to a little constriction anyway – Bunty takes up a great deal of room when she is deeply asleep – and besides, was it actually a politeness to offer one's bed to a guest who knew that there might be a visitor in the night bent upon strangling its occupant?

'I'll be fine on the chaise,' I assured her. 'And perhaps we could draw the screen across in front of it. If anything should happen – if your husband should visit you – I'd like to be hidden from view.'

When I returned in my nightgown, wishing for flannel pyjamas of my own since the open windows let all of the night's chill into the room and the screen shut me off from the fire as well as from the door, Lollie was under the bedclothes with a glass in her hand and had set another on the table by my little bed.

'Brandy,' she said. 'Just a little one to help us sleep, but I couldn't find the soda so it's neat, I'm afraid.' I tried to look grateful, but the thick, dark sherry at six o'clock and the beer with the sausage pie had been followed by the burgundy which Mr Faulds thought really should be drunk up that evening after all so that a long glass of water and an aspirin would have been my first choice for a nightcap.

'How did you meet, you and Pip?' I asked, when I was tucked up, feeling very comfortable against my heap of pillows and under my heap of blankets, feeling – actually – very similar to how one used to feel wrapped in furs on a deckchair during those long Atlantic crossings, especially with the stiff breeze and the feeling slightly queasy.

'At a tennis party,' said Lollie. 'We were partnered by the girl whose party it was, because we were both so terrible no one else wanted to play with us. We got put out very quickly, of course, and spent the rest of the afternoon together. The very next day Pip came to speak to my father.'

'And he gave his blessing?'

'Almost,' said Lollie. 'My father was the last bishop of Brechin.'

'Rev. Percival?' I said. 'I remember him very well. I met him many times.'

'Well, he insisted on Pip becoming an Anglican, but apart from that he made no objections. I was only eighteen, but my mother – she was never strong – had died three years before and my father was fifty when I was born,' said Lollie, 'and his health was beginning to fail, so I think he was glad to know I wasn't going to be alone. Glad to see me settled and secure, you know.' She laughed a little at her own words.

'And *you* must have taken to him,' I said. 'To Pip, I mean.'

'I fell head over heels the moment I saw him,' she said. 'Well, no, not the very moment, but within ten minutes. A bumblebee had got itself mixed up in the tennis net and some of the other boys were taking swipes at it with their racquets. I told them to stop and tried to pick it out, but Pip put his fingers in the holes of the net all around the bee to stretch it and then he blew – very gently – and it flew away. He told me our skin can feel like hot coals to bees' feet. Well, to spiders and all kinds of creepy-crawlies.'

'How . . . touching,' I said, trying not to sound as though I were smiling. Entomology was an unusual route into courtship, but I did not doubt her sincerity.

'We were married the following spring,' she said, 'and we were very happy. We went on cruises and visited lots of exciting places.'

'Visiting relatives?'

'No,' said Lollie. 'There aren't any. Well, there are actually any number of cousins but they're not on speaking terms.'

'He turned even his cousins against him?'

'No,' said Lollie. 'None of *that* was Pip's fault. It was his grand-father – rather a horrible old man. He held the purse strings and so he thought he could tell everyone what to do. And he disowned all his sisters, because of their "disappointing marriages", and the family went its separate ways. No, we just travelled to anywhere that sounded like fun. America and the Indies and we went to Africa but it was shockingly hot – and then we came home and found this house and I was looking forward to . . . well . . .'

'Babies?' I guessed.

'That is, I was hoping for them – we both were – but then Pip started to change, off and on, and things became rather strained between us until, last Christmas, what I told you happened and since then it's been just awful. And the worst thing about it is that sometimes – most of the time even, and always when anyone is watching – he seems just the same sweet old Pip as ever, so that I never know what to expect and I can't tell anyone and I . . . I almost begin to doubt my reason sometimes. I—'

'Sssh!' I said. I had heard a floorboard creak outside on the landing. Slowly I sat up and put my eye to the space between two panels of the screen, peering through it at the door handle. For minutes nothing happened, although I was sure from the very silence that he was out there, listening, as tense as we were, and then I heard a footstep and another going away down the stairs. 'He's gone,' I said to Lollie in a whisper, 'but we should stop talking now.'

It was a remarkably quiet night, I thought, as I lay there. I had never lived in a town and when Hugh and I used to take a London house, before the war and the children, the streets rang with life until the early hours of morning. Here though, on this Monday night in Edinburgh, nothing came in at the open windows except the occasional sound of a policeman's heavy tread as he passed with measured pace along the street and back again. Just after midnight struck, there was some distant shouting and catcalls, and I wondered if somewhere, in some other part of town, the start of the strike was being celebrated or lamented, but it was *very* distant shouting and I turned over and burrowed deeper into the blankets, feeling sleep begin to steal close to me and hearing Lollie's breathing start to slow.

It was light when next I opened my eyes, but in Scotland in May that is no help to one and I squinted at my wristwatch before so much as stretching, in case more sleep might be in the offing.

'Good morning,' said Lollie's voice. 'I was just about to wake you. You'd better get back down to your room before Clara arrives, don't you think?'

I sat up a little, shuddering at the empty brandy glass on the table, and swung my feet to the floor.

'How much time do I have?' I croaked, standing and stumbling towards the bathroom where my clothes were laid. Last night, padding up and down the stairs in the lamplight seemed neither here nor there, but being four flights away from my bedroom in my nightclothes with the household stirring gave me a nasty creeping feeling up the backs of my legs this morning. I dressed hastily, dragged my hands over my hair, stuffed my nightdress into a cupboard until later and let myself out onto the landing.

All was quiet enough up here, but from below I could hear the scraping of a grate shovel as someone cleared a fire and from further below that, there was a sudden dull boom. Yesterday morning I should have been at a loss to explain such a noise arising from what sounded like the bowels of the earth but now I knew it to be the sound of Mrs Hepburn, shutting an oven door with her knee. I stopped at Pip's door on my way past and put my head near to the panelling, but there was no sound from inside so I crossed to the stairway and started down it.

Between the drawing-room and dining-room floors I met Eldry on her way up. She was carrying two trays stacked one on top of the other and was in the striped morning dress which she wore above stairs, but had a capacious brown apron over it. She looked startled to see me, but I carried off the encounter very well.

'Where's Clara?' I demanded. 'It's she whom mistress is expecting.'

'Not feeling very well this morning, Miss Rossiter,' said Eldry, 'so I said I'd bring the trays and do the fires both together.'

I frowned at her. A tweenie should not on any account be carrying tea trays and certainly should not be raking ashes and touching tea things in the same apron. I was surprised at Mr Faulds for letting this pass.

'Couldn't the valet have helped?' I asked. 'Harry?'

'Harry's not up yet, I don't think,' said Eldry and it seemed to me that she was blushing a little. 'Besides,' she said softly, 'I dinna mind.' She turned her eyes towards the back of the house, towards – I thought – the garden and yard and carriage house in the mews, where Harry would be sleeping, and smiled a very small and rather secretive smile. 'I dinna mind taking on a bit extra to spare him.'

Ah, I thought, remembering Phyllis's teasing.

'I'll take mistress's off your hands anyway,' I said. 'She's awake already. No sound from *him* yet, though.' I nodded at the upper-most of the two trays where a teacup, pot and milk jug, along with a rolled-up *Scotsman*, were laid on a plain cloth.

'Good!' said Eldry. 'I hope I can get in and out without him stirring. I havenae got his paper, see?' She sounded rather fearful. 'He takes *The Times* but it never came. And when Mattie went round to the paper shop to get it, they said they had none, cos there's no trains and so they're all stuck in London. No trains at all, miss, nor buses nor trams, and Mattie said he met a man who'd walked up from Leith and the docks are as quiet as the grave and even the gasworks! I never thought it would really happen.'

'Nor I,' I said. 'Not really.'

'So Mattie got a *Scotsman* instead, but I cannae make up my mind whether to take it in or leave him with none.'

'Take him the *Scotsman*,' I said. 'The strike's not your fault. He can't blame you for it.' Eldry said nothing but looked far from consoled by my breeziness. 'Or I tell you what,' I said, 'let me take his tray in to him.' I welcomed any chance to see more of Pip, for I was still far from knowing what I thought about any of it.

'Oh, I couldnae, Miss Rossiter,' said Eldry. 'It wouldn't be right, miss. You're mistress's lady.'

'I don't mind,' I said, truthfully.

'Beg pardon, Miss Rossiter, but you would if you kent him,' Eldry said and flushed.

'So I believe, dear,' I answered. 'Well, how's this? I'll take mistress's and let's leave the doors open and if he gives you any bother when you go in I'll come in at your back and sort him out for you. He doesn't scare me.'

Eldry bit her lip and opened her eyes very wide. It was an expression she often wore and one which did nothing to enhance her meagre claims to beauty.

'He'll put you on notice, if you're not careful,' she said. 'But he'll no' try anything with both of us there, at least.'

We managed the handover of the bottom tray quite smoothly even there on the stairs and Eldry's chin was as high as mine as we processed upwards. I had no worries: it was Lollie who had engaged me and it was only Lollie who could sack me; in fact it was rather odd that he had got involved in the matter of Phyllis, the housemaid. I wondered again what it was she had done.

Upstairs, Eldry made her way to the back landing, to negotiate the night latch which began the circuitous secondary route to Pip's bedside. She managed the little key admirably well one-handed while balancing the tray on the other and I left her to it, knocking softly on Lollie's door and sweeping in, the way Grant always swept into my room when she was dressed and I was not, as though taking match point in some game.

Lollie, though, was in her bathroom and missed it. The water was gurgling and steam was coiling out around the half-open door. I put the tray down on her bed, opened the blinds, plumped her pillows and was turning to leave again – Eldry could come in and light the fire; there were limits to my collegiate helpful-ness and to my domestic expertise – when I heard a scream.

For a second I stood still, listening. Was it inside the house? My eyes flew to the open windows, but then there came another and the sound of running footsteps, footsteps on floorboards – this was no street accident outside. I tore across the floor and out onto the landing. Someone – Eldry – was banging on the inside of Pip's bedroom door, still screaming.

I raced across the hall, through the little passageway, through the bathroom – still shuttered – and swung around into the bedroom through the open door. Here the curtains were drawn back and the shutters folded away, but I could see no one – no sign of Pip – nothing except Eldry beating on the other door, sobbing, begging for someone to let her out.

'Turn the key,' I shouted. 'Eldry, it's still locked – turn the key!' But she was beside herself, tugging on the handle, whimpering now, and she clung to me as I got to her and took her in my arms, feeling her shaking.

'There, there,' I said, as I opened the door for her. 'Shush now. What did he do to you?'

Eldry stumbled out into the hall, shaking her head, and pointed past me. I swung round, thinking he must be coming up behind me, but saw nothing. She slid down the wall until she was sitting, still pointing. Over by the bed, the tray was on the floor, the teapot broken and empty, the sheets of newspaper scattered around. I walked towards it and as I got closer I began to see.

It was a high-set Victorian bed, matching the rest of the furniture in the room, and the footboard was almost as tall as the head, hiding the bed from the rest of the room until one came around the side of it. The blankets were pushed down, but the top sheet was drawn right up over the pillows. I could not clearly see the outline of the man underneath, though, because just where the pillows began the sheet was held away from the mattress, like a tent, around something sticking up there. Where it did touch down again, all around, there was a bloom of red, seeping up through the linen from underneath, spreading like ink into a dampened blotter, and now that I was close there was a smell too, like old coins and like the gamekeeper's cart on the way home after a good day and like the worst of the hospital during the war, which I had almost forgotten.

Leaning over very carefully, I picked up the edge of the sheet and lifted it away. Underneath was more – sickeningly more – red: a lake of red, thick and clotted, darkening to purple at its deepest, spreading across the bed, seeping upwards over the pillows, covering the pyjamas, coating the neck, filling the ears, matting the hair, so only Pip Balfour's cold white face rose above it. His eyes were open, clouded, and his mouth was open too and blood had spurted and run into it, outlining his teeth in rusty orange, and what had tented the sheet over him was the knife, a long, bone-handled knife, lodged to its hilt and standing straight up out of his neck, pooled all around with blood that was almost black. With the back of one hand I touched his forehead, where no blood had spattered; it was cold. I let the sheet drop back down again and retraced my steps to the little passageway.

My fingers were numb as I dropped the latch on the inside of the door and I tested and retested it to make sure I had locked it shut and not open. I locked the door between the hall and the bathroom, then the door between the bathroom and bedroom, and then I crossed the room and took the key out of the main bedroom door, stepped outside, closed the door, locked it and put the key in my pocket.

Eldry looked up at me from where she was still sitting on the floor.

'Is it master?' she said. I nodded. 'He's dead, isn't he?' Another nod. Then she sat up a little straighter and sniffed hard. 'Good,' she said.

'Go downstairs and tell Mr Faulds to telephone to the police,' I said. 'Can you do that? You're not going to faint, are you?' Eldry shook her head and got, rather unsteadily but very determinedly, to her feet.

'I'll hold on to the rail,' she said. 'But can you get the tray, miss?'

'Never mind the tray,' I said.

'I cannae leave it there all dropped and broken.'

'It doesn't matter.'

'But the police,' said Eldry, sounding tearful again. 'They'll find my fingerprints on it and it's right beside the bed, beside the body. I opened the shutters and took it over to him.'

'I'll tell them what happened,' I said. 'Don't worry.'

This seemed to satisfy her and she turned to leave, but then stopped and looked back at me.

'I tell you something, miss,' she said. 'I don't blame her, do you?'

It took me a moment to find my voice and even when I did it was shaking.

'Don't be silly, Eldry,' I said. 'And don't let me hear you saying such things again.'

But my heart was thudding – great dull, painful thuds – as I went back to Lollie's bedroom door and pushed it open. She was back in bed, with a cardigan jersey on over her pyjamas and a cup of tea balanced in her lap. I stayed on the landing in the shadow where she could not see me.

'Clara?' she said. 'Is that you? Tell Eldry not to bother with the fire since she hasn't lit it yet. I think it's going to be a lovely day. Did you hear that funny noise just then? I was running the taps but I'm sure I heard some kind of commotion.'

The greatest actress in the world, surely, could not have

63

summoned such a speech and delivered it in that sunny voice, with that smile, if she had seen what was there in the other bedroom, much less if she had made it happen. And yet, I thought, and yet . . .

I walked forward into the light so she could see me.

'Oh, it's you, Dan— Miss Rossiter, I mean,' she said. 'Did you hear that hullabaloo? Has Phyllis seen a mouse again?' I closed the door behind me. 'Dandy?' she said, looking at me properly for the first time. 'You look terrible. What's happened? What's he done now?'

5

Mr Faulds was purple with rage, but I would not be moved.

'On what authority?' he demanded, standing in front of me, shaking with anger.

'On the authority of an informed citizen, Mr Faulds,' I said. 'And on the authority of the mistress of the house, who is now, following this horrific event, the *head* of the house. And on the—'

'Miss Rossiter,' he said, making an enormous effort to calm down and speak as reasonably as I spoke to him. 'Might I remind you that you have been a member of this household since yesterday, whereas I have run it for the last three and a half years, so I don't give scat for any of your clever-clogs talk. Now, give me that key.' He was bellowing again by the end of the speech and I glanced towards the staircase, where most of the other servants were ranged upon the steps looking through the banisters at us.

'For pity's sake, Mr Faulds,' called out Mrs Hepburn from Lollie's room, where she was administering hugs and, I suspected, more brandy. 'Get away somewhere else if you can't stop shouting!' Her voice dropped again and we could hear the soothing murmur of her comforting Lollie with something close to a lullaby. 'Hush-a, hush-a, hush now, my good brave girl.'

'Miss Rossiter's right, you know, Mr Faulds,' said Harry, and a couple of the maids nodded in support of him. 'The less traipsing about and touching stuff there is, the easier the coppers'll see what happened. If there's footprints or the likes.'

'No' like you to be on the side of the law, Harry,' said John.

'I should have been consulted,' said Mr Faulds. 'It's only what's right and proper. I should have decided whether to telephone the police station. I've no intention of touching anything.' But his actions belied his words; he was shifting from foot to foot, inches from the door, and shooting its locked handle endless darting glances, like a puppy who had been trained not to scratch at things but was dying to.

'Oh, Mr Faulds, please,' I said. 'If you had seen it you'd wish you hadn't. There's nothing right and proper to be done about it any way you look. And I'm not trying to take centre-stage, I assure you. Let's please all go back downstairs and wait for the police. If they need someone to show them round, you can volunteer for that – I'm sure I don't want to.'

At that moment, the question was decided for us by Eldry, who fainted, sinking into her skirts and then half rolling a few steps down the stairs. John and Harry gathered her up between them and fought over her for a moment or two, then John relinquished her with a grin.

'I hope she comes to before you put her down,' he said. 'She wouldn't want to miss this. Anybody else feeling dicky?' he asked, turning to the other girls and flexing his arms.

'Shut up with your stupid jokes for once,' said Harry, turning away and beginning to feel his way down the steps. 'It's not the time.'

John tried mugging to the girls but they threw him their severest looks and trotted anxiously after Harry and his still unconscious cargo. John, his cheeks aflame, followed them. I had been looking at Mattie, the hall boy, who was dangerously white-looking, and I went over to him, put an arm across his back and walked down after the others holding him up firmly.

'Thanks, Miss Rossiter,' he said. 'Sorry to be so—'

'Ch-ch,' I said. 'I've never been closer to fainting in my life, my dear. Don't say another word about it.' In truth, though, I was wondering why he – who had seen nothing of the horrors – should be so affected, but I filed the question away for later; after all I barely knew the child and perhaps this was his norm.

Above us, Stanley was speaking in a low and rather thrilled voice.

'Terrible thing, Mr Faulds,' he said. 'Shocking the way she just waltzed in and took over. I don't want to see it – I'm as sick as a dog just thinking about it – but if you want to get the spare key and go for a look-see I'll stand watch for you.'

'Oh, stop sucking up for once,' said Mr Faulds.

Three policemen arrived at the door and two of them climbed the stairs, sounding very solemn and deliberate as they did so. I was with Lollie, having changed places with Mrs Hepburn shortly after the mass gathering on the landing had broken up. Eldry had been put to bed with a hot bottle and the steady Phyllis watching over her, and Mattie had been given the honour of one of the servants' hall armchairs and the more pertinent remedy of hot sweet tea.

Lollie sat absolutely motionless in a small armchair staring straight ahead of her. She had a shawl over her shoulders and there was a fire in the grate – Mrs Hepburn's work, I imagined – but she was white and pinched-looking and she turned her head only very slowly when a firm knock sounded and a large man in a dark suit entered along with a uniformed sergeant.

'Superintendent Hardy, Mrs Balfour,' he said in a strained voice. Lollie stared back without blinking, but I must have reacted since he turned to me and explained. 'We've suspended leave and called in all the specials while the strike's running, and every one of my inspectors and sergeants is busy organising them so it fell to me.'

'I see,' said Lollie. 'Well, thank you for coming at all, Mr Hardy.'

The large man looked rather grim at that, perhaps seeing an unintended slight or suspecting irony. Actually, I thought Lollie's tone – the careless sound of her voice – arose from disbelief, from a simple inability to take in what was happening.

'I assure you, my dear madam,' said Superintendent Hardy, 'you will receive our utmost attention until this matter is resolved. I shall see to it personally.' His voice and his bulk were reassuring although there was some subtle kind of panic in his eyes. Still, Lollie nodded.

'Of course, of course,' she said.

'Now, it's your husband, I believe?' he said. 'Met with a nasty mishap? Where is he?'

Mr Faulds was hovering behind Superintendent Hardy and he stepped forward now.

'In his bedroom, sir, if you might allow me to escort you.'

'And you are?' Hardy nodded at the sergeant, who opened his notebook.

'Ernest Faulds, the butler.'

'Well, Faulds, if you'll just point us in the right direction we'll take over from here.'

'It's locked, Superintendent,' I said, and he turned to look at me. 'I thought it was best. I have the key, but I'm sorry to tell you that – in all the confusion – I didn't stop to think about prints; I just grabbed it, so there's probably no point in worrying about them now.' I took the key out of my pocket and offered it to him.

'Thank you, Miss . . . ?'

That was the question I had been trying to answer for myself since I first stepped towards Pip's bed and saw the bloodstain. Was this the end of Miss Rossiter? Surely it must be, and yet not only would I give anything to be able to stay in her skin a little longer now that matters had taken this hideous turn, but there was the problem of where my duty lay. As I considered the point, all of a sudden I thought I knew what lay behind the look of unease in Hardy's eyes. His inspectors and sergeants were policing this stupid strike and he had been left nursing the screaming baby, holding the ticking bomb. And if he could not read the shock in a widow's voice – whether it were the shock of grief or the shock of what she had done, if she had done it – could he solve a murder? Could he, plucked out from behind his desk and thrown back into the torrent of an investigation for the first time in years perhaps – and there was something about him, the crisp cuffs, clean nails and careful arrangement of his glossy hair, which made me sure it was years – but anyway, could he be trusted to do it without me?

'Miss . . . ?' he prompted, and the very fact that he seemed not to have gleaned any of what was surging through me, right before his eyes, had almost made my mind up when Lollie spoke, looking awake again, and aware of what was around her.

'Miss Rossiter, my lady's maid,' she said. I shelved the decision, telling myself that the body was their first priority, that it would be an annoyance and a distraction to them to start a long and confusing story about my identity right now.

'Fanny Rossiter, Superintendent,' I said. 'I, with one other, found him, you know.'

Mr Hardy took the key from me and I was glad to see that he – finally – gave me a searching look as he did so. Miss Rossiter's vowels and manner of speaking had completely deserted me and even Mr Hardy must know that I was no ordinary maid.

'This way, sir,' said Mr Faulds, and they left Lollie and me alone.

'Please don't tell them who you are, Dandy,' she whispered to me as soon as they were gone. 'If they know that I thought he was going to hurt me they'll think *I* hurt *him*. They'll think I only asked you to come to give me an alibi and they'll arrest me and put me in jail and I'd die. I couldn't stand to be locked up in a jail cell. Oh, please, promise me. Or ask—' She broke off with a cry. 'I was going to say, ask Pip,' she said. 'He would know what to do. He would be able to help. Oh! Oh, Pip!' Then she put her head down into her hands and began crying hard, sobs racking her chest as though she were choking.

I am afraid to say that although I sprang to her side and comforted her, with a great deal of hair-patting and shushing, I was thinking all the while that the police, looking around themselves and seeing a neatly acquired alibi, would have a point. Her state of shock was convincing enough – no one can make her face go pale at will – and the reality of the current tears could not be questioned, soaking her face and hands as they were and coming complete with a great deal of wet sniffing, but whether they were born of grief, remorse or a healthy fear for her neck was another question. Tears can be turned to account with the greatest of ease if one has a gift for weeping.

At length and after a few horribly deep snorts and swallows, Lollie sat up straight again and pulled away from me. I returned to my seat.

Her eyes were purple-looking now over the pallor of her cheeks, the lashes spiked and sparkling, and, although her nose was swollen and her lips trembled, youth shone out of her. (Had I cried so hard for so long I should have been sodden and wretched and looked ninety.) She tried a smile when she saw me looking at her. It was not successful and a further two fat tears splashed down her front.

'About the question of an alibi,' I began. I thought I spoke kindly and with lightness, but Lollie, tears drying up in an instant, gazed back at me in horror. I decided to plough on. 'I shall, of course, say to Superintendent Hardy that I was in your room overnight and I shall say – which is true – that I don't think you could have left and returned without waking me, but I can't be sure. And as to the question of whether I tell him who I am and why I'm here . . .'

Lollie had recovered herself a little and she spoke up stoutly.

'I don't expect you to lie,' she said. 'You can say this is your first job as a lady's maid and that I had heard about you and wrote to ask if you would come and that it's not what you were brought up to. All of that is quite true. And then you can stay and help find out what happened. Please say you will, Dandy. You must.'

I regarded her in silence. As truths go, the history of Miss Rossiter she had laid out was unimpressive: a forked-tongue tara-diddle of the highest order and if I were to serve it up to Hardy and be found out afterwards I should be lucky to escape arrest, if not a smack on the legs with a hairbrush for the cheek of it. On the other hand, I could not bear to rip myself away from this now. And, I told myself, if she had wanted a simple alibi she could far more easily have enticed Phyllis or Clara upstairs with a story of nightmares. No one, surely, planning to murder her husband would invite a detective into the house, into the very room; I was not only Lollie Balfour's alibi – I was the stamp of

70

innocence branded on her with indelible ink. Still, I had to satisfy the demands of my own conscience too.

'As I was saying,' I continued, just as though the silent tussle had not happened, 'I don't think you could have got out and back. I have to check, though. Would you rather do it yourself or shall I ring down for one of the girls?'

'Do what?' said Lollie. 'Check what?'

'How much noise you'd have made getting out of bed and coming back again. I'm sorry to ask you right now, but I'd like to be able to say to Mr Hardy with confidence straight away that you couldn't have done it.'

'Yes, yes, of course,' said Lollie, already on her feet and making her way to the door. We crossed the landing to her bedroom and slipped inside. I returned to the chaise, pulling the screen across in front of it, and Lollie climbed onto the bed and lay down.

'No, get right under the blankets,' I told her. 'It should be as near as possible as it would have been.'

Of course sound travels further at night, but Heriot Row is a quiet street and today was a quiet day. I could hear, as I lay there, the wheels of a delivery boy's bicycle rattling on the cobbles and some birdsong from the Queen Street gardens and then, just as Lollie began to move, a heavy horse clopped past. After the sound of its hooves and its cart wheels died away I could hear very clearly the sound of the starched sheets being pushed back, the creak of bedsprings and the padding of soft footsteps crossing the floor. The door hinge was silent enough, but the handle clicked twice and there was that dragging sound as the foot of the door passed over the carpet. Then it closed with another pair of clicks, the footsteps sounded again and the bedsprings protested even more loudly as she climbed back in. It was impossible to ignore, but would it have awakened me?

'I tried to be as quiet as I could,' Lollie said softly. 'After all, I would have, wouldn't I?'

I got up and rounded the screen, giving her a reassuring smile.

'Indeed you would,' I said. 'Thank you.' Then we both jumped at the sound of movement out on the landing and Lollie paled again; the little task I had set her had taken her mind away from the nightmare for a moment but now it returned.

'Are they moving him?' she asked. I shook my head.

'No, they won't be moving him for quite a while,' I said. 'The police doctor will have to come. Later today perhaps, but not now.'

'And' – she gulped a little – 'will I have to look at him?' I could not help closing my eyes briefly as the picture of Pip's face flashed through my mind again.

'I don't think so,' I said. 'Someone will have to identify him formally at some point but it needn't be you, dear. It needn't be a relative at all, just someone who knew him. Perhaps Mr Faulds? He's desperate to help in some way.'

Lollie sat back against her pillows.

'Yes, of course,' she said. 'Faulds will take care of it for me. Poor thing. Do you think I'm wicked, Dandy, not to want to see him? Should I, do you think? I've never seen anyone . . . dead before.'

'Don't think about it just yet,' I said to her. 'You might feel different in a day or two.' I went over and stood beside her bed, taking her hand and trying to chafe some warmth into it. 'People will tell you it's best to remember him as he was and others will tell you it helps to see his body, but no one really knows, so don't listen if they pretend to.'

'It all seems like a dream,' said Lollie. 'Not just this morning, I mean. The trouble – you being here, everything I was so scared of. All I can think of now is that bumblebee in the tennis net and how gentle he was and how much fun we always had.'

She looked very small sitting there in her bed, and I squeezed the hand I was holding.

'Isn't there anyone I could telephone to?' I said. 'There must be someone who could come?'

'My Great Aunt Gertrude from Inverness, I suppose,' said Lollie. 'She doesn't hold with the telephone but I could send a telegram to her.'

I did not like the sound of Great Aunt Gertrude from Inverness somehow; in my experience old ladies who do not hold with the telephone tend not to hold with a great deal besides, such as large fires, soft cushions and cocktails. Aunt Gertrude sounded to me like a bracing walk made flesh.

'Are there friends one could summon for you?' I said. I often feel as encumbered by friends and family as a horse is with flies in August, twitching at them to leave me alone and dreaming of tranquil solitude; it was hard to believe that this girl could be quite so alone.

'We were everything to one another,' Lollie told me. 'I never saw the danger in that until now.'

I squeezed her hand again, hoping to head off another bout of weeping, and was glad to hear the heavy tread of feet stumping up the stairs. There was a little quiet murmuring out on the landing and then Mrs Hepburn appeared, carrying a covered basin.

'I've got some—' she said and then stopped and frowned. 'You've never put her back in her bed in her frock, Fanny! Come on, madam, out you get and back into your nightie. I've got some bread soup for you but it's fair hot yet anyway so we've plenty time till it's ready to sup.' I turned to go, but Mrs Hepburn laid a hand on my arm and spoke in a low voice. 'You'll forgive me, Fan, won't you? I shouldn't have ticked you off like that, but I'm just all upside down and it slipped out. I beg your pardon, though.'

'Don't mention it, Mrs Hepburn,' I said, thinking if that was Miss Rossiter being ticked off then there were no words for what Dandy Gilver née Leston had received from the tongues of Nanny Palmer, Madame Toulemonde and Grant over the years. 'I'll get back downstairs to them all if you'll stay with mistress now.'

Mrs Hepburn dropped her voice even further and turned partly away.

'I think you're wanted next door,' she said. 'But see and get a port with brandy from Mr Faulds when they've finished with you.' I nodded. The port and brandy cure-all was a favourite with my own dear Mrs Tilling and, although I had resisted so far throughout childbirths, bereavements and a fire in the attics, I could imagine that today might be the day I succumbed to its charms. I took a deep breath and went out of the bedroom.

On the landing, Mr Hardy was standing with his hands on his hips looking about himself with a furious expression on his face. The sergeant, in contrast, leaned back against the banister rail with legs straddled well apart and a handkerchief pressed to his mouth.

'Ah,' said Mr Hardy, seeing me. 'Miss eh . . . Miss . . . ?'

'Rossiter,' I said.

'And you found . . . ?' He jabbed a finger at Pip's bedroom door.

'With one other,' I said. 'Eldry. Etheldreda, the tweenie. She took the tray in but she didn't lift the sheet.'

'You liftit the sheet?' said the sergeant, looking at me with respect.

'I had to make sure there was nothing to be done,' I said. 'I mean, I could tell there was a great deal of blood but there was just a chance he was still alive. I was a nurse in the war.'

Mr Hardy tugged his coat straight and tweaked his cuffs – girded his loins, in fact, for the task ahead.

'In that case, Miss Rossiter,' he said, 'we'll start with you. Now. Downstairs, I think. There must be a room that's not in use this morning. And Sergeant Mackenzie? You go and find a telephone and get the surgeon and see if there's anyone in the station who can slip along with some fingerprinting . . . things and if not . . . And tell PC Morrison to round up the rest of the servants and keep an eye on them all until we can . . .'

'Right you are, sir,' said Sergeant Mackenzie, sparing Hardy from the problem of ever ending this speech. 'I'll get straight to it.'

I led Superintendent Hardy downstairs and into the back parlour where Lollie had held the interviews. The fire was unlit, which gave a cheerless air to the place, but the day was warm enough to do without one. Hardy sat at the little papier mâché writing table (looking a lot like the big bad wolf looming over the house of sticks) and opened a new notebook at the first page. I sat on the same hard wooden seat as before and reported the story of meeting Eldry on the stairs, of hearing her scream, running to her aid and letting her out of the bedroom door. I was just about to go on and tell the superintendent about what I had seen under the sheet, when he interrupted me.

'What's that?' he said. 'Why did she lock herself in in the first place?'

'No, you misunderstand me,' I told him. 'The main door was still locked from the night before. Eldry had gone through the dressing room – the bathroom.'

'And that was open?' said the superintendent. 'Now, why would the murderer close one door and leave the other open?'

'No, no,' I said. 'They were both locked up tight. The key to the door of the little hallway that leads into the dressing room is kept on the lintel and Eldry let herself in with it.'

'One of these Yale locks?' he said. I nodded. 'And the key of the main door was on the inside when you got there?' I nodded again. 'Good God,' he said and glared at me. 'You see what this means, don't you?'

'I do, sir,' I replied.

'I've been thinking someone must have got in. Even though there's nothing missing as far as we could see. There was quite a bit of disturbance last night here and there. I suppose I thought some devil had broken in but . . .'

'But only someone who knew the house well would know about the Yale key,' I finished for him. 'And actually, Superintendent, the house as a whole was very secure last night. Mr Faulds, the butler, was locking up when I went to bed. He's a bit of a stickler for it by all accounts.'

'Good God,' said Hardy again. 'This is going to be an all-out scandal. This is going to need seeing to.' He could not have looked less keen to do the seeing if he had sprinted for the door and pounded on it begging for release, but he squared his shoulders and sat up a little straighter. 'Right then. I'll need a list of everyone who was in the house and I'll need to speak to them all. I'll need your full name to start with.'

'Yes indeed,' I said. 'Well, then. I'm employed under the name of Frances Rossiter. Miss.' Superintendent Hardy looked up at me with his pencil in mid-air. 'My married name is Gilver,' I went on. 'That is to say, my real name is Dandelion Dahlia Gilver. When I took this job, I changed it. My relations would not otherwise countenance my employment, I don't suppose.'

'Gilver,' said the superintendent, looking thoughtful 'Gilver?'

'It's a prominent name in Perthshire,' I said and Hardy nodded. 'I thought it best to change it under the circumstances.'

Hardy looked at me for a while without speaking and I did my best to meet his gaze square-on. He was not, I thought, an unintelligent man, only rather flustered by this extraordinary day. Perhaps he had come in sideways from the army straight to his desk and had never gathered statements and tracked suspects before. He certainly had nothing cunning about him, but rather the unstoppable look of someone who spent his youth being pushed to the front of the team in games of rugby football. Yes, that was it! If I had passed him on the street I should have guessed that he was a very prosperous and still rather sporting Borders beef farmer; he was completely out of his element sitting here today.

'The circumstances being that you're working as a maid,' he said finally.

'Well, a companion is perhaps a better way to express it, Superintendent,' I replied. 'Mrs Balfour is not – was not – happily married and she felt herself in need of a champion, while she considered what to do about it, but she felt also that her husband wouldn't be pleased to think she had turned to someone for help and so I was smuggled in, I suppose you would say. As her maid. To help.'

There was another long silence to be got through now. I waited it out, trying to look a good deal more confident than I felt.

'And how long have you been here?' said Hardy at last.

'Since yesterday,' I replied. 'I arrived at teatime.'

He put down his pencil and folded his hands on top of the notebook. His jaw, which was square enough even at rest, now stuck out in the most marked fashion.

'You arrived yesterday, using a false name,' he said, and I noticed for the first time how deeply shadowed his eyes were under the strong brow, 'to help Mrs Balfour with the problem of her husband.'

I often tell myself that after years of constant detecting my days of naivety are in the past, that no longer do I put on my red cloak and set off for my grandmother's cottage with a basket of treats, but it was not until that very moment that I saw the forest of trees pressing in all around me and realised that being used as an alibi was not the worst suspicion which could fall upon me.

'Superintendent Hardy,' I said, all thought of subtlety vanished, 'do you know an inspector called Cruickshank from Linlithgowshire?'

'I've heard the name,' said Hardy. 'I can't say I remember ever meeting the fellow.'

'Or how about Inspector Hutchinson, from the Perthshire Force?' I asked. Superintendent Hardy's stern face split into a grin.

'Maynard Hutchinson?' he said. 'Everybody knows him. The stories I could tell you about him would make your hair curl.'

'Well, then telephone to him and ask him about—'

'Mrs Gilver!' exclaimed the superintendent. 'Dandy Gilver?'

'At your service,' I said, letting out a huge sigh of relief. 'Truly, Superintendent: at your service and awaiting instructions.'

'So what was all that about a companion?'

'All true,' I said. 'More or less. Mrs Balfour called me in to help her. To be a witness to her husband's behaviour and a champion of her cause. He was a complete brute, you know. I don't imagine anyone will be mourning him once the shock has passed over.'

'Sounds to me as if she's dropped you right in it, madam,' Hardy said.

I held up my hand.

'Miss Rossiter, Superintendent, please. Not madam. If I'm to stay here and help I need Fanny Rossiter more than ever, wouldn't you agree?'

'Ah now, I don't know what I think of that,' said Hardy. 'You saw him up there – what had been done to him. You could be in grave danger, and I can't let a civilian – not to mention a lady – risk herself that way.'

'Oh come now, Superintendent,' I said. 'Didn't you just tell us that you had called in all sorts of extraordinary manpower to handle the strike?'

'Retired officers and territorial soldiers and suchlike,' said Hardy.

'Well, what's one more? I'll even sign a contract if it would help.'

So it was that Superintendent Hardy allowed the ranks of his constabulary to be swelled by one more volunteer and I became a special constable of the Edinburgh City Police. For all I know, I might still be one; I do not recall any formal release from my duties anyway.

'Here, you haven't got the dog with you, have you?' asked Hardy. 'Don't tell me you brought the dog.'

'I haven't, in fact,' I said. I could only imagine what the caustic Mr Hutchinson had said about my beloved Bunty at whatever policemen's shindig he had enlivened with tales of our adventures.

'Just as well,' said Hardy, and returned to business, with another great roll of the powerful shoulders and another answering creak from the delicate chair in which he was sitting. 'So. Miss Rossiter. Do you have your own room or can you account for any of the other maids?' 'Other' was said with a bit of a twinkle, but I knew that my answer would soon snuff that out. If, that was, I could bring myself to deliver it.

'I owe Mrs Balfour whatever loyalty I can give her,' I said.

'But?' said Mr Hardy.

'But,' I went on, 'as I've had occasion to point out to earlier clients in past cases, I am not a "hired gun".' Hardy's eyebrows shot up. 'My children,' I said. 'Dreadful taste in story papers. What I am, come what may and no matter who is paying me, is a servant of truth.'

'So . . . ?' asked Mr Hardy.

So . . . I told him, feeling like the worst kind of sneak, especially as he clearly thought that Lollie installing me in her very bedroom was getting on for elaborate and roused suspicion rather than quashing it.

'But I don't think she could have got out and back without me noticing,' I said. 'Although . . .' A further and even more damning possibility had just occurred to me.

'Although what?' said Hardy.

'She shoved a nightcap down me with some insistence. If I were to lay my hands on the glass, could it be tested to see if she'd put some kind of sleeping powder in it? I mean, I'm sure she didn't but it would be good to be able to discount it completely.'

Hardy gave me a sharp nod of approval and agreement, then rubbed his jaw again.

'What about washing?' he asked. 'Even if she had you doped up – and let's hope not, eh? – could she have run the hot water without waking the house? I know I couldn't in my bathroom but this place seems pretty plush and maybe the plumbing is silent.'

'Why do you assume . . . ?' I said and then stopped.

'There would have been a fair amount of blood,' said Hardy, confirming what I thought. 'She – or whoever – would have had to wash at least the hands and arms.'

'In that case, I think not,' I said. 'Certainly, I don't think she could have used her own bathroom. And I don't really think she slipped me a powder and I don't even think she killed her husband. But . . .'

'But if it's not her then who is it? I only wish you had been here longer, Miss Rossiter, and could tell me a little about the household.'

'I can tell you a surprising lot,' I said, and this time I felt no compunction. 'I only met Mr Balfour briefly and he seemed perfectly pleasant then but – as I say – he was not well loved, Superintendent. Not by the maids anyway.' Mr Hardy gave me a look which seemed to enquire whether it were the age-old problem. I threw a look back confirming that indeed it was. He sighed. 'And rather an extreme case,' I said. 'There have been two recent departures: a Miss Abbott, my pre-decessor, and a kitchenmaid, Maggie, who flounced off on Saturday night. Phyllis, the housemaid, is on notice as we speak.'

'On notice, eh?' said Mr Hardy. 'That's interesting.'

'But could a woman have done it?' I asked.

Hardy shrugged.

'The doctor will be able to tell us more about that,' he said. 'Have you heard anything from any of those strapping lads down-stairs to make you think one of *them* might have wanted to kill him?'

I thought back to the evening before, John teasing Harry about the use of the razor. Surely he *was* only teasing? Still, I had wondered how someone of Harry's views could bear to be a servant, and a valet at that – the most intimate of servant–master relationships, surely. And then what had been wrong with Mattie this morning? And why was Mr Faulds so very desperate to get into the murder room and so very angry at my preventing him?

'There's a lot of chattering,' I said. 'Probably nothing more than chattering, but still – I think it would be worth your while interviewing *all* of the staff very closely.'

'I'll speak to Mrs Balfour first,' said Hardy. 'Then start on the fainting tweenie. If you would just go and tell them? Also, say to that Mrs Whatsername – the cook – to go and join the others, would you? And don't forget the glass.'

It was gone from where I had left it on the small table by the chaise, but before I chased after it to the kitchens I pulled back the covers on Lollie's bed and scrutinised the sheets, top and bottom, for it had occurred to me that I had seen no more of her than her head before she had hurried off to her bath earlier that morning and, if Superintendent Hardy were right about the blood, there might be traces of it here somewhere. But the linen was white and fresh, hardly even creased, and smelling faintly of lavender and of Lollie's Heure Bleue. The same scents were mingled in her drawers and in the trays of her wardrobe, where nightdresses and underclothes lay in orderly, crisp-edged piles. There was no way she could have stuffed any bloodstained articles in there, even if she could have opened the drawers and doors without wakening me. I went into the bathroom, where there were more neat arrangements, of towels this time, and no sign of anything rolled up or stuffed away where it should not be except my own nightgown. I held her hand towel up to the light from the bedroom doorway and could see not the slightest mark upon it. I turned on the sprinklers of the shower-bath and, as I had suspected, it sounded like rain on a tin roof, impossible for anyone – sleeping powder or none – to sleep through. Even the taps of the hand basin gurgled and spat loud enough to wake anyone in the next room.

There was a photograph of Pip Balfour in a frame on the little enamelled cupboard where the towels were stored. He was standing on the deck of a yacht, his shirtsleeves rolled high and his collar open, laughing and squinting into the sun.

'I don't think she did it,' I said to him. 'Even if you deserved her to.' I stood staring at the picture until all the water had drained away and the bathroom was silent again. Then I shook myself back into motion, turned from him and sped down the flights of stairs to the kitchens, hoping I was not too late already.

'And as to what we're supposed to do for our dinners, Fanny, your guess is as good as mine,' said Mrs Hepburn, striking *in medias res* as I entered the main kitchen. 'If I just sit in the hall all the morning, that is, which I can't, no more than I can work with the rest of them under my feet in here.' She glared at a police constable – Morrison, one presumed – who was trying to melt into the wall behind him and failing.

'The super tellt me I was to keep you all together, Mrs

Hepburn,' he said. 'Just until he's had a chance to talk to you all. He'll kill me if he finds out you're in here and they're in there.' He jerked a thumb at the wall which separated the kitchen from the servants' hall.

'Can't Sergeant Mackenzie stay with the others?' I asked.

'Millie, how many times?' broke in Mrs Hepburn. 'You flour for dough and grease for pastry. Now wipe that off and try again.' Millie, dusted with flour all down her apron, in her hair, on both cheeks and one spectacle lens, dropped her ball of pastry back into its bowl, bobbed and scurried out to fetch a cloth. Mrs Hepburn blew upwards into her hair, took hold of the frilled collar of her dress and shook it, letting a draught in about her neck.

'You've got me snapping at my own niece now!' she said to PC Morrison, who ignored her.

'The sarge is away back to the station,' he said to me. 'He couldnae get a line to ring them.'

'Are the telephonists on strike?' I said. 'I didn't think so.'

'No,' said Morrison, 'but they're overloaded with everybody ringing everybody else to say how they cannae get to wherever they're supposed to be with no buses on and the exchange said to the sarge that half of them are telling her they're the police or a doctor to make her break in and he could go and whistle.'

'I'm sure it will be all right to leave the others in the hall with Mr Faulds to watch them, Constable,' I said. 'I think Mr Hardy probably just meant that we shouldn't be allowed to swarm all over the house.'

'There! See?' said Mrs Hepburn. 'Miss Rossiter thinks the same as me. So let's all go through and have a cup of tea and a wee bite and take that blooming helmet off before you melt.' She picked up an enormous teapot and nodded to PC Morrison to carry a cooling tray of buns, then left at her usual pace.

'Her bark and her bite are both hopeless,' I told the constable, who nodded, smiling but still looking a little scared. I guessed that Hardy's bark was deafening and his bite fatal.

In the scullery, Millie had been distracted and was guddling potatoes in a deep basin of water. The disordered morning was clear to see in the piles of unwashed breakfast dishes ranged about on the wooden draining boards, one plate even still half-covered with rashers of congealing bacon. And there too was what I had been hoping to find: the pair of brandy glasses from Lollie's imposed nightcap the evening before. I could not tell which was mine and so I took them both, holding them down at my sides to hide them. She had been very insistent upon my drinking up and if she had put some kind of powder in my glass to make me sleep through disruptions, there was bound to be a trace of it left in the dregs at the bottom. I slipped out again without Millie hearing me and flitted down to my own room.

When I opened the door, it was to the sound of water and I stood still for a moment and listened. This could not be Millie and her potatoes away in the offshoot at the other side of the house. Very quietly, I turned the handle of the laundry-room door and looked in. Eldry was there, her arms deep in a sinkful of soap suds. For a moment I watched her in silence, but she must have sensed my presence because suddenly she wheeled around. I started backwards, banging my heel against the door jamb and cracking one of the brandy glasses as my hand clenched around it. Eldry was backing away too, pressing herself up against the sink, wiping her hands on her apron and staring at me like a dog which expects to be kicked.

'Please don't be angry, Miss Rossiter,' she said. 'I would have gone out to the wash-house at the back of the coalhole there, but that first policeman said we were no' to leave the house.'

'And what about the second policeman?' I said. 'He was supposed to be keeping you all together.'

'I slipped out,' said Eldry, 'when they were talking in the passageway. He's no' really counted us all up yet, I don't think.'

'I see. And what are you doing, exactly?'

She glanced back at the soapy water and bit down on her bottom lip, making her teeth more prominent than ever.

'Try – trying to get the blood out,' she said.

I felt the hairs move on the back of my neck and I spoke gently.

'What's got blood on it, Eldry?'

'My clothes,' she said. 'My dress and when I took my dress off it got on everything.'

'And how did you get blood on your dress?' I was clutching the cracked glass even tighter now, wondering if I could bring myself to use it if she were to fly at me.

'From him,' she said. 'Upstairs. Master.'

6

I stared at Eldry through the shifting steam in the washroom. Her voice was so faint now that I could hardly hear her at all through the muffled air. 'It must have come off on me when I went to his bedside,' she said. 'Or where else could it come fae?'

I let my breath go. I put the brandy glasses down on the small ironing table behind the door, being careful not to shatter the cracked one, and turned back to her.

'You mean this morning?' I said. 'When you took the tray in?' Eldry nodded. 'I didn't notice it,' I said, trying to get a clear picture of her as she had been during those few short and furious moments of confusion. She had had her back turned to me as she banged on the door and she had sunk down with her knees up; I could not remember having seen her front at any time. 'Are you sure?' I said. 'How could you have got blood on yourself just from walking up to the bedside and away again?'

'I don't know,' she whispered, 'but how else did it get there?'

'I'm sure *I* don't know,' I said. Then her eyes opened very wide and she put her hands up to her cheeks.

'You don't think I hurt him?' she said. Her hands were very red against her white face and her fingers looked like claws as she pressed them into her flesh. 'I could never, miss. All that blood. I could never.' She was swaying slightly and I stepped quickly over towards her and took hold of her hands. They were pulsing with heat, and all of a sudden I was aware of just how steamy and soft the air was here in this little room, and how the distemper on the walls was running with beads of moisture and blistering. I put one finger into the sink of water and yelped.

'Eldry, your hands,' I said. 'Come and sit down. Your poor hands!' I pushed her down into my little armchair and then went back to the laundry room. I pulled on the chain and felt the plug give way at the bottom of the sink. As the water drained, with a horrid sucking sound, a greyish mass rose out of the sinking tide of suds. I turned the cold tap on and once the bundle had cooled a little I began hauling at it, sorting it into pieces. Every stitch she had had on must have been in there. Knickers and vest, bodice and petticoats, stockings, her dress and her apron – white and black, wool and linen all mixed in together. I let the cold tap run and run and when it was icy I filled a deep bowl and carried it very carefully back to the armchair.

'Put them in here,' I said to her. 'Silly girl!' I had decided that brisk but affectionate exasperation was the strong suit here. 'Apart from anything else, Miss Etheldreda, hot water *sets* a bloodstain so nothing will *ever* shift it. A cold water and salt soak is what you need.' I blessed Grant for my crammer course in laundry work on Sunday, during which I had learned this snippet; not only was it a thrillingly convincing line for Miss Rossiter to deliver but it was also true. If there had ever been blood on those ruined clothes of Eldry's I should be able to find it. I decided against trying to feed them through the mangle but simply squeezed the worst out of them and hauled them up over the drying rack, and shut the door behind me. Nothing is more depressing than the sound of dripping.

'I don't want them to think I killed him,' she said to me when I joined her again. 'The police. My mammy would never forgive me if it all came out and everybody knew.'

'If it all came out about what kind of man he was?' I said, guessing. Eldry nodded. 'Did he make a nuisance of himself with you?' I said. She nodded again, just a dip of her chin against her chest. She did not raise her head again afterwards.

'I was a good girl,' she said.

'And a kind girl,' I agreed. 'Taking the tray this morning when Clara wasn't well.'

'We all help each other out,' she said. 'We always do. And Mrs Hepburn is like an auntie to us all – not just Millie – and Mr Faulds is a kind man. He's so fond of Phyllis and he's been good to me too, miss.' She was looking a little brighter now; perhaps it was beginning to dawn upon her, with Mr Balfour gone, what a pleasant establishment his widow's household might be.

'Now, Eldry,' I said. 'No more nonsense. You must be brave and sensible because you are going to be interviewed by the police, dear. They will want to know everything about this morning and about last night too. So why don't we run through it together now and I'll help you decide what to say.'

Eldry was adamant that she could not have crept out in the night without Millie hearing her and when I accompanied her to their shared bedroom I agreed. We were at the front of the house and here the sub-basement seemed very different. The only window was high and rather green and one had to stand right up against it and crane one's neck to see the area steps and the street railings above them. Even in the mid-morning Eldry had to put a light on.

'That's Millie's bed,' she said, pointing towards a rather dishevelled little bedstead with a knitted bear propped up against its pillow. Her own was neater, although by no means the picture of precision mine had been the previous day. Clearly whoever had readied Miss Rossiter's room for her, it was neither of these two. Between the beds was a box with a candlestick, a small prayer book and a couple of photographs, pasted onto board and propped up using opened hairpins. There was a washstand, a large oak chest standing on its end serving as a wardrobe and a small chest at the end of each bed. The floor was stone, but was covered here and there with rag mats. Under the window in the dankest corner of the room a third bed, stripped bare to its mattress, stood neglected.

'That was Millie's until Maggie took off,' Eldry told me, 'then we had a shift around. I hope she does get the kitchenmaid's position and doesn't need to move back again.' I sat down on Eldry's bed and bounced up and down a few times, hearing the grating squeak of slightly rusty bedsprings so familiar from the convalescent home in the war. Back then, the damp which caused the rust had come from windows thrown wide summer and winter to the insidious drizzle and driving rain. Here, the window was shut tight and there was a tiny fireplace with evidence of coal having been burned in its grate, but nothing would ever warm and dry such a subterranean room. When Eldry sat down on Millie's bed, there was another screeching of springs and our knees were practically touching. The girls could have held hands at night without even straightening their arms.

'And I suppose you lock your door?' I asked her.

'In this house,' she said, 'wouldn't you?'

I went over to the door and turned the key, with a scrape and a clunk. Clearly, if either of the two lower maids had left in the night, the other one had to be in cahoots and covering for her. I believed Eldry, I thought, although I would still check her clothes very carefully when they were dry, and I could not imagine Millie – that dewy, blinking little baby doll – driving a knife into Pip Balfour's neck, but I was looking forward to asking her what she made of her master, if indeed she had ever met him to form a view.

'We'd better join the others,' I said, unlocking the door. 'If PC Morrison says anything to you just send him to me.'

Phyllis was skipping down the stairs from the ground floor when we climbed up again.

'Where have you been?' she said, stopping when she saw Eldry. 'That big policeman – what's he? An inspector? – was looking for you, but he took me instead. So I've told him what I know which was nothing and now I'm free as a bird.' She grinned at us and jumped the last few steps down onto the flags then strolled off towards the kitchen. 'He wants Mrs Hepburn next,' she said over her shoulder.

'Well, thank all that's holy for that then,' said Mrs Hepburn, hearing her. 'And after I've said my piece I can get on without thon big lummock breathing down my neck.' She appeared in the kitchen doorway unrolling her sleeves. 'No disrespect meant to you, Jimmy,' she called back, 'I know you're only doing your job, lad. Now come on, Molly-moo. Come with me.'

'Eh, Mrs Hepburn,' said PC Morrison, hurrying out after her. 'It's one at a time. It's just you the now and Miss eh . . . Miss eh . . . Molly-moo after.' He was coatless now and had the glossy look about the mouth of someone who had just eaten a liberally buttered bun.

'Away and get,' said Mrs Hepburn. 'My niece Amelia is only sixteen and she needs her auntie.'

'You can mebbes chum along when Superintendent Hardy calls for her,' said PC Morrison, 'but he only asked—'

'Aye well, he's asked and no one can do more,' said Mrs Hepburn. Millie had joined her and was being firmly brushed, tweaked and smoothed into presentable shape, submitting with great docility. 'But I've no time to be running up and down stairs. I've a fish custard to make for mistress's luncheon – nothing gentler nor more strengthening after a shock – and the rest of them to feed and you two more than likely. We don't all have a canteen we can turn to, you know. Come on, Moll.'

She bore Millie away upstairs leaving PC Morrison mouthing ineffectually after them. Phyllis giggled and stuck out her tongue at him.

'Just as well you're here and not at the pickets if you can't stop Mrs Hepburn getting her own way,' she said. 'That big man Hardy said I could get on with my duties now I've made my statement, and it's my half-day free today – the first Tuesday of the month – so does that mean I can go out and meet my pal after dinner?'

'I'm not . . . I mean, no,' said Morrison. He had blushed when Mrs Hepburn was setting him down and was blushing again now as Phyllis twinkled up at him, his voice climbing up the octaves as he struggled to stamp his authority on the scene.

Phyllis put her hands on her hips and swayed gently from side to side, like a gypsy dancer. All she lacked were the streamers and tambourine.

'We'll see what Mr Faulds thinks,' she said and left us.

'I'd better go back up to Mrs Balfour,' I said, 'and leave you to . . .'

'Herd cats,' said PC Morrison, with feeling. 'It's like no house of mourning I've ever been in before, miss, I can tell you. More like a gala day.'

One could appreciate his sentiments, what with the buns and with Phyllis skipping around like a spring lamb, but there was Eldry as counterbalance. I looked about myself for her, but she had slipped away again.

The front door bell clanked as I was passing through the ground floor and I stopped, hoping to hear who it might be arriving. It clanked again but there was no noise from the down-stairs region at all. Was no one coming? Surely PC Morrison had to let one of the servants out of his custody to answer the door. I wondered where Phyllis was. Then, with a start, I remembered Miss Rossiter and hurried forwards. I had never in my life opened a front door, my own or another's, to a visitor and for a second I felt a cold trickle at the thought that it might be a friend of the Balfours, an acquaintance or neighbour, who knew me.

It was not. It was, in fact, a thin and flustered-looking man in his seventies with a well-polished Gladstone bag in one hand and a slim pocket watch open in his other, the police surgeon, I presumed. Behind him, a young man in a lavishly crumpled suit and wearing a soft hat on the back of his head was leaning against the railings puffing steadily on a cigarette. At his feet sat a large black case of mackintoshed cardboard, bulging out of shape around its contents and held closed by a stout brown leather belt. I could not imagine who he might be.

'About time too,' said the doctor. 'Do you know I had to walk here? All the way from Morningside? And I rang twice.' He had that peculiarly strained sort of Glaswegian voice which makes every utterance sound plaintive. I bobbed at him, which seemed to mollify.

'Please come in, doctor,' I said. 'I'll show you the way. And um . . .'

The other man hefted his case into his arms, holding it like a football, and trailed.

'Prints,' he said, with a grin and an eye-roll towards the doctor. I grinned back.

'I should have an assistant too,' the doctor went on. 'This is all most irregular. Run and get one of the constables, girl, and he can step in to help me.'

'I can't, I'm afraid, sir,' I said. 'There's only one and he's been put to watch over the witnesses until the super's seen them.'

'This is most unsatisfactory,' said the doctor, as I led him upstairs. 'So much for the famous "volunteers".'

'Well, there's usually three of me and I'm not whining,' said the other man. The doctor ignored him and spoke to me.

'Where exactly are we going?'

'I ken,' said the fingerprint man with a wink. 'You might at least have seen to it that he got stabbed in the front lobby and saved us all these stairs. Is this what they would call "the servant problem"?'

I was sorry to see the back of this character, if not of the doctor, when I delivered them to Mr Hardy on the bedroom-floor landing, but Lollie took all my attention when I joined her. Her shock had deepened and was now something I had thought never to see again after the war. She was numb to the point of bonelessness, sitting huddled in bed like a puppet with its strings cut, nursing the photograph of Pip which had been in her bathroom, and so although I longed to be downstairs with the others, I found myself at the little bookcase between the windows looking for something to read aloud as I had done when one of my children had a tooth- or tummy-ache which required distraction. There was a well-thumbed set of Mrs Molesworth and I selected *The Carved Lions*, my favourite of the lot, opening it at chapter one. Before long Lollie uncurled a little, stretching her legs down under the covers and leaning back more easily on the banked-up pillows behind her. After another half-chapter her eyes were drooping and eventually she began to breathe deeply and let the photograph frame fall softly forward against her chest. I read on, quieter and quieter, slower and slower, and then stopped.

As I pulled the door shut behind me and let my breath go at last, the doctor was just emerging from Pip's bedroom, with a roll of oilcloth in his hand and a sour expression on his face.

'Here, girl!' he said, and his face pursed up even further as I put a finger to my lips and shushed him.

'Beg pardon, doctor,' I said, 'but I've only just got Mrs Balfour off to sleep.'

'That's of no interest to me,' he said, in his complaining voice, clearly not one who felt that his Hippocratic oath covered the whole broad sweep of humanity. 'Take this to Superintendent Hardy for me and tell him I'll be with him shortly.' He thrust the little oilcloth bundle into my hands and wiped his own with a large handkerchief. 'You might as well make yourself useful.'

'Is it the knife?'

'It's none of your business what it is,' he replied.

'Should you be giving it to me?' I said. 'Aren't I a suspect?'

'It's been dusted,' he said, forced into an explanation in spite of himself, which made his lips purse so tight they all but disappeared completely, 'and I'm not going to start running up and down fetching and carrying just because nobody's seen fit to give me an assistant. So get on with you and less of your lip.'

With what I hoped was a look of withering pity – for snapping at maidservants really is the mark of a pitiable man – I took the bundle from him and hurried downstairs with it, just in time to see Mrs Hepburn and Millie emerge from the back parlour where Hardy had been interviewing them.

'Much good it did him to put me behind and upset my niece here,' said the cook when she saw me. I was becoming acclimatised to her style of conversation and joined into the stream of this one without any trouble.

'You couldn't tell him anything to help him then?'

'I was tucked up in my bed and Millie was tucked up in hers,' said Mrs Hepburn. 'And you can be sure if I'd heard any goings-on I shouldn't have, I would have been up and at them. It's a heavy responsibility, Fanny, to be in charge of all these girls, and it's not only my Millie I watch out for.' She had been eyeing the oilcloth as she spoke, and I seized the moment.

'You *can* help though, Mrs Hepburn,' I said. 'You'll never guess what this is. The doctor just gave it to me to bring to the super. It's the knife.'

'They've found it?' she said in tones of wonder (not knowing, I suppose, that it had been anything but hidden). I nodded.

'Why would he leave it?' she asked, shaking her head. 'With all you hear about fingerprints and all-sorts like that. You'd think he'd take it away with him again.' Clearly, the import of the locked-up house and the hidden Yale key had not struck Mrs Hepburn yet and she was still imagining some kind of fiendish, and remarkably ungreedy, burglar. 'What did you mean, Fanny, when you said I could help?'

Carefully, and with a glance at the parlour door, I opened one flap and then the other of the oilcloth wrapping and lifted the knife up into the light.

'Have you ever seen it before?'

The knife was still crusted and smeared with blood around the hilt, although its blade had come clean as it was removed and now shone dully. The pale bone handle was black with fingerprint powder, which had come off onto the cloth too. All three of us gazed at it. I was no expert but it looked to me to be an ordinary and rather elderly cook's knife, of the sort used to carve meat in a kitchen or nursery, although not in the dining room. Its blade had been sharpened many times and was now thinner along its length than where it joined the handle.

'That's your mutton knife, Auntie Kitty,' said Millie.

I glanced at Mrs Hepburn to make sure. She swallowed and nodded.

'And when did you last see it?' I asked her. 'Where does it belong?'

'I washed it last night with Eldry,' Millie said. 'I used it to poke the sausages for the pie. It's got a lovely sharp point, Miss Rossiter, see?' She reached out towards it but I drew it swiftly away. 'And then Eldry dried it and we put it back in the knife cupboard.'

'And I locked it before I went to my bed,' said Mrs Hepburn, 'like I always do. Every night without fail and afternoons too when it's my day out or Mr Faulds's.'

'Because you can't be too careful with knives,' said Millie.

'And the key?' I asked. Mrs Hepburn was plucking at her collar again, her face reddening.

'Oh, Fan!' she said. 'This doesn't look good, does it? I don't see how anyone sneaking in through a window could get into my knife cupboard.'

'Who keeps the key?' I insisted.

'Well, I've got one,' said Mrs Hepburn, patting her key ring, 'and . . . Oh my!'

'What?' I asked. I could hear movement inside the parlour and I wrapped the knife up again quickly. 'What is it?'

'Mill,' she said, turning to her niece. 'You trot along back to the kitchen and get started on the carrots for me. Scrape, mind, don't peel – they're as fresh as fresh.'

She drew close to me as Millie disappeared and she spoke urgently.

'Mistress could never have got that knife,' she said. 'There's a spare key and as to who knows and who doesn't, your guess beats mine – there's a couple of they youngsters as sharp as knives themselves and not much gets past them. But there's no way mistress would know.'

'What happened to someone sneaking in?' I said and got a wry look in return.

'That was good enough for the police and the papers,' she said. 'I would have swore on my life to spare mistress any trouble for it – he's no loss and no one will miss him. But if that's the knife then—'

94

The door behind her began to open and she sailed away, moving very fast and remarkably silently on her wooden soles. I started forward to greet Mr Hardy.

'The knife, Superintendent,' I said. 'With the doctor's compliments. It's one of the kitchen knives, kept in a locked cupboard with a key some of the servants knew about and some didn't. I'll try to find out which for you.'

'You do that,' he said, 'and send me up the last maid, would you?'

'There are two more to go actually,' I told him. 'You missed one earlier.'

'Oh no, I've seen her,' said Superintendent Hardy. 'She came in while Mrs Hepburn and the girl were here. It turned into a bit of a party. She came to tell me she hadn't done it.'

'Eldry?' I said. 'A plain girl? Thin nose?'

'She's in quite a state. And Mrs Hepburn isn't so calm as she'd like us to think either.'

'I shouldn't read anything into that, Superintendent,' I said. 'It's been a great shock to everyone.'

'No, you misunderstand me,' said Hardy. 'That's perfectly natural – of course it is. It's the other one that I've got my eye on. Amelia, is it? The one that's in no kind of state at all.'

'Millie?' I asked, unbelieving. 'Surely you can't be serious? You think that sweet girl could have taken a knife and . . .' But even as I spoke I felt a flicker of unease about it. She had indeed been remarkably unperturbed throughout the morning, neither fainting nor crying, and she had bent over the knife with an eager interest which did, upon reflection, strike one as unseemly.

'I'll ask the doctor what he thinks,' said Hardy. 'Whether a girl could have done it at all. I think I hear him coming.'

I took my time joining the others again, dawdling on the turn in the stairs trying to think it through. The superintendent was seeing ghosts in empty corners, I was sure, but *someone* had done it and it must have been someone who slept in the house, since bolted doors could not be reasoned away. I was almost sure that it was not Lollie, although I should have liked to be surer.

Eldry and Phyllis had motives, and Eldry at least was far from at ease, but they would have needed Millie and Clara respectively to cover for them. Mrs Hepburn had no room-mate to outwit and was anything but sorry about the death, but she appeared to suspect her mistress, and so unless that was a ruse she could not be guilty herself. It would be a clever touch, to affect suspicion of another, and I did not know Mrs Hepburn well enough to say whether she were capable of such subtlety. Of Mr Faulds, too, I did not yet know enough to form a view; a matter I should remedy right away.

He was there in his armchair in the servants' hall with the rest of the menfolk and Clara, who was crouched on a fender stool, busy stitching. Stanley was in Mrs Hepburn's seat and PC Morrison sat at the furthest corner of the table from John, Harry and Mattie, staring resolutely into space.

'You're wanted now, dear,' I said to Clara, who leapt to her feet as though I had fired a starting pistol. She hurried towards me and thrust her sewing into my hands.

'About time,' she said. 'Can you carry on with the armbands, Miss Rossiter? I've done seven – five to go.'

'Yes,' I said, clutching ineffectually at the bundle and feeling the needle pierce my skin. 'Now then, what stitch are you using, let me see now . . .' I sank into my own chair, squinting at the tiny stitches in the black cloth. A drop of blood welled up on my pierced fingertip and I sucked it.

'I suppose you'll be next, Mr Faulds,' I said, 'and then perhaps we can all get a bit of peace and quiet to ourselves.' I looked meaningfully at PC Morrison's profile as I spoke. Mr Faulds, though, had clearly not forgiven me for my thrusting behaviour earlier in the day and merely inclined his head with a tight smile. I bent to my sewing again, but I saw that two more drops of blood had come and had dripped onto the strip of serge. 'Bother it,' I said, 'I think I'll need to put a dressing on this.' I held my finger out to show Stanley. (I have often noticed the relish with which servants, like children, will describe and even exhibit any wound, swelling or rash which might befall them and I thought this a very Miss-Rossiterish touch.) Stanley, to my surprise, squeezed his eyes shut and twisted his head away from me.

'Stanley cannae stomach the sight of blood, Miss Rossiter,' said John, from the table. 'Here, Harry, mind of that time I gashed my arm open working on the motor and Stanley had to take his dinner at the kitchen table to keep away from me.'

'Have a heart,' said Harry. 'Don't mind him, Stan.'

'I do apologise,' I said to the footman, who was trying to look haughty but not making a very impressive job of it. 'Is there a first aid box anywhere?'

But even the thought of the first aid box, it seemed, was too much earthy reality for Stanley and it was Harry who got to his feet to show me in the end.

'All right by you?' he asked Morrison rather insolently as he passed. Morrison, who had perhaps been told by now that I was trusted by the superintendent and could be trusted by him, nodded curtly.

'And bring back some smelling salts for Stan, will you no'?' John called after us.

'You hold your tongue,' said Stanley. 'Yelling like that with a corpse in the house. You've no idea how to behave, have you? You don't deserve to be with decent people.'

'Enough,' said Mr Faulds. 'Quit bickering, both of you.'

Harry led me to a small room, no more than a store-cupboard really, stocked with blocks of yellow scrubbing soap and jars of green soft soap, tins of floor polish and boot polish and the great stone jars of marmalade which, for some reason I never understood, always lived with the cleaning supplies.

'Cracks beginning to show, eh?' said Harry, when we were inside and could not be overheard.

'It has been a very trying morning,' I agreed, 'and the more so for you lot, I suppose, just sitting there. At least the girls have had a chance to unburden themselves and get back to work.' Harry nodded. He had found the first aid box – just a large tin painted white – on a high shelf and was prising its lid open.

'We've got some of those sticking plasters,' he said. 'They're no' bad if you don't wind them too tight. Master brought them back from America last time they was over.' He gave me one of the little waxed packets and put the lid back on the tin again. I had never seen one of the things and it took a moment of fumbling before I got it unwrapped and managed to apply it to my finger.

'That was very generous of him,' I said. 'Of Mr Balfour, I mean. He can't have been all bad.'

'He was as bad as they come,' said Harry. 'Not just a mean so-and-so, but useless – they're all useless. Don't know the meaning of a day's work, just play like bairns their whole lives. He played at building toy boats, Miss Rossiter. Did you know that? A grown man and he spent his days making toy boats that didn't even float.'

'And you spent your days dressing him,' I said. This point still puzzled me.

'Not me,' said Harry, 'I'm only twenty-five. I've got plenty days left. If I escape the noose, like.'

He threw me such a challenging look as he said this, almost as though he were daring me to make something of it, that I felt a surge of anger rise up in me.

'John's not the only joker in the pack then,' I said and had the pleasure of seeing that I had surprised him. 'The police know that the back doors were locked and bolted, Harry. You are not under any suspicion.'

'Is that right?' he said. 'They don't think one of the girls would have unbolted a door then?' This brought me up short and for a while I said nothing, remembering how Eldry had told me they all 'helped each other out', remembering how the two house-maids had rushed to comfort Mattie the evening before.

'But Mrs Hepburn would have heard it,' I said. 'Her room is just by the kitchen door.'

'Aye, and yours is right by the one in the sub-basement,' Harry agreed. 'You'd have heard for sure. If everyone was in their beds like good girls and boys somebody would have heard something.' His tone was mocking but he could not, surely, have guessed that I was with Lollie all night and so I ignored him.

'Harry,' I said, 'can I speak seriously to you for a minute?'

'I don't care that he's dead and I don't care who killed him,' he said. 'So if that's what you're on about the answer is no.'

'But presumably, like me, you don't want to see an innocent party accused?' I said. 'Even if you don't mind the idea of the guilty going free.' Harry nodded. 'Well, it's about Eldry.'

'What about her?'

'This morning, when you lifted her up and carried her downstairs, you didn't happened to notice if there was a stain on her dress, did you? Or on her apron? Anywhere really.'

'A stain?' said Harry, looking uncomfortable for the first time.

'A bloodstain. Only she said that she had got blood on herself when she went in with the tray.'

'Well, I didn't see it,' said Harry. 'So I don't think—' He stopped short and stared at me. 'Hang on,' he said, 'how is that "clearing the innocent"? You're checking what she said against what I say – that's not "clearing" anyone.'

'I was hoping you *had* seen something,' I told him. 'Otherwise, I don't know what to think and what to say to the superintendent.'

'And she just come out and told you this, did she?' Harry asked.

'I found her in my little laundry room, washing her clothes,' I said. 'And—'

'God almighty,' said Harry. 'She's never at that again, is she?'

'What are you talking about?' I said, but Harry shook his head.

'Ask one of the girls if you can't guess,' he said. 'That man deserved ten knives in him for what he did, miss, if you ask me.'

'Did he ever do anything to you?' I asked. 'Besides offend you.'

'He did,' Harry said, licking his lips and struggling with what appeared to be an unpleasant memory. 'He belittled me, rubbed my nose in the difference between the two of us as if I wasn't twice the man he'll ever be if you stripped away the accident of birth and the trappings of privilege.'

'Yes, but what did he actually do?' I asked.

'I don't want to talk about it,' said Harry.

'You'll have to tell the police.'

'It's not like that,' he said, looking uncomfortable. 'But I've never told anyone, that's all.'

'We don't get to choose what we tell the police, my boy. Not in the midst of a murder investigation. Even you must see that.'

'But it's just daft,' he said. 'I can't tell that copper – it's just stupid. And I wouldn't even know what to tell him.' I waited and after a pause he blurted out: 'He took my clothes.'

'What do you mean?'

'See? It's daft. He went into my trunk down in the carriage house there and took my clothes away. I think it was after we were talking one time – him and me – about ownership and wealth, him acting all interested and that, drawing me out, and then he took every stitch I had to my name.'

It was, I thought, a neat way to undercut someone's droning on about the sins of ownership but rather a nasty one. I cast a look at what Harry was wearing now and he caught me.

'I got it all back again,' he said, looking down at his shirtsleeves and black trousers. 'But he'd cut the pockets out. And when I went and challenged him he said I wouldn't be needing pockets since I had no time for possessions to put in them. It was late at night and he was drunk and I was . . . I was feart.' He turned out his pockets now and I could see that they were made of mismatched cloth, stitched on the stubs of the pockets which had gone before. 'I fixed them up myself,' he said. 'The girls would have helped me but I never told them. I was feart and I didn't understand why and that scared me even more.'

'Madness is frightening, Harry,' I said. 'I understand perfectly.'

'Aye, madness,' he said, leaping on my suggestion as though it was a stroke of genius. 'He made me feel as if *I* was going mad too.' He shook his head as though to cast it off from him. 'Like how any chance he got he would take the scissors to my coat or snip away at my breeks cuffs. Just wee digs, just to remind me.'

I nodded. This Pip Balfour – creeping about with scissors, snipping away – sounded exactly like Lollie's midnight visitor with the nasty taste in poetry.

'And yet you stayed,' I said, as I had said to Lollie too.

'I did,' said Harry. He had shrugged off the troubling memories and was smiling again. 'And the glorious day has dawned, miss, hasn't it? Not the proper glorious day, but this'll do to be going on with.' With that he left, switching off the light and leaving me alone in the dark.

7

By luncheon, Mr Faulds too had made the journey up to the little parlour and back again and so, with all possible suspects interviewed – for Mrs Hepburn had indeed been vociferous on the topic of her sharp ears and the secure fastening of the house at night-time – PC Morrison was relieved of his watch and was given instead the even duller task of standing outside Pip Balfour's bedroom door guarding the body until the coroner's cart came to take it away to the mortuary. Superintendent Hardy had departed, hurrying off down the stairs to the street, trailing sheaves of notes behind him – and as for Sergeant Mackenzie, he had never returned after his first exit. Lollie was asleep, luncheon was served, all was calm.

'So,' said Mr Faulds, gripping the edge of the table with both hands and looking at his staff ranged up and down the sides, 'I think a short grace is in order.' Eleven heads bowed. Ten remained bowed, but I admit that mine popped up again to watch him. 'Dear Father,' he said, with his eyes squeezed tightly shut and his hands pressed together, 'we thank Thee for Thy bounty and for our deliverance from dark days. We ask that Thou bless this house in its hour of uncertainty and bring peace to the troubled breast of our dear mistress. We pray that Thy mercy be showered on the soul of our departed master and we ask that Thou willst bring us all safely through the storm to a happier future according to Thy holy will. Amen.'

I was speechless, although a chorus of amens rumbled out from everyone else readily enough. Mr Faulds's prayer, if I understood it, could be paraphrased as: thank you for Pip Balfour's death. Please look out for us during the investigation, show Lollie that she's better off without him, make sure no one gets punished and, anyway, he deserved it.

'What happens now, Mr Faulds?' said Phyllis. She was already dressed for her afternoon out in a coat-dress of daffodil yellow and a straw hat, and looked the picture of springtime despite the black armband. 'What will the police do next?'

'Nothing that should be discussed at the dinner table,' said Mrs Hepburn. She had passed a loaded plate up to Mr Faulds at the far end and now turned to me. 'How many slices, Fanny?' It was boiled mutton of all things and I could not help thinking of the knife as Mrs Hepburn forked a thick slab onto my plate for me. 'And take plenty tatties,' she said. 'You've had a draining time of it and you'll need your strength.'

'But d'you think we've seen the last of them?' Phyllis persisted.

'I think,' I said, 'that we'll be seeing quite a lot more of them, don't you, Mr Faulds? Mrs Hepburn?' A few glances flicked towards me. 'They'll keep going until they find out what happened.' A couple of the younger servants glanced uncertainly towards the butler. 'The best way to get rid of them and get things back to normal for mistress,' I went on, 'would be if we could tell them something to help them "crack the case". Help them solve it.' I looked around the table brightly.

'Come up with a story, you mean?' said Stanley. 'That's a thought, Mr Faulds, isn't it? And I could give you some good ideas for it.'

'No!' I said. 'I didn't mean anything of the kind. I meant tell them anything we actually know to help them find out what actually happened – tell the truth and get to the bottom of it all.'

'You don't know what you're saying, lass,' said Mrs Hepburn. 'It maybe hasn't struck you yet, new as you are, but there's only two ways it can be.' I waited while she dished out potatoes to Eldry, Millie and Mattie and nodded at them to start eating. 'Either it was mistress, and we're none of us wanting to see her clapped in jail and the house broken up with all of us on the street, or it was someone sitting round this table. So you just mind what you say.'

I gazed at them all: Mrs Hepburn quite impassive, pulling her meat into shreds with her fork; Mr Faulds watching me with an unreadable look upon his face, one hand around his beer glass; Clara, pale and solemn, sitting with her head bent; John with a little twist of a grin on one side of his face, enjoying the scene; Phyllis in her straw hat looking as though she had not a care in the world; Stanley staring at Mr Faulds, waiting for guidance; Eldry eating quickly but with little enjoyment, jabbing the food up on her fork and snapping it off again with her teeth; Harry, uncomfortable, shifting in his seat and toying with his knife, food forgotten; Millie mashing butter into her potatoes with a small smile; Mattie watching her, grimacing at the sight, or perhaps the sound, of the lumps of butter being squashed through the tines of her fork as though it were something disgusting. Before the silence could grow any more deafening, I spoke up again.

'Are you really saying – all of you – that you would remain under suspicion yourselves to protect . . . whoever it is?' I said. 'Everyone? No one will speak up?'

'No,' said Harry. 'It's not that bad. At least, for me it's not. I don't *know* who it was.' There was a murmur of agreement to this point. 'But I don't *care* who it was either.' At this the murmurs rose almost to a cheer.

'And that's enough,' said Mrs Hepburn. 'Phyllis, where are you going in that hat, eh? What's his name and what does his dada do?'

Phyllis giggled, John took up the tease with gusto and the rest went on wolfing their food or picking at it as their habits or current moods took them.

Presently, Mr Faulds turned to me.

'Miss Rossiter,' he said. 'Perhaps you'd be so kind as to go through to the kitchen and get the pudding. Mrs Hepburn looks dog-tired and we like to help each other. Clara, you go too and fetch in a pot of tea.'

I had only half cleared my plate of mutton but I had no appetite for the rest of it and so I rose and followed Clara out of the room. She walked stiffly, quite unlike the easy, willowy girl who had greeted me at the area door less than a day ago.

'Are you feeling any better?' I said to her as we entered the kitchen. Clara took a cigarette out of her apron pocket and held it against the hot bar of the range to light it.

'Better than what?' she said, putting the cigarette to her lips. 'Want one?' I shook my head.

'Eldry said this morning you were indisposed.'

'Oh!' she said, smiling faintly. 'That. Aye, well, it wasn't a good time for me to go into his room, that's all.'

'Forgive me, dear, but what do you mean?'

Clara gave me a shrewd look out of her little eyes.

'I'd have put you down for a woman of the world, Miss Rossiter,' she said. 'I'd have put money on *Miss* being just for politeness like *Mrs* Hepburn is.' She drew deeply on her cigarette and blew out the smoke in three long plumes. 'Phyllis and Eldry and me took turns of when we had to go into his room, that's all. To make sure we wouldn't come away with no wee souvenirs, see?' I could feel myself blushing.

'Good grief!' I said, and then a fresh thought struck me. 'Phyllis told me that she had escaped his attentions.'

'She was lucky,' said Clara. 'She never got caught by him in one of his moods. Don't ask me why, because . . . I'm not meaning to be nasty but if he went for Eldry he'd go for any— . . . Well, I don't want to be nasty. It must have just been the luck of the draw. He'd have got her in the end.'

'But why didn't you stop going altogether? Harry could have stepped in, surely? Why didn't you tell Mr Faulds and ask him— Well, no, probably you wouldn't have cared to tell Mr Faulds, but why not Mrs Hepburn?'

Clara laughed a bitter laugh. 'Aye, why not just tell everybody everything, eh?' she said, and the way she spoke reminded me of Harry; the same troubled confusion on her face and in her voice too. There was surely more here than she had hinted at so far.

'I do think,' I said carefully, 'that perhaps the worst of what master did was managing to make everyone else ashamed instead of himself.' Clara looked up sharply at me. 'To make everyone keep his grubby little secrets for him.' I paused and smiled at her, trying not to look as though I were holding my breath, waiting. Clara's cigarette burned forgotten in her hand, the ribbon of smoke rippling a little in the waves of warmth from the stove.

'You're right, Miss Rossiter,' she said, speaking in a soft and wondering sort of voice. 'That's just exactly right, the way you said it.'

'When in fact you have nothing to fear from speaking of your troubles to your friends,' I said. 'They all knew him. They know the fault was his and you did nothing wrong.'

With this, though, I had gone too far. Clara came out of her dream with a harsh intake of breath and blinked at me.

'Did I not now?' she said. 'If only.'

'You mean you did do something?'

Clara laughed again but there was no humour in it.

'I didn't stick a knife in him if that's what you mean. You don't really think that, do you?'

Before I could answer there was a knock on the half-open kitchen door and Mattie put his head around it.

'Mrs Hepburn says she's not chivvying you and to say sorry and something else I've forgotten, but John and Harry are ready for their puddings, so I've come to get them.'

'You don't need to knock at the door, daftie,' said Clara. She jumped down from the table where she had been perching and gave her cigarette to Mattie to finish. Then she seized a cloth, opened the oven and drew out a steaming dish of rice pudding bubbling away merrily under a dark russet skin. 'I'll come back and do the tea,' she called over her shoulder, leaving Mattie and me behind her.

Mattie took a tentative puff of the cigarette, grimaced and threw it onto the fire. I thought I should show willing and I took down the largest of the teapots which were ranged on the chimney-piece and gingerly poured in a little hot water from the kettle to warm it through.

'Careful, miss,' said Mattie, then bit his lip. 'Sorry, but you d'ae look fair handy with that, if you'll pardon me.'

'Perhaps you could help?' I said, holding the pot out to him. He beamed with pleasure and took it from me.

'I always make the tea at home, at my mammy's,' he said. 'Been doing it since I was a wee tiny boy.' I looked around myself help-lessly; I did not even know where the sugar and milk might be and I wished I had a cigarette to keep my hands busy.

'So what do you make of all this then, Mattie?' I said. His face stilled again, the smile gone.

'Master?' he said. I nodded. 'I d'ae ken, miss. I'm glad I never saw it. Was it as bad as Eldry said?'

'It wasn't very nice to look at,' I told him. 'But what I really meant was what do you make of . . . what Mr Faulds said? And Harry?'

'I d'ae ken,' said Mattie again. I waited, sure that more would come if I let it. Mattie spooned tea leaves into the pot and then reached up to replace the caddy on the chimneypiece. 'I'm no' sorry he's deid,' he said at last, 'and I'd be right sorry to see any o' them through there deid. Hanged, I mean, miss. Even Stanley.'

'Stanley?' I could not help echoing. 'Why him, in particular?'

'Sorry,' said Mattie. 'Sorry, I shouldnae have said that. Just that him and me don't get on as easy as me and the rest, that's all. He swanks it a bit to the rest o' us. And he can be a wee bit two-faced an' all, miss. He's aye sucking up to Mr Faulds, but you should hear what he says about him when his back's turned.'

'I have,' I said. 'Snippets, anyway. But I have to agree with you, Mattie. I can't think of any of our friends through there that I would see hanged, even after only a day of knowing them. Stanley included.' We shared a smile. 'But I am sorry that Mr Balfour died the way he did, for he did *me* no harm.'

The silence this time was even longer, but eventually Mattie spoke up.

'He didnae harm me either, miss,' he said softly. 'No' really. It was my own stupid fault, being such a . . . nancy. That's what he called it. All it was was he made me wait up for him, up in the wee lobby place, at the front door, when he was out, no matter how late he was out. In the dark there. I'm feart for the dark, miss, and he knew it but he wouldnae let me get Harry or anyone do it instead of me – it had to be me because I'm the only one that was feart.'

'That's beastly,' I said. 'And quite unnecessary too.'

'Well, I had to open the front door for him, miss,' said Mattie, 'and then lock up again at his back, pull his boots off and take them to clean. Only he wouldnae let me keep a light on, so I just had to wait in the dark. Not every night, mind,' he said. 'Only when he was out somewhere. And anyway, I just needed to stop being daft.'

'I can't agree with that, Mattie,' I said. 'No one can say why one person is frightened of the dark and another isn't, but there's no need to go calling yourself unkind names.'

'Oh, I ken fine why it is,' Mattie said. 'It's why I'm here instead of at the pit still, miss. I was in a fall – a collapse, like – and I was trapped until they came to get me out.'

'Trapped down a mine?' I said, grimacing. I could not imagine anything more terrifying, and I could not imagine this child, with his blond hair and his slight frame, ever doing anything so filthy and dreadful as mining.

'I was putting for my big brother,' Mattie said.

'Putting?'

'Dragging the cart,' said Mattie. 'My big brother was at the face and I filled the cart and dragged it back to the road for him.'

'But aren't there lifts?' I said, puzzled. 'Pulleys?'

Mattie nodded, looking just as puzzled, and then he gave a smile.

'The *coal* road, I mean, miss,' he said. 'Underground. Joins the shaft to where the coal face starts. Anyway, there was this wee collapse. Naeb'dy died and it never got in the papers and it was only a few hours but . . . John lost a leg, miss. So I'm lucky really. Only I couldnae go down again, not even for a fortune. It's no' like I didnae try.'

'And master knew this?' I said. Mattie nodded. 'But still made you sit in the dark all alone and wait for him?' Another nod. 'Unspeakable!' But even as I spoke up so stoutly – and truly I was incensed on young Mattie's behalf – there was a question about his story, at least one, which did not make sense. Something about it troubled me. 'Mattie,' I began, but someone appeared in the doorway before I could continue. It was Mr Faulds himself, and both the hall boy and I stood almost to attention.

'What's happened to that tea?' he said. Mattie rapidly filled the pot with water, swiped up a large milk jug from where it had been sitting on a stone shelf under the window and left us.

'Well, Miss Rossiter,' said Mr Faulds. 'Fanny, if I may. You've been talking to Clara and Mattie, have you? And what say you now? Are you getting to think he's no loss?'

'I'm certainly beginning to think you must all love mistress a great deal to stay in a house that had him in it too,' I said. 'And here's another thing, Mr Faulds. You didn't see what was done to him, but you've all heard about it. Aren't you scared to be in the same house with someone who could do such a thing? Aren't you worried at all that now he's started he won't stop?'

'*He*, Fanny?' said the butler. 'Who's this "he"? I'm the only "he" that's had the finger pointed and if it was me who did it, I've nothing to fear, now have I?'

'*Did* the superintendent point his finger?' I said. 'You don't seem unduly troubled by it.'

'The innocent have nothing to fear from the truth,' he said.

With Mr Faulds's permission, and since Lollie seemed set to sleep the day away, I went out after luncheon. I had told the cook and butler as we sat together in the armchairs that I hoped they understood but I just needed to get out into the fresh air and lift my eyes to the hills (this was one of Grant's coded expressions for whenever she feels like sloping off and can think of no actual reason). The cost of my freedom was to regale them with the details of what I had seen, once the youngsters were all safely out of the way and the servants' hall door was firmly closed behind them. Mrs Hepburn merely sucked her teeth, shook her head and continued unwrapping and devouring an endless succession of mint toffees, but Mr Faulds was badly affected by the tale and wiped his neck and forehead several times with his handkerchief before I was done.

'Here,' he said, 'I hope them police will have the cleaning of it all, Mrs Hepburn. I hope them sheets and blankets won't get left for our girls to tackle.'

'I'll take care of them if it falls to us,' I said. 'I was a nurse in the war and I've seen worse.'

Mr Faulds shuddered.

'I've never been any good with the likes of that,' he said. 'Not as bad as poor Stanley, but bad enough. I saw a man hang himself – by accident, this was – in the backstage at the Bristol Hippodrome in my performing days, caught himself up in the ropes and couldn't get free and it was the only time in my life I couldn't go on. I was in my dressing room as grey as a ghost and put to shame with all the chorus and the dancing girls getting on with the show.' Mrs Hepburn tutted again and offered him a toffee.

As I made my way up the steps and along the pavement minutes later, I considered the point; one which had not struck me before. One thinks often of the evil required to do murder and – for want of a better word – the courage, but one cannot ignore the fact that a would-be murderer must also have the stomach for it, at least where a stabbing is concerned. Firing off a pistol at a distant figure or tipping a packet of powder into a glass before melting away are one thing, but driving a kitchen knife into the neck of a man while he looks one in the eye . . . surely I could take at least the screaming Eldry, the gulping Stanley and the quavering Mattie off the list of possible suspects, unless one of them was a very accomplished actor indeed? And Mr Faulds, so he claimed, could not have done it without fainting dead away. Then again Millie, the superintendent's rather peculiar ideas about her placidity notwithstanding, was hardly my idea of a murdering fiend. As to the other three: to have met Clara, Phyllis and Mrs Hepburn in the street and supposed any of them capable of such an act would be hard enough; to entertain the notion after twenty-four hours at close quarters with them was beyond ridiculous. And yet it *had* happened; still whenever I closed my eyes I could see that white face rising up out of a sea of red, beseeching me.

So, here I was, doing what I was ever wont to do: that is, turning to Alec Osborne to beg him to help me. I only hoped, as I let myself into the kiosk at the corner of Darnaway Street and piled up my collection of pennies, that the extra bustle of the morning had died down so that the telephone lines were there for the asking again.

There was a little delay, as it happened, a few extra ticks and thumps and one or two sighs from the girl at the exchange. She asked me if I would not rather try later; I assured her that I had chosen to telephone just when I wanted to. She sighed again, said something I affected not to hear and then at last I heard ringing.

'It's Mrs Gilver, Mr Barrow, for master,' I said, before I could help myself. 'For Mr Osborne, I mean, Barrow, if you'd fetch him.' There was a long, windy silence down the line. Barrow, Alec's valet and, in the absence of a housekeeper, the self-appointed boss of Dunelgar, takes himself inordinately seriously for a man of his age. As well as that, I am never very certain what he thinks of me. Perhaps he is an empire-builder, who looks forward to the day when Alec's household will swell and he will be borne along on the rising tide and finish as butler with valets and footmen to jump when he clicks his fingers. If so, then no doubt he blames me for Alec's continued bachelorhood – a ridiculous notion, for I have been most encouraging on the topic of Alec's settling down, except when I have been downright bossy. There was a whisper of an alliance only the previous winter and I had cosseted it as though it were a kindling fire which I had lit with my last match, but it came to nothing.

Alec picked up the earpiece at the other end and broke in on my meandering thoughts.

'Dandy,' he said, and I heard the click of him resetting his pipe, which meant he was prepared for a long and luxurious chat, if the girl on the exchange would let us have one. 'How goes it across the great divide?' he said. 'Have they seen through you yet? Bunty has settled in like a daughter of the house, by the way. Not fretting at all.'

'There's been a murder,' I announced and managed to get quite a chunk of the pertinent history across in the ensuing silence before Alec came to himself again and started badgering me.

'But the men were all locked out apart from this Faulds character?' he said, cutting me off from explaining that very fact with great clarity. I sighed.

'Yes, and the maids are all two to a room and, as I say, I'm pretty sure Lollie couldn't have done it without me hearing although I'm getting the brandy glass checked to be sure. So I'm stumped and begging you to come and help me.'

'Well, ordinarily, of course,' Alec said. 'Ordinarily try and stop me, but I'm stranded, Dan. I've got enough petrol in the Vauxhall to get down there but not back again, and some of the garages are closed already.'

'But surely garage mechanics are their own bosses?' I said. 'Why should they shut the pumps, for heaven's sake?'

'They've run dry from everyone stocking up,' Alec said.

'Panic buying?' I said. 'How disgusting. How selfish people are. They've forgotten all our lessons from the war already.'

'Quite,' said Alec. 'Also, I never thought of it in time. No, we are *not* finished,' he said in his most commanding voice as the pips sounded and the girl broke in. 'At least another three minutes. At least.' The line changed back from breathy to muffled as she left us again. 'Is there any sign of a motive, Dan? From anyone except the wife, that is?'

'Hah!' I said. 'The place is bristling with motives like a porcupine. You were wrong when you thought him a ninny, you know. Lollie's summing-up was much nearer the mark: a cruel, vindictive, philandering pig. A seducer of the maids and a brute to the menservants. Some of the things he did, Alec, one wonders how he ever dreamed them up they're so lavishly nasty. And Clara the parlourmaid can't bring herself to speak of whatever he did to her even now, so it must be extra specially horrid. No one is sorry he's gone.'

'Still,' said Alec.

'Oh yes, I know,' I said. 'And Lollie at least is keen for me to stay and try to get to the bottom of it for her.'

'Well, if it makes more sense to come at it from this end,' said Alec, 'is there anyone you can put out of the running? Anyone who *didn't* have a motive?'

'I haven't heard anything from Mr Faulds on his own account,' I said, 'although he hated him with a passion in comradeship, certainly. And . . . let me see . . . Mrs Hepburn dropped a very vague hint yesterday but I need to press her. And then there's Millie, the scullerymaid – kitchenmaid in waiting – but I can't think that she would have much to do with him.'

'Oh?' said Alec.

'Have you ever met yours?' I said.

'Good point,' Alec said. 'No, indeed. Although I daresay there is such a creature about the place somewhere. What about the rest of the men?'

'I've yet to speak to John and Stanley,' I said, 'but the thing is that the men are in the clear anyway, because they were locked out, remember?'

'Doors can be unlocked,' said Alec. 'You must be thorough about this, Dan.'

I considered trying to explain to him the difference between his bedroom, muffled with carpet and curtains, miles from any door, and the maids' and cook's rooms with their linoleum over stone, their echoing bareness and the sound ringing along the empty passageways of scraping locks and iron bolts and wooden soles and marble steps.

'Hm,' I said in the end.

'And on another note, what are the police making of it?' said Alec. 'And of you, come to that?'

'Very little so far,' I replied. 'They're rather stretched with all the picket duty – or is it the strikers who one says are on picket duty? Well, you know what I mean – so it was a superintendent who poled up this morning, very flustered and very displeased to be flustered – he is formed for gravitas, really – but he practically had his Big Blue Book for Policemen in his hand, folded open at Murder. So when I debunked Fanny Rossiter and waved Hutchinson's name in front of him he rather fell on my neck.'

'*Fanny*?' said Alec. 'And *debunked*? Where do you get these words? Do you have to pay a subscription?'

'You'll find,' I said, trying to sound withering, 'that debunking comes from Oscar Wilde. When they find out that Algy's dying friend isn't dying.'

'That would be de-Bunburying,' said Alec. 'Do you know when the post-mortem's going to—'

'Phyllis!' I said. I put my hand up to the glass to screen my eyes and peered out along the street. Phyllis the housemaid, unmissable in her yellow coat-dress, was walking smartly along towards India Street carrying a medium-sized suitcase. I spoke into the mouthpiece again. 'Alec, I've just seen one of the other maids with rather more luggage than she would need on an after-noon off. She's making her way towards the tram stop, bold as brass. I think she's heading for the hills.'

'Not by tram she's not,' said Alec. 'But you'd better ring off and give chase anyway.'

I crashed the earpiece back into the cradle and – as I realised later – leaving tenpenceworth of pennies behind me, I slipped out of the kiosk and streaked across the road to the corner where Phyllis had disappeared. Hoping that no one could see me, I flat-tened myself against the wall and poked my head around to peep down the street after her. She was nowhere to be seen. I stepped away from the wall and rounded the corner properly, looking up and down each side, but there was no mistaking it. There were no carts, motor lorries or trees for her to be hidden behind, no more kiosks or even pillar boxes, no shops she might have stepped inside. She was gone. She must have started running, I realised. Perhaps she saw me peering out of the kiosk at her. I went at a very fast walk, almost running myself, to the corner of Jamaica Street and then to the next corner again, where Gloucester Place and Circus Gardens just fail to meet, and looked around in all directions. There was no sign of her anywhere. She could not possibly have rounded two corners in the time it took me to get here and there were no alleys or lanes for her to have dodged into; Edinburgh's New Town is well known for the endlessness and unbrokenness of its many stretches of Georgian splendour.

There was only one explanation, I thought, as I stood there with my hands on my hips letting my breath slow down again. She had gone into one of the houses. Perhaps she had given notice and left, or had simply left – 'flitted', like Maggie – to a new situation already lined up before the events of the morning, in response to Pip's threats of dismissal. But would a maid roll up to her new position in that coat and that hat, looking as though she were going for a walk along a promenade with her young man? Hard on the heels of that thought came another. What if she were indeed going to join a young man, in a flat in one of those houses, escaping from what she had done? What if she had robbed Pip Balfour of some valuable item that no one yet realised was missing and was making off, dressed up to the nines and sure she had got away with it?

'Everything all right, miss?' said a voice. I started and turned to see a rather elderly-looking policeman standing at my side. He was regarding me with an expression more quizzical than helpful.

'Absolutely fine,' I said. 'I was supposed to meet up with a friend of mine but she's given me the slip somehow.' The policeman had reared backwards somewhat when I spoke and was looking at me with outright hostility now.

'Just the one friend was it, miss?' he said. I stared at him.

'As it happens,' I answered. 'Why?'

'Fine and well,' he said. 'I'll take your name just the same though.'

'I beg your pardon?' I said. 'You most certainly shall not.'

'Oh, is that right then?' said the policeman, squaring up.

'It is,' I replied. 'I've done absolutely nothing wrong and I'm surprised, I must say, to find you hanging around here harassing innocent passers-by when your fellow officers are stretched to breaking point with the strikers.' He took a step or two backwards, I am pleased to say. 'Do you know Superintendent Hardy?'

I demanded. He nodded, swallowing hard and making his prominent and rather ill-shaven Adam's apple sink into his collar and bob up again. 'Well, so do I.'

'I beg your pardon, miss,' said the constable, who had instinctively pulled at his coat to smarten himself when he heard Hardy's name. 'Only I *am* minding out for the strike. I'm back in for it – been retired five years, properly. There's trouble down on Princes Street and we're trying to see where it is the gangs are forming. I thought you were standing there in the middle of the junction like that waiting for your pals.'

'Gangs?' I said. 'On Princes Street?'

'By the station there,' said the policeman. 'And a big crowd at the Tron too. Five arrests already and a policeman in the infirmary.' I said nothing. 'And what with you dressed so plain but speaking so fancy – if you'll forgive me – I put you down for one of they intellectuals.'

'I assure you, my dear fellow,' I said, 'that I am neither an intellectual nor a Bolshevist nor any kind of sympathiser.' At that moment, I caught sight of a flash of yellow out of the corner of my eye and turned towards it. Phyllis was shutting an area gate about halfway up India Street. 'There she is now!' I said to the constable. Phyllis hefted her suitcase more comfortably into her grip and made her way back the way she had come.

'Oh, really?' he replied with what seemed to me to be an unwarranted level of interest.

'I'll just run after her, if that's all right,' I said, already beginning to move. 'Keep up the good work, Constable.'

He gave me a knowing look and turned away.

Of course I had no intention of sprinting after Phyllis really, but I did want to see where she had been and try to work out what she might have been doing there. She had definitely come up from below stairs, but if she were merely visiting a friend why had she only stayed a minute and what was in the suitcase? Bloodied clothes would be my first guess and I should like to get inside the place before they were put into a furnace by her accomplice.

It was a grey stone house like any other in the streets surrounding, not so grand as the Balfours' in Heriot Row and ill-kept in a vague way; as I drew nearer, the collection of bright new bell pushes set in by the front door revealed that it had lately been divided into flats. The basement windows were dusty, the area flags brown with dead moss which had been sluiced with ammonia but not scrubbed clear. An unprepossessing place, in all, but it had one feature of great interest to me. In the fanlight above the basement door, there was a crude painting of three brass-coloured balls. Without thinking about what I should do once inside, I opened the gate and descended.

The door was unlocked, but whoever waited inside was well warned of any visitor, for a string of tiny gold bells hanging behind it were set tinkling as I entered. A long passageway distempered in a tobacco colour stretched away in front of me, but on the nearest door, sitting ajar, a cardboard sign proclaimed it to be the *Reception & Showroom*.

A counter had been erected, cutting the room in half, and behind it were countless tiers of shelves, all around and above the fireplace, where the elaborate black-leaded range from when this room was a kitchen still crouched, glowing orange and radiating a most unwelcome heat for such a warm day. The shelves were stacked with brown-paper parcels, done up with string and bearing labels which hung down and fluttered in the rising heat.

On my side of the counter, in contrast to the neat shelves, was such a profusion of objects that one hardly knew where to rest one's eyes. There was a rack of fur coats on wooden hangers, very rusty and stiff-looking fur coats too, with the large flat collars of twenty years ago. There were three tailors' dummies, each dressed in a greying wedding gown and with a hat sitting on its shoulders and a pair of satin slippers resting against its solitary leg. There were glass cases of jewellery: barnacled brooches, dented watches and wedding rings, thin from wear, all set out against velvet. There were tea-chests full of odd golf clubs and a battalion of perambulators each piled high with folded linens. In pride of place were four wireless sets on a walnut table, and around the top of the room – on the high shelf where one would look for the largest of the pie dishes and trenchers, the rarely used platters and pans – there were perhaps a hundred dusty hatboxes, joined together with ropes of spider-web like bunting.

'Help you?' said a voice.

I stepped towards the counter and saw sitting in a low, armless chair with a knitted cover – a nursery chair, I suspected – a small woman in her mid-thirties, but dressed like a grandmother with a piecrust top to her collar and ropes of suspiciously large white pearls hanging down over her boned bodice and pooling amongst her spreading skirts. My first thought was that she was in fancy dress for some reason, but as I noticed the profusion of brooches behind the pearls and the number of mismatched rings on her fingers I realised that she was simply dressed from stock. She was smoothing flat a sheet of brown paper on her lap.

'First time?' she said. I nodded. 'Well, what have you brought me?' She got to her feet and as she came forward at least the spreading skirts were explained for she walked with the rolling gait of someone with one leg much shorter than the other and I guessed that there was a block-soled boot hidden under her hemline.

'What have I brought you?' I said and then hesitated. She regarded me calmly from under a fringe of tight brown curls, slowly winding some string into a figure of eight and stowing it away in a drawer under the counter. I opened my bag, hoping to see something I could press into use to get things started, but it was Miss Rossiter's bag and was empty except for a handkerchief and a purse of money. I took out a ten-shilling note and put it on the counter. The little woman spread her arms wide, showing off the bounty of golf clubs and perambulators behind me.

'Take your time,' she said. 'Jist whistle if you want a case opened.' She was turning away when I spoke.

'I'm not looking for trinkets,' I said. 'I need your help with something and I would like to pay you.'

'Can't help you there, doll,' she said. 'I don't deal in the sticky stuff. Fifty with a chit or twenty-five, sign on the line.'

I did not understand a word of this and told her so.

'I don't have anything to do with stolen goods,' she said, speaking slowly as though to an idiot. 'You can get half the value of your item if you have a receipt to prove you own it or a quarter if you just sign your name and leave an address. You'd be better off doon Leith if that's not to your fancy.'

I took another ten-shilling note out of my purse and put it on the counter.

'The young woman who was just here,' I said, 'the girl in yellow. What did she bring you?' The little woman shook her head, her small brown eyes quite flat with lack of interest in the banknotes. I thought for a moment. If Phyllis had pawned something of Pip's I had to know. If she had pawned something of her own, one had to wonder why she suddenly needed money and to ask oneself if it were perhaps because someone had seen her do something and that someone had to be paid to keep quiet about it. Clara was the obvious candidate for the role, for she alone could have witnessed Phyllis leave her room in the night, but Clara hated Pip enough to forgive his murder and besides, she was not a blackmailer, surely. Hot-tempered, perhaps, and inclined to be huffy, but she was not the kind to sneak and threaten.

'I'll bet,' I said to the little woman, 'that she took twenty-five and signed for it.' Her face remained inscrutable, so I tried another tack. 'She is in my employment, you know,' I said, hoping that my voice would trump Miss Rossiter's good grey serge, 'and I suspect her of stealing from me.'

'That lassie works to Mrs Balfour,' said the pawnbroker. 'What are you at?'

I reasoned to myself that since I would be telling Superintendent Hardy about Phyllis's visit and he would come and get it out of this remarkably stubborn little person in the end anyway, I would be saving him some of his meagre time if I took care of it now.

'You've not heard what happened at the Balfours' today?' I said. 'Phyllis didn't tell you?' She shook her head. 'Mr Balfour is dead,' I said. 'He was found this morning with a knife in his throat and nobody knows who did it, but all suspicious behaviour needs to be explained, don't you see? Now, will you tell me what Phyllis pawned?'

'Nothing,' said the woman, who had paled at the news. 'She was in to redeem today.'

'You mean to take her belongings out again?'

'Aye, that's it,' said the woman. She had opened another drawer under the counter and lifted out a sheaf of paper labels. 'She's a regular here, madam. She has a taste for nice things – well, you can tell that from looking at her – and she's not good at waiting for them either. Here we are.' She had found the label she was looking for and turned it towards me. The pencilled writing on it had been rubbed off to let the label be used again but was still faintly visible.

'One gold ring,' I said, squinting at it. 'Ladies? Lace? What does it say here?'

'One gold ring, large. One gold ring, small. Her ma and pa's, most likely, or grandma's maybe. One silver-gilt prayer book. One black coat, one tweed rug, one set silk nightclothes duchesse satin peach, coffee lace,' said the woman. 'I'd say the nightie and the rug were maybe lifted from the house, would you no'? But I like to give folks the benefit and say they were passed on.'

'And can you tell me,' I said, speaking rather softly as though that meant I were not really asking, 'how much she paid to redeem them?'

'I shouldn't really,' she said. 'And if my ma was here she'd take her hand off me . . .'

'Well, then,' I said, 'before she comes back . . .'

The little woman gave me a sad smile.

'Oh, there's no coming back from where she's gone, madam,' she said. 'It was seventeen pounds Miss McInnes gave me today for redemption.'

'Gosh,' I said, thinking that if this were the going rate for a few baubles and old nighties, there had been times in the past when I could have furnished myself with very useful amounts of pocket money if I had had the nerve to shove some of my treasures over a pawnshop counter. There is a set of Sèvres too hideous to display, much less eat off, which is seeing out its days in a crate in an attic; and much of my grandmother's jewellery is wilfully ugly and just shy of being worth resetting in wearable form. The pawnbroker read my mind and set me straight.

'That's got a fair bit of interest on it, mind,' she said. 'I've had it a good while.' I looked again at the upper shelves of parcels, where the paper was sun-bleached even in this basement room and the labels were curled up like autumn leaves.

'Of course,' I said, hoping that I was not blushing. 'Well, thank you. I shall try to keep Superintendent Hardy from troubling you.'

'No odds to me,' said the woman. 'I've nothing to hide from the coppers.' She gave me a shrewd look as she sat herself down again, gripping the edge of a shelf and kicking her lame leg out as she fell backwards. I wished I had given her more than a pound, suddenly, and did not like to leave such a good little person, all alone in this frankly quite depressing setting. As I let myself out into the passageway, however, I met a youngish man in his shirtsleeves carrying in his arms a fat toddler with tight brown curls and round brown eyes.

'Afternoon,' he said to me, and then to the child, 'Let's see if Mammy's got the kettle on yet, Daisy, eh?'

I put my unneeded sympathy away again and retraced my steps to the kiosk. Inside, seven of the pennies had gone but three were still where I had left them.

'Me again, Barrow,' I said, and then, 'Alec, darling, do you think you might answer the telephone yourself for a while? It's not very sensible to be using up my three minuteses waiting for Barrow to track you down.'

'Yes, yes, yes,' said Alec. 'Stop nagging. What happened?'

'Well, I've had my assumptions about the nature of humanity pleasantly overturned,' I said, thinking of the strapping young man and his crippled wife, and of the two remaining thruppence bits, 'but as far as Phyllis goes, it seems she has suddenly come into funds. Petty cash to the likes of you, guv'nor, but quite a tidy sum to a housemaid. Seventeen pounds, at least. I need to ask Lollie whether Pip kept that kind of money in his pockets and if not we must ask ourselves where else she could have got it from.' Hanging a dog on the strength of a bad name and the sudden acquisition of seventeen pounds is not good detecting, of course, but one could not help the idea that a girl who was fond enough of finery to pawn her grandmother's wedding ring, who could be in as jolly spirits as Phyllis was today when all around was death and calamity, had just the kind of single-minded toughness required of a murderer or indeed a blackmailer of murderers. Who in the house had seventeen pounds lying around to have blackmailed out of him – or her – was another question.

8

Skulking around the streets of the New Town like a private eye in a Brighton guesthouse, I had missed the removal of Pip Balfour's body, but I came upon the rest of the household restoring itself around an open bottle of rum and the inevitable pot of tea.

'A terrible thing,' said Stanley, with his mouth pushed out and his ample chin sunk on his chest. Millie nodded, biting her lip, but Mrs Hepburn flicked him an irritated glance and Clara rolled her eyes at Eldry.

'It's not something I ever thought to do,' said Mr Faulds, 'hold the front door open for my master to be carried out in a black box and put on a cart like something for the rag and bone man.'

'And all them next door out on their steps watching,' said Mrs Hepburn. 'That's the last time I find a packet of butter for her when she's not sent her note in to the dairy in time. The besom! But I daresay I'd have been keen enough to see what was to do if it had been in their house and I shouldn't call her for the same. I'll take some biscuits through to her when they're cooled.'

'I'd better get back up to mistress,' I said, but Mrs Hepburn waved me into my chair.

'You take your rest while you can, Fanny. We've been popping up, the girls and me, off and on, and she's dead to the world. Sleep's the best thing for her today. I've got a jug of toast tea making and I've ordered in some calves' feet for jelly, be ready by tomorrow night. That'll set her right again.'

'Toast tea?' I said and there were a few giggles from the younger servants until Mrs Hepburn fixed them with a glare.

'Just burnt toast steeped in water while it cools and then strained through,' she said. 'And don't you go sniggering, John Petty, because you were happy enough to have it that time you caught the gastric flu and couldn't keep a boiled egg down.'

'Mrs Hepburn, please,' said Mr Faulds, 'don't remind us of it. We were a sorry crew that week, Fanny. Harry and Maggie didn't succumb but the rest of us were laid flat. I couldn't lift my head from the pillow. Ah, but mistress was like a mother to us all, remember, Kitty?'

'Aye, and she made that stew – as if we weren't sick enough already,' said Eldry, to a gale of laughter and a few groans, and then they settled back into a comfortable silence again. I looked around them. No one was tense, no one was anxious. Now that Eldry had recovered her spirits and Mattie had cheered up there was nothing to show that this was not an ordinary afternoon in a well-staffed and under-stretched establishment. The clock ticked, the fire crackled and the only other sound was the click of Millie's knitting needles and the occasional snip of scissors as Clara unpicked a hem for restitching.

'By, but I'm missing my *News*,' said Mrs Hepburn presently. 'It feels that funny not to be catching up with the world at teatime.'

'More power to their elbows,' said Harry. 'And we've got our news anyway.' He waved a printed sheet in the air. 'Official strike bulletin, straight from the TUC District Committee. So we won't need to let another copy of that scab rag over the door.' He gave a pointed look to Mattie who ducked his head.

'I didnae ken,' he said. 'It was for master, not for me.'

'Give it a rest, Harry,' Clara said. 'It's not as if it was Churchill's bloomin' *Gazette*. You'll no' catch germs off it.'

'And I cannae see mistress wanting one of your bulletins,' said John.

'Besides, there's more going on than the blessed strike,' said Mr Faulds. 'I'd like to see what they're going to print about our do today for a start.'

'I won't sit and have it read out to me,' said Harry. 'Nor Mattie.'

'And I won't,' said Eldry, gazing at Harry as she spoke. John snorted, but Harry himself affected to notice nothing.

'I can bring you *some* news,' I said. 'There are gangs on Princes Street. A policeman told me.'

'Gangs?' said Eldry and Millie together.

'Gangs of what?' said Mrs Hepburn. 'Gangs of who?'

'Here, Mr Faulds,' said Clara, 'did you bolt the front door at the back of they mortuary men?'

'Gangs of respectable citizens exercising their right of free assembly,' said Harry loudly over us all. 'See what it says here, Miss Rossiter?' He jabbed his bulletin. '*No attention should be paid to rumours. The official bulletin, which will be issued at least daily, will keep you advised.*'

'I am simply passing on what was told to me by a policeman in uniform,' I said, although Harry looked unimpressed by such credentials. 'But I do appreciate your point,' I went on. 'And our right of free assembly is something to defend most strenuously. They can only dream of it in the streets of Moscow these days.' Harry, who had opened his mouth to spout on some more, shut it again. Hugh would have been proud of me.

I took Lollie's toast tea up to her at six o'clock and found her wide awake, staring up at the ceiling of her bedroom. She gave a faint smile when she saw the glass in my hand.

'Pour that away, will you, Dandy?' she said. 'And then tell Mrs Hepburn it did wonders for me.' I was curious enough to take a sip of the stuff as I bore it off to the bathroom and it was a revelation: the recipe had not sounded appetising, but how a combination of toasted bread and plain water could come to taste so extravagantly vile was beyond me. I rinsed out the glass and returned to Lollie's bedside.

'I'm trying not to think about what's happening,' she said, sitting up a little. Despite her words I could hear that the note of numb disbelief was gone from her voice and it relieved me. 'About what they might be doing to him, right now. I'm trying to think about happier times instead, but I can't help wishing

I had been brave enough, before they took him away, not just to say goodbye, but to see what was done. To see it. So that I shouldn't be wondering. Superintendent Hardy said he had been stabbed. That's the trouble. It's such a very striking word that it's hard not to imagine. Was it in the heart? I keep wondering where would be quickest and least painful. *Was* it in the heart, Dandy?'

'Can't you just put it out of your mind altogether?' I asked, but Lollie's face, as I spoke, told that this was a blunder.

'Oh no!' she said. 'It wasn't quick, was it? It was slow and dreadful and that's what you don't want to tell me and—'

'His throat,' I said, speaking over her and cursing myself.

Lollie lay back down and looked straight up at the ceiling while her breathing returned to something near normal.

'And what kind of knife was it?' she said at last.

'One of the carving knives from the kitchen. Mrs Hepburn recognised it.'

'I see. Well, at least I can be sure he didn't suffer too much then,' she said. 'I mean, if his throat was cut he can't have. What's the name of the big vein – or is it an artery? I never know the difference, do you?'

'The jugular,' I said, and I did not correct her assumption. If she could carry on thinking of a clean cut and instant oblivion, all the better. I wondered if she would have to attend the inquiry, or would choose to attend a trial, were one to come, in the end.

'And Mrs Hepburn,' said Lollie, 'she will throw the knife away, won't she?'

'I should be very surprised if Superintendent Hardy is thoughtless enough to return it,' I said, with a shudder. 'Are you going to get up again today, Lollie? I wouldn't advise it.' Lollie shook her head. 'Well, let me run you a cool bath and then I'll ask Mrs Hepburn to send up . . . what? Some scrambled egg?' I shifted a little before carrying on with the next bit, feeling a heel for even suggesting it. 'Then if you didn't mind, I wondered if perhaps you could do without me overnight. Actually, I was wondering if perhaps I could say downstairs that you felt in need of familiar faces and perhaps someone else could step in completely. It's just that I'd learn so much more if I were down there, on the spot as it were, than up here with you.'

'On the spot,' said Lollie as though she had never heard the expression and were trying to decipher it. 'Do you think one of them knows something about it, Dandy? Do you think one of them let someone in?'

'No, not exactly,' I said, turning for the bathroom again. I did not want to trouble her with all the bothersome details of keys and bolts and overhearings, for I was certain such thoughts would be keeping me awake long into the night and they would certainly stop the widow from resting easy. Besides, until Hardy came back with news of the brandy glass, she was still a suspect and the less I told her the better. 'Don't dwell on it, dear,' I said. 'We shall know more tomorrow when Superintendent Hardy returns.'

'But do swap places, by all means,' she said, 'if you're sure you don't mind them thinking that you've displeased me in some way.'

'Not at all,' I assured her. 'I shall ask Clara then. Or,' I said, speaking carefully. 'Phyllis. When she gets back.'

'Either would be fine,' said Lollie.

'You'd feel safe, I suppose, with them?' I asked. 'You don't suspect that one of them might be mixed up in any of this?'

'Do *you*?' Lollie sat up a little and stared at me.

'I haven't formed particular suspicions at all yet,' I said. 'But I do want to know this, Lollie dear.' I asked her then about Pip's wallet and pocket change and about staff pay and tips and bonuses and any other money that might be left lying around anywhere. (Hugh always keeps the safe in his business room locked up and changes the combination with feverish regularity, but – as he never tires of informing me – not everyone (meaning me) has the good habits of an orderly mind.)

She managed to tell me that Pip kept very little cash upon his person as a rule and tended to walk up to the bank when he needed to, hardly used the safe at all (as I saw would be sensible for a town dweller – and how it flattened me to realise what a country mouse I had turned into not to have thought of that for myself), then she began showing signs of mounting agitation again and I drew the interview to a close.

'I'll go and get one of the girls then,' I said, soothingly.

'No, I'm fine for now,' Lollie said. 'Just send Phyllis up at bedtime, would you?'

Phyllis was compliant enough about spending the night on the little chaise in her mistress's bedroom.

'Good to get away from your snoring,' she said to Clara, who stuck out her tongue.

'I'll fill her hot bottle for you to take up,' I said. I knew that Grant always filled mine, on those many nights of the year when even a sleeping Dalmatian pinning the blankets down upon one was not enough to outwit the perishing cold. 'Nice day out?' I asked tremendously casually, as we waited together for the kettle to come to the boil.

'Not bad,' said Phyllis.

'What did you do?' I said.

'Pictures,' said Phyllis.

'On a beautiful day like this was?' I said, tutting. 'You youngsters and your films!' I reached for the kettle just as the steam started to jet out and carried it carefully to the draining board where the bottle was waiting. 'I thought you'd been on a picnic when I saw you with your big bag.'

'No, not today,' said Phyllis. I screwed the stopper into the hot bottle and wiped it dry. The trouble with being undercover, I thought to myself, was that one could not just keep digging away with question after question as usual; not without gaining a reputation as a nosy parker and making everyone clam up completely. Phyllis took the bottle and left me.

Mr Faulds was locking the house for the night again. He turned the key in the back kitchen door, took it out and hung it on a hook hidden in shadows and almost out of reach. 'Master's instructions,' he said, seeing my puzzled look. 'But I'm with him all the way. I'd no more leave a key in a door inside than out. For one, a thief can slip a sheet of newspaper under and push the key out then pull it back through.' I nodded; I had done this myself to get out of my dormitory and onto the streets of Paris, or rather had watched with fingers crossed as Daisy did it for me. 'But even when the door's too snug-fitted like this one is,' he went on, 'they can reach right in with a pair of pliers and twist the key round from the barrel end. I knew a girl once who did it inside a box in a magic act, and it doesn't take any strength to speak of, it's only knowing the knack like so many things.' He had shot both bolts home, top and bottom, as he spoke and now he tried the handle, giving it a good rattle.

He was at the sub-basement door when I picked my way carefully down the steps minutes later with my cocoa – Mrs Hepburn had whisked the milk to within an inch of its life as it boiled and had added extra cream, so that the cup had a coxcomb of froth like a barber's shaving mug which threatened to spill over at every step – and as he threw the bolts the sound seemed to reverberate through the walls and echo across the arched stone ceiling above us.

'Safe as houses, Fanny,' he said. 'You've nothing to fear.'

Somehow, something about him saying it that way was more disconcerting than if he had said nothing and once inside I found myself peering timorously out into the dark garden and standing quietly behind my locked door listening for the sounds of I knew not what. I heard Clara come downstairs, go into her room across the passageway and lock her door behind her, then I heard the squeak of her bedsprings as she sat down.

It took me well over an hour to finish writing up my notes and by the time I had got to recording my last conversation with Lollie, I was stiff-necked and sour-mouthed with exhaustion, hardly thinking about the words as I scrawled them, scarcely able to believe that this was the end of the same day that had begun with Eldry climbing the stairs, worrying about nothing more than the wrong newspaper for her master.

* * *

Superintendent Hardy arrived at ten the following morning, striding into the house with great confidence and a new lease of energy; or as Clara, who witnessed his coming, described it: 'As if he owned the place and was just gonny paint it.'

He called for me as soon as he had finished with Lollie and I entered the parlour to find him standing looking down along the garden, rocking slightly on his heels.

'All alone, Superintendent?'

'We haven't so much as a constable to spare,' he said, turning round. 'There were two hundred strikers down at Waverley station this morning, all walked in – miles, some of them – to stand on the pickets, and it takes time and men to clear it. You'll have heard about yesterday, I'm sure.'

'The gangs?'

'I've a man in hospital and a police horse dead.'

'Poor thing,' I said. 'What happened?'

'He got hit by a brick bouncing back out of a smashed shop window,' said Hardy, very grim. 'But he'll recover.' I did not like to admit that, of course, it was the horse after which I was asking.

'I think it's very foolish of the Congress,' I said. 'If ordinary people see mobs in the street it will only frighten them and harden their resolve.'

'If you ask me, the unions are as surprised as anyone,' said Hardy. 'And the TUC can't believe what they've started – everybody banging on their door asking to join up so they can down tools for the miners. Teachers was the last thing I heard on the wireless this morning. Teachers! This was from London, mark you, not here.'

'That's something then,' I replied. 'And you seem to have lots of volunteers.'

'Hah!' said Hardy. 'Yes, well, the men at the electric works heard that there were students driving the electric trams and promptly downed tools – didn't want to be supplying the juice for a blackleg service. So now there are students in the electric works too.'

'Oh dear,' I said. 'Is that wise?'

'They're engineering students,' said Hardy, but he looked far from happy.

'And what news of our case?' I asked.

'News indeed,' he said. 'Solid facts – bite down on them and break a tooth, just the way I like it. The doctor was up first thing and examined the body and it's very revealing. There was a good dose of sleeping draught in his stomach, taken with brandy most likely. I asked Mrs Balfour if her husband was accustomed to use such a draught and she told me that no, Mr Balfour was an easy sleeper, never troubled with insomnia or with bad dreams. So that's the first thing. And there was nothing in the dregs of your glasses, by the way.'

'So it begins to look as if the widow's in the clear?'

'Especially since Dr Glenning's considered opinion is that a girl couldn't have done it. Not one in a hundred, he said.'

Here the superintendent flicked through the pages of his note-book. It had filled considerably since the previous day, pages and pages of close, pencilled writing. At last he found what he was looking for and held it up to the light.

'*Not only was the knife driven in with some force, held there and twisted around to open the wound and expedite the flow of blood* – you're not going to faint, are you? Good. – *which would have required considerable strength, but the victim was also held down to allow the attack to take place. There is bruising suggestive of a hand placed very firmly against the victim's right shoulder before decease, effectively pinning him against the mattress. This bruise is four inches in width, five inches in length and with faint finger-marks showing a span of nine inches. The placing of this bruise and the clockwise rotation of the blade inside the wound point together towards a right-handed man.* So there you have it. The murder was done by a right-handed man who was locked in the house over the night in question.'

'Mr Faulds,' I said.

'Means and opportunity,' said Hardy.

'And a motive?' I asked. 'Mr Faulds is one of the few who has *not* told tales of his master.'

'And don't you find that suspicious in itself? The others are incriminating themselves left, right and centre, bathed in innocence, and he's the only one biting his tongue?'

I could not decide whether this showed Hardy shaping up to the task of detecting or was merely an echo of his army days and his desire to have everyone in perfect line.

'I haven't actually got round them all yet, Superintendent,' I said. 'I've still to speak to two of the other men and I haven't had a chance to hear anything from the kitchen staff either.'

'Well, then I suggest, Mrs Gilver, that you – if you'll forgive me – run along and make a start on it. Only send Mr Faulds up to me when you've finished with him, would you?'

'Superintendent,' I said, carefully, 'if *you'll* forgive *me*, should you really interrogate him all alone? I rather thought there had to be two of you.'

'Oh, I'm not here to interrogate him,' he said. 'I'm just here to collect him. I'm taking him into the station for the interview.'

I found Mr Faulds in his pantry, dressed in a long green baize apron and with sacking sleeves over his cuffs, the whole place reeking of Goddard's powder and ammonia. An elaborate table centrepiece lay in several pieces in front of him.

'Our sins will find us out, Miss Rossiter,' he said in greeting. 'Master never liked this, we never used it and so I never cleaned it but all the best'll be laid out for the funeral so I'm taking my chance today and with luck mistress'll be none the wiser.'

'It's pretty hideous,' I said. 'Indian?'

'An elephant parade,' he said. 'And I don't know . . . I always thought it looked quite something all set out down the middle of the table, joined together trunk to tail, all the howdahs full of bon-bons.'

'Was it a wedding present?' I said, thinking that it rivalled the worst of mine. (A gold – solid gold – pickle jar fashioned like some kind of goblin's head. It was Indian too, from a rich aunt of Hugh's who, apparently, hated him.)

'No, it came down to him through the family,' said Mr Faulds. 'From when that branch of the Balfour family were out there.

All right for some, eh?' He looked around at his own surroundings with a half-mocking expression of disgust on his face but I, who had so recently seen Eldry and Millie's dank little lair, could not commiserate with him over his comfortable pantry. It had a pile carpet on the floor – no grey hair and red tape edging for Mr Faulds – and papered walls, and was bright with ornaments and pictures of a quality which would not have disgraced Pip Balfour's own bedroom (and had, I thought, probably started their life there before being passed on). What was even more surprising was the well-stocked little bookcase whose leather-bound volumes of Restoration dramatists, Romantic poets and the essayists of the Enlightenment hinted that Ernest Faulds, for all his music-hall days, was a man of some learning. A man, too, who liked his comforts: a door was half-open onto his bed-sitting room which rivalled anything I had ever heard about gentlemen's clubs for the profusion of leather, oak and dark red velvet to be found there.

'Come now, Mr Faulds,' I said, 'this all seems very commodious. I'll bet you've stayed in theatrical digs that weren't half as cosy.'

'What I could tell you about theatrical digs would make a turn in itself,' he agreed. 'There was one landlady always took in from the Bradford Alhambra used to count the peas. I'm not joking or jesting, Fanny, she counted out the peas onto your plate. I tell you what, we never dared tell her the old joke about the mean landlady from Aberdeen in case it gave her ideas.' I waited. 'Chap complained about the bedbugs one time and she charged him extra for keeping pets in his room.' I could not help laughing.

'But seeing your rooms here,' I said, 'I'm asking myself if I've finally found the one person the late Mr Balfour was good to. I mean, that leather armchair is a real beauty.'

'That's mine and came with me from my mother's when she passed away,' said Mr Faulds, more soberly. I waited but he said no more, just went on polishing with his head down.

'Well, speaking of coming into things,' I said, 'I haven't just missed a bonus day, have I?'

'Bonus day? What's one of them?'

I was surprised that he did not know, for they interest servants enormously and they were a regular part of life in every house I had lived in.

'Master's birthday or mistress's, I suppose,' I said. 'Or the anniversary of the wedding. Birth of sons too, most usually. All the staff get a divi.'

'Now, why would you think that?' said Faulds, eyeing me closely. Before I had thought of a way to allude to Phyllis's windfall, though, he went on: 'Easy to see you didn't have time to get acquainted with Philip Balfour Esquire.'

'So,' I said, 'you're *not* the exception that proves the rule then? With master.'

'Hardly,' he said. 'He was a fair old puzzle. Nice as ninepence one minute and then he would just turn. And a trial to a pretty girl, Miss Rossiter, as you'll no doubt have been hearing. I felt for them all, most acutely. Kitty and me both. But what can you do? When the mantel of privilege clothes a man from head to toe, who's going to listen to you complaining?'

'You sound as though you've been reading Harry's bulletin,' I said and Faulds shook his head, sucking his teeth in a show of sorrow.

'Harry's a young hot-head. Thinks he needs to change the whole world just to rise in it. He'd be better looking to his talents for his fortune and letting the world go its way.'

'That's rather caustic,' I said. 'I'm sure Harry would say he was interested in fairness for all and not just a leg-up for himself.'

'I'm sure he would,' said Faulds, even more witheringly, making me laugh. We were so cosy I even went as far as to say:

'But as to one's talents, and to rising in the world, aren't you rather neglecting both, giving up the stage for butlering?'

I had gone too far. Faulds's smile snapped away as though it had never been.

'Don't concern yourself about me, Miss Rossiter,' he said.

'I do beg your pardon,' I said, blushing.

'Granted,' he said, with a faint inclination of his head. 'Now, if you'll forgive me, I need to get on.'

'Actually, Mr Faulds,' I said, 'I'm afraid you can't. I've enjoyed this little chat but I was, in fact, sent to fetch you. Superintendent Hardy wants you.'

'Well he might,' said the butler, 'but he's not going to get me, Miss Rossiter.'

'I remember,' I said, and quoted him. 'The innocent have nothing to fear from the truth.'

'Exactly,' said Faulds. 'No matter what Harry's bulletin has to say.' And with that he began to unroll his cuffs and prepare himself for the interview.

In the kitchen, Mrs Hepburn too had pronounced it time to begin preparations for the funeral tea to come; she had two enormous pans bubbling on the hotplate of the range and was just plopping into one of them a ham of such girth that one could not imagine how she would ever carve it. From the scullery came sounds of vigorous scrubbing and Millie's voice raised in song.

'Oh, Fanny!' said Mrs Hepburn. 'There's a relief. One less thing to worry me anyway. I'm just crossing my fingers and doing these hams now and if the funeral's held up well then they'll spoil but how I'm supposed to get a ham cooked with no kitchener to cook them on is something they've *won't* tell me.'

'No kitchener?' I echoed, looking at the great hulk of the Eagle which was pulsing with heat as usual.

'Not after today,' said Mrs Hepburn. 'A hundredweight of coal! I ask you! This beastie can burn that up every other day. So I'm switching it off and we'll have to make do with thon useless contraption.' She pulled her chin down and nodded to the far corner where a neat little electric stove sat proudly. It had been covered with a dustsheet up until now and its gleaming blue-grey sides and sparkling white enamel doors suggested that it had never seen active service before today.

'Mistress insisted we had one,' she said, turning her back on

135

it and nestling up to the front fender of her beloved range. 'Nasty scootery wee thing – it looks like something that belongs in a lavatory, Fanny, not a kitchen. Not if you ask me. But it'll boil a pan just the same when all's said and done, so there we are.'

'Indeed,' I said. 'But what did you mean just then, Mrs Hepburn, by a relief?'

She blinked at me for a moment or two before answering.

'Oh!' she said at last, 'Yes, only that Eldry said that policeman had made a beeline for you and I was worried he'd put two and two together and come up with the only new face in the house-hold to pin the blame to.'

'No,' I said, 'none of that. I daresay if it had been the usual kind of thing – trinkets missing, cash mislaid – the new girl would be for it, but murder? Murder's too serious for . . . casual suspicion.' Mrs Hepburn nodded. 'I heard one time,' I said, inching my way towards the question of Phyllis again, 'of a maid – sly little minx – who took to helping herself when a new girl had started, knowing who'd get the blame.'

'Lord!' said Mrs Hepburn. 'There's twisty for you, eh? You'd have to be wicked to the core to think of such a thing.'

'Have you ever been in a house with a light-fingered maid, Kitty?' I asked her, trying out the name for the first time. I was pleased to see that she did not bristle.

'Never,' said Mrs Hepburn. 'I'm glad to say. Or if I have she's been too clever to get caught at it. You certainly don't need to worry about that kind of thing here. And don't be feeling down in the mouth about mistress's funny turn either,' she went on. 'She didn't mean any slight to you, only natural she wants some old familiars round her. Clara's up there now to let Phyllis get the dining room swept out at last, seeing it'd lain two nights and a day as it was.'

Mrs Hepburn was hopping from shelf to table to stove, drop-ping various leaves and little seeds into the ham pot, and would have looked like a witch at her cauldron, but for the pink dress and sparkling white apron.

'I'm not at all offended,' I said. 'It *is* understandable and I'm sure she'll be herself again in time.'

Mrs Hepburn wiped the tip of her nose with the back of her hand and looked at me.

'She'll get the chance to be herself for the first time in years,' she said. 'I've seen her go from a girl to a ghost and I'm looking forward to seeing the woman.' She nodded very firmly and turned back to the range before continuing. 'And I'm looking forward to feeding her too, Fanny, and not have him always finding fault and deciding he can't take one day what he ate without a murmur the day before. *And* not having my good food come back all cut about and wasted so we couldn't even get the finishing of it up. One time, you know, he poured water into the soup and sent it back saying it was cold, then another time he put a mouse – a dead mouse – into a goose I had roasted and called me up to the dining room to show me and tell me what he thought about my kitchen and my "high jinx" or whatever it's called.'

'Hygiene?' I guessed.

'And I asked him,' said Mrs Hepburn, ignoring me, 'I said, Mr Balfour, I said, how do you suppose that goose got roasted and the poor wee mouse stayed cold, sir? And he had no answer for that. But you'll keep it to yourself, won't you, Fanny?'

'Not tell the superintendent, you mean?'

'Well, not tell the girls, really,' she said in a low voice. 'Because . . . well, it was a lovely goose and the wee mouse was only in the cavity and I thought as long as I carved the meat off and threw the carcass away. It wasn't as if I went making stock with it.' Then Mrs Hepburn winked and gave a huge laugh which shook her all over like a good bowl of jellied broth.

'Your face, Fan!' she said. 'I'm just having fun with you. I put the whole thing out to the pig bin and scrubbed the plate with soda near until the pattern come off. And you can tell that Mr Hardy whatever you like.'

'Not that it would matter now anyway,' I said. It was time to tell her. 'Because he told me that the doctor says it was a man who did it. He could tell from the body that a woman couldn't have.'

'A man?' said Mrs Hepburn. 'What man?' Once again as I had seen her do before she took her collar and shook it as though trying to fan away a sudden flush. 'Dear goodness, they never think there was some devil in creeping around! We could *all* of us have been killed in our beds. Does mistress know?'

'I think so,' I said, 'but actually – this is going to come as a nasty shock, Mrs Hepburn, but actually, Mr Hardy suspects Mr Faulds.'

Mrs Hepburn let go of her collar and patted it smooth, frowning.

'Of what?' she said. 'Does he think Ernest didn't lock up properly? Are they blaming him for somebody getting in?' I hesitated and saw her face fall. 'No, never!' she said. 'Ernest? He couldn't have. He didn't – he couldn't have.'

'That's very loyal of you, Mrs Hepburn,' I said. 'Even I think it seems most unlikely and after the length of time you've known—'

'No, no, you misunderstand me,' she said. 'I *know* he didn't. No one could know surer than me.'

'Because . . . you did?' I breathed.

Mrs Hepburn stared at me and made a kind of choking noise that might have been a gasp of laughter.

'Lord, no! God love you, Fanny, what an imagination! No, not that bad.' Now she really did laugh, albeit in a flustered way. 'Bad enough, mind,' she said, and with a glance into the scullery, she went on in a low voice, 'I know he didn't do it because I was with him. All night – and he never left the room.'

'Y-you were . . . ahem . . . I see,' I said. 'Gosh, yes, I see.'

'No, you don't,' she said. 'I can see in your face you don't. I don't myself, come to that. A cook has to be above reproach, looking after all these young girls like I am, and you'd think I'd know better.'

'Well, I must congratulate you on your discretion at least,

Mrs Hepburn,' I said. 'Both of you. I should never have guessed, and I don't think the youngsters know.'

'It's not discretion,' said the cook. 'And there's nothing much for them *to* know. We don't have an understanding as such. Not an engagement, anyway. Oh, we get on well enough and he's a nice enough man and a lot less snooty than some butlers I've known, even if his training isn't all it might be, but that's all. Except that a few times, at night, I suppose you'd say our natures have just . . . got the better of us. And then in the morning it's back to normal and almost like nothing happened at all.'

'Mm,' I said, trying not to smile, for really the thought of the ruddy-cheeked and hefty-shouldered Mrs Hepburn being transported to some netherworld where passion reigned and then returning at dawn to start the breakfasts was highly distracting. 'Well, it's very fortunate, Kitty.' I had no hesitation in employing her Christian name now. 'Mr Hardy has taken him to the police station but with such an alibi he'll be out again in no time.'

Mrs Hepburn dropped down into a chair with her hands covering her mouth. When she took them away her lips were trembling.

'They've taken him?' she breathed.

'Yes, but don't worry. When he tells them you were with him, they'll soon—'

'I know him,' said Mrs Hepburn. 'He'll not save himself. He's too much of the gentleman to save himself.' She clapped her hands on her knees, rose from her seat and started to untie her apron. 'I'd better get down there,' she said. 'Millie! Come through here and keep an eye on the pots. Auntie's just popping out. Bring your trotters with you if you've finished cleaning them and you can get them split in here on the table.' Millie appeared at the scullery door. Her apron was splattered with blood and soaked with water so that some of the red stains had paled to pink, and I found myself taking a step backwards at the sight of her.

'Where are you going, Auntie Kitty?' she said.

'Just running a wee message for Mr Faulds,' said Mrs Hepburn. 'You know what you're doing now, don't you?'

With that she was off. I caught sight of her flying along the passageway to the front area door a moment later with her hat jammed on tight but her coat still open and streaming behind her.

'Auntie Kitty's in a right hurry,' Millie said. She was ferrying a large colander full of pigs' feet to the kitchen table, dripping watery spots of blood on the floor all around her. She tipped them out and they rolled onto the table, one coming to rest against a sugar dredger.

'I'll just tidy up a bit,' I said, hastily moving the dredger, a leather-covered grocer's book and a pile of clean cloths to one of the sideboards.

'Is mistress feeling better today?' said Millie. 'She was all upset yesterday, wasn't she?' With great concentration she set a small saw against one of the feet just where skin met horn and began scraping it back and forward. Her tongue was peeping out and her eyes were squeezed half-shut with concentration. When the saw dropped through and hit the table underneath, she dropped it and winced. 'I should have put a tablet down,' she said, examining the scar on the scrubbed boards. 'Auntie Kitty's told me half a dozen times.' Then she turned to the stove and dropped the sawn-off trotter into one of the pots bubbling there. 'Oh!' she said, looking into the water. 'What's that in there? I thought it was stock.'

'It's a ham,' I told her and she grinned.

'Oh well, that's all right then,' she said. 'That was lucky.'

I had been wondering how to lead her towards the topic of interest to me, but now I thought that surely such a featherhead as this, one who puddled her way through life cushioned against its cares by her own innocence of them, must often find that questions loomed up at her out of nowhere.

'What did you think of Mr Balfour, Millie?' I said. 'Did you see much of him?'

Millie disappeared into the scullery and when she returned

140

she was carrying a cleaver in her hand and looking as stern as her pink and white face and round cheeks would allow.

'Too much, miss,' she said. 'He was a bad man and he did silly things that he shouldn't have.' My stomach turned inside me. Not Millie too! She was a child and had not half the guile of some children one has encountered.

'To you, Millie?' I said, hoping that perhaps she was merely repeating gossip.

'Auntie Kitty said to me not to say,' she said. 'Because what you don't know can't hurt you and if Stanl— I mean, if a nice boy one day asked you anything, then he wouldn't want to know the nasty things that you had done.'

With a sinking certainty, I knew that Millie's hopes regarding Stanley were doomed; he was a young man of great ambition and even greater self-satisfaction and his plans, whatever they were, would not include taking the hand of a simple scullery-maid and making her dreams come true. As I watched Millie centre one of the trimmed trotters on the table and take aim, I wondered suddenly how long she would be able to hang on to that simplicity, where there were good men and bad men and simple right and wrong and what one did not know could not harm one. She raised the cleaver to her shoulder and brought it down so fast that the blade whistled before it split the bone apart with a crack like a gunshot. The two halves dropped away and the cleaver was left sticking up out of the table. Millie bit her lip and gasped.

'I'll get one of the boys to wrench it out for . . .' I began, but Millie had splayed one hand on the table, gripped the handle hard with the other and, after one mighty tug, pulled the cleaver out again. I could not take my eyes away from her hand – spread out broad and strong on the table-top – and could not help hearing again in my mind what she had said about making sure a nice boy never knew the nasty things one might have done. Did Stanley have a reason to hate Pip Balfour, as had so many of the others? Would Millie, blind with love, have gone as far as avenging her beloved footman?

'Now you really must get a board, Molly-moo,' I said. 'Or that table will be kindling by the time you're done.' Millie giggled and wiped her cheek, leaving a smear of blood there, then went to the scullery to fetch one.

9

Lollie was in brighter spirits by the evening. The police had given permission for the funeral arrangements to proceed on the understanding that cremation was out of the question; the will was to be read the next day, allowing Lollie thereafter to begin to make plans for her widowhood; and as for her state of lonely isolation, Great Aunt Gertrude was on her way. How exactly the old lady expected to get from Inverness to Edinburgh, when the nation was at a standstill and strike officials were stopping motorcars left and right to check that they were not carrying blackleg goods, was unclear. It seemed she had left home without maid or chauffeur, but with a full tank of petrol, two cans in the dicky and an unshakeable belief that her long lifetime of getting exactly what she wanted when she wanted it would hold good, whatever pickets, blockades and rioting gangs might be doing to disrupt the lives of lesser mortals than she.

Downstairs, Mr Faulds was safely back in the bosom of the household after Mrs Hepburn's selfless dash to the police station to gather him home, and the amazing news of their tryst (which, to give the two principals their due, they did not attempt to rise above but instead acknowledged with throat-clearings and jaw-scratchings on the butler's side and with blushing smiles from his beloved) gave a larky air to the servants' hall which an uninformed guest would have found quite appalling.

Miss Rossiter's position as a newcomer was most welcome, as it conferred upon her the opportunity to sit rather quietly in the midst of the party (and a party it almost was) watching faces, chasing down glances and listening to anything which was not quite being said. The rest of the servants were gathered around the piano, beer glasses in hand, singing an endless selection of popular melodies from the music halls, and rather saltier ones than Mr Faulds had hinted were in their repertoire too: even as far as something apparently called 'Ta-Ra-Ra-Boom-De-Ay' in which each verse was worse than the last.

'You certainly *have* been practising, Mattie,' said Mr Faulds when the hall boy had got through a complicated run of trills in the lead-in to a love song.

'Aye, I have,' said Mattie, 'but it's more fun to play out loud and no' fret that I'm gonny disturb anybody.' He pressed down the loud pedal and fairly banged the notes out of the thing, and Clara and Phyllis pressed their hands together under their hearts, fluttered their eyelids and began singing.

> *'Oh Cupid, your harp had*
> *me fooled at the start as*
> *it told me his love was for keeps,*
> *but he's scarpered . . .'*

'Take the man's part, Mr Faulds,' said Mrs Hepburn when the girls had got through the first verse and the others had joined them for the chorus (*Oh, pluck my heart out now, why don't you, for everything else you could pluck is away*), but Mr Faulds shook his head and held his hands up, protesting.

'I'm no singer,' he said, 'and John knows this one.' John straightened up and cleared his throat.

> *'Forgive me, my maiden,*
> *you are most mistaken,*
> *if you're telling me*
> *that you languish forsaken,'*

he sang in a fair approximation of the most affected music-hall swain. All he needed was a straw boater on the back of his head and a cane to twirl.

> *'Oh, pierce me through the heart, why don't you?*
> *For everything else is torn in two,'*

sang the company. I wondered if Millie, carolling away merrily, understood the import of this lyric, if anyone did, and I found myself sharing a little sympathy with the only member of our number who was *not* lifting his voice in song; Harry, hunched over his latest strike bulletin, scowling at the din.

'I'm worried that mistress will hear them,' I said to him, going to sit on the next seat to his at the long table. 'It doesn't seem right.'

'She won't,' said Harry, 'she'll either be in her boudoir or in that wee parlour at the back. As long as they pipe down before she goes to her bedroom,' he pointed straight up with his thumb, 'we'll be all right. And anyway, do her some good for a change to see the world getting on without a care when she's miserable.'

This was remarkably callous, I thought, and I could not let it pass unchallenged.

'What has she done to deserve such scorn?' I said.

He had the grace to look uncomfortable as he answered.

'Not her in particular, miss,' he said. 'Just her sort. People like her in general, I mean.'

'Oh Harry,' I said, 'there is no such thing as people in general. Everyone is someone very particular.'

He argued on – his sort will always argue on – but I had stopped listening because a thought which had been nudging gently against me all day now struck me square. Everyone had agreed that no one could open a locked and bolted door without being heard by those in the rooms nearby. Miss Rossiter, however, was not where she should have been that night, close by the sub-basement door. And Mrs Hepburn and Mr Faulds – who ought to have been asleep, one beside each of the other doors – had been cavorting together. Now, had Mrs Hepburn said where they were? I concentrated hard to bring the memory of the conversation back to mind, and I was almost certain that she had used the phrase 'I was with him'. Yes, she had said, 'I was with him,' definitely not 'He was with me,' which meant that her room, above mine, was empty. I sat back.

Of course that still left Phyllis and Clara who would hear the back door, but then Phyllis had come into that seventeen pounds somehow, and perhaps Clara was an unusually deep sleeper and Phyllis knew it – had not Phyllis complained of how Clara snored? – but how could Phyllis know that Mrs Hepburn was at the front of the house, tucked in with Mr Faulds under the red chenille bedspread, and that I was four flights up on Lollie's chaise?

'Are you all right, Miss Rossiter?' said Harry, who had stopped talking quite some time ago.

'Fine, Harry,' I said. 'I think, though, that I shall say good-night.' I needed at least notes if not diagrams for this.

Despite the lusty singing and the glasses of beer which were going strong when I left the room, I had not been in bed long when I heard the party dispersing. Indeed, Harry, Stanley, John and Mattie leaving by the kitchen door sounded like an army on manoeuvres. Mr Faulds locked up after them and shot the bolts with his usual gusto and then I heard Mrs Hepburn enter her room above my head. Mr Faulds and the girls descending the stairs on the other side of the wall was enough to make the water tremble in my bedside glass and, when he secured the sub-basement door, once again the bolts going home rang out all around and above like a hammer on an anvil. I shook my head. No one could possibly have breached this citadel without someone knowing.

Mr Faulds strode away and there was silence, except for the sound of Mrs Hepburn moving around in her stockinged feet, then I heard someone scamper down towards me from the kitchen level. I sprang out of bed and opened my door a crack. Clara was rounding the corner of the passage with her shoes in one hand and a candle in the other, unguarded and guttering.

'Oh! Miss Rossiter,' she said. 'You nearly made me jump out my skin.'

'Everything all right?' I asked her.

'Fine,' she said, her little eyes as wide as she could make them. 'I just had to – you know – go a place before I turned in.'

I frowned at her.

'But Mr Faulds has locked up,' I said. 'If you went to the lavatory, Clara dear, how did you get back in?'

She flushed slightly, I could just see it in the light of the candle.

'Oh well, you know,' she said and started sidling towards her door.

'Didn't he lock up?' I persisted. 'I was sure I heard him. Perhaps I should go up and check.'

'No!' said Clara, taking a step towards me. 'Don't . . . I mean . . . I'm sorry, Miss Rossiter, but that was a wee fib there.'

'A fib?'

'Not a bad one,' she said. 'Nothing to do with . . . what's been happening, I mean.'

I wondered if I could carry off the command that had sprung to my mind. I decided to try it.

'Tell the truth, Clara,' I said. 'And shame the devil.'

She stared helplessly at me for a moment and then, as though giving up some internal struggle, she lifted her hands and let them fall again.'

'Come in, dear,' I said, stepping aside and opening the door wider. 'Sit down and tell me what you wouldn't yesterday.'

'Yesterday?' she said, and then she nodded, remembering.

'Yesterday,' I said, guiding her to the chair. She perched on its edge.

'It's what I said about "souvenirs",' she said. 'I – I fell, Miss Rossiter. A while back now.'

'You had a baby?' I said. 'To master?'

'No,' Clara said. 'I mean to say, I was going to and I never told anyone. I just laced my stays tighter and let out my dress seams, like he told me to, and Phyllis never noticed and then, when it was getting nearly time, it came and it was already gone and then that was that.'

'Your baby died?' I said gently.

'It never even . . . cos you're no' supposed to keep yourself tight-laced, are you, miss? Or maybe it wasn't as close to the right time as I thought. But it was labour, Miss Rossiter, that's for sure. I've seen my mammy labouring and there's no mistaking it. Except . . .

it seems like a dream now when I think back. It's hard to believe it happened.'

'Where were you, Clara?' I asked, wondering how on earth a girl could have gone through such a thing all alone, in this houseful of people, without someone hearing.

'Up in the nurseries,' she said. 'Right up top there.'

'And what did you do with . . . I mean, what did you do afterwards?'

Clara frowned then and shook her head as though trying to clear it.

'Sometimes I think I came down to the furnace,' she said. 'But other times I remember wrapping up a bundle. I don't know, to be sure. Maybe . . .' She lifted her head and stared up at the low ceiling of my room. 'Maybe it's still up there.'

It might have seemed fantastical that she did not know, but I had heard of such things before; there was even a long and ugly name for it which I had, thankfully, forgotten.

'And so tonight?' I asked her softly. 'Were you all the way upstairs on the nursery floor just now, Clara? Searching?'

She lowered her head and blinked at me, then she smiled faintly.

'No, miss. I was in the kitchen.' She screwed up her nose, looking the very picture of discomfort. 'Mrs Hepburn made that chocolate thing for mistress's dinner and she hardly touched it and I asked Millie to set it aside in the scullery for me. I just can't say no to chocolate, miss, and by the time I've paid into my post office book and given something to my ma and got all my doings I've never got a penny spare to buy myself some.'

Of course, I should have scolded her, but who would have had the heart? I opened the door for her to leave, only managing to say:

'You should have torn yourself away from the sing-song and eaten it up earlier. You shouldn't be scampering about at night. Or eating chocolate for that matter. It'll give you nightmares.'

It was I, however, who had the wretched night, reeling at top speed through an endless succession of short, senseless dreams:

in one I was in the wings of a music-hall stage listening to the compère announcing Mr Faulds and me, but I did not know what the act was that we were presenting and I could not speak to ask anyone; in another I was searching through the laundry rooms of the convalescent home in Perth, undoing bundles of soiled linen looking for something I did not want to find and shushing an unknown someone who was whimpering somewhere close by, telling this unknown someone that we had to be quiet, that no one must ever know; in yet another I was sitting in the flower room at Gilverton, which was as close as I could get to dreaming of Miss Rossiter's bedroom, I think (one cannot introduce new settings to one's dream world with swift abandon), and there were men in miners' helmets with their lanterns lit and smoking, and they were trying the door, rattling the handle and then peering in at me through the window mouthing at me to open up for them. Great Aunt Gertrude was somewhere, I knew she was, although I could not hear her. 'Ssh!' I said to Mattie who was banging on a long row of boots and shoes with a drumstick as though playing a glockenspiel. 'Ssh!' I hissed. 'She'll hear you!'

I woke in the cool light of six o'clock and lay gasping, looking around at my room as though at an oasis after forty nights in the wilderness. And here came Mr Faulds to open us up for business once more, the nails in his boots striking hard against the stone floor of the passageway. He pulled back the bolts, giving slightly less than full measure, I thought; certainly it did not ring out in that bone-shaking way it had the evening before. Or perhaps it was just that sounds carried further at night; one often reads that they do. I heard him put the key in the lock, turn it and throw the door wide. This he did with as much brio as he could, sending it bouncing on its hinges.

'Lovely day, Etheldreda,' he called upwards and I could hear Eldry's faint answer.

'Tell Mrs Hepburn two eggs for me this morning,' he said. 'And I wouldn't mind a taste of that ham just to see if it's fit for company.' Whistling, he turned, passed along to the stairs again and skipped up them, making a little tune with his shoes like a tap-dancer.

One of the benefits of Miss Rossiter's life, I thought to myself as I dressed for the visit to the solicitor's office, was the release from all concerns of wardrobe. Had I been appearing as Mrs Gilver, I should have been lucky to get away without several changes before the competing demands of sobriety and decoration were satisfied, for while one would not wish to look jaunty upon such an errand, neither would one want one's black cape and veil to outdo the widow's. Nothing, unless it be wearing white to a wedding, is poorer form than that. As it was, Miss Rossiter got her grey serge, lisle stockings, black shoes, felt hat and armband on in four minutes flat. I was even becoming used to the look of my scraped-back hair and shining, soap-and-water face and wondered whether I were not looking rather better than usual – more youthful, fresher somehow – a possibility I put down to the settled routines and clean living of a servant's life until I realised that between the endless note-making, the rushing about the streets, the nightmares and the way that strong drink punctuated the hours, my two days spent below stairs in Heriot Row had been the least settled of recent memory. Probably it was only the dim light and the elderly looking-glass which gave the effect and if I glanced into Lollie's dressing-table glass upstairs in the sunshine I should be disabused.

'Are you sure you wouldn't rather wait until Great Aunt Gertrude gets here?' I asked Lollie, when I got to her. She simply gazed back at me. The skin around her eyes was yellow and her hands trembled as she lifted her hat onto her head. 'Here, let me,' I said. I secured her hat none too firmly, for they are fearsome things to stick into someone else's hair if one is not accustomed to it, or perhaps just if one has finer feelings than Grant, who wields a hatpin like Captain Ahab with his last harpoon.

Lollie shook her head.

'Mr Hardy wants to know if there's anything of note in it,' she said. Her voice was gravelly as though with exhaustion, very worrying in one known to have slept away the bulk of the last two days, and I determined to get her doctor to her when we returned from our outing. 'Besides, there might be something in it about a funeral – instructions, I mean, or requests, or something. It's best to get it over and done with.'

'Didn't you ever talk about funerals?' I asked her. 'Don't you know what he would have wanted, if you c—'

'If I care?' Lollie said. 'I shouldn't care, should I? And yet, it's hard not to. And no, we never spoke of such things. Pip was twenty-six, why would we?' I had not been imagining long, morbid discussions on their own account, of course, but rather thinking of Hugh and how he always spent the return trip from any funeral in high dudgeon about the mawkish unsuitability of the chosen hymns and the scandalous impropriety of anything – from florists' wreaths to panelled coffins – that his father and father's father and *his* father had 'managed perfectly well to die without, Dandy'. What he would do when this much-vaunted new prayer book finally came out, I could not imagine; I had never seen anyone walk out of a funeral in protest before but I would not put it past him.

'We only ever spoke of it once,' Lollie went on. She was looking at herself in the glass as though she were some sort of puzzling find brought home from a nature walk; she pulled at her eyelids and stretched the skin on her cheeks this way and that. It was disconcerting to watch and I caught hold of her hands, as though to inspect her nails, really just to stop that dreadful, inquisitive mauling.

'When was that, dear?' I said.

'When he went to Paris without me. It was the only night we spent apart after we were married. He made a joke of it; saying that if I were proved right, if the aeroplane went down – that's why I didn't go with him, you see – I would have carried the point and should feel free to bring his body back by boat.' She smiled, remembering, and her skin looked tight and dry as she did so. 'I shouldn't think there are instructions, in the will,' she said. 'Pip was never one to make demands about things. Not at home anyway, or at his tailor's or at his bank. He was the most easy-going man, really, Dandy. Everyone said so.'

I thought it best to remain silent.

'He could get rather impassioned about his model boats,' Lollie went on, 'but even when one of those was broken through a servant's carelessness he just shrugged it off. He was—' She broke off. 'Except he wasn't,' she said, with a harder note in her voice. 'I keep slipping into the most fearful maudlin daydreams, Dandy. As if I'm under some kind of spell. I know very well what he was and so do you.'

'Let's go,' I said, thinking that this robust mood would carry her out of the house and into her motorcar better than any other. 'And don't worry about the funeral. Two horses and "Lead, kindly light". These things practically organise themselves.'

Faulds, sombre of face and – for once – silent of foot, let us out of the front door. John was waiting at the kerb. It was the first time I had seen him in his full livery: a high-collared tunic to match his breeches and a grey cap with a gleaming black peak, his face as impassive as a guardsman's under its shadow. He opened the back door of a very new Rolls-Royce Phantom and between us we helped Lollie up into the seat. John leaned in and put a rug over her knees, then offered a hand to me to help me into the front. I thanked him, finding my voice a little shy, for it was an odd business to be handed into a car by a young man one has seen singing music-hall songs in his shirtsleeves, and an unaccustomed experience to sit beside him, no glass to close between the two of us.

Lollie, behind me, was looking out of the window at the quiet streets. There were nannies, off to Princes Street Gardens with their charges for an hour before luncheon, pairs of girls – the well-turned-out daughters of the New Town – making their way arm in arm to the jewellers' and dress shops of George Street, pairs of matrons – their mothers – on their way to Marshall & Aitken, and upright old men marching to the New Club for the day. What there were not, though, were delivery boys on their bicycles, nor coalmen on their carts, sweeps with their barrows, not even the late postman on the parcel round.

'How quiet it is today,' Lollie said, with a wondering note in her voice, as we came around Charlotte Square. 'The whole world seems to have stopped. Not only me.'

At the west end, a policeman mounted on a horse was standing backed into the doorway of Mather's public house.

'Trying to stop them gathering today,' said John.

'The publican won't be very pleased,' I said, 'to have a great hulking police horse driving away his custom.'

'There'll not be much beer left now anyway, Miss Rossiter,' John told me. 'There's been three nights since the last delivery and there was parties all over the night it begun.'

'I heard them,' I said, remembering the cheers and shouting drifting in the bedroom window in the small hours of Tuesday morning.

'Any excuse for a booze-up,' said John. 'Best night out since Hogmanay.' He winked at me. 'Or so I heard, anyway.' Here he dropped his voice even further in case Lollie could hear him. 'Till the funeral, eh?' He jerked his head towards his mistress. 'Talk about having something to celebrate.'

'Poor master,' I said. 'There are limits, John.'

'He didnae think so,' John retorted. 'And I should know. I spent more time with him than anyone else, except Harry maybe.'

'True,' I said. 'One could hardly drive him around and not get the measure of the man.'

'Aye, I got his measure,' he said. 'And I wasn't feart for him, like some I could name. He was your typical mummy's boy. Sleekit wee bully-boy. Nice as ninepence when anyone was watching and then a right so-and-so when he got the chance.'

'Was he a right so-and-so to you personally?' I asked. John nodded.

'He used to make me sleep in the car,' he said. 'Wasn't so bad in the summertime but once in the winter I near about froze to death.'

'I don't understand,' I said. 'How did he stop you going inside and sleeping in your bed? How could he?'

'No, not at home,' said John. 'This was if he was away out

somewhere and he would say to me to just wait in the car, then he just never came back and the night would go on and then in the end I'd realise that he wasnae *gonny* come back and he'd done it to me again, so I'd just have to doss down until the morning.'

'Where was this?' I said, wondering what these solitary outings of Pip's might be.

'Eh?' said John. 'Oh, you know, here and there. Nowhere special. I can't remember where it was we were the last time it happened.'

His vagueness set a faint alarm bell ringing in me, but at that moment we drew up outside the offices of Murray and Ettrick in Coates Crescent and I had to concentrate on assisting Lollie. We were met at the door by Mr Ettrick himself, as I should have expected given the size of the estate; if Mr Murray had been there brushing flies from our path with banana leaves it would not have been *too* surprising.

'All alone, Mrs Balfour?' he said, his eyes passing over me without stopping and peering at the inside of the motorcar behind me. 'I expected Mrs Lambert-Leslie to be with you.'

'She's on her way from Inverness,' said Lollie, 'but might take some time.'

Mr Ettrick shook his head and tutted, then ushered Lollie up the steps and through the glass doors with one hand in the small of her back and the other thrown wide as though to ward off any harm coming at her in a flanking manoeuvre. I supposed that a solicitor had to be solicitous, if anyone did, and she was a new widow and very fragile-looking, but still as I followed them – Miss Rossiter, of course, was not included in the ushering – the crease of concern between his brows and the way he stooped over her, as well as that arm shielding her from one knew not what, began to worry me.

We crossed a dark hallway, deeply carpeted in blue plush and shining with the gleam of mahogany, the glitter of brass and the wink of polished mirrors, and rose up a set of wide and shallow stairs. Somewhere, deep in the innards of Murray and Ettrick, at least a few typewriting machines were clacking away like crickets, but these front parts – the stairs and the cavernous room we were taken into at the top of them – were hushed and still, free of any modern trappings and looking, with their tall cases full of well-bound books and deep button-backed chairs, exactly like a club library, only less smoky.

I seated myself neatly on a hard bench just inside the door and watched as Mr Ettrick led Lollie to an armchair and settled her into it as though she were a grandmother. As he turned away from her, his frown deepened and he rubbed his palms on his trousers.

'Now . . . Mrs Balfour,' he said, once he had sat down on the other side of an imposing desk, and clasped his hands together on top of it. 'First of all, please allow me to say how very sorry we are. Murray and Ettrick have long been honoured to serve the legal needs of the Balfour family and we feel in our small way some of the shock and disbelief this most dreadful event must have brought to you.' The words were conventional, but Mr Ettrick was an old hand at it and the tone and expression were perfect. Then he faltered. 'Let me say, dear lady,' he went on, looking down at his hands on the desk, 'that we did not draw up your late husband's will, nor did anyone in this office co-sign it as witness. We merely held it. We . . . that is to say, I . . . no one read it until yesterday morning.' At this point Mr Ettrick's discomfort led him as far as to acknowledge my existence. He gave me a quick look and then glanced towards the empty chair beside Lollie. I rose silently and came to sit in it.

'Very well then,' he continued. He wore the usual tall stiff cellu-loid collar of the town solicitor and at that moment it appeared to be strangling him. He gulped once or twice, then took a pair of small spectacles out of his breast pocket and wound them onto his ears with some deliberation. He was a man in his fifties but just then I could see the twenty-year-old he had once been. He drew towards him the green paper folder which was the only item on the desk-top and opened it.

'*I, Philip James Balfour of 31 Heriot Row, Edinburgh, do declare this 5th day of March in the year 1926 that this is my last will and testament and renders all earlier testamentary documents bearing my name null and void.'* Mr Ettrick cleared his throat and gripped the paper a little tighter. *'I hereby give and bequeath everything of which I may die possessed or which may be hereafter due to me, both heritable property and moveable assets, in their entirety, to my cousin, George Pollard, formerly resident in St Mary's Square, Gloucester.'* The solicitor bent his head and I felt Lollie stiffen in the chair beside me. *'This disposition of my estate is in recognition of and recompense for the iniquities meted out from my forebears to that branch of the Balfour family connected by marriage to the Pollard family and to which my esteemed cousin belongs.'*

'He can't do that,' I said, putting an arm along the back of Lollie's chair. 'Mr Ettrick, I must protest in the strongest terms to you subjecting Mrs Balfour to this performance. You know very well that under Scots Law the widow cannot be disinherited.'

Mr Ettrick was holding up a hand like a policeman stopping traffic.

'If you would allow me, Miss er . . .' he said, and bent his head to continue reading.

'I request that this gift and bequest be paid not earlier than two calendar years after the date of my death until which time it shall be held in trust for the said George Pollard excepting the payment of funeral costs and other necessary expenses, for example but without prejudice to the generality, outstanding personal bills.'

'But he can't,' I insisted. 'This is nonsense.'

'Please,' said Mr Ettrick. 'If you would have just a little patience. I am coming to it, I assure you. *I appoint Bertram Ettrick, Solicitor, as my executor and overseer of the trust and request specifically that he expedite with all possible haste the removal from my house at Heriot Row all servants and other residents, including Miss Walburga Percival.'*

'What?' said Lollie and I felt a jolt pass through her.

'There's a little more,' said Mr Ettrick, his voice so quiet now that I could hardly hear it. 'There's a codicil, requesting that George Pollard, after the will is fully executed of course, *ascertain the burial place of my wife, Josephine Beatrice Balfour née*

Carson, born 22nd August 1890 and died 10th July 1924, and erect there a monument, the choosing of which I entrust to him, assured of his affectionate attention in this matter.'

'Who?' said Lollie. She was sitting forward, straining out of her seat, almost keening towards him, trying to understand. Mr Ettrick, unable to bear the look upon her face, directed his gaze instead at me.

'Who witnessed it?' I asked and he nodded slightly, as though acknowledging the sense of my question.

'It was witnessed by a Miss Margaret Anne Taylor and a Miss Jessie Armstrong Abbott. Neither are known to me.'

'Abbott and Maggie,' said Lollie, in a dazed voice. 'My maids, Mr Ettrick. Two of my maids.'

'Ex-maids,' I said, furiously thinking what that might mean, for it had to mean something.

Mr Ettrick had risen and gone to a section of bookcase lower than the rest where a sherry decanter and glasses were set out. He poured himself a stiff measure, swallowed it in one gulp and then refilled his glass and two others. He handed mine to me with a grim look and then placed Lollie's carefully into her hand, wrapping her fingers around it. She put it down into her lap without a glance, but I admit that I knocked mine back just as readily and as indecorously as Mr Ettrick had his first and, I saw, his second.

'I thought you were a maid yourself, madam, at first,' he said to me. 'I do beg your pardon.'

'Not at all,' I said. 'Now, Mr Ettrick, the question is this: is it legal? It's perfectly wicked, but is it legal? Will it stand?'

'Ah!' said Lollie and she raised her hands as though at some spectacle laid out before her, letting her glass tumble down, spilling sherry over her skirt and stockings. '1924! And we were married in 1921. And so we weren't married, were we? I see.' She sounded relieved, happy to have sorted the puzzling words of the will into something that made sense to her; she even smiled a little, but no sooner had the smile left her lips than she swayed back in her seat and then in one fluid movement, like an eel, she slipped downwards and, unless I had caught her under her arms and held her, would have slithered onto the floor.

Mr Ettrick, sturdier after all than the strangulated neck inside the stiff collar suggested, easily took her weight from me and carried her over to a sofa against the far wall, where he laid her down and stood over her, shaking his head and breathing loudly.

'If this earlier marriage to Miss Carson is right enough,' he said, 'and if she really did die in 1924 then, yes, I daresay it's perfectly legal and I'll have no choice but to execute it. The wording is not what I would have written myself, but – most unfortunately – it's clear enough that any objections would be batted away as cavils. If I had known what was in it, it would have been a different matter, though, I can tell you. Murray and Ettrick have never been party to any such thing in eighty years of practice, Miss er . . .'

'What interests me particularly,' I said, thinking back over all that I had just heard, 'is the two years' delay. Have you ever come across such a thing before? Is it usual?'

'Never,' said Mr Ettrick. He stooped to retrieve Lollie's sherry glass and returned it to the tray, taking the opportunity while he was there to pour himself a third measure. 'It's quite common to have a stipulation that a will has to be executed within a year, or two, or five, if there's some doubt as to whether the legatee can be traced, for instance. But as to *waiting* two years, I have no idea.'

On the couch, Lollie shifted a little and moaned softly.

'I'll fetch the chauffeur,' I said. 'She should be at home.' Then I shook my head and laughed. 'Home! She has no home, does she? You are charged to break the household up as soon as you can manage it.'

'Expedite with all possible haste,' said Mr Ettrick, nodding. 'It sounds marvellous, doesn't it, Miss er . . . but Mr Balfour had no legal training and, legally speaking, it doesn't mean a thing. That is, I interpret it as meaning "carry out with as much haste as is commensurate with the comfort and convenience of all affected parties". Yes, indeed, that's what it means to me.'

Mr Ettrick, in other words, was that fabled beast: a lawyer with a heart of gold. He was in Pip's employ and could not resign from it, but he was in Lollie's corner. He was a small mercy in all of this and I thanked heaven for him.

10

'And you had no idea, madam?' said Superintendent Hardy. He was sitting on the dressing stool in Lollie's bedroom looking like a shire horse in a hat shop against the lavender silk. Lollie had gone straight to bed upon her return and when I had tried to get her up again, tried to persuade her that it was highly improper to summon the policeman to her bedside, she had only laughed a rather hysterical laugh and asked me why she should care about what was proper now. She laughed again as Hardy spoke to her

'Not "madam",' she said. '"Miss"! I'm not a married woman. I'm a . . . I'm a . . . I don't even know what the current term is for what I am.'

'Mrs Balfour,' said Superintendent Hardy, who must have been squirming but was hiding it very well. 'My dear madam. Let us pay no attention to any of that until we see what's what. I for one don't believe it.'

'Then why would he have said it?' said Lollie. 'Written it? Put it in the most serious document anyone ever writes in his life?' I was standing beside the window looking out along the street for her doctor, to whom I had sent an urgent message to attend. Lollie, I feared, was beyond the reach of toast water, fish custard, or even port and brandy now, and as pitiful as her tears had been in the first throes of grief, as worrying as her blank, pale face and toneless voice had been when the shock had benumbed her, this was worst of all. Now her eyes glittered and her voice had a rich chuckle in it, and she made me think of a child's balloon dancing at the end of its string as the breeze tried to twitch it away. I only hoped the doctor would come soon with some kind of stout medicinal tether for her.

'It seems perfectly in character to me, Lollie dear,' I said. She and Hardy both turned towards me. 'He did have a weakness for rather cruel little practical jokes, didn't he? The goose with mouse stuffing? Perhaps this will was another of them. Perhaps he meant to show it to you. He can't have expected to die at twenty-six, after all. He probably meant to enjoy your distress then tear it up and write a new one, a real one.'

'What goose?' Lollie said, and I found it far from reassuring that out of all I had said, *this* was the point she chose to question. With relief, I saw out of the corner of my eye a tall man with a large leather bag striding confidently along the road. He took the steps to the front door of Number 31 at a bound and as he disappeared from my view I heard the unmelodious clank of the bell sounding far below.

'That's the doctor,' I said. 'I'll go down and meet him.'

But outside the door, Hardy laid an arm on mine and drew me into the boudoir.

'Let one of the maids go tripping up and downstairs with the doc,' he said. 'You've more important business to see to. Now, as Mrs Balfour asked you: what goose?'

I told him as briefly and as dispassionately as I could, about the mouse in the goose, the chopped-out pockets in Harry's clothes, the nasty way Pip Balfour had had of stranding people alone at night in the dark and the cold. 'I don't think there's a single person in the household to whom he wasn't thoroughly callous at some time,' I said, counting them off on my fingers. 'Actually, I don't know about Stanley, the footman. I haven't spoken to him. But the men are immaterial. It's the girls we need to worry about. They were in the house.'

'But Dr Glenning said a girl couldn't have done it,' Hardy reminded me.

'A typical girl couldn't have, perhaps,' I said, thinking of Millie, 'but that's not the point. I was already thinking that one of the girls might have let someone in, let him in the back door unheard by Mrs Hepburn and unheard by me, since neither of us were where we should have been. Only I didn't know which girl and couldn't imagine *who* she had let in. I was thinking along the lines of a swain come to avenge her honour, I suppose. But we can cast the role now, Superintendent, wouldn't you say?'

'George Pollard?' said the superintendent. 'Does he even exist? I thought you didn't believe in that will. I thought you said it was a joke.'

'There's *something* very odd about it,' I said. 'Something I can't quite put my finger on, but I'm afraid when I dismissed it I was only trying to calm Mrs Balfour. I think it's real enough. And if Pip Balfour's cousin knew its terms, then he had the strongest possible motive to persuade someone in this house to open up the back door one night and let him in.'

'But would he know?' said Hardy.

'He might have,' I answered. 'There's something . . . I'm *sure* he might have but I don't know why I'm sure.'

This was just the kind of Easter egg hunt in which Alec and I revelled – chasing down a little wisp of an idea one knew was there – but Superintendent Hardy plucked at his watch cover and kneaded his hat brim as though in some kind of unbearable distress as he waited. Then of course, he tried to argue.

'I don't agree,' he said. 'There had been a rift in the family. You said yourself Pollard was identified by a *former* address. The two men might not even have known one another.'

'That's it!' I said. 'Oh, thank you, Superintendent. That's what's been nibbling at me. Pip Balfour knew George Pollard. Definitely.'

'How do you know?' said Hardy. 'What told you?'

'The will itself,' I said. 'Balfour referred to Pollard as "my esteemed cousin" and talked about "affection" and one can't esteem someone one doesn't know, much less feel affection for him. Clearly, Lollie knew nothing of him, but Pip certainly did.'

Hardy sat back in his seat, causing some creaking in the delicate silk panels which formed its sides, and gave a nod firm enough to crack a walnut under his chin.

'Good,' he said. 'We can go on that.' Then he blew out hard.

'You wouldn't catch me telling some cousin that I had left him my fortune,' he said. 'Asking for . . . well, a knife in the neck, in this case, don't you think?'

I nodded, but I was still feeling troubled. I had relieved for a moment the little tickle at the back of my mind which always tells me I am missing something, but it had already returned; clearly, I had not thought my way through to the end of this yet. Alec would have read my face and doubled back to meet me but Hardy was another matter.

'So you were just making sympathetic noises to poor Mrs Balfour?' he was saying now. 'I can see your reasoning – she's in a bad way – but it's going to be harder for her in the end.'

'I'm not so sure,' I said. 'If the whole thing is a joke – if the will's invalid – then Pip Balfour died intestate and . . .'

'Ah,' said Hardy. 'Mrs Balfour inherits.' He gave another final sort of nod.

'And if the will is good and if Cousin George, with the help of someone in this house, did for Cousin Philip, then he – George, I mean – can't benefit from his crime, and once again Lollie scoops the lot.'

'Right,' said Hardy. 'That's all tied up then.'

'Except for this Josephine person,' I said. 'The first wife. The *only* wife if the dates are right.'

'Oh yes,' said Hardy. 'Her.' He sounded pained again.

'Although . . .' I said, thinking it all over. 'I shall have to check, or perhaps you might, but I think, as long as George Pollard is guilty and is cut out of the will because of that, and since Josephine Carson is dead, and so long as she and Pip had no children . . .'

'Lord, that's a thought!' said Hardy.

'But there's nothing to suggest that they did,' I reminded him. 'So, Pollard guilty, a childless Josephine long gone, even without a will Lollie inherits. I'm almost sure she does. On account of her irregular marriage. What's called in England a common-law marriage.'

'They don't exist,' said Hardy. 'There's no such thing.' The definite nature of this point seemed to please him.

'*They* don't,' I said, 'but Scottish irregular marriages certainly do. By declaration, by habit and repute or by consummation. I should say Lollie has two out of the three, wouldn't you?'

Mr Hardy blushed at that but I sailed on.

'I daresay a judge would look most favourably on Lollie's claim, especially in a case like this, where if she doesn't get it there's no one else it can go to except the Crown.'

'Good luck to the poor judge who had to pick his way through it,' Hardy said.

As I passed the telephone in the hallway on the ground floor minutes later, I felt a sudden wild desire to ring up Hugh and tell him that I had just astounded a police superintendent with my superior grasp of Scots Law. I fought it.

Hardy had gone, in faint hope, to look for a George Pollard who might, despite that 'formerly', still be lingering in St Mary's Square, Gloucester, and if not to order a search for Pollards with a Balfour connection and track down marriages of Balfours to Carsons. He was thus playing to his strengths. And I to mine: I was to hand-feed a few carefully selected titbits of news to the others and had also been set the task of a little actual, Holmesian, sleuthing, not quite with a magnifying glass and a tin of finger-print powder but very much along those lines. I looked forward to it; perhaps after a short interlude of snooping around for clues with my mind engaged on such tangible matters as gates and walls and doors and keys, whatever it was that was troubling me would dislodge itself from the recesses where it was lurking and allow me to . . . cough it into my hand and see what it was? I really had to find a different way to describe it to myself before I tried it out loud.

At that thought, my shoulders drooped a little, for there was only one individual imaginable to whom I might ever relate it. If I could only have ten minutes with Alec, I thought, then the niggle of the will, the tangle of the servants and their alliances, and the various other cobwebs which had brushed lightly against the edge of my attention for a moment each before falling away again would all be brought to bright light and clarity. Of course, I was romanticising; Alec and I can blunder around together in the twilight, beset by cobwebs, as readily as can I alone, but two heads, as Nanny Palmer always used to say, are better for knocking together than only one.

I was still staring at the telephone when it rang, and when my feet touched the floor again after a short leap into the air I was convinced it would be Alec at the other end, somehow coming to help me.

'Good afternoon,' I said, in my most carefully modulated accent. 'The Balfour residence.'

'The what?' said a penetrating voice. 'Who the dickens is this? And who taught you how to answer a telephone? Balfour residence indeed! Who are you?'

'Mi-iss Rossiter, madam,' I said, for whoever this was it was most definitely a madam.

'Who?' bellowed the voice. 'Where's Faulds? And where's my niece?'

Illumination spread over me. It was Great Aunt Gertrude.

'Mrs Hampton-Hayley,' I said, sure of my recollection, 'I'm afraid Mrs Balfour is seriously indisposed this afternoon. Would you like to—'

'Who? What's going on? This is Mrs Lambert-Leslie speaking.' I had been close but hardly accurate, then. 'With great reluctance, I might add, because I detest these damnable machines. Fetch my niece at once.'

'As I was saying, madam.' I had an aunt of my own for whom I had perfected the technique I was now employing: that of holding the earpiece a foot from my head to dull the booming and putting my face very close to the mouthpiece to try to break through it. 'Mrs Balfour has her doctor with her just now and she's very unwell indeed. If I might take a message, perhaps?'

'Nonsense,' said Great Aunt Gertrude, although I was unsure which part of my contribution she was dismissing. 'This is becoming utterly farcical. I'm ringing to say that I've run out of petroleum and I'm only halfway there.'

'I'm terribly sorry to hear that, madam,' I said. 'Mrs Balfour is in great need of succour.'

'Can't think why,' said Aunt Gertrude. 'My second husband came off and went half a mile with his foot caught in the stirrup, bashed to bloody bits, and I watched the whole thing through my field glasses and didn't go looking for any succour. What she needs is jollying up and setting straight. But I'm stuck halfway, and not a drop of petrol to be had. I'll tell you, young woman, I wish I'd brought my gun.'

The words, when she repeated them, went in at last.

'Halfway?' I said. 'Halfway between Inverness and here? Where exactly are you, Mrs Lambert-Leslie?' She drew away from the mouthpiece and I heard her shouting to someone in the distance. I did not hear the reply, but when she spoke into the telephone again, the sun shone. 'Ballinluig,' she roared. 'God-forsaken spot. I thought Inverness was bad but this is worse, I can tell you.'

'In that case,' I said, 'you are in luck. You are five short miles from some petrol, if you will consent to carry a passenger to town.'

It took rather more explaining than one might have imagined, because Great Aunt Gertrude was one of those individuals who, rather than be told what the teller knows and she does not, fires questions, guesses and objections as rapidly as she can think them up and listens to nothing. Eventually, however, we established to her grudging satisfaction Alec's name, address, school, regiment, father, mother and – crucially – grandmother's sister, whom Great Aunt Gertrude had met in the days of her youth and remembered fondly.

Alec Osborne is the other kind, in this as in every respect, and he took less than a minute to cotton on.

'Gertrude Lambert-Leslie,' he said. 'Battleaxe. Arriving in ten minutes. Right-ho. I'll pack for a week, Dan, because God knows how I shall ever get home again. Now what about the dogs? Shall I bring them?'

'Don't tease me,' I said. 'How can you? But if she's there, right there, right now, put her on for a moment, would you?' There was some scuffling and whistling at the other end and the sound of extravagant sniffing came down the line to me. 'Bunty?' I said. She whined. 'Oh, darling! Hello! Hello, my darling!'

'*Miss Rossiter!*' Mr Faulds was in the dining-room doorway, having entered it from the servants' door in the breakfast parlour. He had a piece of the elephant train centrepiece in each chamois-gloved hand, and looked so aghast that he was lucky not to have dropped them. Stanley, hovering behind him, pulled a frown of which Superintendent Hardy would have been proud.

'Oh, Mr Faulds,' I said, and I could hear Alec laughing as I crashed the earpiece back down and leapt away from the telephone. 'Please forgive me. I don't know what came over me. I was speaking on the telephone to mistress's aunt and when she rang off, I just . . . called up my young man. I can't account for it.'

'Mrs L-L was this?' said Faulds, his face softening. 'Well, she'd send anyone flying to the arms – or even the ears – of a protector.' Stanley, by the looks of him, was more shocked by Faulds's calm reaction than by my outrage itself. He stared at the butler's back, shaking his head in a kind of delighted disgust, his eyes threatening to pop right out of his head and roll away.

'She's coming,' I said to Faulds. 'She's in Perthshire. She'll be here by tonight.'

'Lord love us, as if we hadn't got enough on our plates,' said Faulds. 'Well, you run and tell Phyllis to air the back bedroom and get a fire lit for her.'

'Certainly, Mr Faulds,' I said, happy to ignore the cheek of a butler telling a lady's maid to 'run and' do anything, if it would put me in the black again. Stanley did not miss the impropriety, though. He tutted in a very missish way. 'Then, I'm going to want to speak to you.'

'To me?' said Faulds. Stanley was quivering with interest.

'To everyone. At tea. I've got to tell you all something that I heard today.'

But before that, I had my sleuthing to do. I left Phyllis and Clara at the linen closet, looking out the best guest sheets and groaning at the prospect of Great Aunt Gertrude, and after a quick look into the servants' hall which showed me John and Harry sitting down in their shirtsleeves, I stole downstairs and out of the garden door. There was no one on the walkway above and the scullery window was misted up with steam, so Millie would not see me even if she were bent over her sinks as ever. From the coalhole, directly under the scullery, there came the rhythmic sound of a cob-hammer. Mattie must be busy in there, although it occurred to me that if I were in charge of the household I should have suspended the practice of breaking coal cobs into dainty little pieces for the drawing-room scuttle while we were held to a hundredweight a week (and who knew when it would be reduced even further). Great lumps like boulders might be inelegant but they burned with a marvellous lack of speed, and it was May after all; no one was going to catch cold for want of a good blaze.

Beyond the cherry tree, a grass path led between washing ropes where the long aprons of the kitchen staff and the rough shirts and undershirts of the male servants were pegged out in the sunshine. Then there was a little garden, ten feet square, of brick paths and flowerbeds, which must have been a herbiary in the first days of the house but was now left to its own devices and growing a profusion of weeds with one or two leggy shrubs struggling through them. Further on again through a gate lay a small yard centred around a pump and drinking trough, with room around its rim for half a dozen horses – although the clean cobbles and the layer of weed on the surface of the water spoke of how long it had been since any carriage horses stood to refresh themselves there.

At the far end of the yard, the carriage house closed off the garden completely from the mews. The stable doors were boarded up but there was a small door to one side still usable and I tried its handle. It opened onto a passageway with a staircase leading up to the sleeping level, a door on each side and a door at the far end, along the bottom edge of which I could see a slit of light. The door on my left was half-open and the edge of a roller towel rail hinted that this was the 'men's arrangements'. The door on the right was just ajar too, and when I stepped towards it I saw a large dim space and the bonnet of the motorcar from that morning. The big garage doors, I could see, were shut and bolted. The door at the far end of the passageway with the light showing beneath it was not bolted, although it was locked – the key hung on the inevitable high hook to one side – but the bolts were shiny from touch and ran easily when I tried them, suggesting that the carriage house was kept fast at night. Could one of the maids have come all the way to *this* door to let in a murderer? Would she not have been heard? I looked up at the ceiling over my head, wondering if any of the boys slept right above this bolted door.

The stairs creaked horribly as I went up them, and my feet sounded like clapping coconut shells on the bare boards above. There were only two rooms up here, each with a window onto the mews and another into the gardens. They had no fireplaces and I thought that these days, not a single horse downstairs warming the air with its breath, winter would be without much comfort. As to who slept where, it was hard to say; there was a bottle of brilliantine in one of the rooms which might have been Harry's, and, near one of the beds, an elderly coachman's cape which was surely John's by rights was hanging on a nail, but in any case the partition walls were simple lath and plaster and even the wall which divided this carriage house from the one next door and the servants of another household sounded, when I knocked it, like a single layer of brick. If someone had got in through the mews, I did not see how all of the menservants could have failed to hear him.

I had not glanced out of the garden window during my time upstairs and had not seen the figure coming down the drying green, along the brick path and over the yard, and so the sound of him entering the passageway beneath me set my heart hammering. There was no way out and nowhere to hide so I stood my ground, feet planted stoutly, and it was Stanley who jumped and gasped when we met, not me.

'Miss Rossiter?' he said, his pop eyes rolling about this way and that as he tried to see what I might have been doing. It did not appear to take him very long to come to a view. 'Leaving a little note on his pillow, are we?' he said, nodding at the bed nearest to where I stood. 'Couldn't you get his attention away from the bulletin any other way?'

'I don't appreciate your tone, Stanley,' I said. 'You have a very impertinent manner and I would remind you that a footman owes respect to a lady's maid.'

'You're no more a lady's maid than he is a valet,' said Stanley. 'I'm the only true-trained servant in the place, I think sometimes.'

I rose up.

'If you can't keep a civil tongue in your head I shall be forced to speak to Mr Faulds about you,' I said.

'Mr Faulds?' said Stanley. 'Oh yes! A great head of staff he is.'

'Don't be such a prig,' I said.

Stanley put his thumbs into the armholes of his waistcoat and rocked back and forwards on the balls of his feet.

'I wasn't talking about the famous liaison,' he said. 'But now you mention it, it's—'

'A private matter,' I finished, 'and one I have no desire to discuss.'

'But they didn't keep it private, did they?' said Stanley, growing almost oily in his glee, and quite repulsive.

'They were overtaken by events,' I said. 'I think Mrs Hepburn should be applauded, actually, in not letting any silly modesty deflect her from doing the right thing. I found it courageous. There's more to life than a petty guarding of one's reputation. And if you really want to know what I'm doing here in the carriage house – not that I owe you an explanation – I was trying to see if the murderer might have got in this way.'

'Got in where?' said Stanley, suddenly looking very nervous and glancing about himself.

'Where do you think? Into the house. From the mews. Through here.' The grin returned then.

'Oh, so you think somebody came in from outside, do you?' he said. The rocking had started again. 'Where did you get that one, then?'

'Look, do you actually know anything or are you just being annoying, as usual?' I asked him and was rewarded with a trace of a frown passing over his face. He really was a most unappealing young man. 'If you know something, it's your duty to tell someone. Tell Superintendent Hardy if you want the glory of it. Tell mistress and she'll no doubt reward you. But you must tell someone.'

'Help the police? I'd no more help a dog bite my own backside. That rotten devil deserved everything he got.'

'Why?' I said. 'What did he do to you?' I felt a small flutter of triumph. If Stanley had a tale to tell of misuse at the hands of his master, I should have got the full set.

'He refused to give me time off to visit my own father when he was at death's door,' said Stanley, and his large eyes glistened with instant tears. 'Not even a day.'

'Oh,' I said, regretting the sparring at once. 'That was unspeakable of him. I'm very sorry.'

Stanley sniffed and nodded in acknowledgement.

'I never forgave him,' he said. 'He told me he couldn't risk me bringing it into the house and if I went home to visit I needn't bother coming back again. And I knew a widowed mother would need whatever I could send her, so I stayed put. My father could have died without me ever seeing him again.'

'Could have?' I said, latching on to this clue that Stanley was overdoing his tale.

'He rallied, as it happens. But master wasn't to know that and I'd have got called all the names under the sun at the funeral.'

'That certainly is a consideration,' I said, drily, thinking it would only occur to the most monstrously self-centred of sons. From sheer dislike, I wished I could suspect him of the murder, but his squeamishness and his servility – each undoubtedly real, as well as the very habit of dropping sly hints, combined to trumpet his innocence. No murderer in his right mind would dare to be so infuriating to those around him.

'But he threw it off in the end,' Stanley said. 'And he has forgiven me. I never told him why I didn't come, of course.

A good servant would never carry home tales that reflect ill on his master. And I daresay master couldn't help being a fastidious man.'

Even though it came from Stanley, I could not help boggling a little at this. How could anyone rejoice that the rotten devil was dead and still praise the same man for being a ninny over a germ or two?

'Was it the flu?' I asked. Pip and Lollie had only been in Heriot Row four years but I could not think of anything else contagious enough to excuse such precautions.

'Consumption,' said Stanley.

'But that's ridiculous,' I said. 'You can't catch consumption as easily as all that. Why, I can't count how many soldiers I saw through it in the war.'

'That's why I'll never forgive him,' Stanley said.

11

'So, Fanny,' said Mrs Hepburn, 'Ernest tells me you've got something to say. No. not like that, Mollie-moo. Watch Eldry and copy what she does.' The tweenie and scullerymaid were engaged on some mysterious task at the table, with sheets of waxed paper and large pairs of scissors. Millie put down her scissors and her paper – in tatters after her efforts – and bunched her hands together under her chin. She gazed at Eldry with devoted attention and Eldry, snipping neat fringes into her own paper strip, could not help beaming back. Really, I thought, every servants' hall should have a Millie, someone to make the others feel suave and competent and give them scope to be kind.

Mrs Hepburn was holding the enormous teapot over the collection of cups, with her head cocked, and as soon as she heard Clara's clogs on the passageway flags she started pouring.

'Mattie,' she said. 'So weak it's not worth dirtying a cup for and no more than three sugars mind, for that Calvert's powder cannot work miracles and I'm not sending you back to see your mammy with those wee pearlies all ruined.' Mattie smiled as he took his cup of dishwater tea; he did indeed have sparkling white teeth and I sympathised with Mrs Hepburn about the guarding of them. Clara arrived with a large platter covered in a teacloth and set it down.

'Miss Rossiter?' said Mrs Hepburn, with the pot poised.

'I'll have a good dark cup today, Mrs Hepburn,' I said, for I had fast learned that the strident Indian blend beloved of the servants' hall could not be outwitted by dilution and was best got over one's gullet strong, milky and sweet, so that one might pretend it was not tea at all but some kind of exotic soup.

Mr Faulds reached across from the head of the table and twitched the teacloth from on top of the plate, revealing a mountain range of warm scones, flour-dusted, current-studded and steaming gently. There was a murmur of appreciation from all around the table as the scent of them wafted over us, and Phyllis began dishing out tea plates, a large pat of cold butter on each one.

'Food of the gods, Kitty,' said Mr Faulds as he bit into his first one. 'I never thought I'd say it, but I don't miss jam and cream when it's your scones under my butter.'

John gave a snort of laughter and, indeed, there was something inexplicably lewd-sounding about the compliment. Mrs Hepburn tutted, but with a twinkle in her eye.

'Make the most of the scones *and* the leisure,' she said, 'because there'll be no more of either after today.' She filled another three cups and Harry pushed them across the table to their destinations. 'I've two cakes to mix when the tins are dressed and they hams to glaze and the whole house to get ready for the funeral with no kitchener, and there's you-know-who on her way. I'll tell you this, Fanny, that woman doubles the work of the house single-handed.'

'Mrs Lambert-Leslie?' I said.

'Aye, Great Aunt Goitre,' said Clara. 'Maybe she'll have learned to use a handle by now, eh?'

'Some chance,' said Phyllis. 'You know, Miss Rossiter, she shuts every blooming door and drawer and cupboard with one of her big fat hands flat against the wood. Smears the mahogany in her bedroom like you wouldnae believe if we told you.'

'And it's your turn to do her feet this time, Phyllis,' said Clara, 'because I did them at Christmas and wrote it down and got Mr Faulds to sign it.'

'Please, girls, not while we're eating,' said the butler. Stanley was looking pained and moved a mouthful of scone from one cheek to the other without swallowing any.

'And if she's brought a boot-load of washing with her she can raffle it,' said Mrs Hepburn. 'Treating this place like a laudnry and never leaves a penny tip behind her. But there, she's an old woman on her own and nobody presses a lace edge like Eldry, so let's see if we can't look after her even better this time. She's mistress's only living relative now.'

'Speaking of which,' I said, although whether I meant living relatives or witnessed documents I could not say, 'mistress has said I can tell you what happened at the lawyers' this morning. And Mr Hardy wants you all to know too, before he speaks to you again.'

'Well?' said Mr Faulds. He had his curled fists resting on the table, looking like the chairman of the board.

'Master's will had a very nasty surprise in it,' I said. 'Mistress has been cut right out altogether.' I paused to allow this to sink in.

'The devil,' said Mrs Hepburn. 'Oh, the fiend!'

'What, cut off with nothing?' said Harry. 'Not a shilling?' He was frowning at me. I had determined to gloss over the matter of Josephine Carson, trusting that no one of the servant class would be acquainted with the details of testamentary law, but now I wondered whether the valet knew too much about wills and succession to let this go by.

'Surprised you care,' said John, saving me from having to answer. 'Many's the time I've heard you calling her and him both for sitting back on their what's-its instead of earning a day's pay.'

'My poor mistress,' said Mr Faulds, and then in the next breath. 'Here, Fanny, what about us?'

'Nothing,' I said. 'There were no bequests to anyone.'

'Not even a wee minder for any of us?' said Clara. 'After four years?'

'That's cold for you,' said Mr Faulds, 'but it's not what I was getting at. I meant what about us, Number 31, the household, if mistress has been left without a penny?'

'So where's it all gone then?' said Millie and the others turned to look at her. In her simplicity, she had not frittered off into questions of just deserts and repercussions, but had kept her whole mind squarely on the pot of gold.

'Exactly,' I said, and as one they turned back to me. 'He has left it to a relation, by the name of George Pollard. A cousin, it seems.'

For a short moment no one spoke and then the clamour began.

'A cousin? What cousin? He's never been here. Pollard? I've never heard of him. Has mistress met him? Does the lawyer know him? Will he be running the house then? Will we still have our jobs? Who is he? Why should he come in for a fortune?'

'So,' I said, carefully looking around at them all, one by one. 'No one knew?'

'Us? Why would we know? Think we would know and not tell mistress? What are you hinting at?'

'Simply,' I said, 'that Miss Abbott and Maggie witnessed the will and I thought they might have mentioned something about it. I'm sure I couldn't have bitten my tongue if it were me.'

Harry sat forward.

'Maggie and Jessie Abbott?' he said. 'Them that left. Why would that be, then?'

'Ah, but Miss Rossiter,' said Mr Faulds, ignoring him, 'they needn't have read what was in it. Probably never even saw it. I believe it's customary to draw a blank sheet over the page and leave only the bottom portion where the signatures go.'

'How would you know that, Mr Faulds?' said Phyllis, rather pertly.

'Oh, we all know Mr Faulds has led a full life,' said John. 'Eh, Mrs Hepburn?' But this was going too far even for such an affable butler as Ernest Faulds and he scowled the grin off the chauffeur's face in a way of which my very own Pallister would have been proud.

'As for your jobs,' I said, 'the will was very clear. The house is to be sold.' There was a collective gasp at that and Mrs Hepburn put her cup down hard in its saucer. 'Everyone has to leave and the money is to be held until George Pollard comes forward to collect it.'

Harry was the first to speak.

'Your jobs?' he said. '*Your* jobs, Miss Rossiter? Do you think mistress will be keeping a lady's maid then?'

I bit my lip at the blunder but said nothing as Harry continued.

'Is that why you're passing all this on, like so much cosy gossip? "I'm all right, Jack"? So much for solidarity, eh?'

'Don't be a clown, Harry,' said Phyllis. 'Don't be so rude to everyone all the time.'

'Miss Rossiter was quite right to tell us,' said Mr Faulds, 'if mistress asked her to. And you said something about Mr Hardy too, Fanny?'

This was the point I had been leading up to and dreading. This was the moment when below stairs at Number 31 Heriot Row would cease to be the snug little burrow where all could gather together for pronouncements about the doings of those above over buttered scones and tea.

'Yes,' I said. 'Mr Hardy has taken me into his confidence quite remarkably.'

'Spotted you for one of his own,' said Harry sourly, but the others shushed him.

'Indeed, Harry,' I said, 'he's under considerable pressure with the strike and this case is exactly what he didn't need on top of it all, so I daresay he has been less . . . professional than he might have. He knew that I, unlike the rest of you, had no quarrel with Mr Balfour and no reason to want him dead and so he knew he could talk to me.'

'Now, here, wait a minute,' said Mrs Hepburn. 'You've no call to be talking that way, Fanny Rossiter, even though, mind you, it's true enough, true enough. You carry on and finish your piece.'

'I think everyone here felt ill disposed towards master to some extent, although some have been more discreet than others.' I bowed in acknowledgement to Mr Faulds, who accepted the compliment with a court bow of his own. 'And everyone said that they couldn't care less who killed him and wouldn't want whoever it was to be punished for it.' My mouth was dry and

I took a sip of tea. 'But that was when you thought one of your number had struck back, had lashed out in protest, or self-defence, or revenge for some injury you could all imagine.' They were in the palm of my hand now. 'Only that's not what Mr Hardy thinks happened. And I agree. What he thinks is that George Pollard got wind of his inheritance and killed Mr Balfour for it. And – here's the rub – he thinks someone let him into the house and that can't have happened – couldn't have – without someone else hearing something or seeing something of what was going on.'

There was perfect silence now in the servants' hall.

'So,' I went on, 'any of you who is perhaps keeping quiet about . . . anything: someone not where they ought to have been, or being where they oughtn't; a noise you couldn't account for; a key out of place or a door that should have been locked left open . . . what you need to see is that you're not protecting one of your friends who suffered as you did. You're protecting someone who is quite happy to see you jobless, out on the street, all of you.'

Clara and Phyllis were both staring at me fixedly and did not see Mattie glance quickly between the two of them. John saw it, though, and tried to catch Harry's eye. Stanley was drilling a look down towards the floor that could have shattered the stone flags there, and Millie and Eldry avoided looking at one another so studiedly and with such a deep pink bloom on their cheeks that they might as well have stared and pointed.

'Well,' said Mrs Hepburn. 'You could cut the air in here with a knife and tile a roof with it. You've set the cat amongst the pigeons now, Fan.' She cast her gaze around her staff, frowning. 'What's to do with you all, eh?'

'They're just upset, Kitty,' said Mr Faulds. 'Overwrought, as are we all, I'm sure. Miss Rossiter, do you really think that someone could be so lost to goodness that he – or she, of course – would protect one murderer but not another? I hardly think any of our young people is as calculating as all that.'

'Self-preservation is a powerful force, Mr Faulds,' I said. 'Just to be as plain as possible and make sure everyone understands,' – I was thinking chiefly of Millie here – 'if George Pollard did it and he gets caught, then the will is ripped into little pieces, Mrs Balfour – as the widow – inherits, and this house carries on just as before, only better by far for the loss of master. So the choice for someone who knows something and could tell is protect one or save all. It's as stark as that.'

There was another long silence then. The upper servants as far as Phyllis and Stanley had collected themselves, and were now wearing poker faces of admirable rectitude; well-trained in the art by their years of standing at the edge of intimate domestic scenes as untouched by what passed between master and mistress as a lamp post is by the lives of those who walk through its light. Millie, Eldry and especially Mattie were quite another proposition, never having needed to develop impassive faces in scullery, laundry and coalhole. Mattie looked close to tears and the kitchen girls were still flushed and fidgety.

'Well, let's not dwell on such things unduly,' said Mr Faulds, addressing us all. 'I'm sure that Superintendent Hardy and Mr Ettrick between them will see mistress right and she'll do right by us too. But if any of you does have something to say to Mr Hardy when he returns, you should say it, and God forgive you for not saying it straight away on Monday like you know you should have.' He shot a look at me as though to see if that would satisfy me. I gave a tight smile and a suggestion of a nod. 'Now, it's Friday tomorrow,' he said. He dabbed up a few scone crumbs with his finger, chewed them daintily and then wiped his mouth with the back of his hand. 'And it should have been Maggie's day off.'

'Oh, can I have it, Mr Faulds?' said Phyllis. 'It's not fair having a rotten old Tuesday for my free afternoon. Let me swap it, and I'll do Great Aunt Goitre and not complain – promise.'

'You're doing her anyway,' said Clara. 'It's your turn.'

'I've decided that Miss Rossiter should step into Maggie's free days,' said Mr Faulds. 'Sorry, Phyllis. Fanny, if that's all right with you.'

I could not have been more delighted, for Alec would be here by the following day and a free afternoon was more than I could have hoped for to spend with him. We had not arranged how to meet but later that evening, with the greatest imaginable fuss and uproar, Mrs Lambert-Leslie finally arrived. Mr Faulds went out to meet the lady, Stanley helping to ferry a great many bags and boxes up the front steps, Clara – caught on the hop – rushed upstairs with the water jug and hot bottle for her bedroom, Lollie rang down to ask if that was Great Aunt Gertrude arriving, Phyllis sped to her side to say that it was and her passenger got out of the motorcar, let himself in at the area steps and pushed a note for Miss Rossiter through the letter box. Miss Rossiter was in the servants' hall at the time and saw the three sets of legs come down with the note and go up again: one pair of legs in grey flannel bags and town brogues, four liver and white legs with soft fringes, and another four, long, smooth, beloved, spotted legs which brought a lump to my throat as I glimpsed them.

'Damned fellow brought his dogs,' Great Aunt Gertrude was saying, as I stepped into Lollie's boudoir with a tea tray, 'all the way from Perthshire with two tails whipping in my face. Pretty little spaniel and a Dalmatian bitch with even less sense than most. Tea?' she enquired, seeing me. I nodded and bobbed. 'Oh well, why not,' she said, 'as long as there's a drink on its way soon. And I smelled ham when I came in. Run down and get Mrs Hepburn to cut me a sandwich, would you, girl? And one for my niece. I don't like this peaky look of hers.'

No one, I thought, could describe Mrs Lambert-Leslie as having a peaky look. She was a large pink person, with plain features gathered all together in the middle of her face and a great deal of cheek and jowl and forehead around them. Her hair was white and fluffed up into a fan-shape at the front, leaving a sparse little bun, very neglected, at the back, just above her collar. It was not an attempt at a fashionable hairstyle which had gone woefully wrong, nor even a relic of some earlier arrangement which had survived and mutated as one often sees in ladies of a certain age. It was inexplicable and could only have been carried off by a woman of titanic self-confidence. Great Aunt Gertrude, needless to say, managed.

'Who was it who gave you the lift anyway?' said Lollie, and I was interested to hear that her voice was calm and sounded neither flat nor suspiciously animated. The doctor must have mixed up a magic potion out of his bag which had dulled her down and picked her up and left her in the middle. 'You didn't just stand by the side of the road and wave your stick, did you?'

'Wouldn't be the first time,' said Great Aunt Gertrude with a shout of laughter, 'but no. He's Millicent Osborne's sister Daphne's grandson. Dorset. Good family. Although there was something about him . . . I forget what now . . . came into an estate somehow that wasn't quite the thing. But it's a neat enough place. Of course, I only saw the drive and the hall, but you can tell a lot from gravel, I always say. And he's not married. So I've invited him for dinner. You were too young last time of course, but you can't hang about now. Here – girl! What are you standing there for? Sandwich, sandwich. And you can take the smaller of the two bags with the straps on downstairs with you. All that's for washing.'

I glanced at Lollie again as I left to see how well she was standing up to this extraordinary person and her outlandish suggestion, but either the doctor's powders were potent ones or she was too used to her aunt to be shocked by anything, for she gave me a mild smile to send me on my way and turned back to listen to the report of the journey which was just beginning.

I half expected a timorous knock or two on my door that night or the following morning, as one or other of the junior staff wrestled with their consciences and decided to give up their secrets. I even made sure that I was busy in the little laundry room so that I might not miss the knock when it came, and listened intently whenever I heard a pair of feet descend to the sub-basement. There was a great deal of traffic up and down for, as well as the usual commerce of the house and the extra burden of our exacting guest, Mr Hardy had indeed returned and all the servants trooped up to be grilled by him once more.

All I got for my pains, in the end, was a pile of rather limp underclothes – Lollie's (I drew the line at 'the smaller of' Great Aunt Gertrude's strapped bags which was not much smaller and was stuffed to bursting) – as well as a crick in my neck and very sore knuckles from scrubbing wet cloth between them. There was presumably some knack to this which Grant had neglected to pass on to me, but I consoled myself that dishpan hands, as they call them in the cold cream advertisements, were an authentic touch for Miss Rossiter and I should take them out on my free afternoon with pride.

After luncheon – haddock and egg pie, fried potatoes and pickled beetroot followed by steamed ginger sponge and custard – I tidied my hair, put on a cameo brooch and a pair of fine stockings, jammed my copious notes into Miss Rossiter's best bag and left by the area door, to meet Alec – as his letter had suggested and as was most fitting for a lady's maid on her free afternoon – under the Scott Monument in Princes Street Gardens.

I set off with head high and heart stout, but by the time I had crossed George Street – the spine of the New Town – and was descending again, my footsteps had started to falter as I imagined what I might see when I emerged onto Princes Street, with who knew what gangs gathered there and what scuffles brewing.

There were indeed a dozen or so men standing arm in arm at the top of the steps which led down to Waverley station, with perhaps a dozen more marching up and down in front of them carrying signs on sticks. Three policemen stood in the road, very still, simply watching, but they had their whistles between their teeth: even at this distance I could see the glint of the chains which fastened them to their breast pockets.

And how could three policemen stand still in the carriageway on Edinburgh's busiest thoroughfare on a Friday afternoon? Quite simply because aside from the little tableau they made with the pickets and the sign wavers, Princes Street was empty. Oh, the shops were lighted and open and there were customers going in and out, but very few, and they walked quickly with their heads down and their voices low and, besides, the pavement with its window displays and awnings and tempting doorways, which would draw the eye on any other shopping street but this one, is always – even on ordinary days – belittled by the great broad flat road and, on its other side, the green sweep of gardens falling away and then rising up to the jagged skyline of the Old Town and the hulk of the Castle Rock. Today, with the road deserted, tramlines still, bus stops unpeopled, rabble of motor lorries and taxicabs and horse carts gone like ghosts when the lamp snaps on, a handful of shoppers scurrying in and out with their parcels were like sand-hoppers on the tideline against the expanse of emptiness behind them, and so the emptiness was all one could see and all one could hear was the silence.

I felt a fluttering in my throat as my pulse quickened. I had laughed at Hugh, even at Harry, but this was no Edinburgh I had ever known, this was no country of mine, and just for a moment, I feared for us all.

Then I heard a shout from the other side of the street and, looking over, saw Alec silhouetted under the arches of the monument waving wildly at me. I looked to both sides for traffic – for one cannot suppress these instincts – and crossed the deserted street towards him, towards the whining, circling bundle of pent-up ecstasy on the end of the lead.

'My darling!' I sank onto my knees and let Bunty yelp and sniff and lick my hat and trample her paws all over the front of my coat and skirt and wipe quantities of her stiff white hairs onto me and wheel away to gallop off some of her joy and then come back to do it all again. Eventually she dropped down, rolled onto her back and wriggled this way and that with her eyes half-closed and her tongue lolling out of one side of her mouth and I stood, brushed myself and resecured my hatpin.

'Well, I can't compete with that for a welcome,' said Alec, 'but it is good to see you, Dandy.'

'And you,' I said, returning his quick hug. 'Hello, Millie.' Alec's spaniel, sitting primly at his side, waggled her bottom briefly.

'Shall we go down out of the breeze? I said, for it was rather gusty.

'If we can get past the doormen,' said Alec, pointing to the top of the steps where two policemen were standing shoulder to shoulder, their mouths set and their eyes grim.

Of course, both policemen stepped aside and one touched his hat as we passed them, and we descended to the lower level and claimed an empty bench, one looking down over the railway lines which emerge from the glass roof of the station and briefly bisect a portion of the gardens before disappearing into a tunnel which runs under the rest of them. Princes Street Gardens, I thought as I looked around, are at their best in May, crowded with tulips and pansies and wearing fresh new cloaks of green on the ground and in the air. (Later in the summer the green grass would turn yellow if it were dry or wear through to the earth from the tramp of feet if it were rainy, the green leaves of the trees would darken with smuts from the trains, the growers of the bedding plants would have outdone themselves for double and treble and quadruple begonias all of monstrous size and unlikely colour, and the benches would be dusty and sticky so that even if one were not actually sitting amongst picnic litter with spilled lemonade under one's feet, it always felt that way.)

'Very odd with no trains, isn't it?' said Alec. 'You get used to there always being a few chuffing away at the platforms. It's like being in a summer meadow today.'

'Apart from the shouting,' I said. From the station I could hear voices and what sounded like a drum being beaten in slow threatening time. I jumped as a particularly lusty yell reached our ears.

'Don't worry,' said Alec. 'There are so many special constables in the station there's hardly room on the tracks for the strikers and they were sharing out cigarettes and playing cards together when I looked in on them.'

'You went down there!'

Alec grinned at me. 'I told the bobbies I was a volunteer.'

'*Are* you going to volunteer?' I said. 'Do be careful.'

'I don't think so,' said Alec. 'I just put a ten-shilling note in the strikers' collecting tin at Platform 3, so it would be rather inconsistent. Oh, don't look at me like that! The Prince of Wales sent them a tenner. Now, Dandy – fill me in.'

I heaved in a huge breath, planning to expend it on the start of my tale, but long before I had decided where to begin I had to let it go all in a rush, for fear of bursting. The same thing happened with the second breath. Bunty, who had come to rest her muzzle in my lap, looked up at me with wrinkled brows and blinked at the draught.

'A hippo in a mudhole,' said Alec. 'Top marks.'

'Sorry,' I said. 'Very well, I shall try and you must make of it what you can. You knew already what sort of husband Pip Balfour was, but what I've discovered is that it wasn't just Lollie. *Everyone* hated him, with very good reason too, except . . .'

'Except?'

'Except . . . I don't know. I can't put my finger on it. Look, he forced his beastly attentions on several of the maids. Clara, the parlourmaid, a high-spirited colt of a girl, long legs, long nose – prettier than I'm making her sound, though – got the worst of it, since she, as she put it, "fell".' I saw Alec's puzzled frown and translated. 'Was made with-child, darling, which – at Pip's insistence, I should add – she successfully concealed with tightened corsets and bigger aprons.'

'Really? Is that possible?'

'You'd be surprised,' I told him.

'And what happened to . . . it?'

'It was stillborn. She crept off on her own to the attics, Alec, and never told a soul.'

'Dear God.'

'He also pounced on Eldry, the tweenie,' I continued. 'Rather an unfortunate girl. Pitifully plain, all bones and teeth. Edith Sitwell, except that she arranges her hair like a character from Beatrix Potter and so only draws attention to herself. Also Millie, the scullerymaid, *truly* a character from Beatrix Potter – round and pink and guileless, and by the way absolutely besotted by the most unattractive young man – Stanley, the footman.'

'What's wrong with him?'

'Fastidious,' I said. 'Faints at the sight of blood or the mention of it.'

'He can't help that,' said Alec.

'Also pompous, boastful, ostentatiously servile, insinuating and sanctimonious. I'd love to be able to suspect him, but no one who pales at a drop of blood on a pricked finger could have wielded that mutton knife, you know. And no one who wasn't innocent would dare to drone on so about what he knows and could tell.'

'What *does* he know?' said Alec. 'What *could* he tell?'

'Nothing, he's just one of those annoying hinters. He had good reason to revile Pip, all the same. Pip refused him leave to visit his father when everyone thought he was just about to peg out from TB. And threatened him with the sack if he went AWOL. And he'd do it too, because Phyllis, the housemaid – she of the pawnshop visit – was on warning for cheek and would have been out on her ear if Pip hadn't died. That was Phyllis's particular complaint. She can't even say, with any certainty, what it was she did, so one suspects she did nothing.'

'He just wanted rid of her? What's she like?'

'Delightful,' I said. 'Little impish, freckly thing with those very round blue eyes. Irish, perhaps.'

'Doesn't sound like the kind of girl one would cast easily aside,' said Alec, with rather unguarded honesty it seemed to me. 'Do you really believe she can't think what she did? Clumsiness? Breaking the Meissen? Pilfering? Corrupting the grocer's boy?'

'Well, pilfering is a possibility,' I said. 'I never did manage to work out where she got that seventeen pounds, after all.'

'That's not pilfering,' said Alec. 'That's theft. Fingers as sticky as all that would have got her much more than a warning.'

'Yes, but I wondered if perhaps she was in the habit of a little very minor pinching – the pawnbroker thought the rug and nightie – and then after Pip's death she swooped in and pocketed the seventeen pounds she knew was lying around.'

'But that would be senseless,' Alec said. 'To do something to draw suspicion towards one when one knew there would be policemen sniffing about.'

It did sound unlikely when he put it that way.

'Well,' I said, 'perhaps she did it to get the rug and nightie back, in case there was a search and they were missed. And then found. In the pawnbroker's.'

This sounded even less convincing and Alec was kind enough to pass on without commenting.

'So that's the young girls,' he said. 'And Stanley.'

'So let's have the rest of the men. Mr Faulds is more discreet about Pip's deeds than the rest but he didn't hide his feelings for a minute. Good news about the death, let's all stand together and what's next, was the order of the day.'

'Who's Mr Faulds?' said Alec.

'Oh! The butler,' I said. 'Faulds. Ernest. He's a dear. He lays down the law to the youngsters when he remembers but his heart isn't in it. Mostly he hands out drinks and instigates sing-songs. He has a music-hall background, you know, and is teaching young Mattie to play the piano. Now, Mattie is the hall boy, also a dear. White-blond hair, deep dimples and a stammer when he's nervous. He comes from a family of miners but had to give it up after an accident. Can you imagine, Alec, being trapped down a mine for hours? It's left him with a crippling fear of being alone in the dark and yet Balfour – blister that he was – insisted on Mattie waiting up in the dark hall to let his master in on late nights out. Similarly, John the chauffeur was left to sleep in the car countless times when Balfour might easily have organised for him to have a bed wherever. And he's the usual strapping type that people employ as chauffeurs too – not built

187

for curling up on the back seat. And as for Harry, Balfour's valet – well, there the tricks begin to get so silly they seem quite mad. Balfour stole the poor chap's clothes and gave them back with the pockets cut out.'

'Eh?' said Alec.

'I know. It's like something from a fairy tale. But actually, it makes some kind of sense when one considers that Harry is the resident communist.'

'Does it?'

'Well, you know, can't really make a fuss about his possessions since he thinks no one should have any.'

'A communist valet,' said Alec, as wonderingly as I had. 'Rather an odd choice of occupation, isn't it? Odd enough to be suspicious, do you think?'

'Hang on,' I said. 'I've forgotten someone. Faulds, Harry, John, Stanley, Mattie. Clara, Phyllis, Eldry, Millie and . . . Oh! Mrs Hepburn. Of course. Kitty Hepburn, the cook.'

'Interfered with like the rest of the girls?' said Alec.

'Not by Balfour,' I said. 'But she and Faulds have a bit of an understanding. In fact, they were together on the night in question and provided one another with alibis.'

'So does she have some other reason to have loathed Balfour?'

With a shudder I told him about the dead mouse in the goose and the other insults to her cooking.

'Hm,' said Alec. 'It's nasty – especially the mouse, which you might easily have kept to yourself, Dandy; I may never eat roast goose again – but it's better than what happened to all the young ones.'

'Ah, yes,' I said, 'but there's the thing, Alec. One of the many things. It didn't.' Alec waited, eyebrows up and head cocked to one side. 'It didn't happen to all the girls. It didn't happen to Phyllis. The prettiest one and one who – as housemaid – would have been in and out of the family rooms all day every day and would have been readily . . . well, accessible, I suppose, if that weren't a repugnant thing to say.'

'And yet, Edith Sitwell . . .' said Alec.

'Eldry, yes. Far less attractive and – since she was the tweenie – hardly ever in any place where Pip Balfour could pounce on her except in the early mornings to light the fires. Not to mention Millie, who was *never* anywhere he could easily have found her. She spends her days in the scullery with the cook – her Auntie Kitty, no less – planted in the kitchen between Millie and the rest of the world.'

'Auntie Kitty?' said Alec. 'Is that a term of affection?'

'Well, Mrs Hepburn is kind to all of them, but she is actually Millie's aunt.'

'And yet she brought her niece into a household where the master was known to be a ravager of maidens and kept her there?'

'Exactly,' I said. 'Another thing that makes no sense at all. As well as the question of how he got close enough to Eldry and Millie and, in poor Eldry's case, why? And if Eldry then why not Phyllis? And . . . and . . .'

'What?' said Alec. 'What is it? You're having one of your ideas, Dandy, I can tell. Start speaking before it goes away again.'

'Shut up before you chase it away!' I said. 'It was what I just said about how he got close enough to the girls to . . . Aha! That's it. It's Mattie. How on earth would the master of the house come to know that the hall boy was afraid of the dark? How could that be? What do you know of your hall boy's fears and demons, Alec? Hm?'

'I don't have a hall boy,' said Alec. 'What about you?'

'Well, hall, boots and under-footman combined,' I said. 'And all I know is that his name is George and he sniffs. Do you see?'

'I do,' Alec said. 'There's something very odd about all of this.'

I was nodding furiously.

'The story of the stolen clothes too,' I said. 'Even if Balfour got into the carriage house and out again with his valet's clothes, where would he put them so that his valet couldn't just take them back? Are we saying he hid them in the attics? Or got a luggage locker at the station or something? The whole story just makes no sense.'

'No more sense than the idea of a communist sympathiser being a valet in the first place,' Alec said. 'This Harry might be making up his story to fall in with the others. And doing a pretty poor job of it.'

'But it's not only Harry,' I said. 'That's the point. It's all of them. Take Stanley and his father.'

'No, no, I must disagree with you there,' said Alec. 'That little tale was only too believable. Oh, what is it?' I had clearly been unable to prevent a look of smug triumph from spreading over me.

'Just this. I don't believe it. I don't believe that Stanley would have gone within a mile of someone with consumption. Stanley? Clamouring to go to the bedside of someone coughing up blood into a hanky? Never. I mean, have you ever seen anyone with advanced TB?'

'Of course I have,' Alec said. 'And I can imagine what it's like to be stuck in a dark mine too. Except in my case it was a dark foxhole and it wasn't TB making my sergeant cough up blood and he didn't have a hanky either. And we were being shelled, just to add to the fun.'

'Sorry,' I said, reaching out and giving his arm a quick squeeze. Bunty put her paw up on my knee. If ever there are tokens of affection being handed out, she likes to make sure she gets one. 'I had no idea. You never speak of it.'

'Would *you*?' Alec said. 'But at least we got called heroes for it. And given medals and parades. Not like Mattie and his brethren – told to do it again, for longer hours and less pay, and called nasty names for objecting.'

'Have I told you recently what a lovely man you are?'

'You hardly ever tell me,' said Alec. 'And very sketchily when you do – no details. So Mattie has my commiserations for his long nights in the dark alone and even the chauffeur – nothing makes one as miserable as trying to sleep when one is really chilled to the bone.'

'Hah!' I said. Bunty took her paw back and sat with it in mid-air watching me.

'A problem?' asked Alec.

'It's all beginning to fall into place,' I said. 'Or out of it rather. I *knew* there was something wrong when John told me. And it's this: Lollie said that she and Pip had only spent one night apart in all the time they were married and that was when he went to Paris in an aeroplane. Unless she's lying I don't see how he can have left John languishing in the motorcar all these times he's supposed to have. And Lollie said something else to me in the same conversation. What was it? Oh, why don't I write things down?'

Alec laughed, sharply enough to wake the placid Millie who was lying over his feet.

'*You?*' he said. 'Not write things down? What, pray tell, is in that bulging article you've lugged along with you today?' He nodded towards Miss Rossiter's bag, which had a few corners of writing paper peeping out around its straining clasp.

'Well, yes, all right, but I wish I could be like a policeman and keep my notebook on my knee, rather than having to store it all up until I'm alone again. She was talking about Pip and she said he never went away on his own and he . . . what?'

'Would never snip the pockets out of other chaps' clothes?' Alec was teasing but I smiled and clapped my hands together.

'Yes!' I said. 'Well, almost. Thank you, darling. What she said was that he was no trouble, not fussy, never complained about anything.'

'Such as?'

'Well, I'm thinking about his food, really. If a man sent back his dinners often enough to enrage his cook, how could his wife say he was easy-going? And do you know what else? When I mentioned the mouse in the goose—'

'As you do with surprising regularity,' said Alec. 'Once would have been enough for me.'

'Lollie didn't know what I was talking about.'

'Are you sure?'

'Would you forget it?' I said. 'Could someone mention mice and geese together to you ever again without you remembering?'

'So,' said Alec, nodding slowly to acknowledge my point, 'what we're saying is that we don't actually believe a word that any of the servants said about him?'

'And we don't have any proof that Lollie's story has a scrap of truth behind it either, when you get right down to things. And for what it's worth, the two times I actually met Pip Balfour I couldn't believe it was the man I'd been hearing about.'

'But Lollie *was* scared enough to come to you,' Alec said. 'No, I think Mrs Balfour's tale of threat and treachery is solid enough, just not any of the others. Dandy, what do you suppose is going on?'

Once again, I was counting off the residents of the servants' hall on my fingers and did not answer him. Was that really true? Could it be? Had we argued away every single instance of Pip Balfour's villainy in inconsistencies and implausibilities? Even that most likely, most everyday, villainy of lust and its brutal fulfilling? I did not believe that anyone who would ravage Eldry would overlook Phyllis, and I did not believe that Mrs Hepburn would let her niece stay in a house where the master had harmed her, but that still left one of them.

'Clara,' I said. 'There's nothing to contradict what Clara said and what he's supposed to have done to her is the easiest to believe and – oh God, Alec – it might be the easiest to check. Clara thinks she might have swaddled the baby and hidden it, up there in the nurseries. Lord, I'm going to have to look.' I shuddered at the thought of it. 'If someone had told me five years ago the kind of thing I'd find myself doing, I'd have—'

'Thinks she might have?' said Alec, interrupting me. 'What do you mean? Doesn't she know? If she can't keep her story straight why should we believe her?'

'She was *in extremis*,' I said. 'She has a vague idea that she went to the furnace but she also seems to remember hiding a wrapped bundle. Neither memory is clear, under the dreadful circumstances.'

'Well, I suppose I can sympathise with that,' said Alec, and I thought of the foxhole again.

'She might have done both, one after the other,' I said, 'or she might have hidden the little body and burned soiled sheets. And anyway, her confusion – her derangement – makes it all the more likely that she could have been turned murderous. Yes, I'm sure of it. I think what Clara told me was true.'

'And . . . what? The others made up all the rest of it like a haystack to hide the needle in? In advance? Because they knew that she was going to kill him and they supported her? But if he was not the fiend to them all that they said he was why would they?'

'I've no idea.'

'And why in the name of heaven didn't she just leave? Before the baby, after the baby, whenever. Why didn't they all just leave? Why, if any of what they say is true, is there a single servant left in the place?'

'I don't know,' I said. 'I thought we'd got somewhere, but it's only made the whole thing more mysterious than ever. If the stories are true, why didn't they leave? If the stories *aren't* true, why didn't they care that Pip was murdered? And could Clara have done it? The police surgeon reckoned it was a man and Clara has anything but masculine hands.' We sat in silence for a while. 'Although, it's not true to say that no one ever left,' I said at last. 'Maggie the kitchenmaid left and Miss Abbott who was Miss Rossiter's predecessor took off too.'

'So what was different about them? What did he do to them that's worse than the fates of the others?'

'I don't know what was done to them. But they are different, in point of fact. They witnessed Pip Balfour's will. And let me tell you, Alec, the will is another barrel of eels altogether.'

'A barrel of eels?'

'Isn't that the phrase? A sack of monkeys? A box of worms?'

'Dandy, you're gibbering,' Alec said. 'Tell me about the will.'

Five days I had been in the servants' hall at 31 Heriot Row but it had changed me. I could not, I told Alec, contemplate even beginning on the will without a pot of strong tea and a plate of buns, thickly buttered and spread with jam. I only regretted that I had no hip flask with me from which to slop in a good dose of something more strengthening still.

12

Crawford's tearooms were doing brisk trade, as might be expected on a Friday afternoon when all the public houses had been closed, and we had to wait, shuffling forward in the queue every few minutes and trying to ignore the plaintive moans of Bunty and Millie who had been left tied to a lamp post but who could still see us and, more importantly, could smell cakes. We could not even carry on a conversation of any usefulness while so many silent fellow queuers pressed in on us before and behind. At least the pause gave me time to compose my report, though, and when we were finally shown to our place I was ready.

'Sorry about the table, sir,' said the waitress, peeping up at Alec and smiling. She had swept one practised glance over me and had clearly concluded that Alec was free to be simpered at. 'But it's all we've got.' The table was indeed small, in a far from commanding position at the side of the empty band stage and, I noticed as I sat, none too steady on its feet.

'Not at all,' said Alec. 'This is perfect. Exactly what we're after.'

The waitress, thinking she had misjudged the matter – for why would anyone want to be so secluded except for wooing – gave me a look of insulted envy, Alec one of pity and flounced away.

'You should have flirted back,' I said. 'She'll pretend to have forgotten us now.'

'Good,' said Alec. 'Now then, Dandy.'

I told him everything; all about George Pollard and Josephine Carson, the two years' delay, the break-up of the household and the casting of Lollie into the harsh, cruel world.

'Golly,' he said, when I was done. 'Is someone checking it? The earlier marriage, I mean. And has this Pollard been found?'

'I'd be very surprised if he let himself be found,' I replied. 'I rather think he must have done it. With the help – of course – of what the spy stories call "someone on the inside".'

'If he knew,' said Alec.

'Ah, but I think he did,' I said. I was still feeling rather proud of this piece of deduction. 'I think that at the very least he was in touch with Pip Balfour, that they had met and spoken. They were cousins, but not long-lost ones – or if they had been they'd found one another again.'

'Because of the high esteem and all that,' said Alec.

'Well, that's part of it,' I said, trying not to look crestfallen, 'but also – and this has only just occurred to me – because he left the fortune to George Pollard outright. Just to him. Not to his heirs and successors and there was no mention of what would happen if Pollard was no more.' Alec was frowning at me. 'I mean to say, darling, if you were to leave your last penny to someone you'd have to know that he was still alive to get it.'

'That doesn't make any sense at all,' Alec said. 'You've been misled by hindsight, Dan. You're thinking about it in entirely the wrong way.'

Of course, it was at that moment that the waitress reappeared with her little notebook to take our order. I was vaguely aware of Alec listing our requirements but even though I left it to him and thought furiously I could still see no problem in my reasoning by the time she had gone.

'Oh come on, Dandy, this isn't worthy of you,' he said when he turned back and saw my knitted brows. 'Why didn't Pip Balfour bother with survivorship and all that?'

'Because he knew Pollard was alive and well,' I said. 'I told you.' We stared at one another in silence for a minute until Alec gave in.

'And knew that Pollard would still be alive and well when he himself died because he knew he'd be dying soon?' I could feel the flush beginning and did not even bother trying to hide it. Besides, I was soon distracted from my embarrassment by the new puzzle Alec had unearthed out of the old one.

'So . . . why would he have written it that way?' I said. Alec shrugged his shoulders.

'Makes no sense to me,' he said. 'Seems completely insane.'

'And therefore completely in character,' I said. 'Another of Pip Balfour's silly little teases? *Did* he mean for Lollie to find out about the will and spend her life worrying over it? If so, we're back to the theory that George Pollard – not to mention Josephine Carson – doesn't exist at all.'

'But we just decided we didn't believe in Pip's teases, didn't we?'

'And I was sure that this George Pollard character must have got into the house and done the murder.'

We were sitting in blank stupefaction when our tea tray arrived and the little waitress looked delighted; she must have thought our tryst had descended into a quarrel.

'Oh, heaven!' I said, as Alec poured a thin stream of straw-coloured China tea into my cup. 'Mrs Hepburn's brews could be eaten with a knife and fork. And no milk, thanks. No, no sugar, nothing.' I blew into my cup, took a long fragrant sip and smiled at him.

'What about these two maids who witnessed it?' Alec said at last. 'Perhaps they'd be able to throw some light on matters?'

'How?' I said, remembering what Mr Faulds had thought about the unlikelihood of them seeing anything except the signature itself.

'I don't know,' Alec said. 'I'm casting around for anything, really. Odd that they should both have left, though. If they knew what was in the will and they knew George Pollard – from his coming to the house, perhaps – and one of them told Pollard for a cut of the money . . .'

'But he didn't come to the house,' I said. 'None of the servants remember ever hearing of him. And anyway, if Miss Abbott or Maggie had done that, they'd never have left. They'd have stayed. To let Pollard in. Because someone must have. No, I think the fact that the witnesses both left their jobs is far more suggestive of the will being a joke on Lollie. Pip wasn't ready for her to find out and he made a concerted effort to get rid of the two people who could tell her that he'd written a new will in case she somehow persuaded the solicitor to let her see it.'

'And he wrote it in March,' Alec said. 'Is that significant? Did anything happen in March?' I shrugged. 'And what was he waiting for, do you suppose? When *was* he going to tell Lollie about it? Was there some significant time to do that for any reason?' I shrugged again.

'Was there any significant timing in any of it?' I said, and then I stopped chewing my mouthful of bread-and-butter.

'Dandy?'

'Yes,' I said, through crumbs, 'there was. Miss Abbott and Maggie witnessed the will. Miss Abbott left Lollie shortly afterwards. Maggie left on Saturday. Pip was killed sometime during Monday night, as soon as both witnesses were out of the house. I've no idea what it means but it can't be a coincidence, surely.'

'Well, they must be found,' Alec said. 'All three of them. Abbott, Maggie and Pollard.'

'If there is such a person,' I reminded him. 'He's popping in and out of existence like a jack-in-the-box.' I put my elbows on the table and my head into my hands and groaned. 'I thought you'd clear everything up for me! I thought if I got up into the air and talked it all through, things would be revealed in simple outline. And you've only made it madder and more confusing than ever and – worst of all – I know there's something not right that I was closer to realising before today than I am now. I almost got it lying in bed last night, or was it this morning? It's something to do with lying in bed anyway. Now it's completely gone.'

'What do you mean, "up into the air"?' said Alec, which was very kind of him, for he might easily have taken offence at my sharing out of the blame in the way I had.

'Hm?' I said. 'Oh, just life below stairs, you know. I hadn't expected it to feel so literal, but to eat and work and sleep in a sub-basement with a whole house pressing down upon one is not conducive to leaps of reason. I just think if I could climb a high hill and look down I'd be able to see more.'

'Well,' said Alec, 'I don't think we can manage a hill, but we can certainly get you up into the air. Look, you wrap two cakes in your hanky and I'll wrap two in mine.'

'Four cakes?' I said. 'Didn't you have any luncheon?'

'One each,' said Alec. 'You – as befits the boss of this little outfit – have been marvellously focused but I'm far more easily distracted and I can't stand it any more. Listen.'

When I did, I could hear the duet from the pavement: low, sustained howling and a series of percussive little yips.

'She's a very bad influence on Millie,' said Alec, grinning. 'Come on, let's take them up the Scott Monument and tire them out for the evening.'

The Scott Monument – erected in honour of Sir Walter specifically and not, as I had long believed, to the general and misspelled glory of the Scots race – was a kind of airy turret in High Victorian Gothic style, not attached to anything but just rising up out of the grass as though some ecclesiastical architect had lavished all of his attention on the decorative touches but forgotten to build the cathedral itself. 'Better than the Albert Memorial' was the best one could say about it, and it was smaller, too – and sooty black, like everything in Edinburgh which cannot brush itself down or send itself to the laundry – so at least it did not draw the eye.

I had never climbed up it before, had in fact congratulated myself on not letting my sons find out that one could (for they would have badgered me to death on every shopping trip if they had known), and should have realised, from the fact that I had never noticed anyone else scaling its heights, that the staircases were hidden away at its core. As Alec, Bunty, Millie and I toiled up the darkest, narrowest, steepest spiral staircase imaginable, breathing in the sharp stink of damp, tarry stone, I could not help thinking that I could have reproduced the experience in the six floors of Number 31 in far greater comfort, and saved my sixpence.

'I'm expecting a helter-skelter at the end of all this,' said Alec, sounding rather out of breath, and I laughed. We had arrived at the first landing and while Alec investigated the little room in the centre I paraded the terrace which wrapped around it. At least, I tried to; one could not actually walk all the way round because at one corner there was a door blocking the way.

'It's locked,' I called to Alec.

'Probably a cupboard,' he replied, but I had crouched down to peer into the keyhole and I could see light.

'No, it goes through,' I said and rattled the handle. 'It's certainly locked though. I wonder why.'

'Never *mind*, Dandy,' Alec said. 'There's air and light as requested.'

'Not nearly enough,' I said, shaking my head. 'Let's go up again.'

The staircases got even steeper and narrower as they rose and by the time we stepped out onto the little terrace at the crow's nest I did indeed feel a lift in my spirits to be looking across the rooftops at a far horizon instead of out of my barred window at the cherry tree.

'I think I might be missing Perthshire,' I said. 'I think after all these years of distant forests and hilltops it's finally got to me.'

'Right,' said Alec, who was still at the top of the stairway, examining the stonework and ignoring the panorama. 'Now that you're up here looking down,' – at this he gulped – 'what do you see?'

'Well, give me a minute,' I said, 'it's not like putting a penny in a slot machine and getting a bar of chocolate.' I craned around the corner, trying to see beyond a jutting buttress. 'You must get a good view to the Old Town too.' I put my foot on a kind of stone skirting board and hoisted myself up.

'Dandy, do be careful,' said Alec, and put a firm hand around my arm, squeezing really quite tightly. 'There's a pathway round – you don't have to clamber.' I looked down at him. His lips had disappeared and although he had not looked tired a moment ago there was now a purple patch under each eye.

'Are you all right?' I said. 'You look very peculiar.'

'Heights,' he said, through gritted teeth. 'I always forget.

Now for God's sake come down, or I shall faint and you'll have to roll me down all those stairs again.'

I hopped down and stood beside him, feet squarely planted, while his colour returned to normal.

'Now, please try to concentrate,' he said. 'You told me this idea was in reach when you were lying in bed. Is it about Pip's bedroom? Something you saw near his bed? Something out of place in Lollie's bedroom?'

'Hush,' I said. I was looking down at the view again now, at the long empty street, its tramlines shining like snail trails, and the few people scurrying about on the pavement, all looking very similar under their hats from up here. I could not tell which of the rooftops was 31 Heriot Row, for the fronts of the houses were hidden behind the trees of Queen Street Gardens, but I trained my gaze at where I thought the house must be and thought hard. I almost had it. I could almost touch it, just out of reach.

'Say it,' said Alec, very loudly in my ear.

'Say what?' I said. 'Alec, I'm trying very hard to think and you're making it harder.'

'I was trying to help,' he said. 'I thought if you just blurted something out perhaps it would turn out to be the clue that unlocks it all. Psychology, you know.'

'The locked door,' I said. Alec tutted but I shoved him to shut him up. 'Not the one downstairs. I mean, The Locked Door. In general. That's what this case would be called if it were Sherlock Holmes's. The case of the locked door. That's what I hear last thing at night and first thing in the morning, lying in my bed; Mr Faulds, locking the doors. And Pip locked his bedroom door. And Lollie can't sleep in a room with a locked door. And the mews door was locked in the daytime and one assumes that the back mews door – the garden door – was locked up at night. And Mattie had to stay in the vestibule to open the locked front door for his master and then lock it again after him. There's something about all these locked doors.'

'How would he get out?' said Alec. 'On the late nights, I mean.'

I shrugged. 'I suppose he went out earlier, when the house was still open or at least when Faulds or Stanley were still about.'

'No, not Pip,' Alec said. 'The hall boy cowering in the dark. What's his name? Mattie. After he let Balfour in, how would *he* get out to go to bed in the carriage house?'

I leaned over and kissed him roundly first on one cheek and then on the other.

'That's it,' I said. 'Alec, you are a genius. That is it. How did Mattie get through a locked and bolted door in the night? That's what's been pricking at me.' I beamed at Alec but his answering smile was so uncertain as to be hardly deserving of the name. 'What?'

'Nothing,' he said, most unconvincingly, 'only hadn't we agreed that the story of waiting in the hall wasn't true? No more true than the TB visit or the trouser pockets or, indeed, the will? I mean, it's good to have these loose ends cleared up but it doesn't get us anywhere we hadn't got already.'

'I'm not so sure,' I said, and put my hand up to stem the tide of argument which began. 'I know. I know what we said, but Mattie certainly knows something, I'm sure he does. Clara, Phyllis *and* Mattie. When I asked them all about locked doors and people creeping around in the night yesterday dinner-time the two girls stared at me as though butter wouldn't melt in their mouths and missed poor Mattie trying to catch their eyes to see if he should speak up or stay silent.'

'Well, those three *would* be rather jumpy, wouldn't they,' Alec said. 'If Clara's story is the only real one and the other two are just made up.'

'Although, to be fair, John was discomfited too, Stanley squirmed like a worm on a hook, and Millie and Eldry blushed to the roots of their hair.'

'Are you sure?' said Alec. 'Are you absolutely sure you weren't imagining things? Or wait: perhaps they were all staring and blushing because they had heard the cook and butler creeping around in the night and couldn't believe you were being so indelicate as to ask about it.'

'I'm still going to lean very hard on Mattie,' I said. 'Those two girls are as tricky as a bag of knives – Lord, I simply cannot remember that expression! – but Mattie is the weak spot. If I manage to get him on his own he'll never be able to hold firm against me.'

'You sound very fierce,' said Alec. 'I'm glad it's not me keeping secrets. What can I do to help you, here on the outside, as it were?'

'I should have thought that was obvious,' I replied. 'Find the missing persons. In case – as I fear – the police get nowhere with it. Start with George Pollard.'

'No such man,' said Alec.

'Well, check at least. And the same for Josephine Carson. That should be easy enough. There will be a marriage certificate and Pip was twenty-six so you'll only have to look through about eight years' worth at the very most.'

'Oh, so breezy when it's not you!' said Alec. 'Only eight years' worth indeed. What if they weren't married in Scotland? How am I supposed to get to London to Somerset House? On a donkey? And what if they were married abroad?'

'Maggie and Miss Abbott then,' I said. 'I'll ask Lollie where the lady's maid moved on to but I know that Maggie went to North Berwick to work for a baronet. She should be easy enough to find.'

'North Berwick?' said Alec. 'Might as well be the North Pole right now.'

'Nonsense,' I said. 'Harry told me this morning that there's petrol to be had again. He was complaining, of course, saying that "that toad Churchill" – not kind but not inaccurate either – has got soldiers delivering petrol all over the big towns. Actually, he was saying that there are vans marked "Petrol" delivering – oh, I don't know – larks' tongues and long-stemmed roses, but there must be some petrol getting through too. Enough for North Berwick, anyway.'

'So what are we doing rambling around public parks and up and down monuments then?' said Alec, heading for the top of the stairs as though there were not a moment to lose.

'I didn't know Maggie and Miss Abbott were crucial before we talked it all through,' I reminded him.

'Can't think why,' he said. He was plunging ahead, already out of sight, and surprisingly for one with a fear of heights he seemed to have no qualms about racing down a dark, twisting staircase with a lively spaniel tugging him to go even faster. I, on the other hand, had never been more sorry for Bunty's poor training and when she had almost pulled me off my feet for the second time I am afraid that I unclipped her lead and let her slither down to catch up Alec and Millie, with only a 'Watch out!' to warn of her arrival.

I was returning early, thanks to Alec's eager departure, and turning the corner of Heriot Row I met Clara sauntering towards me, swinging a duffel bag. She stopped when she saw me.

'You're back sharp,' she said. 'Are you no' feeling well?'

'Just run out of things to do,' I said. 'I've no family to visit and my friend that I was meeting had to go.' She gave me a pitying look at that; one surmised that she would never run out of amusements on a May afternoon. 'Where are you off to?'

'The baths,' said Clara. 'It's not my day or anything but Mrs Hepburn said I could go. My afternoon free is on a men's day, see? So I'd never get there else.'

'Mrs Hepburn is very kind to you all,' I said. I had fallen in with Clara and was walking away from the house again.

'Are you . . . ?' Clara began, eyeing me warily. 'Are you chumming me, Miss Rossiter?'

'If you don't mind,' I said. Clara gave a tight smile and said nothing. She could not have sent a stronger signal that she dreaded Miss Rossiter's awkward questions if she had tried.

'Of course not,' she said, 'but they don't hire out towels. You can borrow mine, though.' I laughed and shook my head.

'I don't have a bathing suit with me,' I said.

'Oh, they hire out costumes,' she said. I tried not to show what I thought of this idea.

'Yes, a very kindly soul is our Mrs Hepburn,' I said again. 'I'm not surprised that Mr Faulds is captivated, are you?'

Clara had one of those faces upon which every thought passing through her mind is played out. Now, an impish amusement and natural taste for gossip fought with an equally natural suspicion (and disapproval) over an upper servant like me sucking my teeth with a lower servant like her about my equals and her betters. Or perhaps the disapproval was for two such ancient persons as Mrs Hepburn and Mr Faulds giving in to passion.

'Well, I was surprised, Miss Rossiter, to be honest,' she said. 'They've been awfy discreet. And I thought I could tell when Mr Faulds liked a girl – you know – *that* way. I mean, he's always had a right soft spot for Phyllis and he never hid it better than a boil on his—'.

'Nose?' I said quickly. The usual expression had always struck me as rather nonsensical; a boil where Clara had just been about to place one is hidden for much of the time in the ordinary way of things.

'Miss Rossiter, you're terrible,' she said. 'I thought when you first turned up you were a right old stick-in-the-mud.'

'It's my face,' I said. 'And these clothes, but I assure you I'm not, dear.'

We tramped on for a while, down sweeping crescents and along endless quiet rows of tall houses, until it occurred to me to wonder where we were heading. After all, Mattie was set to walk nine miles to his village on the morrow.

'Where exactly are these baths?'

'Glenogle,' said Clara. 'Stockbridge. We're nearly there.' She cleared her throat. 'Miss Rossiter?' I waited, trying not to perk up too visibly. 'Do you really think they'll put mistress out? And the rest of us? Mr Faulds says no.'

Now, in truth, Alec and I had all but decided that the will was nonsense and would not stand, but if Clara needed an incentive to do her duty, then *my* duty was clear.

'Absolutely,' I said. 'I'm afraid. Unless the police can catch the man who did this – if it's Cousin George, that is – then it's a grim lookout for all of us.'

'Poor mistress,' Clara said. 'Poor us an' all. I'll never get another parlourmaid's job in a house with all that company. Not in Edinburgh, anyway.'

'No indeed,' I agreed. 'I shall be very lucky to be a lady's maid and not a cook-general.'

'Can you cook, then?' said Clara. 'I cannae even do that. I'll end up in a factory. Or a shop. Living back at my mammy's in the middle of nowhere. She ayeways said that Balfour job was too good to be true.'

'Let's hope that someone saw something and will speak up, then,' I said trying to sound like justice raining unstoppably down, but only succeeding in sounding like Nanny.

'I suppose,' said Clara, 'but even if it brings no good to mistress or to me, I just can't see myself helping to punish whoever killed him. I'd have killed him myself if I'd thought of it. And I just don't give a—'

'Tinker's cuss?' I said.

'You have a wonderful way with words, Miss Rossiter,' she said. 'As good as Mr Faulds when he gets his music-hall patter going.'

'But you're not protecting anyone in particular, Clara, are you?'

'Like who?' said Clara.

'It might not be that you saw someone covered in blood leaving master's room, you know,' I said. 'It could be something else entirely. Someone who perhaps . . . oh, let's say . . . suddenly had extra money she – or he, of course – shouldn't have.'

'What money?' said Clara. 'Where does money come into it?'

'Well, if someone opened the door up to let George Pollard into the house, she – or he, of course – might have been paid for it. That's all.'

Clara had stopped walking and turned to face me. 'But no one could open a door without somebody else hearing,' she said.

'True,' I said. I looked along the street and then back at her, standing there in front of me like a statue. 'Shall we go on?'

'We're here,' said Clara. 'This is it. Come in and have a wee look. See if you fancy it for another time.'

We were on one of those Edinburgh streets, of which since the city clings to the side of a steep hill there are many, where sunlight never reaches down between its high walls and the road is carved deep like a fissure. To the natural darkness was added an extra measure of gloom from the dark, red stone of the baths, mossy and wearing little sprouts of fern like buttonholes here and there. Inside, beyond the turnstile, the tiled passageways were just as dark and even damper and smelled of floor soap and chlorine. The chlorine, at least, was a smell which had nothing but happy memories for me, making me think of lidos in the south of France and a hotel Hugh and I had stayed in once in Italy which, despite the endless sunshine, had a covered swimming pond under a glass roof beyond its foyer – for the Italians, one supposed, who could find it too chilly for the sea and could look glamorous in cashmere wraps when I and the other Englishwomen were hot and red in limp cotton frocks with our waves melting.

The pool at Glenogle was under a glass roof of its own, but was otherwise as unlike the pond at the Miramalfi as my own tin bath before my bedroom fire at home. Wooden changing cubicles were ranged up and down its sides, most of their doors left open onto inelegant heaps of discarded clothes and, on hooks outside them, the kind of demoted bath towels – thin and grubby – that mothers hand out to children to take swimming. In the pool itself, a flotilla of girls and women bobbed around looking, in their rubberised bathing hats with the straps firmly buckled under their chins, like a squadron of pilots after an unfortunate water landing.

Clara disappeared into an empty cubicle and pulled the door closed behind her. I sat down on one of the wooden folding chairs laid out for spectators and prepared to wait and then to watch Clara for a polite few minutes before leaving but, when an arc of water sent up by some athletic girl diving in a few feet away from me soaked my skirt through, I thought the better of hanging around at all. I could see Clara's head over the door of her cubicle and, since she was already wearing her cap – dark red and most unbecoming, I surmised that she had finished changing and went over to say goodbye to her. When I popped my head over the door, however, it was to discover that, to my horror, she had put her hat on first and was only now struggling into her suit, had in dreadful fact only got it unrolled as far as her hips. I stepped back very sharply, almost skidding on the wet floor.

'Oh my dear! I do apologise. How dreadful you must think me.'

'Eh?' said Clara, peering out at me over the top of the door, her bare shoulders just visible. 'Why? What have you done?'

'I – um – I didn't mean, that is, well, if you are not the modest sort, then nothing. Forgive me.' Clara only laughed and shook her head and I felt all of a sudden very old. I remembered clearly the river bathing with my sister at home, as naked as eels in the sunshine, and the late-night sessions in the dorms at finishing school in Paris with Daisy and Freddy, which we spent 'trying on': trying on one another's dresses and shoes and nightgowns and even underclothes, for my own calico shifts and knickers – my mother's penchant for Nature stopped at no threshold – sent the other two into shrieks of laughter as they paraded up and down in them and I, of course, thrilled to the unaccustomed touch of machine lace and milanaise as I modelled theirs. But it had been years since anyone except Grant had witnessed my dressing and undressing, and she with a sheet held high between us and her face turned away from the sight of me, and I had forgotten the easy ways of girls.

I had not, however, forgotten everything about girls. I had not forgotten what they looked like, and as I left the echoing hall and the damp corridors and re-emerged onto the Glenogle Road I was slowly coming to terms with what I had just seen in the changing cubicle. That girl, Clara, had never had a child. She had the untried, untrammelled body of a child herself, a bud, still waiting for flowering and fruitfulness but untouched by it so far.

And so, I thought to myself as I paced along, not one single one of the stories of Pip Balfour's treachery was left standing.

I listened at Lollie's boudoir door for a long time before knocking, thinking that if Mr Hardy were not in there I would rather not announce myself and get embroiled with Great Aunt Goitre. It was impossible to tell, however, whether *anyone* else was in there with the lady: her voice boomed on and on, asking no questions and pausing for no replies. She might have been talking to her own extraordinary reflection in the glass, for all one could say. When at last I tapped and entered, though, she did draw breath.

'Knocking on doors, Walburga?' she said in tones of high astonishment. 'Where do you find these servants of yours?' Lollie did not reply (from her wan face and unfocused gaze I could guess that the endless pronouncements and rambling anecdotes had long since beaten her into hopeless silence). Of course, *I* could not come back with a retort although I had to bite my cheeks to prevent one, for a boudoir on the bedroom floor is not a public reception room and knocking on its door is perfectly proper. I scowled at Great Aunt Goitre who, unfortunately, saw me.

'And don't you give me that kind of look, young woman,' she said. 'That's exactly what I was saying, Walburga, my point in a nutshell. The very reason I've always resisted hiring a companion. The only ones I've ever come across are pert and lazy and I'm not the woman to pay good money and see nothing for it.'

'No, Aunt,' said Lollie.

'So you see, when you come to make your home with me we shall both be the better for it,' continued Great Aunt Gertrude. 'And I shan't expect any more than the most ordinary gratitude. Nor shall I be selfish, my dear.' Here she gave a simpering little smile, quite horrid to behold. 'I still move in the highest Episcopalian circles and there's many a curate and vicar sent overseas all alone who'd be happy to have a steady wife along with him.'

I cleared my throat and broke into the stream then, thinking that I had to crack that will and save Lollie from such a future.

'Can you tell me where Superintendent Hardy is, madam?' I said.

'Pip's room,' whispered Lollie. I bobbed and opened the door to leave.

'Oh, and . . . can you tell me, madam, where did Miss Abbott go when she left? Do you know?'

'What? What?' said Great Aunt Gertrude, unable to bear having to listen to snippets of conversation she could not join.

'Abbott?' said Lollie. 'Why . . . ?'

'I have some of her belongings to send on,' I said.

'Can't you ask one of the other maids?' said her aunt, almost at a roar. 'Where were you trained, girl?'

'Mrs Ruthven,' Lollie said to me, ignoring her aunt. 'In the Braids.'

I entered Pip's bedroom with some diffidence, expecting to find the superintendent standing there, communing with the spirit of the dead and hoping for inspiration, and unsure whether he would want a witness while he did so. The room, though, was empty, the bed bare, even the mattress gone. I shivered, not just from the cold – the window was thrown wide to air the place – but because ever since the wards a stripped bed means death and looks both pitiful and brutal in its bareness, conceding defeat and moving hygienically on to other things.

I finally ran Hardy to ground in Pip's *other* room, the library on the first floor, following the scent of his cigarette smoke and finding him seated behind a desk which was strewn with papers he was studiously ignoring. He lay back in the chair and blew smoke straight up at the ceiling.

'Miss Rossiter,' he said, looking down his nose and making great exhausted-sounding hisses out of both parts of my assumed name.

'Mr Hardy,' I said. 'How goes the investigation? Have you discovered anything new? Have you found a George Pollard?'

'Hah,' said the superintendent. 'A George Pollard? *A* George Pollard. I found six and then I stopped looking.'

'Where?' I said. He clearly thought that the unearthing of six suspects was an embarrassment of riches, but to my mind having only six suspects when that morning we suspected the population at large was a great stride forward.

'Well, when I say I've found them, I mean I've found their names. Found out that they exist. But not in Gloucester. Oh, no, that would be far too easy. Where did I put my notes?' He stirred the papers on the desk with his pen and picked out a loose sheet covered in inky scribbles. His neat notebook was forgotten, it seemed. 'Now then. Balfour's great great great great grandfather, James—'

'The banker?' I said.

'Just so,' said Hardy. 'He had a brother who moved away to take care of one of the family's many business interests, and this brother had a daughter who married a Pollard and had a son named George. This George Pollard had a George of his own, as well as a Philip, who himself had a son named after his brother: George.'

'But they'll all be long dead, Superintendent,' I said. 'You just need to follow the pieces of string to the end and see where they lead you.' He was shaking his head, and so I subsided.

'George's George had a George to go with Philip's George – these are second cousins, now, same generation as Balfour's grandfather although older since the original daughter married her Pollard very young – and between them they had a pair of Philips and a pair of Jameses too, and every James and Philip and George in time had a George of his own. Making six George Pollards in total who could all be called cousins of Philip Balfour. They're every age between seventy and forty-five. All married, none dead yet as far as I can tell.' He threw the paper down. 'I'm used to facts being a help to me,' he said. 'I can't be doing with this – it's like a comic operetta.'

'And what about the next generation?' I said. 'Surely six married Georges must have had some sons.'

'They did,' said Hardy. 'Three. Including two Georges.'

'Just two?' I said. 'The great days of Georges are over then. Don't you count these as cousins? What would they be? Third cousins? Or cousins twice removed? I never know the difference, do you?'

'Oh, I'd have to count them all right,' said Hardy, 'but they're dead. The war. There are no more Georges to bring yet more Georges now unless one of them remarries and starts again. I tell you, I'm sick of the lot.'

'And how did you find all this out since yesterday?' I said. 'It's miraculous when your men are so stretched.' I looked around at the tall cases of leather-bound books. 'Is there a family history?' I asked. 'Is it all set out in one of these volumes here?'

Hardy looked up very sharply at the bookcase behind his head.

'By God, there'd better not be,' he said. 'I found out by telephoning to my sister-in-law in St John's Wood and sending her in to Somerset House to do my work for me. I'll never hear the end of it.'

'She must be a remarkable scholar,' I said. 'I always thought it took weeks of toil and wheedling of the porters to trace back as much as all that.'

'I had her sworn in,' Hardy said. 'She's now a special constable of the London Constabulary, Northern Division. So she got the curators or whatever you call them to hop to it and got the job done. She'll probably refuse to turn in her armband ever again. She's one of these new women. Well, I beg your pardon, for you're probably one yourself. But I can just see her out on the street tonight, boxing strikers' ears and telling them to go home to their beds.'

'She sounds like Great Aunt Gertrude,' I said. 'Have you met that lady, Superintendent?'

Hardy nodded and crossed his arms – an involuntary attempt to defend himself against her, I thought.

'You know she's offered Mrs Balfour a home?' I said. 'We have to overturn this will.'

Hardy, with a determined glint in his dark eyes, gave the sharp single nod I had come to know, but then immediately after it he groaned.

'Back to the Georges, then,' he said.

'I would bet that all of them have sound alibis,' I said. 'Having a George Pollard – no current address – named in the will when there are so many of them to choose from sounds exactly like

Pip Balfour. Like one of the horrid little jokes he played on his wife.'

'And everyone else,' said Hardy.

I took a deep breath. This was going to take some explaining, and Hardy was not going to like it.

'No, Superintendent,' I said. 'Not everyone else. Not anyone else. Listen to what I worked out this afternoon.' To his credit, he did, clearing up the mess of papers on the desk as I talked, saying nothing, taking no notes, just nodding now and then. When I had finished he offered me a cigarette, took one himself, lit both and stared at me.

'So what the devil are they up to?' he said at last. He sat up and looked around himself, ready to take hold of anyone he could find and shake it out of them. 'Pretending that a man who's cruel to his wife is cruel to his servants too, when he's not. Are they covering for her?'

'Not all of them. But going by significant looks and general squirming when I told them about Pollard, I'd say the kitchen girls are sitting on some sort of secret. The valet and chauffeur too. And the footman. Not Mrs Hepburn and not the butler. But definitely – most definitely – Mattie, Clara and Phyllis.'

'Ah, Phyllis,' said Hardy. 'Our friend with the bulging purse.'

'Did you get anywhere with the mystery of the seventeen pounds, by the way?'

'She denied the whole thing,' said Hardy. 'Acted as if the very idea of a pawnshop was beyond her. And I couldn't pursue it without "blowing your cover".' He looked tremendously proud of having delivered this choice morsel of vocabulary. 'I'm delighted to hear that you think it's worth me pressing her again.'

'And Clara too,' I said.

Mr Hardy rested his cigarette in the ashtray, laced his fingers together, then turned his hands palms outward and flexed them with a series of sharp cracking sounds. 'I shall press with the greatest pleasure. I don't like the feeling that someone has got one over on me; it's not a feeling I'm used to. And' – he unlaced his fingers and picked his cigarette up again – 'while I'm not used to having to do everything myself these days – I've been a superintendent ten years now – I'm beginning to remember what a good way it is to get things done.'

'Quite,' I said, wondering if he knew how terrifying he was when he spoke that way, lips thin and brows lowered. 'But if you will permit me, I have a plan to press Mattie myself and I'd like to pursue it. I think he might dissolve if one pressed him too abruptly, but I'm going to put him in a vice and turn the handle so slowly he won't know what's happening until all of a sudden the truth pops out.' Mr Hardy looked terribly impressed, as well he might, for such a plan would have been pretty hot stuff, but in reality I was only trying to make sure that he stayed away from Mattie and left him to me. The dissolving was only too likely and, besides, I could not consign that stammer and those dimples to a man whose knuckles cracked in such a fearsome way.

13

'Mistress says you're off out again today, Miss Rossiter,' said Phyllis at breakfast the next morning. It was eight o'clock and, tea trays delivered to Lollie and her aunt, bedroom fires lit, morning room and breakfast room swept and ready, we were gathered around the long table in the servants' hall for bacon, eggs and ebony tea. Mrs Hepburn was grumbling and apologising in equal measures for the state of the food, which had come from 'thon useless contraption' now that the range was cold, but it all tasted the same as ever to me.

'I am indeed, Phyllis,' I replied. 'Mistress has Mrs Lambert-Leslie to attend to her and she's sending me on an errand.'

'Aye, but in the wee car though,' said Phyllis. 'All right for some.'

'You'd better not be blacklegging,' said Harry.

'And what would Miss Rossiter and mistress be blacklegging?' said Mr Faulds. 'You're tilting at windmills, Harry boy, with this strike. You're getting a . . . thingumijig . . . over it.'

'Monomania,' I supplied.

'That's the one,' said Mr Faulds. 'You've a proper head for knowing, Fanny.'

'But here's another thing,' said John. 'How come you're getting to drive Goitre's wee car instead of me taking the Phantom? First I've heard of a maid doing that, I can tell you.'

'Great Aunt Goitre to you, John,' said Mr Faulds, causing much laughter.

'I'll be next,' said Phyllis. 'Nothing I'd like more than to tootle away down to Portobello on my free day. Good on you, Miss R.'

'I'm not driving it myself,' I said. 'Mrs Lambert-Leslie's chauffeur is accompanying me.'

'Ohhhh,' said Clara. 'Great Aunt Goitre's "chauffeur". I see.'

'I don't know,' said Mrs Hepburn. 'It's always been a free and easy house and no one happier for it than me' – here she flushed a little – 'but these things can go too far.' She gave me a stern look and although she said no more I took her meaning.

The evening before, after all, I had committed a below-stairs solecism far greater than tucking up with the butler when no one was looking. I had slipped out to a tryst with – as we used to call them in my mother's day when they were absolutely forbidden in the servants' hall at home – a follower.

We had been ensconced as usual, Mr Faulds, Mrs Hepburn and I in the armchairs, Mattie at the piano, the girls clustered about the lamp sewing, the boys spread around the table reading and laying out Patience, when the sound of the area gate opening drew our ears. John, who was nearest the window, leaned back in his chair and craned upwards.

'Who's this then?' he said. 'Some toff with two dogs. What's he after?'

I rose and hurried out to the passageway.

'I'll see to him,' I said over my shoulder. 'I was needing to stretch my legs anyway.'

Mr Faulds, in his shirtsleeves, was happy to let me and, although Stanley huffed and puffed a little about whose job it was to greet visitors, he did not go so far as to stand up and race me for it.

'What on earth are you thinking, Alec?' I hissed when I had opened the door to him. 'Shush, Bunty! There's a good girl. You can't just tool up here and knock. Miss Rossiter will be put out with no character.'

'Needs must,' said Alec. 'I had to talk to you. I've been to North Berwick.'

'And?' I said. 'Settle *down*, Bunty.'

'Can't you come out for a minute?' said Alec. 'She'll never shut up unless we walk up and down. Really, Dandy, I have to agree with Hugh sometimes – you have spoiled her.'

I drew the door over behind me and, hatless and in my cardigan, followed him up the steps and out onto the street.

'Well?' I said when we were a few steps away from the house and the servants' hall window, at which I was sure all were gathered by now. 'You've been to North Berwick and . . . ?'

'Maggie,' said Alec, 'never arrived.'

I halted and was pulled off my feet by Bunty. Alec caught my arm.

'She was expected on Sunday,' he said, 'but didn't show up. No sign of her on Monday either and when Sir George's housekeeper – Sir George Finlayson; he was, as you suggested, easy enough to find – telephoned to the Balfours on Tuesday it was to be told of Pip Balfour's murder. After which, understandably, the housekeeper didn't think she could press the matter any more.'

'I don't like the sound of this,' I said. 'She needs to be found. And we must check on Miss Abbott too. Lollie told me she went to a Mrs Ruthven in Braid Hills.'

'Where?'

'South Edinburgh, beyond Morningside – geographically *and* socially. Terribly genteel.'

'And has she been heard of? Did she write to anyone to say how she was settling in or anything?'

'I don't think she was particular chums with any of them,' I said. 'No one has said much about her since I arrived.' We had got to the kiosk on the corner of Darnaway Street now. 'Do you have any change? No time like the present and I've got the most horrid feeling about this.'

I asked the girl on the exchange for Ruthven of Braid Hills and was put through quite promptly. The bell rang out five or six times and then was answered by a servant of exquisite reserve and even more exquisite South Edinburgh vowels.

'The Ruthven residence,' she intoned. 'To whom am I speaking to?'

'Hello,' I said. 'My name is Gilver and I'm calling in connection with a Miss Jessie Abbott, who I believe began employment with you a few—'

'Well, you believe more than you've leave to then,' said the servant, abandoning the reserve and the vowels both. 'And if you're a friend of the besom you can give her a message from me and tell her she'd no business leaving my mistress in the lurch that way with no more than a scrap of a note to excuse her.' Alec was watching me and I shook my head at him as I listened.

'I don't suppose you kept the note?' I said into the mouthpiece.

'What? Who is this?' said the voice. 'What's it got to do with you what anyone in this house did with anything?'

'If you can lay your hand on it,' I said, 'I think the police' – I kept speaking through the inevitable squeak this produced – 'might want to see it. Superintendent Hardy will no doubt be ringing you up or coming to see you. Perhaps you might warn Mr and Mrs Ruthven.' I put down the receiver and Alec and I stared at one another until someone waiting for the telephone knocked on the kiosk window and made us both jump.

'Right,' said Alec. 'I'll go straight to the police station and tell Hardy – if he's still there at this hour. Or try to get whoever is there to ring him up and tell him. You go back – and for goodness' sake keep your head down.'

'Certainly not,' I said. 'There's plenty I can ask about Abbott and Maggie leaving: if anyone remembers anyone hanging around or if either of them voiced any worries.'

'I absolutely forbid it,' Alec said. 'Unless you promise me that you'll say nothing, I shall go back into that kiosk, tell all to Hugh and get you hauled off the case and back to Gilverton before you can blink.'

I could not help smiling at this, but he was not to be swayed.

'Two women have left that house and never been heard of again,' he said. 'Superintendent Hardy can ask all the questions in the morning.'

I gave Bunty her second passionate farewell of the day and stood with my hand on the area railings watching them carry on along the street. Before they disappeared from view, though, a thought struck me and I raced after them calling out Alec's name.

'Get Hardy to ask who the housekeeper at Berwick spoke to,' I said. A third farewell and they were gone. I descended, let myself in and returned to the servants' hall and the inevitable teasing. My pink cheeks and breathlessness were, of course, the result of the last-minute sprint but there was no use telling that to Phyllis and John, who joshed me mildly for the rest of the evening and were rewarded with smirks from the others. As to the equally inevitable questions about the identity of the toff with two dogs, my brainwave had been to pass him off as Great Aunt Gertrude's chauffeur, mystifyingly not staying in the carriage house while his mistress was *chez nous*. This only set off more questions and caused more ribaldry in the end, as they wondered aloud what he wanted with me and hazarded opinions as to whether he were really a chauffeur at all.

'He's too posh,' said Clara. 'Did you see his shoes?'

'And too good-looking,' said Harry, causing John to kick him under the table.

'Maybe he's her "companion",' said Phyllis.

'Or a relation down on his luck,' said Eldry.

'Oh, you mean like a "nephew",' said Phyllis, which puzzled Eldry and made John and Harry hoot with laughter. Mrs Hepburn, with a frown towards Millie, shushed her.

'Great Aunt Goitre?' said John. 'Never!'

So, in the morning, when I revealed that my errand was a shared one with this mysterious stranger the giggles and wondering looks were no surprise and I showed great stoicism as I endured them.

Still, I was glad that there was no one about in the mews when I emerged from the carriage house to find Alec, Millie and Bunty waiting there in Great Aunt Gertrude's Sunbeam: he did not look much like a chauffeur.

'Back or front?' said Alec as he got into the driver's seat. 'Where *would* Miss Rossiter sit?'

'She'd sit in the front with her bag clutched on her knees,' I said. 'But I'm going in the back, of course. The dogs can go in beside you. Now, Mattie turned left at the top of the steps, so I imagine that he'll be heading straight up the Bridges and out of town on the Peebles Road towards Penicuik.'

'Yikes,' said Alec. 'The east end and the Tron? Fifty-six arrests there last night, Dandy.' I gulped and he took pity on me. 'It'll be quiet enough this morning again, though. And the police won't bother the likes of you and me.'

The police did not, it was true, but the combination of a man in front in no kind of chauffeur's uniform and a woman in the back in no kind of hat for a grand lady rang false in the eyes of the strike stewards who were waiting halfway over the North Bridge. This did not occur to me until afterwards; at the time what happened was as inexplicable as it was terrifying. Two men, grim-jawed and cold-eyed, flagged Alec down and a string of them stepped out and joined arms across the road in front of us. Feeling my pulse begin to thump, I looked around for a policeman or even a special constable but saw none.

Alec wound down his window.

'Taxi service is it, sir?' said one of the men who had pulled us over. He wore an armband with initials on it and had some kind of badge on his coat lapel but I did not recognise either of them.

'Private journey,' said Alec, effortlessly slipping into the same laconic style.

'Oh aye?' said the man. 'Of what nature?' He was looking me up and down with a disdain I had not encountered since the death of Nanny Palmer and even she saved it for when I had been very bad in ways which left damage not soon mended. I could feel my initial panic begin to recede and be replaced by anger.

'Visiting friends,' said Alec. 'This lady' – he jerked his head back at me – 'doesn't care for dogs.'

'Aye, I thought the dogs were a nice touch,' the man said.

'Now look here,' I began, but Alec talked over me.

'I'm not a working man,' he said, 'but I wouldn't break your strike. You'll just have to take my word for it, I'm afraid.'

'You'll not mind us jotting down your number and taking your name then?' said the man.

'We most certainly wou—' I said, unable to believe my ears, but again Alec spoke over me.

'Alexander Osborne of Perthshire,' he said. 'But Dorset originally. I was once in a clay pit when I was a boy – just for an hour, you understand, just to see it.' The man had jerked his chin up at this and he gave Alec an even more searching look. 'But an hour was enough. I wouldn't break your strike.'

After another long pause, the chap jerked his head at the rest of the men and they broke apart and returned to the pavement.

'Not a minute on the day!' they chanted, as we started up again. 'Not a penny off the pay!' Alec, pulling away, touched his hat and gave a toot on the horn.

'Well!' I said. 'I would not have believed that possible.' Alec said nothing. 'Where are all these celebrated specials when one needs them? I thought you were going to have to hand over hard cash for a moment there.'

'If I had offered him money, Dandy, we'd never have got through,' Alec said. 'And I'd be on every TUC blacklist in the land.'

'Really?' I said. 'Do you think so? You seem to have got a very romantic view of miners from that hour in the clay pit years ago. Or was that just a story? Splendidly quick-thinking if it was, I must say.'

Again he said nothing, his silence going strong until we were well onto the South Bridge, where we saw another collection of men at the side of the road outside the university. 'We might just slip straight through here if we're lucky, Dandy,' Alec said, 'since they're concentrating on the student volunteers, but you'd better get in the front seat beside me anyway, just in case. I'm sure that's what made the last lot think I was a taxi.'

'No need,' I said. 'There he is now – look.'

Up ahead of us I had glimpsed the white-blond hair and the determined set of the thin shoulders and indeed it was Mattie, weighed down by two huge baskets from Mrs Hepburn, half a mile into his nine-mile trudge home to his mother for the day. Alec touched the horn as we drew up beside him and Mattie smiled at the two dogs who were standing on the front seat, with their heads nosily out of the side window. Then he frowned in puzzlement as he glimpsed me. I opened the back door.

'Hop in,' I said. 'I'm coming with you, Mattie. Mistress's idea – mistress's orders, in fact. We'll take you there and back and have a nice chance to talk without those girls listening.' I gave him a bright smile and although his face fell he knew that argument would be fruitless. Pushing his baskets in in front of him, he joined me.

After that, although we were stopped by another three checkpoints before we made it out of town, Mattie was the golden key which unlocked all doors. He only had to mention his surname – MacGibney – and say where we were bound and the linked arms unlinked themselves and rose in the air to wave us on our way.

'Very good of you too, sir, madam,' said another of the badged leaders, not half so grim-jawed or cold-eyed as the first, now that we had Mattie to our credit. 'And you tell your grandad that Wullie Armstrong was asking for him, son, eh?'

Between all these stops, there was less time than I had imagined to pin Mattie back against the upholstery and begin to extract from him the secrets I was sure he was keeping, but leaving him to stew with nothing more than my confident assertions and vague threats for his mind to work on would, I told myself, lead to a greater unburdening in the end.

'It's the doors, you see, Mattie,' I said. 'Mistress and I and Superintendent Hardy have been talking over and over this terrible business and we know that there's something fishy going on about the doors.'

Mattie gave a fearful look at the back of Alec's head.

'Don't worry about Mr Osborne,' I said. 'He's helping Hardy get to the bottom of all this for mistress. Anything you want to tell me you can safely say in front of him. And if you don't tell me today, it'll be Superintendent Hardy tomorrow, maybe in the house but maybe in the police station. So be a good sensible boy. I know you know more than you're telling.'

'You're wrong, miss,' said Mattie. 'I d'ae ken nothing about what happened to master that night. Not a thing. Swear on my life.'

'You know something you *think* is nothing to do with what happened to master,' I said. 'But you must tell me – or Mr Hardy tomorrow; that's your choice – and we will decide whether what you know is important.'

'I d'ae ken nothing,' he said again.

'We're here,' said Alec from the front seat. 'Best leave it for now.'

We had to pass right by the colliery to get to Mattie's village and, although Alec cruised along quite unconcerned and Mattie even waved out of the window at his acquaintances, I could not help drawing back into shadow at the sight near the gates to the mine. There were perhaps a hundred strikers there: wiry, hard-bitten, dirty-looking men in caps which hid their eyes. Some were singing in rough and raucous voices and some were silently smoking thin, home-made cigarettes but all had their fists clenched and were beating time against their legs and stamping their feet too. Once again, there were no police to be seen, only three men in the grey suits and round collars of clerks, whistles around their necks and sticks in their hands, watching the strikers with impassive faces from inside the chained gates.

We passed this dreadful tableau and followed a bend in the road to find ourselves at one end of three long rows of brick terraces with washing strung between them, filling their little yards. It was unlike any village I had ever seen: no shops, no real streets, and no church spires nor inns nor schoolhouses – nothing except those three long straight rows set down at the edge of some rough fields. Women began to appear at the doors and come out into the yards at the sound of the motorcar, and when Alec pulled up and Mattie stepped down one of them rushed forward and gripped his arm.

'Whae's this?' she said. 'What have you done now?' She looked too old to be the mother of the boy but was surely too young to be his grandmother and no one else would grip his arm and shake him in that way.

'They're chums, Mammy,' said Mattie, standing up well to the grabbing and shaking I thought; clearly it was no more than he was used to. 'Miss Rossiter is one of the maids at ma work and Mr Osborne is mistress's auntie's chauffeur that's gave me a lift.'

Mattie's mother let go of his arm and brushed his hair back, just once and rather briskly, by way of an affectionate greeting. I felt a flush of guilt at my first reckoning because, on closer inspection, she was probably younger than me, only rather tired and ill served by her coiffure and her toilette in general. She had Mattie's fairness, and such looks take careful managing in the middle years.

'And look, Mammy,' Mattie said, dragging one of the baskets out of the motorcar. 'From Mrs Hepburn. Cakes and pies and cheese and all sorts.'

At this a few of the neighbour women who had drawn close to watch, shifted from foot to foot and looked sharply at Mrs MacGibney.

'Well, that was good of her,' she said. 'That's the wifie that's the cook, eh no? That's very kind. Well, you take one and maybe Mr Osborne would take the other one and get them over to the institute for sorting.'

The women who had been watching her stepped back a little then and seemed to let go of a collective breath. Mrs MacGibney did not miss it and she turned on them.

'What?' she said. 'Did you think I would jist . . . Tchah!'

'I have a few bits and pieces in the boot too,' Alec chipped in. 'Where is the institute, Mrs MacGibney? Perhaps I could just drive right to its door.'

Unseen by us all, a man had joined us, a fair-haired, stringy man, resting on a crutch and with one trouser leg swinging empty below his knee.

'Bits and pieces o' whit?' he said. 'We'll have none of your blacklegged muck in our village. Who are you, anyway?'

Alec went around and threw open the boot. The women clustered in and the man with the crutch, surely Mattie's brother, hobbled over to peer at a perfect cornucopia of loaves, waxed butcher's parcels and bottles of beer.

'It's all from the Co-operative Society,' said Alec. 'And I've got the chit if you want to see it. I told them it was for you out here and they let me take as much as I could carry.'

The wiry man pushed his lips out and in for a minute or two and then, tucking his crutch further under his arm, he held out his hand to shake Alec's.

'John MacGibney,' he said. 'Much obliged, brother.' Then his face finally cracked into a grin. 'It was the beer that swung it, mark you.'

'Now, get you away in and say hello to your grandad, Mattie,' said Mrs MacGibney, 'and I'll get over to the gates and get the sorting committee off the picket to see to this lot. We cannae leave meat to spoil, the warm day it's getting.'

Mattie ran ahead into one of the cottages, taking the dogs (they had been a great hit with him), but I dawdled, keeping step with John MacGibney on his crutch.

'Is it as bad as all that then?' I said. 'Already? Are there no shops nearby?'

Mr MacGibney gave me the kind of look one would bestow on an idiot child.

'Mr Mair that manages this place shut the shop when he locked us out on Monday,' he said. 'And between the two wee shops in the toon there' – he gestured over the hills with his crutch although no sign of a town could be seen – 'one willnae serve any of us – it's one of the Scott chain and Mr Scott plays golf with Mr Mair – and the other one's full of blackleg stuff they've got they bloody students bringing in from Leith so it would choke us. Pardon me, miss, eh?'

'So you've no food?' I said.

'Not so bad as all that,' he said. The way he spoke told me that his pride was pricking him and I kicked myself. 'The Congress have been good to us – sent a Co-op van out on Wednesday and the weans get their piece and milk at the school but it's no' long running out again.'

'I knew the stories of striking teachers weren't true,' I said. 'Yesterday's bulletin said the teachers were more likely to be spreading propaganda for Churchill than coming out in sympathy.'

Young Mr MacGibney gave me a sideways look and for the first time I saw a trace of Mattie's fine looks about him.

'You've been reading the bulletin?' he said. 'And you a lady's maid.' We were halfway along the row of cottages now – the front row facing out onto the fields and hills – and John turned in to an opening between low walls and pegged across the few feet of tiled yard which made the front garden of the MacGibney residence. The door was open onto a small porch and in it, hung on nails, were two sets of clothes, black as soot and smelling like it too, three cracked and blackened boots resting below them. There were sheets of newspaper pinned to the wall behind to keep the distemper clean.

I edged past the bundles and stepped into a small kitchen-cum-living-room where Mattie was standing in front of a fireplace range, still holding the dogs' leads while Millie and Bunty submitted to a thorough patting – what, in parts of Scotland, with some accuracy, they call a 'good clap' – from an old man sitting there.

If I had seen him in the street I should have guessed at a sailor, from the white beard and the two layers of knitted jerseys, one buttoned tightly over the other and a woollen scarf tucked down inside both. Something about the curve of his pipe had a nautical air too, unlike the usual straight cob pipe of the Perthshire villager I was used to seeing at home. But whenever he coughed, as he soon did and continued to do throughout our visit, it was the cough of a miner; deep, reaching, painful to hear (let alone to produce) and not a souvenir one could possibly have brought home from a life in the salt breezes.

As soon as the paroxysm had passed, he put his pipe back in his mouth and looked up at me out of two very small, very round black eyes (I found it hard to resist the fancy that they were little nuggets of coal pushed in amongst the wrinkles and shining there).

'And who's this fine lady you've brought home to us, Mattie?' he said.

'Fanny Rossiter, Mr MacGibney,' I said, bobbing a curtsey. 'One of the maids.'

'I'm Mr Morrison,' said the old man. 'Trudie's faither, but call me Grandad, hen, like everyone and you'll no' go far wrong.'

My smile was not merely a performance of Miss Rossiter's, judged to be required and delivered accordingly. For one thing, my own grandfathers were a distant memory and I had not used the word for many years. For another, I could not help warming to the easy mucking in and shaking down of the lower orders as I had found them. There were proprieties to be observed, it was true, but it was far from the minefield I had foreseen. Grandad Morrison's next words confirmed my view.

'Aye well, you've picked a bad time to come looking for a bun,' he said to me, 'but there's tea to spare, so you get it made like a good girlie and I'll take mine black with three sugars, please.'

'Grandad!' said Mattie. 'Miss Rossiter is mistress's lady's maid. She disnae even make her own tea in the house, never mind here.' But I had taken off my gloves and, grunting a little, had heaved the enormous black kettle off the range and over to the sink to fill it. I was determined to make a good job of this, for the MacGibneys might have tea, but I was sure they did not have *anything* 'to spare' and I would not be the one to waste what there was. I had just balanced the kettle on the edge of the sink to rest my arms when Mrs MacGibney's voice came from behind me.

'What?' she said. 'You've nae need to be tipping that water oot, it's this morning's and it's fine yet.'

'Of course, of course,' I said, flustered. 'I wouldn't dream of such a thing. I was going to fill right up and make a good potful.' Of course it was at that moment that I noticed the lack of any tap spouting out into the little china sink under the window, noticed the two tall cans standing on the wooden draining board at its side, realised that there was no piped water in the MacGibney kitchen and saw that I had just, with my assumption that there would be, played the grand lady far worse than if I had sat down, crossed my ankles and snapped my fingers for my tea. Mattie's mother had two patches of red across her tight cheeks as she took the kettle out of my hands, set it back on the range and topped it up from one of the cans, all without speaking.

'So, what can we dae for you?' said John, ending the silence at last. 'What brings you out here the day?'

'Was it not you driving the car then?' said Grandad. 'I thought you'd given wee Mattie a hurl.'

'I came with Mattie,' I said, 'because mistress didn't want him to be alone. He's been very upset.' It was the only thing I could think of in time.

Mrs MacGibney stopped with a half-full bottle of milk in mid-air (she had been sniffing it to see if it were fresh enough to put in our tea).

'What's wrong?' she said. 'What's happened noo?'

The old man made a noise almost like spitting and John shook his head at Mattie.

'You need to toughen up, wee brother,' he said. 'If you cannae frame tae work at this, what's left for you?'

'It's no' that,' Mattie said, speaking softly and aiming his words towards the floor.

'It's the murder,' I said.

'Murder?' said Mattie's mother. Grandad removed his pipe and sat with his mouth hanging open.

'I assumed you would all know,' I said. 'Mr Balfour – the master – was murdered on Sunday night. I'm sorry. I naturally assumed that you would have heard by now.'

'Heard how?' said John. 'We've had no paper since the *News* shut down.'

'But surely it was on the wireless?' I said. 'It was so brutal. I can't believe it wasn't reported on the news.' Of course, this was the water tap all over again. After I spoke, I looked around the kitchen for a wireless set at which to gesture, and took in the rough table and chairs, the makeshift curtains shutting off the box-bed in the corner, the tin bath hanging from a nail on the back door.

Mrs MacGibney, with a transparency which tied a knot inside me, went to stand with one hand stretched up to rest on the chimney-piece above the range, where a walnut-wood clock, highly polished, sat between two china dogs facing one another from each end, the three precious objects together forming the only sign of luxury in the entire room.

Thankfully, Alec interrupted the silence before I was forced to think of what to say. He entered with three bottles of beer clutched in one arm and gave John MacGibney a broad wink.

'Your father and the others insisted,' he said. 'These haven't gone on the book at all and nobody's complaining.'

'Mattie's too young for beer,' said Mrs MacGibney.

'Of course he is,' said Alec. 'The third one's for me.'

14

My stock rose a little when, after the tea and beer had been drunk – and I did quiet penance by insisting that I took my tea without either milk or sugar and drinking the horrid stuff to the last drop without a shudder – I volunteered to go with Mattie on an expedition to pick gooseberries, which Grandad had been nagging his daughter about all week but for which Mrs MacGibney did not herself have time.

'Aye, well, you've your washing to do, I'm thinking,' the old man said, but his daughter stuck her chin out and shook her head at him.

'I am not taking they work claes and washing them,' she said. 'They get washed every other week and they've only done one. It would be bad luck and I'll not do it.'

John gave a mirthless laugh and explained it to me.

'Ma and the other wifies think if they wash the black claes and put them away it'll be like saying there'll never be work again. So there they hang stinking the house out.'

'Nothing wrang wi' the smell of coal,' said Grandad. 'That stink brought your mammy up and it brought you up too.'

'Oh aye,' said John, flipping his empty trouser leg. 'It did the world for me.'

'Let's go then, Mattie,' I said, standing. 'We can take the big baskets you brought with you. No harm in being hopeful.'

'And I'm going back over to talk to the men,' Alec said. 'There might be another wee message I can run while I've got the car here today.' I stared at him. I had known for some time that he paid more heed to his servants than was proper, and I knew that he found the Scots tongue more delightful than did

I, but to hear him talk of running a wee message was a new departure again. None of the MacGibney clan, however, seemed to mind his patronage and the three of us – leaving Bunty and Millie behind with their new friend and his energetic caresses – exited together.

The gooseberries were to be found along the side of the railway line some three fields distant and so off we trudged, Mattie carrying both baskets, one over each shoulder so that they formed a shell across his back, as though they might be armour against me.

We passed a collection of shaggy little ponies which were being patted, fed tufts of grass and – in some cases – ridden upon by a troop of small children.

'I don't suppose they mind the sudden holiday,' I said.

'Except their food's locked up down in the stables and we've no' much money to buy more with,' said Mattie. I gave up looking for a silver lining then.

'Right then, young man,' I began. 'I am going to give you the benefit of the doubt and say that you don't realise the import of what it is you know. You will not be punished for withholding it, I assure you, but you must tell me.'

'I went to my bed and went to sleep and got up and the first I knew at all was when Eldry come doon the stair in the morning like a ghostie and tellt Mr Faulds to get the police,' Mattie said.

'All well and good,' I replied. 'I believe that. But it's these nights when master was out – the nights you told me of, if you remember – something about them is puzzling me.' I waited but Mattie said nothing. We had reached the edge of the first field and were taken up with clambering over a post-fence for a moment or two. 'How did you get out?'

'Eh?' Mattie said, in that infuriating way that children do.

'After master returned and you locked up behind him, did you knock up one of the girls or get Mr Faulds to open up? And lock up again behind you?'

'Eh?' he said again. 'The girls did nothing.'

'Well, someone must have locked and bolted the kitchen door or the door in the sub-basement,' I pointed out to him. 'Surely, you didn't leave the house open all night?'

Mattie was looking at me with an expression of apparently genuine puzzlement on his face.

'That would be daft,' he said.

'So . . . ?' He simply shook his head and then returned his gaze to the ground where the going was rough and needed a little attention. 'And how did you get into the carriage house?' I asked him. 'Did you have a key? Isn't that door bolted too?'

'There's a key in it,' he replied. 'Or – well – hanging up beside it in the passageway.'

'But how did that help?' I asked him. 'How did you get in if the key was on the other side?'

'I can't remember,' Mattie said, almost as infuriatingly as just saying 'eh'. 'I'm confused. You're tying me up in knots, miss, and I d'ae want to say the wrong thing and get anybody into trouble.'

'Yes, you are in a tangle, aren't you?' I replied. 'Perhaps this question will be easier for you.' Mattie's eyes were wide but he kept his head up, even if he did have the appearance of someone waiting for an axe-blow. 'How did master ever find out that you were scared of the dark, Mattie?'

'He—' The look of puzzlement came back into his eyes. 'I d'ae ken,' he said. 'That's daft too, miss, eh no? That cannae be right.' We had stopped walking now and were standing in the middle of the field like a pair of statues. 'Or you know what it is,' Mattie said at last. 'It's just different there. It's all . . . different. And here it's hame and it's all fields and that and things are no' the same so's you cannae remember what it's like when it's . . .' I was nodding, because although his stuttering attempt to explain was far from eloquent I recognised it as kin to the feeling I had had with Alec the previous afternoon when I had wanted to get up into the air, where I could see things, like Mattie was suddenly seeing things, out here in the field, in the open.

Not too far off from us was the unmistakable ridge of a railway siding, a few children dotted about its slopes with sacks in their hands, busily picking at the bushes growing there.

'Let's get the berries for your mother,' I said, 'and come back to all of this on the way home.'

Mattie's eyes, I was astonished to see, filled up with tears until they were brimming and he shook his head roughly to scatter them before they could roll down his face.

'You're being dead nice to me,' he said. 'And I hate having to be no' nice back, but I cannae tell on . . . anybody that's been just as nice and let them down. I never wanted to let anybody down, ever.'

I had to tread very carefully now.

'Your mother and grandfather,' I said, 'and your brother too, even if they are not always . . . nice, as you call it, even if they are not always kind, they do care for you. And just because someone else is kind, Mattie, that person does not necessarily care any more deeply. Certainly no one who *truly* cares for you would ask you to keep secrets for them which weigh so heavily upon you.'

'They don't,' he said. 'They're no' heavy secrets, miss, honest injuns they're no'. It's me keeping my mouth shut that's making you think they are.'

Inwardly, I was cheering, but on the outside I remained calm and kept the kindly look on my face. Being nice to Mattie was what would swing all this in my favour, I knew. I turned and walked to the edge of the field where a chestnut tree most obligingly provided both shade from the sunshine and some canker-swollen roots for us to sit upon. Mattie followed me like a gosling, shrugged off the baskets and sat down.

'I really, really, really hate being all on my own in the dark, miss,' he said. I nodded and even put a hand out to squeeze his arm. 'And I really, really, really love playing the piano. Only I never get the chance to practise it. Cos if anybody's in the mood for a sing-song, Mr Faulds knows more tunes than me, from when he used to hear them in his music-hall days, and if nobody's in the mood for music then they're no' in the mood for hearing me practising either, are they?'

'But I've seen you practise making no sound at all,' I said. Mattie grinned at me.

'I learned how to do that in the night-time,' he said. 'They let me in, and I go to the servants' hall where it's still nice and warm and sometimes I read the song sheets and sometimes I practise, and I don't make any noise.'

'Who lets you in?' I said. His face clouded again. 'I promise that you won't get anyone into trouble,' I said, mentally crossing my fingers behind my back.

'Clara,' he said, with a spasm of the pain it caused him flashing across his face. 'Or Phyllis. One of the two.'

'And how do they do it without Mr Faulds or Mrs Hepburn hearing them?' I said. Mattie gave another grin at this, fainter but full of glee.

'When Mr Faulds is locking up at night,' he said, 'he always does the kitchen door first, and one of the girls always stays up there and when he turns the key in the sub-basement they know he's just about to shoot the bolts there and when he does, they shoot the bolts back again in the door upstairs.'

Instantly, I was back in my little bed in Miss Rossiter's cosy bedroom, listening to the resounding clang of the bolts at night and the mysteriously less resounding clang of the bolts in the morning.

'Of course,' I said. 'My God, Mattie. You know what this means, don't you? The house was open all night – lying open, all night, every night, including the night of the murder.' Mattie was shaking his head so hard that his flaxen hair flew out around it like ribbons from a maypole.

'No, it's still locked,' he said. 'It's just the bolts they open for me. But there's a key, hidden in a wee hidey-hole in the bricks, away up high, and I can get in and then I can lock up again when it's safe to leave, see?'

'I do,' I said. 'Not quite so bad then. But doesn't Mrs Hepburn hear you?'

'She—' Mattie bit his lip. 'She's another one that's been dead, dead kind,' he said. 'That's why I always stayed. All the girls and Mrs Hepburn were that good to me even if the boys werenae. She said the girls were her business and the boys were up to Mr Faulds to keep in line and since it was me she knew there was no hanky-panky. And that's the truth, miss, because Harry and John and Stanley never knew about that key and they still don't and Phyllis and Clara told me straight if they ever found out that would be the end of it, because I'm a good boy and like their wee brother but they others are *men*.'

'So the other three lads know nothing about it?' I said. 'They couldn't have got in without someone knowing.'

'I d'ae think so,' Mattie said.

'And they don't even know that you sneak out?' I asked, thinking that the three of them had to be extraordinarily sound sleepers.

'No,' said Mattie, without meeting my eyes. He was still hiding something; I was sure of it.

'So, the night master died. What did you see? Or hear?'

'I wasnae there that night,' Mattie replied. 'I stayed in the carriage house and never went nowhere.'

It was very hard to settle for this; almost impossible to face that I had cracked Mattie's great secret only for it to lead precisely nowhere. I supposed it was something to suggest to Mr Hardy that he find this key in its hidey-hole in the brick and test it for fingerprints. Further than that, I was at a dead-end again and it was with a clod of disappointment inside me as heavy as a sandbag that I trailed off to the gooseberries at last.

I had quite forgotten what a torturous thing a gooseberry bush is and since the little girls with the flour sacks had done the sensible thing and stripped the fattest and easiest-reached fruits before we arrived, Mattie and I were left to stretch deep into the thorny interiors to snag the little green pellets which remained. My grey serge, by the end of an hour, sported a great many loops of thread and puckered grazes which I am sure Miss Rossiter would have known how to remedy but which I simply rubbed at feebly as though the coat, like the arm underneath, might simply heal itself given time.

When I could stand it no longer, I began to extricate myself.

'Come on,' I said to Mattie, going over to where he was picking. 'We've got a good lot and you've got roses in your cheeks already before you've even eaten a single one.'

His smile faltered. He really was the most sensitive child, whom even a bracing reference to his health struck as some kind of fault-finding. Then there was the fear of the dark struggling against his love of the piano. He had what would be called, if he were more gently born, an artistic temperament. And there was some kind of courage in his putting the art above the fear, I supposed; at least, my mother would have thought so. Picking my words very carefully to avoid hurting him again, I tried to tell him so but he only put his head down as low as ever and I could see a flush spreading over him.

'It's no' really like that, miss,' he said, and although he refused to elaborate, something he had let slip before came back to me.

'Do you mean,' I said, 'that you got into the house at night, even though you hate to be alone, because the boys tease you? Or are cruel to you somehow? You said the girls and the girls alone were the kind ones.'

'I d'ae want to get anyone into trouble,' Mattie said and he put on a spurt of pace – we were recrossing the fields towards the cottages again – and left me behind him.

'But if someone is being mean to you, surely he deserves no loyalty,' I said, puffing a little as I caught up.

'Naeb'dy's being anything,' he insisted. 'They do what they want and I just have to lump it. Same as ever, same as anywhere.'

Slowly, very deliberately, I put down my basket and stood with my feet planted well apart and my arms folded in front of me.

'I am not moving until you tell me the rest,' I said in the coldest voice anyone with a heart could turn on this child. It was a considerable effort too, because I wanted to clap my hands and click my heels at the discovery that there was a 'rest', that Mattie's tale had not run out into sand after all. 'I'm quite willing to stand here until Mr Osborne and your mother come to see what's happened to us.'

'My mammy'll skin me alive,' said Mattie.

'I know. I'll help her.'

He gave a huge sigh and started walking again.

'I really, really hate being on my own in the dark,' he said again. 'And John and Harry and Stanley know it. But . . . they go out, miss. They go out at night, all three of them, and I'm on my own, and that's why I go to the servants' hall and play the piano. Because even though I'm on my own in the room, there's Eldry and Millie underneath – and Maggie too before she left – and Mr Faulds through the wall, and Mrs Hepburn and Clara and Phyllis and Miss Abbott and it's better than the carriage house by a long chalk, I can tell you.'

'And where, pray, do the three of them go?' I said. 'Do you know? Can you tell me?'

'The three of them d'ae go anywhere,' Mattie said. 'John and Harry go to the Free Gardeners' or else to this club that Harry knows that serves drink after time, except on Monday night it was shutting at midnight cos it's that kind of club but they went to watch the start of the strike, with the fireworks and all the speakers and the singing and they didn't get back until all hours. And Stanley went out too. But he always goes on his own.'

'So why did you stay put?' I said, remembering this. 'You assured me that you weren't in the house that night.'

'I wasnae,' Mattie said. 'I was looking out the windae to see if it was safe to come out, but it wasnae so I just had to bide where I was and I fell asleep in the end.'

'What do you mean, "safe"?' I said.

'Well, Stanley,' Mattie said. 'Stanley didn't get out of the way, miss, if you must know. He was in the back garden in the way of me getting in the basement door. He's no' usually.'

'But what on earth do you mean?' I said. 'What was he doing? What does he usually do?'

'Nae harm,' said Mattie. 'No' really. He looks in at the windaes, miss. He likes to look in.'

'What windows?' I said, although I could guess already.

'Well, Clara and Phyllis's,' said Mattie, 'except they're fly to him and they stop up all the wee holes in the shutters wi' twists of paper. And he used to look in at Miss Abbott sometimes and I've even seen him taking a wee peek at Mrs Hepburn, but mostly he goes over the garden wall, to the other houses, where the maids d'ae ken him and maybe don't shut their curtains so careful. But that night he didnae go over the wall. Like I said, he stayed in the garden at Number 31.'

'Peering in?' I said. 'Since there was someone new to peer in at?'

Mattie bit his lip and nodded and I felt a flood of revulsion pass through me.

'A peering tom?' I said. Mattie flushed again. 'And you kept it a secret?'

'He held it over me, miss. About how I went out too, on account of how sometimes he was back before me.'

'And the times he was back before you,' I said, speaking slowly as I thought it through, 'he might well have watched for you and he might very well have seen you coming out and hiding the key and—'

'No,' said Mattie. 'I was careful. And if Stanley had known he would have used it himself, miss. That's what he's like. If he'd been able to get into the house he'd never stick at windaes – he'd have been inside peeping through keyholes instead. And he'd have hinted. He cannae stop himself hinting.'

'Yes, hinting is Stanley's favourite pastime,' I said, unable to keep my lip from curling.

'Aye,' said Mattie, quietly. 'And he's hinted . . . I mean, he's let on . . . Honest, miss, I d'ae ken nothin' about that night but Stanley does. He tellt me.'

'Oh, Mattie!' I said and his head drooped like a wilting flower.

'I didnae want to get him in bother,' he said, his voice trembling. 'And it wasnae much anyway. It's was jist that he said . . . it was when you were talking to us about how somebody must have let somebody in. Remember, miss? When you said that? Stanley was grinning like a cat and he said to me – really quiet – that you were wrong. That's all – he jist said you were wrong.'

'That's enough,' I said. 'I knew someone must have seen something. I *knew* it. Well, let's see Stanley getting away with "hinting" to the superintendent, eh? He'll crack like a nut.'

'But . . . you dinnae think Stanley killed him, miss?' Mattie said. We had reached the cottages again and he rested his basket on the low garden wall and turned a troubled face to me

I took a long moment and then answered only very grudgingly: 'No. He had no apparent motive, he doesn't have the stomach for it, and if he were guilty he'd keep his silly mouth shut. The teasing and hinting and hugging himself might be infuriating for the rest of us, Mattie, but it's the stamp of innocence for Stanley. Now, come on. Let's go in.'

Alec and I were invited to share the MacGibneys' luncheon – bread, margarine and potatoes fried in yesterday's bacon pan – and, astonishingly enough, after my morning of tramping the fields and struggling in the gooseberry bushes, I was able to make a good show of repaying them with a clean plate. Nanny Palmer would have been proud of me.

Mattie's father had come home for his dinner and when it was eaten he, John and Grandad all lit their pipes and Alec joined them. In such a small room with such a low ceiling and with only one very little window – and that fastened tight – I should have been glad to leave the table and join Mattie's mother at the sink, but she showed me with a glare that I was to keep away. (I supposed she did not foresee much skill with a dish-mop and did not want to risk handing her good plates to me to dry either, not in a room with a stone floor.) I should have been even gladder to leave straight away and return to Heriot Row to furnish Mr Hardy with my little bit of news – a way forward at last in all of this tangle – but we could not drag Mattie from his mother so early in the day.

'My, that's grand-smelling baccy,' said Mr MacGibney Sr when Alec had got his pipe going well.

'I like it,' Alec said. 'I wish I'd thought of bringing some more.' All three generations of men shook their heads in unison.

'You couldn't bring tobacco on a Co-op chit,' said John, 'nor spirits neither. You'd need a licence for them.'

'I meant as a gift,' Alec said, but the head-shaking went on.

'Cannae be too careful about "gifts", time like this,' said Mattie's father, and I remembered what Alec had said about giving money to the men on the blockade.

'Cannae believe we've come to this,' said the old man. 'We won that war for them. Broke our backs on fifteen-hour shifts we did and kept this country going. And now look what they're at! Importing German coal. *German*! Reparations, they say. Well, I've got a different name for it.'

'Wheesht, Faither,' said Mrs MacGibney. 'Dinnae upset yourself.'

'I dinnae care for me,' said her father. 'But what about the young lads, eh?'

'Me and Mattie are no' exactly carrying the torch,' said John.

His father did not look at him, but spoke very firmly.

'You might be on the surface now, lad, but you're still a miner. *You've* nothing to be shamed for.' There was just the slightest emphasis but it was enough to make Mattie's head drop low.

There was a long silence. The MacGibneys were sunk in gloom, Alec was smoking steadily and looking sympathetic, but I writhed. My early training at tea parties, my instruction at finishing school, my two decades of adult life: all had instilled in me a horror of silence in any social setting.

'The German element *is* shocking,' I said. 'Talk about insult to injury. But . . .'

Alec took his pipe out of his mouth and stared at me. All the MacGibneys looked towards me too.

'But what?' said John.

'But,' I said, swallowing hard, 'if their coal is cheaper than ours then ours has to come down too and everyone must just pull their belts in.' I was quoting Hugh to a certain extent, but this part of his philosophy had always seemed above argument to me. Mrs MacGibney spoke up from the sink, without turning.

'Everyone?' she said. 'You think Old Man Mair's pulling his belt in to live off two pounds a week? You think if he said no he'd be down to five shillings strike pay?'

'Two pounds?' I said. 'Two pounds a week? But it says in the papers . . .'

Now she did turn to look at me and she was almost laughing.

'What papers have you been reading then?' she said. '*Tatler*, is it?'

All the men laughed out loud at that. I did not mind; at least we were talking again.

'You're from another world, hen,' said Grandad. 'You need a wee lesson.'

Mattie and John groaned.

'Oh, here we go,' said their father.

The old man took his pipe out of his mouth and gestured to where his grandsons were sitting. 'Turn they chairs round and show the lassie, boys.' Mattie and John rolled their eyes but stood up. John leaned against the wall – his crutch was out of reach – while Mattie set the two chairs close by each other, sideways on to Alec and me. 'See that here,' said Grandad, pointing again, at the chair legs. 'Could you fit yourself through there, hen?'

I looked at the gap between the front and back legs, below the seats, wondering where this parlour game might be leading to.

'I daresay,' I said. 'It would be a bit of a squeeze, but I think so.'

'Try it for a mile and a half,' Grandad thundered, 'pitch black but for a candle on your helmet and sweat running off you with the heat. Not a stitch on your body and scraped red with the rock and when you get to the end where you left off, there you've seven hours chipping out wee lumps wi' a hammer and pushing them past you to your laddie to drag to the shaft for you and then a mile and a half back again and the same again the next day and the next day and—'

'Dinnae upset yourself, Faither,' said Mrs MacGibney again, 'and let they boys sit back doon.'

241

'I always imagined caves,' I said, and the smiles showed me that I was not the first to have said so. 'And was that what it was like when the roof collapsed on you two?' I said to Mattie and John.

'Not so bad,' said John. 'That tunnel was high enough to sit up in.'

I could think of no adequate response to this, and indeed spent the rest of the visit in near silence. The others talked until shortly after four o'clock, when Mattie's mother asked him when he had to be getting back again. We could have stayed longer – Mattie certainly could have – but we could not in conscience take another meal from the woman so I did not demur, and Alec and I left Mattie to his goodbyes. (I noticed Alec's baccy pouch tucked discreetly down beside the chair where he had been sitting.)

There was just one more vignette of pithead life for us to be treated to, unexpected, unlooked for and – whatever Alec's frame of mind might have been after the hours in the little cottage kitchen – quite unnecessary to me. As we were making our careful way over the ash lane which led away to the road, with a wave for Mattie's father who was back at the picket now, we heard the sound of another engine and a large motorcar of a type I could not name came along the lane towards us. It was driven by a chauffeur in uniform who drew up in front of us blocking our path. Almost before the motorcar had halted one of the back doors opened and a bulky man in a striped suit stepped down. I felt Mattie freeze at my side.

'Are you the one that's been driving in and out of here all day?' said the man, striding towards the car and treating Alec to a glare. He caught sight of Bunty and Millie and stopped in his tacks. 'Dogs?' he said. 'Dogs, is it now? Who the hell are you? Who's that in there with you?'

He had arrived at our side now and was looking at us with angry puzzlement. Mattie seemed to puzzle him more than anything.

'You're not from the union,' he said to Alec, 'driving around with women and children. Who are you?'

'I can't see that it's any of your business,' replied Alec. 'Who are *you*? You start and I'll see if I feel like joining in.' Beside me, Mattie was shaking.

'I? I?' said the man. 'I'm the boss and I'm not going to be spoken to that way by some bloody do-gooder coming causing mischief on private land. Now get out of it before I call the police on you.'

'Ah, Mr Mair, the manager,' said Alec, making it sound as though he were playing Happy Families. 'My name is Alec Osborne and I am neither a union representative nor a do-gooder. So we have that much in common, sir, but nothing else. I, unlike you, am a friend of the MacGibneys and have been visiting them in their time of need, as friends do.'

'MacGibneys?' said the man. 'Matt MacGibney and those useless sons of his?' Mattie let out a whimper, and I put my arm around him. 'Five of them living in the lap of comfort in a good cottage and only one of them doing a man's work for it. You have strange taste in friends, whoever you are. Now get off this land.'

As Alec stared back at him, breathing like a bull and struggling for a response, help came from the most unlikely quarter. Bunty – quite out of character and driven by who knew what noxious cocktail of terror, shock and cold fury rising from the three human occupants of the car – suddenly leapt, baying, for the open window and made a creditable attempt to take Mr Mair by his fleshy neck, snarling like a hound of hell. Alec stamped on the accelerator and got us away before she could actually connect with him, which was just as well, and Mattie, amazingly enough, was not further petrified by this latest turn but was un-accountably delighted, whooping and clapping and lunging over the front seat to hug Bunty hard.

'My God,' said Alec, laughing as well once he had recovered himself. 'Dandy, what on earth? Has she ever done that before?'

'Never!' I squeaked, feeling weak from the parade of extreme emotions. 'Whoever heard of an attack Dalmatian? Oh, why couldn't Hugh have been here to see it? He'll never believe me!'

Mattie had stopped laughing and was now hugging Millie, who

had pushed her head in between him and Bunty when she felt that her friend had hogged the limelight for long enough.

'Who's Hugh?' he said. 'And why did you call Miss Rossiter Dandy, Mr Osborne?'

Thankfully, though, there was too much else going on for him to pursue such points, and after just one panicked glance between Alec and me in the driving mirror the questions sank without reply.

15

Back at Heriot Row, when we slithered out of a six-inch opening to prevent Bunty from surging out after us (and it was excruciating to leave her without saying goodbye, especially after such heroics), there was a sharp rap above. I saw Superintendent Hardy standing in the drawing-room window beckoning to me and without so much as going to my room to take my hat off, I sprinted up there with Alec behind me.

Hardy met us on the landing and gestured into the library.

'I have something to tell you,' I began as soon as the door was shut behind us.

'You shall have to wait your turn,' he said. 'I have a great deal to tell you. Good solid results. I've had two men trying to trace Miss Abbott and Maggie all day.'

'Oh, please tell me you've found them,' I said, and then as he hesitated I realised that there is something worse than being missing and I hoped that he had not found them, that they had run off and were living high on the hog together somewhere.

'I hope not,' said Hardy, confirming my fears. 'But let me tell you in an orderly fashion. Maggie's family haven't missed her yet, or at least they hadn't until a police sergeant rolled up to tell them she wasn't where she should be. Her mother said she usually gets a letter on Wednesdays but thought nothing of it, with the new position and the strike too. The bad news, the very bad news, is that the body of a young girl was found drowned off the Brigs of Fidra on Monday.'

'The what?' said Alec.

'On the road to Berwick,' said Superintendent Hardy. 'A well-nourished and healthy young girl dressed in a manner suitable

245

to a servant, and no one has come forward to claim her as their own. We're taking Maggie's father and brother down there just as soon as we can organise a car.' He shook himself all over like a dog in the rain. 'I'm glad it's not me going along with them,' he said.

'And Miss Abbott?'

'Now, Miss Abbott *was* missed,' said Hardy. 'Her sister, a Mrs Light, of Trinity, has been trying to find her since shortly after she disappeared in April. She sent several letters to this house but got no reply.'

'Lollie never mentioned any of them,' I said.

'Mrs Balfour didn't get them,' Hardy told me. 'They were sent to her husband. But if he got them, they weren't among his things.'

'Faulds and Stanley might remember them,' I said. 'And actually, Superintendent, that's what I was going to say: you need to speak to Stanley. He saw something that night. He knows something. He's often out at night-time – well, they all are. All four of them from the carriage house, at it happens. Mattie creeps out to his piano practice if you can believe it,' – Hardy's eyebrows lifted a little – 'letting himself in with a key hidden outside the back door. John and Harry frequently go out on the town after lights out and did so on Monday night.'

'I know that much,' Hardy said. 'Eldry and Millie told me. Eldry is in the habit of sitting at her window watching for a glimpse of Harry's legs as he passes. Millie sometimes joins her, but *her* beloved has yet to be seen.'

'At the front anyway,' I said. 'Stanley doesn't go anywhere near the street. He creeps around the back gardens looking in at maids' windows.' Mr Hardy drew his head back sharply as though at a nasty smell. 'And Mattie tells me – apropos of the murder night – that Stanley was out in the back garden, at Miss Rossiter's window, and knows that "no one needed to be let in". I think that's very significant, don't you?'

'Peeping tom, eh?' Hardy said. 'Never mind speaking to him, then. I can take him in, and have a proper go at him.' He strode to the fireplace and tugged the bell-rope, looking like an executioner releasing the guillotine.

Faulds answered the bell and sent a puzzled glance around the room, at the incongruous sight of the superintendent, Lollie's lady's maid still in her outdoor clothes, and rather dishevelled ones at that, and the young man who might or might not be Great Aunt Gertrude's chauffeur. I was standing very properly with my hands folded and my eyes down and Alec was sitting forward on a hard chair as befitted a servant in one of the upstairs rooms, but one could still see Faulds trying and failing to make sense of it.

'Send the footman to me, please, Faulds,' said Hardy, 'and tell him to bring his hat and coat, won't you?'

'Stanley?' said Mr Faulds, shifting from foot to foot. 'Well now, sir, I can't do that right now, I'm afraid, but I'll leave word that you want to see him.'

'I beg your pardon?' said Hardy in dreadful tones. Mr Faulds swallowed hard but spoke without a tremor.

'We can't seem to find him,' he said. 'It's not his free afternoon, but he's gone, sir.'

'Gone?' said Hardy. 'What do you mean?' Alec and I frowned at one another.

'Well, they sometimes slip out after tea if there's nothing planned for the evening,' said Faulds, wilting a little under Superintendent Hardy's gaze. 'At least Mrs Hepburn lets the girls and so I don't want to come the heavy and stop the lads doing the same, so long as they don't take it too far, you understand, but I must say, Stanley is a very proper young man and he usually tells someone if he needs to pop out and says when he'll be back and all that. I assure you this isn't like him, not at all.' Mr Hardy had started moving towards the desk telephone before this speech was halfway through and jiggled the button up and down with fierce jabs of his finger.

'Gayfield police station,' he said. 'This is Superintendent Hardy and I don't want your opinion on the matter, young lady. Just put me through.' While he waited he turned to Mr Faulds again.

247

'When was he last seen? Who saw him? Has anyone been through his things to check whether anything's missing? Send anyone who knows anything up here to me. Osborne,' – Hardy scribbled on a scrap of paper and shoved it at Alec – 'you go to his home address and ask them there if he's been seen. Miss Rossiter? Go to the carriage house and search it.'

'Now, sir,' said Mr Faulds. 'Really, Miss Rossiter could not possibly be expected to go poking around in the men's quarters. I shall take care of that myself.'

'Well, do it then!' roared Hardy and turned his back on all of us to speak into the telephone.

Faulds, moving faster than I had ever seen him go and looking quite unlike a butler, dashed away down the stairs and slammed the green baize door behind him.

'I can't believe it,' I said, to Alec, as we hurried after him. 'Stanley? Stanley? It can't be true. All that blood?'

'But if he's skipped,' said Alec.

'And *why*?'

Alec only shrugged. We were down in the servants' quarters now. Alec made for the area door. Mr Faulds, emerging from his pantry in a mackintosh, on his way to the carriage house, laid a hand on my arm before we parted.

'Try to keep it from them, won't you, Fanny?' he said. 'Phyllis and Kitty and the others. Don't upset them before we're sure, eh? I'll go and see what's what in the mews, but I'm sure I'll find nothing amiss. I mean, not *Stanley*. Stab master? Never, Fanny. I don't give scat for Mr Hardy and his ideas. I've known that lad nearly four years and I'd stake my life on it.'

And yet, I thought, he had jumped to exactly that conclusion without Hardy ever actually saying it out loud.

Mrs Hepburn and the girls were in the kitchen, Millie and Eldry busy and the other two maids perched up on the dresser, huddled close like a pair of little birds.

'I thought I heard you a while ago,' said Mrs Hepburn, 'but with all the rushing about, upstairs and down, I couldn't be sure it was you. Where have you been?' When I failed to answer, she looked up and her eyes widened. 'Fanny, look at the state of your hat! What have you been doing to yourself? And your coat's ruined.'

Phyllis giggled.

'You do look a sight, Miss Rossiter,' she said. 'We've had a terrible day too, Clara and me, with that policeman, but we've come through it better than you.'

'I need to ask you all something,' I said. 'It's about Stanley.' Millie looked up. She was pushing cloves into the scored glaze of a ham and she stopped with one finger pressed against it like someone leaning on a door bell.

'Is he all right?' she said. Phyllis giggled again. 'He's gone out without telling us where he's going.'

'And who saw him last?' I said. 'Mr Hardy wants to know.'

'Superintendent Hardy?' said Millie. 'Does he think Stanley's in danger? Oh! Oh! Auntie Kitty!'

'Now hush, Molly-moo,' said Mrs Hepburn, glaring at me. 'Miss Rossiter didn't mean anything of the sort. Don't upset yourself. We all saw him at dinner-time, Fanny. You tell that to the policeman.'

'I saw him after dinner,' said Eldry. 'I saw him going to the front area door. At least at the time I thought he was going to Mr Faulds's pantry, you know, to get a job to do or maybe to get his chamois apron or his silver-gloves or something that he keeps in there, but that must have been him leaving.'

'And what time was this?' I said. Eldry bit her bottom lip and pushed out her top one.

'I was just coming out of the china store,' she said. 'I'd been getting the sweet dishes for tonight's dessert. When was that, Mrs Hepburn?'

'Half-past two sort of time?' said the cook. 'I sent you for them as soon as the custard was cool enough to pour without them cracking. Half-past two, Fanny. Tell the copper it was then.'

'He's been gone an awful long time then, Auntie Kitty,' said Millie and the rest of the girls glanced at one another, for this was true.

'Who cares what Stanley does, Millie-Molly-moo,' said Clara. 'I've always said you're too good for him.'

I left them to try to persuade the stubborn Millie of this self-evident truth and slipped out again. At the stairs, I hesitated and then hurried down instead of up. If I really looked as frightful as Mrs Hepburn said, I wanted to make a few hasty repairs before seeing Hardy again.

In my room, I flung off my hat and my much-abused coat and shrugged into the neat little black slub jacket I had taken to wearing in the evening, then I elbowed open the door of my washing room, meaning to splash my face and damp down my hair, but stopped short in the doorway, looking into the dark.

The shutters were closed but I could see that someone was in there, bent over the sink, and my first thought was that whoever it was was drunk – helplessly, disgustingly drunk – and had had the nerve to come to *my* room, to use *my* sink, for the inevitable aftermath to take place in comfort and privacy. Then I realised three things all at once, or so quickly in succession as made no difference: that it was Stanley – his striped trousers, his black shoes; that the smell in here which had made me put my hand up to my mouth after the first gasp was not the smell of drink and sickness, but something worse and only too familiar; and that he was not bending over the sink, but slumped there, his round little stomach resting against its front edge, his legs slightly bent and his feet dragging sideways on the tiled floor, absolutely still.

I stepped towards him and all I could see was darkness instead of the white gleam of the china sink that should have been there. I returned to my bedroom and lit a candle.

Now I could see it all: the dark head hanging down, the deep, dark red pooled in the bottom of the sink and turning black there, the pudgy hand lying half-open in the deepest part of the puddle with the razor slipping from its grasp. I bent down close to his head, holding my breath, my hand shaking so that everything danced in the candlelight and even Stanley seemed to be moving.

His face had not fallen against the sink but was hanging down into it with just the tip of his nose touching and his chin was . . . I held the candle up and looked more closely, then stepped back so sharply that the candle, in the sudden movement, snuffed itself out. His chin was hidden, had disappeared into the cut in his neck, or the cut in his neck had gaped open and swallowed his chin; either way it was a sight I could not bear to have seen but one which, no matter how I squeezed my eyes shut and scrubbed at them, would not leave me.

I did not have to explain to Superintendent Hardy.

'I found Stanley,' was all I said and his face drained until it was as ghastly and as grey as I felt sure mine must be. Together we went back down and he waited while I fumbled the lock open, not offering to do it for me, suspecting perhaps that his hands would be no more steady than my own. I hung back once we were inside and let Hardy enter the little washing room on his own.

He was very quiet in there, not even so much as breathing heavily, much less uttering the ugly sounds of disgust I feared had been torn out of me at the first sight of it. His shoes squeaked now and then and I imagined him bending and craning for a closer look, but that was all until he cleared his throat and said:

'My dear? Is it his writing?'

I stirred myself and I too had to cough my voice back to life before I could answer.

'I'm sorry, Superintendent – what?'

'Is this Stanley's writing? I've never seen it, but perhaps you might have.'

Reluctantly, I edged towards the door and looked in. Hardy had relit the candle and was holding it over the slatted wooden board beyond the sink, peering down at a piece of paper there. He turned round and beckoned to me. 'Forgive me,' he said, 'I don't want to move it until I have a cloth to wrap it in. We shall need to dust it for fingerprints, naturally.'

I put a hand up to the side of my head to shield my eyes from another sight of Stanley and walked, rather unsteadily, over to Hardy's side. The paper was a single lined sheet torn from a cheap pad, rather rough, with blue lines across it:

May 8th 1926

I am not sorry for what I did, but I cannot face what will happen to me if I am found out. The world is a better place without Philip Balfour and it will do very well without me.

Stanley Drumm

'I can't tell you,' I said. 'Mr Faulds would know. Shall I . . . shall I fetch him?'

'No,' said Hardy, putting a hand under my arm and leading me back out into my bedroom. 'The fewer people who see all this the better, I think, don't you? There's no reason to doubt it anyway.' He had lowered me into the armchair and now sat down heavily upon the bed. He put his hands up as though to rub his face and then jerked them away again, plucked a handkerchief out of his breast pocket and wiped it over his palms. I put my hand to the place on my sleeve where he had touched me. There was a little dampness there.

'So,' I said. 'I was wrong. I always thought that Stanley hinting and boasting was a mark of innocence on him.'

'And the blood phobia was nonsense,' said Hardy. I touched my sleeve again and nodded, shuddering.

'And no matter what Mattie thinks, Stanley must have known about the key. And used it that night.'

'Yes,' said the superintendent, 'I suppose so.'

'And he did after all often deal with the post-bag and answer the telephone, so he could easily have fobbed off Mrs Light and the Berwick housekeeper.'

'Who said – as a matter of fact, madam – that it was a man she spoke to when she rang.'

'So the only question left is why,' I said. '*Why*?'

'Well, that sort of character,' said Hardy, 'a peeping tom? He wouldn't need the kind of motive that would make sense to you or me.'

For some reason, I could hear Nanny Palmer's voice, on the subject of hanging dogs and bad names, which made no sense at all. I shook my head to silence her.

'Do you know, Superintendent,' I said, 'I am probably the only one of the upper servants who doesn't have a bottle of something handy in my bedroom somewhere.'

Hardy nodded, acknowledging the attempt at a joke, and then looked around.

'Bedroom?' he said. 'Yes, of course. Well, you must gather what things you will need for the night, my dear, because I shall have to lock up at least until the morning.'

The thought was not to be entertained of sleeping here ever again and so it took some effort to prevent myself from bundling up every last stocking and hairpin and fleeing, but I managed to restrict myself to my notebooks, my nightgown and a change of clothes for the following day and followed Superintendent Hardy upstairs again, feeling like a refugee.

We had hardly had time to tell Lollie and Great Aunt Gertrude the news when Alec returned, mounting the stairs at a gallop and bursting into the room.

'There's—' he began and then checked himself when he saw Mrs Lambert-Leslie and Mrs Balfour there as well as Hardy and me. 'Forgive me, ladies,' he said.

'Out with it and never mind your pretty manners,' said Great Aunt Gertrude. 'We're past all that now.'

'I've got some news,' Alec said. 'I went to Stanley's house out at Shandon and they haven't seen him, not since his last free day – but here's the thing: I *did* find out that he's a model of filial devotion, never misses a week, certainly didn't stay away for any long stretch because his father was ill. They didn't know what I was talking about when I mentioned it. So I think, I really do, Superintendent, that the whole story about a fear of blood is nonsense and Stanley might well be our man.'

He did not get the expected response at the end of this and when he looked around at our faces to try to find out why, I think he saw them properly for the first time.

'What's happened?' he said. 'Dan – Miss Rossiter, I mean, are you all right?'

I turned beseeching eyes upon Mr Hardy but before either of us could speak, Great Aunt Gertrude steamed in and summed it up neatly.

'Stanley's the one, all right. He confessed and then cut his own throat like a white man.'

Alec frowned at the boorish phrase but said nothing, only turned to me and enquired with a look whether I agreed. I shrugged and nodded.

We arranged that I should spend the night in a room on the third floor of the house, the unused nursery floor, and I left to deposit my bundle of books and clothes there. Alec came out of the drawing room behind me while Mr Hardy stayed to summon mortuary men and a police surgeon to attend Number 31 once more.

'I don't like this, Dandy,' he said, as we climbed the narrow staircase together. 'In fact, I'm going to have to insist that if you spend another night in this charnel house – and on a deserted floor at that – I do too. I shall bunk down between you and the stairs and I'm bringing the dogs in – don't tell me otherwise. That lot down in the servants' hall already think I'm Mrs L-L's fancy man – you should have heard the maids giggling – so it won't be any shock to them that I get special favours.'

'You and I agree then,' I said. I had put down my things on a blanket box on the landing and was opening doors, looking for a suitable room, feeling a little like Goldilocks in the empty cottage, for Lollie had already fitted up her nurseries for the children who would never be and there were short beds, low to the floor, and a crib with lace hangings, but nowhere that would be just right for me.

'Agree about what?' Alec said. 'Here we go, Dandy. The nursemaid's room. You and Bunty can sleep here and I'll take the floor in the outer nursery.'

'Like a bear at the mouth of a cave,' I said. 'You know it too, don't you? Even though you don't know how you know or what you know. No, don't scoff! Listen – if Stanley is the murderer and Stanley is dead then what do I have to fear and what do you have to fear for me and why are you not going off to supper and a night in an hotel?'

'I'm just rattled,' said Alec. 'There's no rhyme nor reason to it and in the morning it'll be gone, but I'm spooked by it tonight – please, Dandy; humour me.'

He was not alone. The servants' hall was the most subdued I had ever seen it once the news spread below stairs. Millie, as might be expected, was quite undone, and sat bellowing like an abandoned calf with tears rushing unchecked over her cheeks and dripping from her chin. At least, though, the sound of her howls drowned out the tramping feet of the doctor and the fingerprint men and, a little later, the heavier tramp of the mortuary attendants as they removed the body. Millie was facing away from the area, thank the Lord, and those of us who were not managed to compose our expressions before she noticed and turned around.

No one objected when Mr Faulds broke up the gathering. He bid Clara make up a cot for Millie beside her Auntie Kitty and – very thoughtfully, in my opinion – told Eldry she could do the same in the housemaids' bedroom, so that she would not be alone. He even asked me if I thought I would manage to sleep up in the nurseries and did not seem entirely convinced when I assured him that I should be fine.

'What an end, eh?' he said, shaking his head in great sorrow. 'What a waste of a life, Fanny.'

'Four lives,' I said without thinking.

'Four?' said Mr Faulds, looking at me sharply. 'I suppose you mean master and mistress? But not Millie, surely. She'll get over it soon. Kitty will talk her round.'

Mrs Hepburn reappeared at that moment and joined Mr Faulds and me before the embers of the servants' hall fire.

'She's off like a lamb,' she said. 'Tired herself out with all that crying, so I'll just leave her a while and not start creaking and splashing until she's deeply gone.' Mrs Hepburn cleared her throat. 'Well, to tell you the truth, Ernest, I could murder a drop of something and that's no lie.'

'Only natural,' said Mr Faulds. 'And someone should raise a glass to poor Stanley anyway. No matter what he did. His passing can't go unmarked.'

Mrs Hepburn closed her eyes and nodded very gravely.

'Do you really think he *did* do it?' I said. Mrs Hepburn opened her eyes again. 'Can you really believe it of him?'

'It does you great credit that you can't, Fanny,' said Mrs Hepburn. 'But he left a note. He confessed to it all.'

'I wish he had said in his note *why* he did it,' I replied. 'I think I'd be happier if I had any idea why.'

'Oh Fanny,' said Mr Faulds. 'You've led a sheltered life if that can puzzle you. The truth is, when one man sets his mind to murder another, there's no "reason" anywhere to be found.' I nodded reluctantly and Mr Faulds carried on. 'I remember a pair of comics on the halls with me,' he said. 'Brothers they were – Valentine and Gallagher O'Malley: Vally and Gally. They toured their cross-talk act for twenty-five years until one night in Swansea they came off after their bow and encore and went to their dressing room and Val killed his brother, strangled him with his dressing-gown cord, and then called the stage-door to get the police and put his hands out for the cuffs to go on them. And when the copper asked why he did it he said Gallagher had dropped fag ash in the cold cream once too often.' Mrs Hepburn tutted and shook her head. 'Fag ash in the cold cream, Fanny,' said Mr Faulds, 'without a word of a lie.'

'But we don't even have that much of a reason in this case,' I said. 'I know what Stanley *said* about master, about his cruelty, but it wasn't true. That's one thing that's come out from the police digging around. There's no reason at all – not a spot of ash or anything.'

'What are you talking about?' said Mr Faulds. 'What's this the police have dug up?'

'Oh, Ernest, please,' said Mrs Hepburn. 'And you too, Fan. Can't we just leave it be? I'll be greetin' worse than Millie if I have to keep going over it now.'

Mr Faulds, the thought of his beloved in distress taking precedence over everything else, clapped his hands, stood up and announced that he had a bottle of Rémy Martin in his pantry and we were all to go there now and drink to Stanley's memory. I tried to demur, not wanting to be a gooseberry, but he would not brook a refusal and in the end Mrs Hepburn left before me, fearing that Millie would waken and find herself alone. I meant to follow on her heels, but somehow the time passed and it must have been long after midnight when, full of brandy and music-hall tales and slightly cloudy, I climbed all the way to the top of the house, bade goodnight to Alec and climbed into the little iron bed to join Bunty.

16

Bunty woke me with one of her most luxurious yawns, one which slid down several octaves from a whine to a growl, and I was glad to be wakened; my sleep had been plagued by the kind of unpleasant dreams one cannot quite remember but cannot quite shake off either. Alec called my name and I opened my eyes and gazed around the little room. It was awash with morning light and alive with dancing dust motes at which Bunty started snapping, trampling over the bed without regard to the tender parts of her mistress under her paws.

'One moment,' I called back and sat up, shoving Bunty off the bed with my feet. Perhaps it was not a dream, this thing that was nagging at me, but rather something I had forgotten or something I had to do and deep down was dreading. I looked around the room for clues, but I knew even as I did so that it was not that sort of a something, not a watch I had not wound nor a letter I had to answer. After all, I thought, shaking my head, I did not even know if this nagging something was in the past or the future. It was, somehow, neither. It was, in a very odd way, somewhere else entirely. It must, I decided, be a dream after all.

Besides, my work here at 31 Heriot Row was done. It had not been my finest hour. I had suspected Stanley from the start, had watched him, had become more and more sure of his guilt every day and yet had done nothing about it until it was too late to bring him to justice. Even if I had really been Miss Rossiter, Mrs Balfour's new maid and nothing more, I should have spoken up and told Superintendent Hardy that very first morning to take Stanley in and press the truth out of him. As a so-called detective, supposed to be helping, I could not account for how I could have let it end this way.

There was a soft knock on the door and Alec put his head around it.

'Dan?' he said. 'Are you all right? I can hear you sighing from out here.'

'I'm fine,' I said. 'Well, of course, actually, no, I'm not fine. I'm kicking myself.'

'Can't think why,' Alec said, 'but – having slept on it all – have you at least accepted that the mystery is solved and the case is closed?'

'Yes, I suppose so,' I said. 'I mean, yes, of course.'

'So we can go home?'

'Home?' I repeated. 'Yes. Yes, I think perhaps I should. This place . . .' I looked around myself again. What *was* it?

'This place what?' Alec said.

'I don't know,' I answered. 'I feel rather odd this morning, that's all.'

'Bad dreams?'

'That's probably all it is.'

When he had gone, taking Bunty and Millie with him for a turn around the garden, I made every effort to shake myself. (Nanny Palmer, in full epigrammatic flight, had once shared with me the view that if we spent all our time looking back at yesterday, we would be roundly spanked by tomorrow – and although I had had to suppress my giggles at the time, I had come to see the wisdom.) And perhaps Stanley's guilt had not really been so very clear at the time as it was now, with the glare of hindsight shining upon it. No! I told myself. Stop that! It *was* clear. It had been perfectly obvious to me from the start and I would not allow myself to wriggle out of my discomfort by pretending otherwise. Besides, I could not edit my memories to suit myself because I had a record of them.

I laid a hand out and picked the topmost book from where I had left them on my nightstand. My much-ridiculed notebooks, I thought, as I flipped through the pages. There were my first impressions of the household: Lollie – *sweet and confused, inclined not to believe her own experiences but rather to cling on to her hopes even in the face of bitter experience to the contrary;* Mrs Hepburn – *sharp-tongued but good-hearted, kind to her charges* and a later note squeezed in – *food sent back and tricks played – soup/water, goose/mouse;* Eldry – *shy, easily frightened, PF foisted attentions against will. Unstable – stains/washing find out more?;* and Pip Balfour himself – *unassuming, friendly, shirt-sleeves! Model yacht!! Hard to see beast L. speaks of. Seems absol. unexceptional & pleasant yg man. Brilliant actor???*

Stanley must be further on. Yes, that was right, I had not set down my thoughts about him until after the meeting in the carriage house that day. I picked up a second and a third note-book and found it at last. I turned the page towards the window and began reading.

Stanley. Footman. Smug, boastful (esp. re superior training), ingrati-ating, hates blood. Hints but knows nothing of import. Hates PB, because father/TB/visit. This had been scored out and changed to: *would never pay TB visit – fears blood. Could not stab someone. Conclude: innocent as has always seemed (more's the pity).* I stared at the page in front of me. I traced the words with my finger and spoke them under my breath. 'Innocent as has always seemed'?

So where were the notes about my suspicions? About what I had thought of Stanley all along? I got out of bed and walked up and down the bare floor staring at the journal in my hands. How could such lies be there in my book, in my writing, when I had not written them and never would write them, and where was what I *had* written, what I must have written, about all of his blunders and my growing certainty? I stopped pacing and threw the book down onto the bedcovers.

I was still standing in the middle of the floor when Alec came back to the door again.

'Dan?' he said. 'Are you still in h—?' He came right into the room and took my arms in his hands. 'Dandy?'

'Alec,' I said, and I was surprised at the smallness of the voice that came out of me. 'Something is wrong.' I led him over to the bed and sat him down on it, opening the notebook and laying it on his lap.

'I didn't write that,' I said, pointing.

Alec skimmed the page quickly and then looked up at me.

'Are you sure?'

'Quite sure.'

Alec shut the book and looked closely at the cover.

'It's your book, though, isn't it? I recognise it.' I nodded. It was certainly mine. Alec opened it again and peered at the binding. 'It's a proper page,' he said. 'It hasn't been bodged in with glue. And it's your writing, darling. I'd know it anywhere. I always said you take too many notes. And now there are so many you can't even remember writing them. Lesson for next time: less writing.'

I nodded. Writing, I thought. Handwriting. Names signed in writing. I was close to it now; I had almost caught hold of the end of it. And yes! There it was.

'Listen,' I said. 'Listen to this.' A will in Pip Balfour's writing, referring to a cousin no one has ever heard of and a wife who probably did not exist, and bearing the signatures of two women who cannot be found. And a note in Stanley's writing accusing himself of a crime he could not have committed – because of the blood – and left to prove a suicide he could not have committed – more blood – and now this. A journal entry in my own writing which I did not write, saying things I did not think and omitting things I did.'

Alec whistled.

'I'm sure I'm right,' I said. 'Alec, there's a forger at the bottom of this.'

'Hang on, though,' Alec said. 'The will, I grant you, is worth forging and the signatures to it, obviously. And the confession. But why would anyone forge a note in your personal papers?'

'I don't know why. I'm very confused about things this morning. I feel almost . . . drunk.'

'Well, you looked at least "almost drunk" when you came up from your cosy time in the pantry last night,' Alec said. 'Perhaps it hasn't worn off yet. What were you drinking?'

'I can't remember,' I said, and ignored Alec's tutting and rolling eyes. 'But I'm sure about this.'

'A forger, though,' he said. 'I always thought that a forger had to copy what lay before him and that it took long hours of practice and draft after draft to get it right.'

'So?'

'Well, just that that would do for a will that could be worked upon in secret for as long as it took to perfect it, but could a forger dash off a suicide note or slip an entry into a journal without a single crossing-out or false step to betray him? It seems more like some kind of party trick or magic turn, not part of a carefully planned murder. Sorry, darling, I think this particular leap of genius can be cured by two aspirin and a prairie oyster.' He gave me a very unsympathetic grin and left again.

His words, though, had left their mark upon me. Party trick, he had said. Magic turn. Words which sent me scurrying to put on my clothes, drag a brush through my hair and fly down and down and down the four flights, back to the servants' floor. If anyone had heard of such a thing it would be Mr Faulds, I told myself, for had he not spent the last part of the evening before regaling me with tales of impressionists and ventriloquists, mind readers and spirit writers, and all the ways there were to fool a gaping audience about who one was or where or what one could see or touch or do? If this feat of forgery were possible, then Mr Faulds would surely have come across it somewhere along the way. And besides, the thought of pouring even a little of this out to Mr Faulds was as comforting as a warm blanket and a mug of cocoa. Mr Faulds would help me.

He was at the head of the table, in his waistcoat with a cotton breakfast napkin tucked into his collar against splashes of yolk on his black tie, but he gave me a sunny smile as I rushed in and did not hesitate to follow me out into the passageway when I said I needed a word with him. He ushered me into his pantry with the utmost courtesy and I sat down again on the seat I had occupied the previous evening.

'It's about writing,' I said. 'Gosh, this is all so muddled. But it just occurred to me that no one who saw the will being written is here to confirm it. And obviously, poor Stanley is not here to say whether he wrote the note that was found beside him, and there's another thing too – it doesn't signify but it started me wondering – and I just think that maybe there's something peculiar about all this suspicious writing of things and I wondered if you had ever heard of anything like that, in your music-hall days. One of these clever tricksters you were talking about last night or something? Could such a thing be done, do you know?'

Mr Faulds was staring at me with his eyes very wide and his mouth just slightly open, but I could see that behind the frozen look on his face his mind was whirring just as fast as mine.

'What?' I said. 'What have you thought of? Has something struck you too? What is it?'

'What on earth put such an idea into your head?' said Mr Faulds.

'Am I right?' I said. 'Have I solved it?'

'Solved it?' said Mr Faulds. 'Why on earth would you be looking to solve anything, Fanny?' He was gazing at me with the oddest expression and I remembered that Fanny Rossiter was not in the business of solving things. He did not seem to disapprove, though. His regard was sorrowful, as though I had filled him with some regretful sadness of some kind.

'Fanny,' he said, 'listen to me. Just listen. I never heard of such a thing. And you can be sure I would have.'

'Oh,' I said. 'Really?'

Mr Faulds tapped his fingers against his cheek and thought hard, but he was soon shaking his head.

'You must be thinking of the spirit writers I was telling you about. But they had huge sheets of white card and the "spirit pens" – all done with a wire, you know – were great black things that made writing you could see from the back of the gallery.'

'Oh,' I said again. 'I really thought I'd got a hold of something there.'

'Listen, Fanny,' he said again. 'Just hush now and listen to me.'

But before he could go on there was a rap at the door.

A spasm of annoyance passed over his face as he barked out permission to enter. It was Eldry, looking startled at his tone.

'Beg pardon, Mr Faulds,' she said, 'but that Osborne, Aunt Goitre's chauffeur, is asking urgently for Miss Rossiter.'

Mr Faulds looked very slowly between Eldry and me before he replied.

'You'd better run along then, Fanny my girl. But you need to tell that young man how to behave himself when he's a guest below stairs in another man's house. You tell him from me.'

'*He's* in a funny mood this morning,' said Eldry when the door was shut behind us. I nodded but did not reply. Alec was standing in the open garden doorway, smoking, and turned round when he saw me, throwing his cigarette out onto the grass and starting up the stairs. I followed him. When we were out of Eldry's earshot I asked him what the trouble was.

'I was worried about you,' he said. 'Phyllis said you came panting in and dragged Mr Faulds from his bacon and eggs and disappeared with him. I didn't know where you'd got to.'

We were on the ground floor and I veered off the stairway and into the small back parlour which I knew would be empty once the fire was laid for the day.

'Never mind where I *had* got to,' I said, when we were inside with the door locked behind us, 'ask me where I've got to now. I've got a lot further in the last five minutes, I can tell you. I went to ask Mr Faulds about the forgery because last night he was telling me all about card tricksters and voice throwers and people who could guess objects held up in the audience when they were blindfold and all that sort of thing. Now, he was adamant he had never heard of such a thing. He thought long and hard and drew a blank. But I've just realised something.'

Alec gave a loud tut and rolled his eyes, for he hates these dramatic pauses when I do them even though he does them himself every chance that comes.

'Mr Ernest Faulds,' I went on, 'has said that he has no singing voice, and has "heard" lots of music-hall songs over the years – "heard", mind; not "played" – and spoke of comics as though of a separate race and said he had no time for magic acts and is not much of a dancer and in short . . .'

'In short, has never said outright what it was he did onstage,' said Alec.

'Precisely. And did not like it one little bit when I started talking about trick writing. And here's another thing: one time I teased Faulds about "neglecting his talents" working as a butler instead of treading the boards and he shut down like a trap. I couldn't understand why I had offended him so, but now I see.'

'How could forging handwriting make a stage act?' Alec said.

'How can card tricks?' I countered. 'The question is how can we find out? Or do we just go to Hardy with what we've got and tell him Faulds is the man? That he forged the will and the suicide note and killed Pip and Stanley?'

Now, Alec actually screwed his face up, so little did he think of my brilliant leap of reasoning.

'I shall come to the police station with you and wait outside,' he said, 'but if you want to march into Hardy's office and shout "Ta-dah!" it will have to be a solo act, I'm afraid.'

'What a shame it's Sunday,' I said. 'I could have telephoned to the stage-door of the Swansea Alhambra or the Leicester Whatever and asked if anyone remembered him. Ernest Faulds the Forger. It even sounds like a music-hall turn.'

'Well,' said Alec, 'I really don't think this is going to go anywhere, Dandy, but if you're determined, you should know that Sunday is the busiest day backstage, all hands on deck for the departure of the outgoing artistes and the arrival of the next lot for the week to come. And also, if Fabulous Faulds the Forger played Leicester and Swansea then he would surely have played the Edinburgh Empire too.'

'Will you come too?' I said. 'I've never knocked on a stage-door before.'

'Nor have I!' said Alec, just too emphatically to be quite plausible, and I smirked, wondering which curled and powdered little songbird had tempted him into hanging around with red roses and invitations to supper. 'But I'll happily tag along.'

There was indeed a great deal of activity in the lane behind the Empire Theatre, with trunks and hampers being carried out to carts waiting at the roadside, and stagehands trotting up and down between the backstage proper and the workshop which lay at the farthest end of the lane. There was even the inevitable argument going on out front on Nicholson Square, between the men in the carts and the men in the armbands.

'I'm nowt to do wi' no carters' union,' said a pugnacious-looking little man who was holding one end of an enormous trunk whose other end already rested on the flat bed of his cart. The horse in the shafts was looking back at the commotion with eyes which had seen it all. 'I work for Moss's Empires and I'm already having enough trouble today trying to get this show over to Glasgow with no bloody trains and no bloody buses and not even a barge on the canal. And so help me if you don't get your neb out you'll not recognise it next time you look in a glass, I can tell you.'

Alec and I sidled past as casually as we could and just as casually mounted the stage-door steps and entered the theatre. I sniffed deeply, expecting some romantic aroma from all I had heard and read on the matter, but there was just must and paint and lamp oil and I concluded that one would need to be devoted already to all things theatrical for such a smell to quicken one's blood.

'Name?' said a voice at our side, making both Alec and me jump. We turned to see an elderly man wearing a velvet blanket around his shoulders like a shawl, clutching a tattered sheet of paper and looking at us over the top of a pair of half-moon spectacles.

'Mrs Gilver,' I said, 'and this is Mr Osborne. Are you the stage-manager?'

'No, no, no,' said the little man. 'I'm the door-keeper. What name'll we have you down by? Here – you're not amateurs, are you? We haven't come to that?'

'Oh, no – you misunderstand,' I said, ignoring Alec's quiet chuckle. 'We're not an act. Goodness me, no! We've come to talk to . . . well, you, I suppose. How fortunate that we came upon you right away.'

'You're not an act?' said the man, looking between the two of us and the two dogs. 'Pity. I'd have liked to see it. And God knows what we'll end up with Tuesday night, because half our next week's show was coming up from Bradford and the other half was coming down from Dundee and now Mr Moss is having to scrape up what he can from round-about. But no amateurs so far, I'm glad to say.' He turned away in the middle of this and shuffled back towards a small office, more of a cubby-hole really, set to one side of the door. His shawl, at the back, trailed almost to the floor and ended in a tassel. At second glance it might have been a curtain; certainly one edge showed puckered fading as though it had been gathered onto tape in an earlier incarnation. This, I thought, boded very well, for surely toddling about draped in old curtains was the sort of thing one would come to after long years. If he had taken this job the month before and was just settling into it, such behaviour would not have occurred to him.

He let himself down into a battered armchair inside his little kingdom with a rheumatic groan and puffed in and out a bit until he had recovered from his excursion.

'So what can I do for you?' he said. 'Autographs, is it? Who're you after?' He gestured around himself at the walls where photographs, half-covered with fading endearments in looped handwriting, were tacked up six deep almost to the ceiling. Right behind his head in pride of place was a garishly tinted portrait of Marie Lloyd blowing a kiss.

'We're after someone in a manner of speaking,' I said, 'but not an autograph. We're trying to find someone, or find out if he ever appeared here.'

'Well, you've come to the right place,' said the man. He stuck out his hand and gripped first mine, then Alec's, then a paw each of Bunty and Millie. 'Joe Crow,' he said. 'Fifty years and counting.

I was here the night the old Empire burned down and I was first back in after the painters left when they finished the new one. There hasn't been an act through here since 1876 that I don't remember.' He tapped his head (a remarkable red colour for anyone, let alone someone who was seventy if a day). 'It's all up here. Ask away.'

'You are a godsend,' said Alec, wringing his hand again and this time passing a folded banknote as he did so. This is the kind of thing one is always very glad to have Alec around for; I could never manage it without fumbles and blushes. I didn't see what denomination of note it was but it caused old Joe to turn up the gas ring under a tea kettle and to gather three cups, wiping them out with a corner of his velvet curtain.

'It's a man by the name of Ernest Faulds?' Joe shook his head. 'Or perhaps he used a stage-name. But we do know what the act was. It was forgery of some kind. Copy-cat handwriting. Off-the-cuff, perhaps taking members of the audience and mimicking their hands?' Joe was shaking his head again, very determinedly.

'And this act said he did a turn at the Empire?' he said. 'Someone's been having you on, missus. I've never seen it. I'm not saying you couldn't work it up to an act if you put your mind to it – that would all depend on the patter – but I've never seen such a thing. Not here.'

He sounded horribly sure and I looked at Alec only to find him gazing back at me.

'Ernest Faulds,' I said again, slowly, hoping that something would jog a memory out of the old fellow. 'A Cornishman. Very pleasant-looking chap, turned-up nose, red lips, twinkling eyes, wavy black hair.'

'Sounds like a comic,' said Joe.

'No,' I said. 'I know he's not a comic or a song-and-dance man. I only wish I had a picture of him to show you.'

The kettle was boiling and Joe was spooning great heaps of tea into a battered pot.

'Coals to Newcastle, that would be,' he said, 'I've a picture of every act that's ever trod the Empire stage. I put the cream of the

crop up on my walls, like Miss Lloyd here.' He paused in the act
of pouring in the water on top of the tea and shook his head. 'I
still can't believe she's gone,' he said. 'Can't believe I won't ever
see that little face looking up at me and hear that little voice,
always with a chuckle in it. "What do you know – it's Joe Crow!"
she used to sing out whenever she stepped inside the door there
and saw me.'

Alec and I murmured in sympathy and after a respectful pause,
I led him back to the point again.

'The cream of the crop are on your walls as you said, Mr
Crow, but what of the others? Where are they?'

'In my albums here,' he said, patting the table where the teapot,
caddy, milk bottle and packet of sugar lay. 'Well, scrapbooks really.
I've saved every one. Even managed to get them out the night
of the great fire.'

I was puzzled, but Alec leaned forward and lifted the table-
cloth and then, with a sinking heart, I saw. It was not a table at
all but a stack of cardboard albums, three across, as many deep
and half-a-dozen high with a cloth thrown over them.

'It would be a very great inconvenience, I know,' I said, 'but I
don't suppose you would let us look through them to see if we
can spot the chap, would you?'

Joe's eyes, still glistening from his thoughts of Marie Lloyd,
filled to the brim again, and for the third time he pumped
Alec's hand.

'My eyes, missus, sir,' he said. 'You've no idea how happy
you've made me today. It's been years since anyone's wanted to
look at my pictures and hear my stories. You've made my day
for me. Now, just take your tea – and drink it while it's hot,
mind you – and let me get this lot cleared off. Will we start now
and work our way back or start in the '70s and go through in
proper time?'

I tried as gently as I could to nip this in the bud, telling him
that for now we would have to begin five years ago and work
backwards for perhaps twenty before we would be forced to admit
defeat in our quest.

'But if you would be so kind,' I said, 'another day I should love to come and look at the very oldest ones. What a treat! And I can bring a drop of something too, for us to share. You just name your poison, Mr Crow.'

For all the velvet shawl and the shuffling he was admirably efficient once he had got the spirit of our enquiry and he found the book for 1921 within a minute or two. Then – thank the Lord! – he was called away to his business (a very dramatic-sounding voice hailing him from the stage-door) and Alec and I were left to flick through the heaps of pictures on our own.

Joe looked in on us now and then and was unperturbed by the growing disarray of his little domain as the 'table' was dismantled and the albums we had finished with grew up into tottering piles all around and, until he was called away again, would lean against the door-jamb having a quiet smoke and making little observations about the faces as we turned them over.

'Flirty and Gertie,' he said. 'They could hold the splits through an entire song. Three verses with a chorus in between each. Don't recall him – fine set of muscles, though, eh? Ah, Miss Allakamba and her snakes. She was a lovely lady. And who's that? Another comic? What does it say his name is? Oh, yes, I remember him like my brother. And that's Sarah . . . Sarah . . . Oh, now, Sarah . . . ?'

The main impediment, in fact, was that we were only inter-ested in the men and Joe only remembered the names of the women, and so every Sarah and Gertie and lady with her snakes which we should have laid aside without a glance had an associated chuckle and reminiscence to be waited out before we could get on.

'Sarah Pretty!' said Joe. 'How could I forget that? You only have to look at her – Oh, you've moved on, have you, missus. Well, you go back and see if it's not Sarah Pretty that signature says, now you know what you're reading.'

After half an hour when my hopes were beginning to flag, Alec gave a cry, plucked a photograph from a page – ripped it right off its anchoring – and held it up, letting the rest of the album slide off his lap onto the littered floor.

'Got him!' he said. 'Hah! Got him.'

I snatched the photograph out of his hand and felt a surge spread through me, for it was indeed Mr Faulds; there was no mistaking it. He was dressed in a turban with a long feather and a satin tunic of rich ornamentation, and was staring out of the photograph with a piercing gaze.

'We've found him, Mr Crow,' I said. 'This is him! We've got him now.'

Then Alec and I met one another's eyes, both remembering at the same time that really we had got nothing. We had already known Faulds was on the stage. Finding a picture had got us nowhere.

'Unless . . .' said Alec. He nodded towards Joe who was peering over my shoulder at the picture of Faulds.

'Indeed,' I said. 'Now Mr Crow, if you please. What was this man's act? Can you remember? Was it anything to do with handwriting of any kind?'

Joe Crow shifted from foot to foot and rubbed his finger along under his nose.

'Oh, it's all up here,' he said. 'Never you fear. Now. Now then. You just read me what it says on the picture there, missus, for these aren't my reading specs I'm wearing.'

I looked in dismay at the faded ink of the signature and the message above it. It was a scrawl, like a ball of wool after a kitten at play, and I could imagine Mr Faulds, halfway out the stage-door, late for his train, dashing off a word for 'old Joe on the door' without a moment's real attention.

'*To* . . .' I began, pretty sure of that much. 'And then the next bit is probably *Something Joe. Dearest*, Alec? Could that be *dearest Joe*?'

'Ah, he was a sweet laddie, I remember,' said Joe, making me want to kick him.

'*With something something.* Actually *with somethingest something* . . .'

271

'*Fondest regards,*' said Alec. '*From . . . ?*'

'*Mister,*' I said. 'The next word is definitely *Mister.*'

'And then *something something something hands,*' said Alec.

'Handwriting?' I said. 'No, it's not, is it? It's just *in something hands*. Could that be a reference to handwriting? *Writing in many hands?*' Alec screwed his face up and I had to agree; this was stretching things.

'Anyway,' he said. 'I think it's *in my hands*, don't you?'

'Mister, mister, mister . . . ?' said Joe. 'I remember him well. He threw it all up, you know. Left the stage behind him.'

'His name starts with *Mes* or *Mis* or perhaps *Mef* or *Mif,*' said Alec.

'*To dearest Joe with fondest regards Mister mifsomething. Something* – maybe *your?* – *something in my hands.*'

'His own name was plain enough,' said Joe. 'It's on the tip of my tongue. And here's another thing – he lives in Edinburgh now. I met him on the street once and passed the time of day.'

Alec and I both turned to stare.

'He does,' I said. 'That's right, Joe.'

'Didn't I just tell you?' said the old man. 'It's all up here. I remember everything. He was a clever enough act but he couldn't give up on the high life he was born to. Now, money, you see, wouldn't be no good to most in this game – top billing and your name in electric bulbs is something it just can't buy – but he went back to it in the end. Back to his family. Oh, his name's on the tip of my tongue.'

'No, he's not with his family,' said Alec. 'He took a position here. A live-in job.'

'And why would he be doing that when he was in for a fortune? I'm telling you, he lives with a relation. A cousin, he told me. And his real name's . . .'

'George Pollard,' said Alec and I together, and Alec went on, under his breath, 'My God, Dandy. We've got him.'

'George Pollard!' said Joe. 'That's him. You might have told me if you knew it all along. That's the chap. Georgie Pollard – from Cornwall – came from a rich tin-mining family down there.'

'And his act, Joe?' I said softly, hoping that now the floodgates had opened it would all come pouring.

'Mister Mesmero,' said Joe. 'That's the one. "Your mind in my hands". Best stage hypnotist I've ever seen. He could twist you round his little finger and you never knew a thing about it.'

17

The police station at Gayfield Square was buzzing like a hive, with special constables – undergraduates in high spirits and armbands – milling around and getting under the feet and on the nerves of the desk sergeant. So while, on an ordinary Sunday morning, it might have taken some fast talking to get two strange and breathless civilians, a spaniel and a Dalmatian upstairs to the superintendent's private room, today the poor man just lifted the counter and waved us through.

Hardy was sitting with his head in his hands staring down at a desk covered with sheets of paper, and when he looked up we could see that he had transferred great patches of carbon ink from his hands to his cheeks. I strode over to the desk and put the photograph down on top of the litter.

'George Pollard,' I said. 'Balfour's cousin. A hypnotist.'

'A what?' said Hardy. He peered at the photograph. 'This is Faulds, isn't it?'

'A mesmerist, Superintendent,' said Alec. 'A brainwasher. He used to do it as a music-hall act eight shows a week and now he plays a longer game for higher stakes.'

'You can't be serious!' Hardy said. 'You think he could hypno- tise a man into changing his will? Hypnotise another into cutting his own throat?'

'No, not that,' I told him. 'But into writing a suicide note and then bending obligingly over a sink and letting someone else cut it. Certainly. And into believing one had been assaulted and was carrying a child, had been made to sleep in a cold car, had been threatened with the sack . . . he even hypnotised me last night. I woke up this morning convinced that I had suspected Stanley all along and I still can't shake it off even though I *know* it didn't happen. I read the report in my own handwriting that *told* me it didn't happen.' I shook myself. 'And when I tried to ask him this morning about . . . Good Lord, yes, about odd things in people's handwriting, he started again. Look into my eyes, he said. Listen to my voice. But Eldry disturbed us and told him Mr Osborne was looking for me, otherwise . . .'

'It doesn't bear thinking about,' Alec said, squeezing my arm. 'Please hurry, sir. Goodness knows what he might be doing if he's really feeling the rope begin to tighten on him.'

'It all sounds quite unlikely,' said Hardy.

'I can't help that,' I snapped back. 'It might well sound unlikely but it's true. And even if you don't believe me, at least believe that Ernest Faulds's real name is George Pollard. We have a witness who will say so.'

Hardy nodded, just once, very curtly and picked up his telephone.

'Go back to the house,' he said. 'Make sure everyone keeps out of his way. I'll be right behind you.'

Lollie and Mrs Lambert-Leslie had gone to church with John driving them, Mrs Hepburn told me. She was in the kitchen, with Eldry in attendance, preparing a joint of meat and a rhubarb pie for luncheon. It was Phyllis's free Sunday, I knew, but the rest of the household was in the servants' hall. Harry – nothing to do, with his master dead and gone – sat in Miss Rossiter's chair, hunched over the inevitable strike bulletin. Mattie was polishing the maidservants' shoes on some old newspapers spread on the floor and Clara was over by the window, sewing in the best of the light. Millie, with a hot bottle at her feet and a cup of cocoa on the fender at her side, sat in her Auntie Kitty's armchair, looking as though she had not stopped crying for a moment since the loss of her beloved Stanley the day before. Her nose was red and bulbous and her eyes were almost lost between purple lids, tears sparkling on their lashes even now. Did I only suspect that Mr Faulds, sitting opposite her, was gazing with something like remorse at her puckered brow and that he winced at each sob that was wrenched out of her?

'Where on earth have you been, Miss Rossiter?' Clara said with round eyes, as Alec and I entered the room. 'I had to get mistress dressed for church myself and Aunt Goitre's ready to string you up.'

'Blooming cheek,' said Alec, sitting himself down at the table and shrugging off his jacket. 'It was Old Goitre herself that sent us off on a wild goose chase in the first place. You can't be in two places at once, Miss Rossiter. And if you end up moving to Inverness with Mrs Balfour, you'll need to take a firm hand with the old—'

'What wild goose chase?' said Mr Faulds. I busied myself with my gloves, hoping that Alec had an answer and was not expecting me to catch the lob and run away with it.

'Flowers,' Alec said. 'Corsages for church for the two of them. And for one thing it's Sunday and for another thing, there's been no flowers delivered all week anyway.'

'And they'd be blacklegged if you could get them,' said Harry.

'Exactly,' Alec said.

'With mourning?' said Clara.

'I know,' I said, rolling my eyes. 'That woman is stuck in the days of the old Queen. Whoever heard of mourning corsages these days?'

'I never heard of them at all,' said Clara who was looking very suspiciously between Alec and me. 'And mistress never said a word about any— Hello?' She turned and looked out of the window. 'Mercy! There's the police again,' she said. 'Coming to the area door this time.'

'That was Stanley's job,' said Millie with a great wuthering breath in and a snort as she exhaled it. 'Stanley always answered the area door.'

Mr Faulds gave her a pained look and stood up.

'I'll get it myself,' he said. Alec caught my eye. He must still think himself safe, if he were willing to answer the door to the policemen. Still, I was careful to watch that he did turn to the front

276

outside the servants' hall and not to the back to make an escape to the garden and away through the mews or over the wall. When the front door had opened and shut and the butler's pantry door too, Alec dropped his act, and turned to me.

'Get Mrs Hepburn and Eldry in here, Dan,' he said. 'We'll be best all together.'

'What?' said Harry, but I was gone.

I did not even have to speak to the cook and tweenie, but just laid a finger on my lips and then beckoned them to put down the rolling pin and larding needle and follow me, and it was not until the servants' hall door was locked and we were all inside that I let my breath go.

'What's going on?' said Harry.

'The police have come to arrest Mr Faulds,' I said. 'But as to what's going on . . . I hardly know where to begin.'

'Arrest him for what?' said Mrs Hepburn.

'Killing Mr Balfour,' I said. 'And Stanley and – I'm very sorry to have to tell you this but – Maggie and Miss Abbott too.'

'Stanley didn't leave me?' Millie said.

'No,' I told her. 'Stanley was murdered, because – I think – he couldn't resist hinting to Mr Faulds about what he knew. What he saw when he was peeping in the back windows on the night Balfour died, hoping to see Miss Rossiter undressing.'

'Why do you say "Miss Rossiter" as if she's someone else?' said Harry.

'What did he see?' said Mrs Hepburn.

'We don't know for sure,' said Alec, but I interrupted him; I had worked it out.

'He saw you, my dear lady, going to bed on your own in your own room,' I replied. 'And he knew that Mr Faulds was lying when he said you were in his room with him.'

'But I – I was,' said Mrs Hepburn. 'I'm sure I was. I remember it cl— no, not clearly, but I remember it.'

'You remember it, but not clearly,' I repeated. 'And remembering it puzzles you, doesn't it? It's not like other memories. Like your memory, Mattie, of the nights you spent in the front

277

hall and why you were scared there when you were never scared in here at the piano. And like Phyllis's memory of why she was put on warning, which is very hazy indeed.'

'Aha!' said Alec. 'I've just realised something, Dandy.'

'What are you talking about?' Clara said. 'And why does he keep calling you that?'

'When Mr Faulds was on the music halls,' I told them, 'he did a hypnotism act. Do you know what that means? He has brainwashed you all. He made you believe that Pip Balfour was some kind of monster, cutting out pockets and interfering with girls and putting dead mice in geese – but none of it's true. He planted all those horrid ideas – he tried it on me last night – and almost worse than that, he planted the idea that you shouldn't tell, that you should be ashamed and secretive and guilty. So you all thought you all had motives and suspected one another and you all hated master so much you were willing to ignore them. But hear me and believe me – not a scrap of it was true.'

Clara gasped.

'None of it?' she said. 'Not what I thought either?'

'It didn't happen,' I told her. 'Nothing happened. Not a thing.' Clara put her sewing down and hid her face in her hands.

'And I've just thought of something that confirms it,' Alec said. 'Phyllis is Mr Faulds's favourite, isn't she? And she's the only one of the girls he didn't force to believe that Balfour had had his way with her. He gave Phyllis a pretty harmless little memory compared to the others.'

'How do you know all this?' said Harry. 'Who are you?'

I wondered how on earth to explain it all, thinking it would take an hour at least, but Alec showed me I was wrong.

'Private detectives,' he said. There was a stunned silence and then Clara broke it at last.

'I knew you were a hopeless maid.'

'Phyllis was Mr Faulds's favourite,' I repeated slowly. 'Yes, of course, Alec. She hinted that she knew something and Faulds gave her – well, you know what – to keep her quiet.'

'But then when *Stanley* started making insinuations?' said Alec.

I nodded. 'It was a very different matter. Mr Faulds had no time for Stanley and he saw his chance to get rid of the problem and shift the blame.'

'How could Stanley have been so st—' Clara bit off the word, with a glance at Millie. 'So reckless? Hinting away to someone he thought was a murderer.'

'Perhaps he didn't,' I said. 'Perhaps blaming Stanley and killing him was part of the plan right from the start. We'll never know.'

'Stanley's a kind of hero, then,' said Millie, raising her chin for the first time and gazing at me.

'Well, a martyr anyway,' I said and Millie nodded dreamily, quite happy to settle for that.

'And Ernest Faulds is a villain,' said Mrs Hepburn. 'And all those nights that seemed like dreams . . . *were* dreams?'

'They were, Mrs Hepburn,' I said.

'But here's the question, Fanny – or whatever your name—'

'Fanny will do,' I said, smiling.

'Why did he do it?' she said. 'If master wasn't all those nasty ways he made us think, why would Ernest kill him?'

'For money,' I said. 'Ernest Faulds isn't his real name. His real name is George Pollard. He's master's cousin.'

'But hang on,' said Harry. 'Isn't the will just so much faddle?'

'Of course it is,' Alec said. 'He must have been brainwashed into writing it. But probably Pollard – Faulds – was going to wait until the house was broken up and then find Mrs Balfour and do away with her. And do you know what, Dandy?' He turned to me. 'That way, when the two years had gone by, the wife would be dead and the question of whether she was a real wife or a bidey-in would be moot and then Pollard would turn up at the last minute and no one would connect him with Ernest Faulds the butler.'

'A bidey-in?' said Mrs Hepburn. 'Mistress?'

'I think you're right, Alec,' I said. 'He would only have had to get Lollie on her own and start mesmerising her and she could have gone the same way as Stanley. It's not as though anyone would have been surprised at her suicide after everything that's happened to her.'

'That policeman better watch himself then,' Clara said.

'What?' I said. Alec had swung round to face her.

'Mr Hardy,' said Clara, gesturing out of the window. 'That's who's in with him now.'

I was out of my seat.

'Just Hardy?' I shouted, fumbling with the lock. 'Why in God's name did he come alone?'

'Oh *hell*, Dandy,' Alec said as the lock released and the door swung open. 'He didn't believe you. He probably couldn't get men at short notice, not easily anyway, and he didn't see why he should try.'

Faulds's door was locked but Harry, with one mighty kick, splintered it open and there was Mr Hardy, sitting on a chair in the middle of the room, fast asleep, with his chin sunk on his chest.

'Hardy!' Alec said, taking the superintendent by the shoulders and shaking him. 'Wake up. Where is he?'

I galloped into the bedroom, banged opened the wardrobe, tested the window, wrenched the covers aside to look under the bed and then streaked back to the pantry again. Superintendent Hardy was looking around himself blearily, rubbing his face.

'Wha—?' he said, but his eyes were already beginning to roll up again.

'Take him into the bedroom and lie him down, Alec,' I said. 'Then ring for a doctor. He might be drugged.'

Alec nodded and began hoisting the superintendent to his feet.

For a second, Harry and I stood staring at one another, then he said:

'Garden door.' He wheeled around and sped out of the room. 'He can't have got far,' he shouted back to me as he ran along the passageway. 'I'll catch him.'

I started to follow and then stopped. I looked at the door Harry had kicked open, its lock hanging loose on the splintered board. It had swung wide and was lying back against the wall, across the corner. I put out my hand and pulled it towards me.

'Watch my face, Fanny,' said Mr Faulds, 'and listen to what I say.

You'll understand if you listen. You'll understand I only wanted what was mine. Only what was mine. Just listen and I'll tell you. Just listen to my voice, Fanny. Just look at my face and listen to me.'

'Yes, but you see, the thing is,' I said, 'my name isn't Fanny any more than yours is Ernest Faulds. So really I'm surprised you managed to hypnotise me at all.'

He took a step forward then and, without thinking, I shoved the door hard and heard the thud and crack as it hit him.

Postscript

Two days later, I was sitting in Lollie's boudoir once more, in a rather wonderful raw silk coat and skirt in the palest imaginable amethyst (which was overdressing a little, but I had to make up for Miss Rossiter's serge somehow and, as Grant had assured me, amethyst is purple and purple is mourning). Bunty was fast asleep over my feet and I could feel hairs unattaching themselves from her skin and attaching themselves instead to the nap of my pony skin town shoes. Great Aunt Gertrude was still there, with a black mantilla arrangement secured to her head behind the white fan of hair. This had puzzled me at first. Why should her mourning have deepened? Her manner to Lollie offered a clue: it was solicitous and even approaching thoughtful, with her natural flights of opinionated interference frequently choked off and replaced by beatific smiles. I gathered that a bereaved niece who might make a free companion for her aunt and a bereaved niece who was now rich enough to buy and sell her aunt ten times and not notice the outlay required two very different kinds of aunuly sympathy.

'Poor, poor Pip,' said Lollie, with a glance at the table nearest her, where a large photograph of Pip Balfour had been placed, with a red rose in a silver bud-vase at its side.

'It's absolutely shocking,' said Mrs Lambert-Leslie, sleeves, earrings and chins all a-waggle. But Lollie, I noticed, was less shocked now than she had been in the dreadful week between Pip's death and Faulds's – Pollard's – capture. I could understand that, in a way: the wrenching away from her of her beloved husband by a man who was greedy and evil and no concern of hers was orders of magnitude more easy to bear than the wrenching away by Pip's own madness and cruelty, with his death only the final horrid chapter. Pip was restored to her heart and could be mourned there.

'I must say, though,' Lollie went on, 'that the Balfour ancestor who just whipped all his money out of the Cornish tin mines and the Nottingham coal mines and left his relations – his own family, Dandy! – to make their own way from scratch again . . . Well, if it had been him who had been punished instead of my darling Pip I should have said he deserved whatever befell him.'

'Nonsen—' began Great Aunt Gertrude and then coughed. 'I mean to say, I don't think I would go that far, Lollie my dear, but your generosity of spirit, unflagging, most admirable, dear me, yes.'

'And I feel the responsibility,' said Lollie.

'For what?'

'Not *for* anything exactly,' Lollie said. 'Just the responsibility of so much money. All that money. When Mr Ettrick came back to see me yesterday and told me the figure . . . in cold hard pounds sterling . . .'

Great Aunt Gertrude was as still as a statue, quite breathless, waiting.

'And especially at a time like this when one only has to look out of one's window to see the most wretched plights that tattered humanity could endure . . .'

I turned my eyes to the window onto Heriot Row and the railings of Queen Street Gardens, thinking that tattered humanity did not make a habit of enduring its wretched plights just there. Great Aunt Gertrude was breathing again – in fact, almost panting.

'One must be prudent, dear,' she said. 'One cannot let one's tender heart lead one to . . .'

Give away any of that lovely loot to anyone but Great Aunt Gertrude, I guessed to be the end of the sentence.

'It's poor Stanley's family, you see,' said Lollie.

'My dear Walburga,' said Great Aunt Gertrude, 'no one in the world could lay that at your door. You needn't let it trouble you for one second, truly.'

'I *needn't*,' said Lollie. 'But I shall. Maggie's parents and Miss Abbott's sister too – Mrs Light. She's terribly distraught and I think a cruise would be the thing for her.'

Her aunt, soothed by the inexpensive sound of this, smiled fondly. Then Lollie dropped the bomb.

'And I was wondering,' she said, 'about buying a mine. A coal mine. They don't have any other kinds around here. And I could probably get one on quite reasonable terms just now.'

'I shouldn't doubt it,' I said. I did not trust myself to look at Great Aunt Gertrude, from whom gurgling sounds could be heard. Bunty lifted her head and gave the old lady an enquiring glance before going to sleep again. 'But do be careful, Lollie, won't you? Take advice, dear.'

'I shall,' she said, 'but I'm determined to carry on the Balfour tradition and going against the tide of popular thinking is very much the Balfour way. It's something I should like to pass on to my children, if I marry again, even though, of course, they won't actually be Balfours, but perhaps if I had a son I could give him Balfour as his Christian name, if his father didn't mind too much of course, and then Pip *will* carry on, in a way.'

She seemed to be skipping ahead rather lightly for a woman whose husband was not yet in the ground, but she was twenty-five and rich with reddish curls and blue eyes and so I supposed that husband number two would not, indeed, be very long in arriving and might easily agree to all manner of things.

'Now, Lollie dear,' I said, shoving Bunty off my feet and giving my shoes an ineffectual rub with my hanky, 'if you will excuse me, I really do want to pay a visit downstairs.'

I had only been away two nights, but stepping through the door under the stairs opposite the dining room and descending those stone steps onto the flagstones felt like something from a half-forgotten dream.

There they all were, what was left of them anyway: Mrs Hepburn and Eldry in their pink dresses with their aprons on, Clara and Phyllis in black with lace caps for serving the tea, and Mattie in a waistcoat and striped trousers.

'You look very smart,' I said, smiling at him.

'Look who's talking,' said Mrs Hepburn. 'Not that I should speak to you that way now, madam, I don't suppose. But you're Fanny Rossiter to me for all time and you've only yourself to blame so you can lump it. And you were a lovely girl to have around and that kind and brave so I'm sorry I spoke that way.'

'I've got to answer the door now, miss,' said Mattie. 'I'm the only man left in the house now. If you think that John's the chauffeur and he's outside really.'

'Where's Harry?' I asked.

'Sacked,' Eldry said, sounding mournful. 'Or at least let go. He wouldn't take on the footman's duties so there was nothing else for it.'

'Well, my goodness,' I said. 'There are going to be a perfect stream of interviews, aren't there?'

'You don't half sound funny,' said Clara, and she mimicked me. 'A perfect *stream*!'

'Mind your cheeky tongue,' said Mrs Hepburn. 'No, madam. Mistress hasn't the heart. She's keeping us on and she says she'll get a housekeeper too if I can't manage the cooking and the running of it all with just Eldry to help me – Millie's away home to her mammy, you know; she didn't have the makings of a maid and even I who love her to pieces knew it really. But she says she'll never have another butler and she doesn't want the fuss of a footman and that what did she call it, Phyllis?'

'Flummery,' Phyllis said. 'I didn't think it sounded quite nice but it's in the dictionary. And I've seen enough of butlers to last me a lifetime, so I'm happy. I'm mortified, so I am, to think that black-hearted devil had the cheek to *like* me.' Clara gave her a friendly shove and told her not to be a daftie but Phyllis shook her curls and pursed her mouth, comical in her indignation.

'You should be grateful you were such a favourite with him,' I said. 'Or you could have ended up like poor Stanley.' Phyllis clutched Clara's arm and stared at me.

'What?' she said. 'What do you mean?'

'I've been puzzling over this, I have to tell you,' I said. 'I know you went to Mr Faulds and I think you must have let slip that you knew something, but he didn't harm you, did he? He . . . distracted you. With gifts. Didn't he?'

'What?' said Phyllis again.

'That very first day after master was killed,' I said. 'You went out for the afternoon in your pretty yellow coat and hat, remember? And Mr Faulds had given you a little gift.'

'I did go to Mr Faulds that day,' said Phyllis, 'and asked him for a wee sub so's I could get my black coat and my prayer book out for the funeral. Is that what you mean?'

'Get them out?' said Mrs Hepburn. 'Oh Phyllis, you're never at that lark again. You promised me and I promised your ma. I could take my hand to you sometimes.' She sighed. 'Aye, but it's hard for you all these days with them pictures showing you all what you've not got. I wouldn't be young now in this world of ours for a fortune, you poor loves.'

'And he *gave* you this "wee sub"?' I said, leading Phyllis back to the point again.

'He gave me a whopping great big sub,' said Phyllis. 'I cleared my slate.'

'So the question that interests me,' I said, 'is why. Can you remember what exactly you said to him?'

Phyllis screwed up her face, thinking, then shrugged.

'Nowt,' she said. 'I mean, we were talking about what had happened – of course we were – master and all that and I might have— Oh!' She clapped a hand over her mouth and above it her eyes were wide open.

'You might have what?' said Mrs Hepburn.

'I was moaning about Stanley,' Phyllis said. 'Like we all used to, didn't we? Even if it sounds bad now he's gone. I told Mr Faulds he'd said he kent something and he was being a pain about it, you know the way he was? Dropping hints and thinking he was it?' Clara and Mrs Hepburn nodded, but Eldry and Mattie – innocent youths – looked unwilling to malign the dead in this way. 'And I asked Mr Faulds if he thought I should tell the policeman about it.'

'Oh Phyllis!' said Mrs Hepburn and Phyllis's eyes brimmed.

'And Mr Faulds said no and not to worry my head about it and that he'd see to Stanley himself.'

'See to him!' said Mrs Hepburn. Two great fat tears like goblets slid down Phyllis's face.

'And he gave me . . . a fiver,' Phyllis said. She did not look at me.

'He gave you a fiver and you never wondered why?' said Clara. Still Phyllis would not meet my eye, for I knew it had been much more than that and if a fiver should have set alarm bells jangling then seventeen, or probably twenty, ought to have been as good as a signed confession.

'I didn't think,' she said. More tears followed the first two, and faster. The others said nothing.

'Don't dwell on it,' I told her, trying to speak kindly but not quite managing, I fear. 'It's too late now.'

'And anyway,' said Mrs Hepburn. 'Stanley, after all, I mean to say, he only had himself . . . and it's Mr Faulds that should be . . .'

'Thoughtlessness born of innocence is not a crime,' I said, taking pity at last. 'It's a virtue.' Phyllis smiled her thanks.

'Exactly,' said Mrs Hepburn. 'Well said, Fanny my girl. And it's all over now. We can leave all that behind us when we go.'

'You're moving away?' I said.

'That's right,' Mrs Hepburn said. 'We're away up north to the lodge tomorrow afternoon, or maybe Thursday if it takes them until then to get the trains straight again.'

'The strike's definitely going to end then?' I said. 'I didn't think that stupid Astbury ruling could possibly stand.'

'What's that, miss?' said Phyllis.

'Judge Astbury said it was illegal,' I told her.

'Aye,' said Mattie, with his face very solemn. 'It's ending tomorrow, right enough.'

'Well, that's good news,' Phyllis said. 'Your father and brother back at work again.'

The others, me included, looked at her with pitying looks.

'Eh no, Phyllis,' said Eldry. 'The strike's finishing – all the trains

287

and buses and the newspapers and all them – but the lock-out's carrying on. The miners'll just . . .' She glanced at Mattie and bit her lip.

'The miners'll just be on their own now, fighting for themselves,' he said.

'Don't fret, Mattie,' said Mrs Hepburn, 'Mr Baldwin will make it all better. He said so. He's going to . . . what was it he said?'

'Ensure a square deal, to secure even justice between man and man,' said Eldry, who was reading from a piece of paper she had been holding folded up in her hand. Phyllis giggled, and Eldry flushed. She must have copied it out, perhaps as a little billet doux to give to Harry upon parting.

I said goodbye to them all then and, for the last time, pulled the door of the servants' hall closed behind me. I did not go upstairs to where Bunty was waiting, though, but down.

Miss Rossiter's bedroom door was open. The door to the little washroom was closed, and I left it that way. The grate was swept and bare, the bed stripped down, with its pillows and blankets folded in a pile at its foot, and the wooden chimneypiece was empty again. I looked around. I had only spent four nights there, between the first night on Lollie's chaise and the last night in the nurseries, but I would never forget it and might even miss the view out of the window where the cherry tree was already turning green as the grass beneath it turned pink with fallen blossom. I peered out, seeing movement. Harry was coming up the path in a smart suit and hat, carrying a small case and looking quite unlike a valet, not even trying to. I knocked on the window and waved to him, and instead of taking the steps to the kitchen door he let himself in on my level and came to my room to say goodbye to me.

'Well!' he said, once he had shaken my hand. 'So this is the real you, then? Underneath that brilliant disguise.'

I laughed.

'Hardly,' I said. 'If it hadn't been for events taking all the attention off me I shouldn't have lasted even the week I did. You made a much better job of it with less effort, if you don't mind me saying so.'

'I wasn't in disguise!' said Harry. 'I'm a working man and I was doing a job that plenty of working men are forced to do, even if it is one that demeans the worker and the master both. Twelve of us, Miss Rossiter, twelve able-bodied workers toiling away all day every day to keep two more able-bodied people fed and clothed and pampered like babies.'

'*Toiling*?' I said. 'We spent half our time in the servants' hall drinking our way through Pip's cellar. A cook-general and boot boy might have toiled, but we had a very comfortable time.'

'Not as comfortable as the two of them upstairs. It degrades all sides the same.'

'So why did you do it?' I asked him. 'And are you going to do it again with another master now?'

Harry looked at me, with a twinkle in his eye.

'I can't tell you that,' he said, 'you of all people.' I waited, knowing he was teasing. 'Ask John about the club we used to go to. He went for the beer and the dartboard but I went for the talk, Miss Rossiter, and he must have heard some.'

'I worked out for myself that it was a socialist club,' I said, feeling very much the woman of the world to know that there were such things and to mention them so casually.

'Communist club,' said Harry. I gasped, not so worldly after all. 'Soviet Comrades of Scotland. We infiltrated many a house in Edinburgh, from below stairs, waiting and listening.'

'Waiting and listening for what?' I said and I knew that my voice had turned hoarse, for my throat was dry.

'The call to arms,' said Harry. 'The uprising. The start of the revolution. I really did think last Monday that that day had dawned.'

'And now?' I said, in a whisper.

'They've lost their nerve,' said Harry. He looked over my shoulder and stared into a mythical distance, shaking his head. 'They never found their nerve. The TUC was that busy keeping it small, keeping it manageable, stopping their brothers from joining up and joining in . . . they did the government's job for them. And today they're going to sign on the line and it'll be over by the morning. They're giving in, letting go of the greatest groundswell of workers' solidarity this country has ever— but you don't want to hear this, do you?'

'I certainly don't,' I said. 'I can't believe it. You mean to say that you were hiding out here, you and all your . . . comrades . . . in people's houses waiting for the moment to . . . put them up against the wall and shoot them, just for being rich? Pip Balfour? Lollie too? *Me*? My husband has spent the last ten years telling me that people like you are all around us and I've spent the last ten years telling him he's imagining things and— How can you be laughing?'

'I'm having you on,' he said. 'It's not me and all my comrades. It's just me. My father was a valet and brought me up to it, but I went into the printers' union and ended up a newspaperman, then about three years ago or thereabouts I went freelance. I'm going to write a book. About the twelve of us and the two of them. Only now, of course, I can't decide between the book I was going to write and the one I found myself in the middle of. I know which one would sell more.'

I could not help my eyebrows rising.

'Ah, yes,' I said. 'The idea of making a bit of money does have a universal appeal.'

Harry's grin snapped off again.

'Anyway,' he said. 'That's my story and I'm sticking to it. So don't go telling your friends in the police about cells of spies in the servants' halls because I'll deny I said any such thing and no one will believe you.'

'Well, I shall keep an eye on the review pages,' I said, 'and I look forward to reading whichever book you write in the end. It's bound to be pretty thrilling stuff.'

'Here,' he said, giving me a very hard stare, 'don't you go stealing my thunder and writing your own.'

'I?' I said, pressing my hand to my heart. 'I shan't have the luxury, Harry my boy. I shall be onto the next job. I'm a working woman, you know. We can't all be freelance like you.'

And so we parted, Harry and I, Lollie and I, the rest of the servants and I, none of us unchanged by those nine tumultuous days. How, I asked myself, could I begin to describe my part in them to Hugh, if he should ask me? As I pulled the door closed and climbed the stairs to fetch Bunty, I decided to stop off at Alec's on my way home.

Facts and Fictions

The Balfours' house at 31 Heriot Row is mostly 3 Moray Place and some 5, 6 and 7 Charlotte Square, with just a hint of 29 Fitzwilliam Street, Dublin, which was where I first had the idea for this book.

The Balfour family is entirely fictitious, as is the account of their various banks, mansions, mines and oilfields around the world. I was, for once, following the good advice of Jim Hogg and 'just making it up'.

The details of the strike are based on accounts in the TUC-produced *Strike Bulletin* and the one Edinburgh newspaper which was published during the nine days.

The miners' village and colliery where Mattie's family live and work, although imagined to be near Smeaton in Midlothian, are not based on any of the pits which made up the Lothian or Dalkeith Companies.